LORD JANUARY

Year of the Sword Book One

DAKOTA KROUT

ACKNOWLEDGMENTS

I will never stop being amazed by my wonderful readers. You all make my life so much more fulfilled and awesome.

A massive thanks to all of my Patreons, who help me make this book the best it can be, and a specific thanks to Michael Matteucci, Zeeb, Garett Loosen, William Merrick, and Samuel Landrie!

PROLOGUE

Random Messenger Number Six stopped for a moment, hands braced upon his knees; ragged breaths entered his lungs as he looked for the courage to carry on. Pain made him focus, just enough that the whine of an incoming elemental spell didn't distract him from his objective. His gaze flashed over the area, a massive tundra that had once contained flowers and small but powerful monsters.

All that remained was mud, blood, and the sharp tang of ozone from the elemental lightning spells that flashed through the area. No one would come to the rescue of the few cultivators that were still groaning in pain, not this far out in no man's land. They remained where they fell, desperately hoping that a stray spell would give them an honorable—a quick—death.

The messenger's eyes landed on his destination, still a distant and dangerous target. A red tent dominated the crown of a shallow hill in the distance. Rings of smaller shelters and a swarm of campfires crowded the space around it, practically leaning toward the scant protection the command center afforded them. With a deep breath, the messenger found a hidden reserve of energy and started running once more. Slick mud made the journey treacherous; the faster he ran, the more the mud clawed at him, trying to drag him down into its warm embrace. Still, he couldn't stop: the message *must* get through. He could end this war of god-like cultivators if he could just *get* there.

Streaks of blue-white light arced across the night sky, similar to the streaks of tears that ran down his own face. Even at this distance, the thud of the artillery spells as they connected with the ground shook his weary bones. The messenger sprinted onward, muttering a mantra of, "It'll all be over soon. I'll be a hero!"

A glowing white flag emblazoned with the sigil of a royal messenger floated above his head and provided some comfort, along with a much-needed pool of soft light to guide the way across the sea of mud, bodies, and shattered equipment. The command tent was the last bastion of Lord December and his army. Despite being the most powerful Wielder in the world, and the Regent of the Calendar of Months, he was no Calendar *King*. No matter how much he acted like it, or wanted the power.

His latest grasp at power had led to this moment, a world-wide war in which December was assaulted from all sides by the eleven other Lords and Ladies of the Months. Their beacons soared into the heavens from wherever they waited in their own outposts, the solid pillars of light spanning all colors of the rainbow—and then some. Only the frosty white beacon that represented Regent December's power was hidden from view.

After what seemed like an age, the messenger stumbled to the perimeter of the camp and was met with a sword to the throat before he could blink. The cultivator on duty glanced up at his flag and nodded, retracting his sword and moving aside to allow him passage after searching him for hidden weapons.

The messenger stepped through the makeshift gate, and the world became brighter than the sun in the sky.

In the space of a heartbeat, the guard that had stopped him turned to ash. Air turned to plasma, and the ground beneath was vaporized—along with everything else within a ten-foot radius. The shell-shocked messenger landed fifty feet away, blinded and ears ringing. Only the protective shield provided by the white flag had stopped him from sharing the fate of the guard, but blood still dripped into his eyes as he staggered to his feet.

Anyone watching would have witnessed a silhouette momentarily floating in a sphere of incandescent light before it was catapulted across the camp. Random Messenger Number Six came back to himself quickly, shaking off the confusion and searing pain from his fuzzy head. The light of the artillery spell still clouded his vision, but at least he could see enough to finish his task.

He hobbled toward the command tent that stood pristine amongst the maelstrom, pulling back the heavy tent flap before crossing the threshold. Outside of this space, war raged, the iron tang of blood assaulted the nostrils, and artillery formations were slapped back and forth in a godlike game of catch. Wielders and cultivators alike hastily cast spells to protect the camp from the intensifying volley, rushing to fill gaps where searing magic spilled across the ground to engulf random soldiers or wielders in liquid fire.

Inside the tent… the *lack* of sensory stimulation assaulted him, and he nearly passed out from the relief that flowed through his body. He felt transported to an entirely different world.

Equidistant globes floated at head height, filling the cavernous tent with a soft glow. Dense, intricately patterned rugs carpeted the floor. He felt guilty dragging mud across them, but as he stepped toward the lone figure sitting cross-legged in meditation, the rugs somehow remained pristine. Even as a war was coming to an end, mana was being devoted to *cleaning* magic? Random Messenger Number Six shook his head at the games those in power tended to play for no real reason.

The walk seemed to take an age, and his eyes darted from one treasure to another. Piles of scrolls littered an enormous oak table, along with a map. He gasped aloud as he saw the map. It was a *living* map. Small dots moved around, along with streaks of light that crossed it in an instant; obviously the tracks of artillery spells. The colored pillars of light that represented the other Lords and Ladies were quickly closing the distance toward the camp marked at the center.

They didn't appear to be converging on the command tent, but another location nearby. As he passed, he couldn't help but stare a little too long at the mound of scrolls. The top one glowed, and a summarized projection appeared above, framed in purple:

Quantum Computations of Astral Projection—Level IX. Prerequisites: Quantum Computations of Astral Projection: Level VIII Astral Primer.

His eyes darted away. It was *forbidden*—and more-so, life-threateningly dangerous—to read scrolls and spells above one's level. He was just a lowly single-method cultivating messenger. The only magical abilities he had been granted were to renew the messenger's protection, an auto-identification spell that had to be cast *on* him, and a passively enhanced level of stamina.

Tearing himself away from his thoughts, he crossed the remaining space and stood a respectful distance away from the kimono-clad figure maintaining a lotus position. "Random Messenger Number Six, Regent December, here to deliver a message from the Lords and Ladies of the Months."

As with the living map and the scrolls, he struggled to tear his eyes away from the deceptively simple katana with an unadorned ivory handle lying on Regent December's lap. An informative projection started to appear, thanks to his auto-identification, so he *slammed* his eyes shut. As much as he wanted to learn about the Regent's fabled Wielded Weapon, December First, he didn't particularly care for the idea of being sliced in half for his audacity! The messenger had heard about this weapon. All the Lords had their unique weapons of power; Wielded Weapons that focused and channeled their magical abilities beyond what any other cultivator could hope to achieve.

Regent December sat motionless, either unaware—or unconcerned—with the disturbance. After several minutes of waiting patiently for a reply that did not arrive, the messenger cleared his throat and continued. "I now speak the decree of the Lords and Ladies of the Months."

His voice changed as he accessed the confidential message, and eleven voices spoke as one. "The war is over, Regent December. In our infinite wisdom, we have formed an alliance to dethrone you. It has been decided that it is for the best that you stand down as Calendar Regent. We do not believe in the threat you claim to protect us from. We will be waiting at the Stone Circle for you to peacefully relinquish your stolen crown and Wielded Weapon. Enough blood has been shed. For abusing your power and the trust of the people, you will be exiled from this land."

Clenching the hilt of the katana with knuckles as white as the ivory hilt, Regent December's eyes shot open. A pillar of eye-searingly pure white light engulfed him as his power was unleashed and his beacon was lit. "Message received, Random Messenger Number Six. I shall give them my answer… personally."

He turned to face the messenger, who started leaking fluids from several places. With an amused smile, the Regent calmed the too-young man down. "Don't worry. I don't intend to destroy you for this. I never kill the messenger. If you have somewhere you want to return… I suggest you *run*."

With that, Regent December took a step out of existence, and a pillar of white light slammed into the center of the Stone Circle, which was fully surrounded by the Lords and Ladies of the Month. Regent December emerged from the light, then bowed before his unimpressed audience. "Thank you for meeting me here… my old friends."

"We have all had enough of you and your prophetic *tales*," the Lord of March snapped, slamming the end of his diamond-topped baton onto the Stone Circle. "The power you have been hoarding should be used for the benefit of *all* the people. I hope you came here to surrender, December. Not for me, but for my people. They have begun rebelling, their lives militarized for too long. They want to relax for nearly the first time in over half a generation. As for me… I believed in you, once upon a time. Killing you would bring me no pleasure."

"I'm glad to hear that. Truly, I am." Regent December looked at the Nobles surrounding him and shook his head slowly, refusing to relax. "But I have explained my reasoning. I *don't* do this for myself, but for the *people*. The fate of the world depends on it."

"So. You. Say." Lord January drew a sword that matched December's in simplicity of design, yet being a broken mirror of the Regent's own. Holding his blade in a guarding stance, he edged forward. "Twelve *years* have passed since you were appointed Regent. The cycle of twelve, and the prophecy didn't come to pass. We want *freedom*. Starvation is overtaking even *my* lands!"

"No, my fine Lord January. All you want is to wield my power, and then hide it away so that you can live in luxury. I wish that we all could do the same, and I would freely give the power away if I could… but the threat is too great. Work *with* me. The time of change is at hand!" December's attempt at a rousing speech was met only with silence or scoffing.

Lady August stepped forward. "We will not warn you again. Relinquish your Wielded Weapon, and we will allow you to go into exile. Leave now, and you can even keep your kimono."

"I'm afraid…" A few of the Lords laughed mockingly at the Regent's slow admission. All took a step toward him, Wielded Weapons outstretched and crackling with energy. December looked around and swallowed, quietly finishing his statement, "...that you leave me no choice."

Before the powerful cultivators had a chance to make a move, he sliced the palm of his hand and smeared the blood along the length of the katana's simple blade. Realizing the threat, coruscated beams of vibrantly colored energy shot toward him from each and every one of the Lords' and Ladies' weapons. Each magically-infused beam held enough power to level a city, and together, they would end this dictator once and for all.

Or so they thought.

Time slowed as Regent December began to Blade Dance. The katana's edge sliced through the air. As it passed, it left behind a thread of magic imperceptible to those untrained in Spatial magics. The simple katana shed its basic form, seemingly becoming a shard of purest ice. It eagerly drank the magic seeping from the gaping wound in the Regent's hand, transforming it into a complex network of threads and filaments. In the space between heartbeats, a glowing structure began to emerge: a primal spellform from a bygone age, not seen even during the darkest part of the Wielder Wars.

Acutely aware of the incoming beams of light bearing down upon him, despite his warping of space time, December made the final touch to the first sphere. He then spun his blade furiously, funneling the Lord of January's brown magic into the container he had conjured.

Saturated light flowed through the fine filaments, giving them newfound strength and solidity. The dance continued. He leapt and spun, avoiding the writhing beams of light while adding new levels of complexity to the framework. Orange, then red, were captured in quick succession and became no more than angry, buzzing fireflies bottled safely away.

The Lords and Ladies couldn't begin to imagine what Regent December was working on. As far as the eleven of them knew—as they were moving through time normally—he was currently in the process of being blasted to pieces by their combined might. Once the red light had been captured, the construct was visible as a three-dimensional structure. The Regent winced in pain as violet light struck him from behind—thankfully only a glancing blow—before he managed to capture and spin it into the system.

He wrote a series of symbols in the air, grinning to himself as the violet light reflected off the shimmering surfaces and looped back upon itself. With four powers captured, control of time and spatial magics became… *easier*. December sped up everything within the sphere to the point that the outside world appeared to have paused. Now working with all the time he would ever need, he calmly captured the remaining spectral frequencies and worked on fine-tuning each of the ruler's fragments of reality, taking what would have been *days* in the normal world, as he added support structures, backup mechanisms, wards, and shields.

Days turned into weeks, and not a single time did he slow.

Finally, his masterpiece was complete, and time returned to normal. The Lords and Ladies appeared perplexed as their much-weakened power returned to them. They still stood in a circle—together, yet apart—and expected to find, at most, a pile of ash where Regent December had once stood. Instead, each was now separated by a wall of shimmering light spreading from Regent December and traveling as far as their eyes could see.

"What have you *done*?" Lord June bellowed, attacking the newly-created barrier only once before knowing that it was futile.

"I did what had to be done. For all of us!" With that statement and a forceful downward stroke, December severed the remaining filament, the one grounding the dimensional spell-construct to this reality. The last of his pure white magic pulsed within this new creation, beating as if alive. The beacons had been depleted, and the world had been split into twelve equal Districts; separated by a shimmering curtain of light that spanned the poles of the world.

Ignoring the raging, the screaming, the realization of power lost… December turned away. He was weakened; *all* of them would remain this way until the barrier itself fell, but he had enough power to do what must be done. The Lords and Ladies of the Month were wrong. He *knew* they were wrong.

The prophecy *was* beginning... and Regent December had work to do.

CHAPTER ONE

"My valiant knight!" Big Betty Arabella, daughter of Lord January's second cousin twice removed, breathlessly trailed her sausage-like fingers along the sharply defined musculature of Grant's chest. Her hand wandered down, lightly resting on his sign of wealth and prestige: his enormous gut. "You were *wonderful* today!"

"Everything that I did was to win the tournament… and your hand, my Lady!" Grant had a wide grin plastered on his face as he lay on purple sheets of the finest silk in District January. He wiggled his shoulders, allowing them to be engulfed by plump goose-feather pillows. Even the recovery couch he was forced to remain on was plush, a testament to how much the District valued their warriors.

"No! No man has accomplished what you have this day. You were attacked from all sides by Vassals and Wielders. Lightning bolts struck you, and the swords…! Somehow you managed to deflect them, taking down another Vassal mid-strike! I was so worried!"

Grant grasped her hand and pulled her closer to him. "I have trained all my life for this day. What I did is the result of tireless training, day after day. I would do it all again for my prize… to take whatever you'll give me."

"In that case," Betty pressed a finger to Grant's lips to forestall any more honeyed words, "it's time for your reward! Are you ready?"

"Yes! After waiting so long, working so hard… this is what I've been waiting for!" Grant started salivating instantly, his eyes never leaving her.

Betty backed away and giggled, disappearing into an adjoining room in the royal hospital suite. Moments later, she came back, wearing a flour-coated apron and a fitted chef's hat, which fully covered her hair. In her hands, she held out a platter of scrumptious-looking scones. She came closer, and powdered sugar began floating all over the combination reclining couch and feasting table. "This is just a sample of what's to come! As victor of the January Tournament, you have won an all-you-can-eat-in-a-year supply of baked goods from Big Betty's Bakery!"

He could practically taste the delicious scones already. He watched as Betty bit into one and rolled her eyes in pleasure, then stepped toward him with her eyes remaining focused on his. Grant could feel his pulse quicken. She smelled of roses in full bloom, and sweet sugar. Her lips approached his awaiting left ear, and she whispered softly, "First, there is something I want to tell you…".

"I'm listening, my lady." Grant closed his eyes. "*Anything-*"

"*Moo~o~o!*"

"What the…!" Grant was unceremoniously jerked awake by Daisy the dairy cow, her face inches from his, and her tongue lapping into his left ear. "Come *on*, Daisy... could you not have waited another five minutes? I've been dreaming about those scones for months, and I almost *got* them this time!"

She gazed at him beneath long eyelashes, bobbed her head, and answered, "Moo?"

"I suppose it isn't your fault." He looked out of the opening in the barn and squinted into the late morning light. The sun had already been up for a few hours. Daisy, as patient as she normally was, had just reminded him that she hadn't had breakfast. That meant it had to be later in the day than he thought, which might be an issue. Someone of his station did *not* get to sleep the day away.

Grant stood and went to stretch but immediately fell down with a splitting headache. With a growing sense of horror, he remembered *why* he had fallen asleep next to the dairy cow. Instead of cleaning up his master's feasting table as he had been ordered, Grant had quaffed as much fermented apple cider as he could manage last night. No one had noticed, since he had only drained the last dregs in the cups, but any of the potent liquor was still far more than he was used to drinking.

"I can't tell if I'm happy that no one notices me, or…" he muttered bitterly, fists clenched. Yesterday was New Year's Eve, and he had wanted to celebrate, even if it was by himself. Even so, he was paying the price right now. He had always heard that drinking was the same as stealing happiness from the next day, but now he knew what that saying actually meant.

"*Moo*!"

"Yes, yes. I know that *you* see me, Daisy. Thank you for making sure I didn't freeze to death last night. Now, I need to catch up on my chores before my 'caretaker' notices that I have been shirking my duties. I don't think even *you* kick as much as he does!" Trying to pull himself together, Grant got up, *successfully* this time, and splashed handfuls of frigid water from the trough onto his face. The cold slap of water instantly brought him back to the reality of his life.

The last hints of the beautiful dream faded as he looked down, half expecting to see a finely chiseled chest and a huge belly, but was instead greeted by only his usual barely-even-husky physique. His slightly rotund shape caused him no end of grief, no matter where he went; it was obvious from his small size that he was *poor*. It only took a glance, and he was avoided as though he were coughing blood.

Most people in the District were *grotesquely* obese, and the most wealthy even had to be carried around on palanquins or wagons. The less they needed to do, the more powerful they were, the more resources they could bring to bear, and the more important they were to the District. His situation guaranteed that he didn't have access to the sheer quantity of food that most people did. He actually knew for a *fact* that he was even a little thinner than some of the homeless people in the cities he had heard tales of.

He would stuff himself like that if he could afford to do it; he tried to convince himself that being poor wasn't the reason he was stealing scraps of food and drink from the feasting table last night. Grant *needed* food! He had *goals*! He would never become a knight, valiant or otherwise, if he lacked the strength and stamina to swing a sword or wear armor! That was why he did whatever it took to bulk up. His plan: get powerful, learn to use a sword, get rich and marry someone, then spend his newly acquired vast fortune on food and luxury, just like everyone else in the District of January.

"I'll make it happen. Someday. Until then…" Grant shook his coarse woven shirt, brushing off shards of prickly hay. Last night, it had acted as a makeshift bedsheet, providing limited protection from the sharp grasses below. Shirt and britches as clean as they were going to get, he strode through the barn door and into the light of the new day. He informed the clucking chickens and the world in general, "*This* year will be my year! A year that will be remembered in the history books, in ages yet to come!"

He'd said pretty much the same thing every year so far, but it still sounded impressive to his ears. Today was January first, year nine hundred ninety-nine AB, or Anno Barrier. Nine hundred and ninety-nine years had passed since the erection of the barrier which had split the world into twelve equally sized Districts. Each District was controlled by the Lord or Lady of the Month: the most powerful Wielder in each District.

Though he knew it was a fool's hope, Grant wanted nothing more than to become a Wielder. The reason it could only ever be a dream was obvious: being a Wielder meant becoming Nobility, and the only way to become Nobility was to attract the attention of a Noble House of the Week. For that, he needed to become a powerful cultivator, then a Vassal—Vassals were cultivators that had been chosen to serve the Nobility, and had been granted a portion of their power—and finally be brought into a Noble house as a full-fledged Wielder… instead of the previous Wielder's heir.

Grant shook his head and chuckled at his wild imagination. "Am I still asleep? I can't even become a cultivator. Where in the world would I get a cultivation manual? Or even a cultivation *method*, for that matter?"

Though Grant didn't have a deep understanding of cultivation, other people would rub their superiority in his face often enough that he understood that a cultivator was someone who was able to gather the energy of the world around them. A cultivator was able to take this 'outside energy' and use it to boost their 'cultivation achievement level' and 'characteristics'. This could make them hit harder, think faster, defend easier, or even—if they were Nobility—cast high-powered spells. It was a well-known fact that only Wielders and Vassals had been able to use spells after the barrier went up, though anyone with a proper cultivation method could gain levels and physical power.

So, since becoming a cultivator was the first step—and already impossible for him at this point—becoming a Wielder was *wildly* beyond his grasp. Becoming Nobility was only a part of the process; being a Wielder was different than being a cultivator. Yet, as far as his limited understanding went, there were similarities.

Both were able to increase their cultivation in four directions: physical, mental, weapon, or armor cultivation. Increasing any one of these allowed a cultivator to become far *more* than human. Most methods were narrowly focused, and made it near-impossible to cultivate a second method at the same time, but an average Januarian was usually at least lucky enough to have a family cultivation method that allowed them to wield *one* of the four. Unsurprisingly, the most powerful cultivation methods that were referenced in mythos allowed for all *four* methods to be cultivated.

Wielders had an additional advantage over cultivators: they commanded a Weapon of Power, known as a 'Wielded Weapon'.

From what he had gleaned over the years, there were three hundred and sixty-five Wielded Weapons; one for each day of the year. Each Wielded Weapon apparently had some kind of strange power which the Wielder was able to tap into, and bonding with the weapon automatically made the Wielder a part of the Noble class. Unless the entire lineage was wiped out, Noble houses only *ever* passed their weapons to their heirs; just another reason that his dream this morning had been ridiculous.

The truth of the matter was that Grant would be happy with just a simple single-cultivation method. Being able to increase even *one* of his characteristics would eventually allow him to stand on his own two feet in the world, and a *single* cultivation achievement level would also allow him to gain *skills* for the work that he did every single day, like tending animals and plucking fruit in the orchards. Everything would become easier. Literally… *everything*.

Grant forced himself to stop thinking about it before he had a mental breakdown; he got to work on his chores.

Everyone else in the District had January First off of work as a holiday, in honor of Lord January. Despite this, Daisy and the chickens needed to be fed, and the pigsty was… more of a pigsty than usual. The pigs seemed to magically produce vast quantities of excrement, and who else would clean it out but him? A couple hours later, the jobs were complete, and he was dripping with sweat from the exertion. "Ugh. I'm gonna get even *thinner*."

Grant slumped against a fence post. It protested, creaking under the load, but held. He took a deep swig from a water jug, quenching his growing thirst. He paused mid-swig and nearly choked, "Oh! That's right! A new year! My status!"

Somehow, between the chores, lucid dream, and hangover, Grant had forgotten to check his status! He shook his head in wonder, excitedly squeezed his eyes shut and thought *status*. A status sheet materialized, shining bright blue in his mind's eye.

Name: Grant Leap
Class: None
Cultivation Achievement Level: 0
Cultivation Stage: None
Inherent Abilities: None
Health: 50/50
Mana: 0/0

Characteristics
Physical: 0
Mental: 0
Armor Proficiency: 0
Weapon Proficiency: 0

Grant's shoulders slumped. The initial excitement at checking his stats was gone in an instant. At one point in his life, he had held out hope that he would be able to cultivate properly, growing strong, powerful, and respected. However, without a cultivation method—or better yet, a full cultivation manual—it was impossible to increase the base stats and levels. As an abandoned orphan, he didn't even have access to the most basic family method. Those were precious, and every single one of them was unique. No family was going to risk their secrets to help a random person. Many rumors stated that if you knew how someone cultivated, you would know how to topple them and their family.

"At least I can see my status. No one can block me from doing *that*." The viewable system was a side effect of the barriers put in place by Regent December just shy of a thousand years ago to save himself from Lord January; the man that was *supposed* to become the true Calendar King.

Before the barriers were erected, there had been no restrictions on growth. *Anyone* could use spells and fight to enter the Nobility based on power alone. In short, nothing stopped people from advancing, but there was also no clear way to quantify the growth you did achieve. The result was a blood-soaked, worldwide conflict over the pursuit of power, the Wielder Wars.

Now, the 'System' allowed everyone to clearly see their growth and potential, even a lowly Leap: the last name given to the rare few cursed like him, those born on the day of the leap year: February Twenty Nine. That was another sore spot, and another way that he could be controlled by his 'caretaker'. Unlike normal orphans, who would get the last name 'Spring' when born in the Districts of January, February, or March, a 'Leap' was legally considered a child their entire life; only becoming an adult after sixty-four years, on their 'sixteenth' birthday.

Grant rubbed at his aching arms; the effort of shoveling out the pigsty and stables made him want to sit and relax for a while. But it was a new year, and he wasn't one to give up or let obstacles get in his way! He was an achiever! Or rather, he *wanted* to be. Standing tall, he strode over to his sword, a roughly-shaped block of wood that was once a fence post.

"Someone *had* to have created the first cultivation manual! I can figure this out; I can make my own, if I try hard enough." He bent over to pick it up with one hand and winced; almost putting his back out due to the weight of the woody weapon. Rather than feeling frustrated, this just made him more determined to *somehow* achieve the first level of cultivation. He picked up the sword and held it in a two-handed grip. Swaying a little, his weak body threatened to topple over after all that work. Grant focused, remembering his inspiration for weapon cultivation.

A few years ago, a Calendar—a squad composed only of

cultivators, Vassals, and above—had passed through the village. Grant had been visiting the market at the time, selling produce from the farm. The Vassals weren't the lazy kind that were common across the District; these ones looked *deadly*, their bellies encased in gleaming armor that made them look like wrecking balls, with a two-handed sword or polearm attached to each of their mounts. One Vassal in particular had caught Grant's attention. While the others were laughing loudly and playing cards beside a fine carriage, this knight was making unusual motions with his sword.

Sword and arm were one. The man moved in mesmerizing patterns, so much so that Grant had stood there gawping, mouth slack, hypnotized by what he was witnessing. Never in his short life had he seen the like. With his feet planted shoulder width apart, the knight thrust his sword forward, impaling an imaginary foe. The gleaming metal was brought overhead and swung in a downward arc. Impressive, but nothing compared to what Grant would witness next.

Despite the weight of his armor, the knight sprinted forward, sword in hand. He leapt into the air, completed a forward somersault, and swung the sword down with a whistling cry.

A wave of pure power was unleashed from the sword as it connected with a training dummy, coating it in a burst of blue flame. Then there was silence, apart from the whine of dogs clearly distressed by the thunderous sound. The knight—who Grant later learned was actually a Wielder, and therefore a *Noble*—knelt on one knee with his hands resting on the pommel of the sword as he panted for each breath.

It was at that moment that Grant decided that he would do whatever it took to become a weapon cultivator.

The cluck of chickens brought him back to the reality of the farm and the wooden stick, a poor replica of the knight's sword. Feet wide, Grant thrust the sword forward, mimicking the witnessed sword form. The attempt was followed by a crash as he toppled over, landing in a heap amongst the straw and dirt.

He dusted himself off, picked up a significantly lighter weapon—the handle of an old broom—and made *much* better progress. At the end of ten minutes practicing sword forms—or was that broom forms?—Grant was completely spent.

Breathing heavily, with heart hammering, he collapsed in a sweaty pile; tired but happy. With consistent daily training, he would achieve his goals. "Even when I feel like giving up, I just have to keep going. One small step at a time."

This was the mantra he lived by. Doing his best to ignore the facts of his life, Grant fervently promised himself once more that he would never allow himself to fall into despair.

It was a promise that got harder to keep every time he opened his status sheet.

CHAPTER TWO

The smile dropped off his face in an instant as Grant remembered what sleeping in meant on a day like today. *Market day*. He had forgotten to take the day's produce to town! "Regent's cruel eyes, I'm gonna get *flogged* for this!"

His caretaker wouldn't be happy if he found out. Grant *could* just do it tomorrow; he had a stash of coins saved up in his... house. Shelter. Lean-to. He shook his head, maybe he could just hand over a few...? "It's a day off, for Regent's sake! I..."

"No... I have to head to the market." Knowing his luck, someone would go out of their way to mention that they hadn't seen 'that Leap boy'. Leaving everything in a pile outside the barn, he collected the eggs and milk and loaded them onto a rusty handcart. The wheel soon squealed in protest, and the eggs rattled in their basket as Grant pulled the cart down the bumpy lane at the highest speed he could manage.

Half an hour later, Grant arrived at the village nestled below in the valley. It was the first day of spring, according to the calendar, but the cold of winter wasn't ready to give up its hold just yet; clearly shown by the sweet cedar wood smoke puffing out of chimneys. Grant felt his heart sink as he peered down and saw that the market was nearly empty, as it would be on a regular weekday.

That was a surprise; despite it being the first day of the year, traders would have been up early to set up their stalls and sell goods to a waiting crowd. Servants had to do the hard work of preparing the daily feast and vast quantities of delightful snacks for the evening's entertainment. Normally, Grant would have been there with them, up at the break of dawn to complete his list of daily chores. He trundled forward, cart leading the way.

"Hey, Leap! It's the Leap, guys." Grant ignored the dark laughter hidden in the voices and pushed the cart calmly toward the stall at the far end of the market. It was one of the few stalls still working at this time of day. "You *ignoring* me?"

Splat.

A projectile thudded against the back of his head: an over-ripe tomato, from the smell and the juice sliding down the back of his neck.

"Aww, yeah! Great shot," another voice congratulated the first. Grant hunkered down, making his bulky profile as small as possible as he continued onward with clenched teeth.

"We'll be waiting for you, *Leap*," the first voice taunted Grant as he hurried away. The threat made the blood drain from his face, but he resolved to ignore it like everything else today. Moments later, he arrived at the stall he'd been aiming for. An ancient woman sat humming a tune, her beaky nose poking out from behind a black shawl.

"Good day, Madame Mercredi. This insignificant one apologizes for their lateness. I have some eggs and milk to sell, if you have a spot for them!" Grant's words were rushed and breathy from the fast pace he had needed to keep up.

"Eh. What was that? Speak up, girl. I can't hear too good. Ma hearin' ain't what it use' to be." Madame Mercredi squinted up at the figure looming above her.

"This one… it's Grant, Madame."

"Oh, *Granite*! Why didn't you say so? I was wonderin' where you'd gotten off to, lassie." She chuckled to herself as she motioned for the goods. "You have such an odd name for a young lady. Have I ever told you that?"

"Once or twice." Rather than go through the process of correcting her—again—Grant went to the cart to gather the perishables. He placed them carefully on the table in front of her, but his heart sank when he realized that half of the eggs had broken in the mad dash to the market. At least the milk was okay, being sealed within the jug. He dropped his head into his hands and started to break down: he couldn't ignore this.

Despite her rheumy eyes, Madame knew that there was an issue. She grinned at Grant, patting his soft hand with her own wrinkled one. "Don't worry, dear. I can make an omelet for ma snack. You just saved me the trouble of breakin' the eggs, look at that! I must be movin' up in the world, don't even need to prep my own meals these days!"

"That is very… kind of you." He squinted up through the fog of tears and bowed deeply. "This one doesn't know how best to express gratitude."

"That's one Hour and thirty Minutes for the groceries this last fortnight… and here is another ten Minutes for yourself." Madame Mercredi dipped into her purse and carefully counted out a small pile of coins, placing them one at a time into his palm. She flashed a toothy grin up at him and winked. "Eat somethin', girl. No man is goin' to want to marry you if you don't put some meat on yer bones first."

"Thank you." Now he was doubly glad that he hadn't corrected her earlier.

"Oh, and Granite. Happy New Year to you. You *rock*!" She cackled, pleased with her small burst of inspired humor. "You are goin' to do great things this year."

"Happy New Year to you, Madame Mercredi." He took the previous day's empty milk jug and was off with a wave. Even though she was sweet, he never let himself get attached to her. Grant knew the truth of the matter: she was only friendly to him since she couldn't see clearly enough to read the system-generated nametag that hung over his—and everyone else's—head. If she realized he was a leap-year child, she would have avoided him like the plague. He was sad to admit that her near-sightedness was the reason he went to her each time: it was the only way to get a fair deal.

Pulling his now-empty cart up to the only other stall still open, Grant contemplated avoiding the stall and the merchant behind the table that only held a few goods; most had sold in the morning rush. The obese merchant raised his head and smiled broadly to the newcomer, pudgy fingers spread wide in welcome. The smile quickly faded and the arms snapped shut like a bear trap. "Oh, it's *you*! No customers buying breakfast this time of the day, so I need nothing from your filthy barn. Move along. Now. I don't want to be associated with your type, Leap. Go on. Beat it. Quickly, now. A *valuable* customer may appear at any moment!"

The man made a shooing motion, trying to get rid of the pest. Grant glanced around at the empty area. The market was deserted, and both of them knew that no more customers would be visiting today, but even so, he sketched out a bow. "Pardon this one's intrusion, great sir. I have Time."

"Time? *You* have Time to spend? Hmm. Well… I do have this old loaf of bread. It's starting to go stale." He waggled the loaf in front of him. "It's yours for only thirty Minutes."

Grant gasped at the extortionate price. The normal price for a loaf of bread was *five* Minutes. His stomach was rumbling, though, and it was unlikely he'd have anything apart from fruit or milk until tomorrow. Gritting his teeth and taking a deep breath, he slapped the coins on the table. "This one will… gladly accept such a generous offer."

The merchant scooped up the coins and suddenly sneezed. Rather than use his sleeve to wipe his nose, he used the loaf of bread. "Whoops! No worries; I won't even charge extra for that!"

Grant almost walked away, but he had already paid. He took the moistened loaf and placed it on his cart without commenting or meeting the other man's gaze. This wasn't the first time he'd had to wipe off his food before eating, and it likely wouldn't be the last.

CHAPTER THREE

Grant had been quickly walking along the path for the last ten minutes, but started to slow down as three bulbous silhouettes loomed ahead, blocking the path he was on. This was the only route back to the farm that he could take the cart on, a choke point he couldn't just go around. The only viable alternative path would take him on a two-hour detour through streams and woods, forcing him to abandon his caretaker's equipment.

"Leapster, we thought you weren't going to show up!" The tallest of the three boys laughed playfully. "If we had to wait any longer, we woulda needed to leave and catch you another day. Larry here is *mighty* hungry, aren't you, Larry?"

"Mmm, yup. Momma has a feast waiting for us. Greasy pheasant, venison sausages, and cakes... oh, the *cakes*. Sponge cakes, cream-filled eclairs, and my favorite, the chocolate fountain. I like to put my face under it; Momma says it's a great way to build up my body." His squat frame quivered in anticipation as he licked his lips hungrily, imagining what waited for him.

"I'm surprised your head can fit!" Curly playfully elbowed Larry. "I wish *my* parents were merchants for House Thursday!"

Grant pushed the cart slowly forward. "You'd better get

back, then. This one would hate to be the cause for a spoilage of appetite."

Larry nodded in agreement and turned to leave, only to be cuffed on the back of the head by Mo, the leader of the band. "Now, *Leap*, I know that you are only four years old, but trying to play tricks on poor Larry? It seems we need to educate you once again."

All three chuckled as they edged in on him. Mo gave the order, "Grab him, boys!"

Grant sighed and went limp, resigned to his fate. As a zero-level Leap, this terrorizing was a near-daily ritual he went through. The faster they tired themselves out by beating him, the quicker he could get back to the farm. The more he fought, the greater delight they had in tormenting him. Hefty digits locked around his arms, holding him with more strength than Grant could possibly muster. Larry and Curly were level one cultivators, and Mo *Tuesday*, of the Noble House Tuesday, was level *three*.

His plans of just getting beaten up were defenestrated as soon as he realized that he wasn't getting hit. Instead, Mo was carefully walking toward him with something he clearly didn't want to spill.

"What is that?" Grant begged and began to struggle as Mo uncorked the bottle that was clearly marked as 'dangerous'. He didn't know what was coming, but it wasn't likely to be good. Grant strained unsuccessfully against the hands holding him. "You can't-!"

"We *were* going to give you this gift on your birthday next month, but now is as good a day as any. Praise be to Lord January." Mo spoke first, then Curly and Larry parroted the phrase most commonly spoken in the District, particularly on the first of January. Grant could smell Mo's breath, the garlic of his last meal lingering in the air as he closed in.

Mo upended the small bottle and started splashing it across Grant's face and arms; drenching any exposed flesh. "Do you know how hard this was to find? It took a week to gather the ingredients, and getting someone to put it together cost me an entire eight Hours! Hope it's a good investment and gives us a decent show. Oh, just so you know... this is *Itchious Dermificus.*"

"Look, Mo, it's already working!" Curly pointed gleefully at red welts that were appearing anywhere the liquid connected with bare skin.

Grant writhed in agony, unable to scratch at the unendurable itch. He found power in his pain and rage, managing to yank his right arm away from his distracted bullies. He grabbed the closest thing to him, the milk jug, and swung it with all his might. It smashed against Mo's face, and his health bar flashed as Grant attacked again.

Damage Dealt: 5 blunt. (1 blunt x2. Critical! Sneak attack!)

Multiple chins rippled in confusion, and a tooth flew out of Mo's shocked face upon receiving the second blow. The young man staggered and collapsed against a nearby rock. Bewildered and panicking at the sight of blood, the other two boys let go... giving Grant the opportunity to make a run for it. He left the cart, doing everything he could to ignore the itch while he sprinted up the path.

Grant was almost out of sight of the confused pack of young cultivators when the full itchiness of the potion kicked in and started driving him insane. Scratching furiously as he ran, he tripped on a rock and tumbled to the ground in a cloud of dust. He lay there, dazed and in terrible pain. No matter how vigorously he scratched at the growing lines of welts, the itch just wouldn't relent.

"Drag him down here," Mo's voice was dark and filled with a quiet fury that terrified Grant. Blood flecked his shirt as he spoke, and the others quickly ran to obey; pulling Grant by the feet along the gravel and dirt path. The gravel bit into his flesh, actually giving a little respite to his inflamed skin by scratching the itches that he couldn't reach. "You will be sorry you were ever *born*, Leap. Looks like I finally have *cause* to put you down like the dog you are."

Blood dribbled from the newly-gap-toothed smile. Mo

launched his hand forward and punched Grant's stomach over and over, relentlessly pummeling his battered body. Grant struggled to catch a breath between the meaty jabs and pain of the itching potion. "Join in, boys. Don't mess up his face. We want people to *know* that this pathetic stick was Grant Leap."

Each hit did between one and four points of blunt damage, depending on whether they landed a critical or not. The only positive was that all three quickly tired, unused to this level of activity. Usually, the most exercise they got was lifting pies and cakes up to their faces. Grant closed his eyes, hoping that his impending death would at least make the itching vanish... but then a potential savior appeared.

"Hey! What are you *doing*? Leave him alone!" a voice in the distance shouted. The owner of the voice ran over to the sweaty bullies. Seeing the state of the bloody, welt-covered figure on the ground, she gasped, "Lord January preserve us!"

"Stay out of this, Becky." Mo demanded threateningly. He pointed up at the toothy gap, his bottom lip quivering. "Look what he did to me!"

"I'm sure it was well-deserved! Let him go before I call for the Peacekeepers. You think your *father* would allow this?" Becky stood her ground, even as the chunky lads tried to loom over her. Registering the steel in her gaze, the boys eventually looked away.

"Fine. We've had our fun... for today. Don't worry, Leap. We will be waiting for you tomorrow!" They laughed before sauntering off toward their waiting feasts. As they walked away, Grant's status flashed in front of his eyes.

Quest failed (Survive the Bully). Objective: Placate your bullies by letting them beat you up. Reward: Live to fight another day.

Hidden Quest Complete (Beat the Bully). Objective: Give the bullies a taste of their own medicine. Inflict 5 damage against a single target that is attacking you. Reward: Live to fight another day, 5 hours cultivation, 20% boost to cultivation for 1 hours. Error: no cultivation method detected. Retracting rewards.

"Grant, is it? Are you okay?" Becky came close to him, stopping just out of arm's reach and hesitatingly putting out a hand that he flinched away from.

"This one has had better days." He tried to laugh, resulting in a coughing fit that added more blood to the burst welts on his chest.

Becky inspected his skin critically, and her voice shifted to a professional tone. "From the look of those boils, they used a simple itchiness potion. Depending on how potent it was, I'd say it will itch for anywhere from four to six hours."

Grant groaned at the thought of it lasting that long. She fumbled through her satchel, pulling out a large leaf. "Here, take this. It'll take some of the itch and pain away."

"I offer my thanks, Lady Becky. As useless as it is." Grant squinted up at the system-shown name displayed above her head, confirming what he had heard and adding an honorific. He smiled gratefully at her while rubbing vigorously with the leaf, losing the grin when he caught the slight disgust on her face as they locked eyes. "Ahh…!"

Name: Grant Leap
(Poisoned: Approximately 3 hours remaining)
Class: None
Cultivation Achievement Level: 0
Cultivation Stage: None
Inherent Abilities: None
Health: 15/50
Mana: 0/0

As he rubbed with the leaf, the health stat which was flashing red in warning slowly started to shift. A green plus symbol pulsed next to his name as the length of his poisoning was reduced. Becky smothered her aversion and smiled down at him as he gasped in slight relief, "It's nothing. One of the perks of being an herbalist. This leaf will slowly get you back up to half health, but you will need a rest if you want to heal fully. Is there anything else I can do for you?"

"Please, no. Asking anything more would… could you help this one to stand so as to return to tasks and my caretaker?"

"Sure." Becky promptly held out a hand, then put the empty milk urn back in the cart, wincing as she spotted Mo's lost tooth. "After losing this, maybe they will be less likely to bother you again. Or… they might be more reckless. Be careful. See you around, Grant."

"Maybe. I offer my thanks once again." He waved and trotted up the road as quickly as he could. Fortunately, the cart acted like a crutch and supported his weight. It bounced along until the gravel ended and he passed to the rough dirt path. Rather than go straight on to the farm, he took a left toward his caretaker's estate.

His destination was at the edge of the grounds. Grant kept spare Time hidden in his small shelter—his lean-to—a few planks of wood and some furniture he had salvaged. Most of the time, he preferred to sleep in the barn, near the animals, rather than trailing across to the farm and risking running into anyone. It was easier that way. There was the added benefit that he could do his chores and practice his sword forms in peace before most people had even awoken.

It dawned on him only as he got to the edge of the property that Becky had called him *Grant*, not 'Leap'! He was universally despised. At the absolute *best*, he was tolerated. Even then, it was only because he performed a lot of odd jobs that no one else could be bothered with doing, so this was something truly worth noting. "One nice thing really *did* happen today. A new year's miracle?"

Trundling the cart through the entrance to the estate, Grant was relieved to finally reach his destination… all the way until he looked up and was greeted by his caretaker, Randall, standing at the entrance to the lean-to with ham-sized fists planted firmly on his hips. "I've been looking all over for you, boy. I almost missed mid-afternoon tea and crumpets! After all I have done for you? Ungrateful wretch."

"This one *profusely* apologizes, sir. As an excuse, this one can only offer the fact of becoming waylaid at the market." He pulled the top of his shirt down, highlighting the welts and bruises which were starting to blossom in shades of pink and purple.

"Hmm. Well, that's no excuse. I'm sure that you deserved every last one." Randall grinned at the thought of Grant in pain. "It was payment day; where's my *Time*?"

A fat hand shot out; heavy gold rings dripping with colored jewels encircled each meaty digit. Grant snatched the coin purse hidden in the cart and darted over, spilling the contents into the waiting palm. "Here. Sir."

Slowly and carefully, Randall counted out each and every coin, and Grant realized that he was in for a beating. He hadn't gotten a chance to replace the missing Minutes from being overcharged for the bread. He had received one Hour and forty Minutes, including the ten as a gift from Madame Mercredi. After paying for the bread, he was twenty Minutes short.

"Do you take me for a *fool*?" Randall roared as he got to the last coin, spittle flying in all directions. His eyes started to turn yellow; as far as Grant knew, a side effect of his cultivation method. When he got mad enough, the man went into a berserker state. Grant could feel energy coming from the caretaker, and the fine hairs on his arms stood to attention. He didn't know what was making Randall so angry, but he didn't want to be on the receiving end of a berserker beatdown. "You've been stealing *my* Time!"

"No, sir! This one only bought a loaf of bread and was on my way to my shelter to replace the missing coins."

"You mean *these* coins?" Randall took a familiar pouch out of his pocket, and Grant's heart sank in his chest. "As I said earlier, I went looking for you in the room I *allow* you to live in, and this was what I found. Twenty-three Hours, forty-two Minutes! How do you explain *that*? Thieving like any other Leap, no doubt!"

The energy built in intensity and the man got closer. Orange threads pulsed along Randall's veins, and Grant was turning desperate, "Sir. Please! That is all the Time this one has in the world, from doing odd jobs for *years*. Sometimes at the market, this one earns little tips for fast service, all in an attempt to better myself!"

"Hah!" Randall paused and let out a laugh. Then another. When he finally finished, the yellow had dimmed from his eyes, and his veins no longer pulsed visibly. "Leap, you will never be *anything*. You were born nothing, and you will die nothing. Only the *cow* will mourn you. As your caretaker, I will requisition this Time toward your upkeep. By law, you are under my care until you reach sixteen! As a Leap year child... I'm sure you understand that will take quite a while."

"But I've already been here nineteen years..." Grant stood there, dumbfounded, as the Time went back into Randall's pocket. It had taken ages to save up that meager stash. Once he finally leveled up, he was going to use it to make a new life for himself.

"Then there is the other matter!" Randall reached into the lean-to for a moment, pulling out a copper cup. He waggled the cup accusingly, rings clinking against the metal surface.

Grant shook his head furiously. "I can explain-"

"*I*? You *dare* slip into non-formal speech around *me*? When I was the person who expended the effort to teach you your place? I found this in the barn, and thought to myself, 'how did that get there'? Then I smelled the cup, and it reminded me very much of the cider we enjoyed last night. Were *you* invited to the party, Leap?"

"No-"

"Indeed you were not! Come with me." Randall jabbed a finger toward the main door of the estate, then walked inside, expecting Grant to follow. The young man sighed and trailed along, unsure of what to expect. He glanced nervously around the spacious kitchen. Half-finished plates of rich food lay strewn across tables and countertops. A small, somehow familiar-looking onyx figurine on the mantle above the hearth caught his attention.

"This way," Randall's muffled voice called. Grant tore his gaze away and looked down a flight of stone steps, tentatively making his way down. Globes of light, apparently powered by magic, lined the stairs. At the bottom, he was greeted by a cellar. Row upon row of oak casks lined the underground vault. Numerous varieties of red and white wine… and cider. "Sit."

"Please, sir. This one simply desired to have a little fun. Celebrate the New Year. It was only the leftovers; this one *never* took from-"

"Do. *Not.* Force me to repeat myself." Grant quickly ran to obey, plonking himself down on a stool. Randall jabbed a fleshy digit repeatedly against Grant's forehead. "You may have picked the apples, Leap, but the cider does not belong to you. I own *you*, and I own everything *else*. Do. You. Understand?"

"Yes." Grant nodded vigorously, attempting to defuse the situation. "Can this one go to think over his mistakes, sir? Tomorrow will be an early day-"

"You will leave when I say you will! Now, as you apparently like cider… help yourself to as much as you can drink."

"This one is not thirsty, but thanks you-"

"I. Said. *Drink*!" Randall slammed the copper cup on the table. It was filled to the brim with frothy cider, fresh from the barrel. Grant took the cup in a hesitant hand and started drinking, pausing only to scratch at his welts. He normally enjoyed the flavor, but couldn't under these circumstances. "Come on, *Leap*. You will do better than that."

Randall grabbed him by the scruff of the neck and forced the cup to his face, pouring the frothy liquid straight down his throat and all over his face. Cider blocked Grant's nose, choking him. "Don't spill any, now. I don't want to get a drop on my new shoes."

Grant spluttered in agreement before trying to come up for breath. He had a moment's respite, then another brimming cup was waiting for him. Then another, and another. He lost count of the number of cups he'd drunk. He struggled to focus, feeling dizzy and light-headed. Randall smacked him, "Had enough? Are you *sure* you don't want to drink any more of my cider, Leap?"

"N.... no. Never again." It took all of his effort to hold the souring alcohol-infused apple juice down. "Sir."

"Good. I have one more task for you today. Then you can enjoy the rest of this fine holiday, in honor of Lord January." Grant nodded numbly at Randall's oddly kind words, in his delirium just glad to get away. "Take the large wheelbarrow and fill it to the brim with cow pats. To. The. Brim."

Each word was accentuated by a jab to the forehead. Randall smiled warmly and patted him forcefully on the head. "Once you have completed this task, we can forget this little indiscretion. You are lucky that I am such a *generous* caretaker, boy."

As Grant was barely able to stand, Randall grabbed him under the arms and forcefully showed him the way up the stairs. Outside, the cart stood waiting. Grant stumbled against it, displacing the tarp. Randall strode forward and snatched up the loaf of bread, then ripped off and devoured several large chunks "So, that's what *my* Minutes bought, huh? This will tide me over until afternoon tea. Go. Start collecting."

With a laugh, he slammed the door, leaving Grant alone outside. Despite everything—his welts, itchy and beaten body, even his drunken stupor—Grant took great pleasure in knowing that Randall was scarfing down the snot-soaked bread. He laughed and scratched as he walked an unsteady path toward the wheelbarrow.

"That went *way* better than expected."

CHAPTER FOUR

Grant pushed the wheelbarrow with purpose out of the estate, then promptly released the acidic contents of his stomach in a nearby bush. The world spun as he clung on to the wheelbarrow, taking in great lungfuls of air. He had to press on. The sooner he had collected the cow pats, the sooner he could forget this day had ever happened.

"Sta... tus." He managed to get the slurred word out, wondering what condition he was in.

Name: Grant Leap
(Poisoned: 1 hour remaining. Intoxication: 3 hours remaining)
Class: None
Cultivation Achievement Level: 0
Cultivation Stage: None
Inherent Abilities: None
Health: 23/50

Quests (1 active)

Hovering over the Quests tab, under active quests it showed:

. . .

Common Quest (Cow Pat Collector)

Objective: Collect 50 cow pats and deliver them to caretaker Randall. Only solid, old cow pats. No one likes warm ones! Cow pats are a valuable resource and can be burned as fuel in the colder months of Winter and Spring. Reward: 10% increase to Physical Cultivation speed for 1 hour. (Cultivation method required for rewards.)

It was late afternoon by now, and the January sun was getting dangerously low in the sky. As much as he wanted to lay down and have a nap, Grant had to continue on if he wanted to make use of the last of the day's light. The last thing he wanted was to put his foot in a still-warm cow pat, or fall asleep and freeze to death in the field.

That actually may have been Randall's intent, now that he thought about it.

Grant staggered past the farm and headed up the hill toward the woods. By the time he reached the top of the hill, he was panting heavily from the effort of pushing the empty barrow. He slipped on the loose dirt, but forged on toward his destination. Using the shovel, he scooped up a dried old cow pat. It wasn't that bad of a job. As long as they were old and dry, they were more like bricks than turds! Everything was going well until the sun sank behind the trees, then **shloop**. "Ugh!"

His foot sank into a warm one. As it did, he managed to overbalance the wheelbarrow and cover himself in old cow pats. He righted the barrow and filled it back up, adding one more to the already heavy load with a sigh. Just then, a commotion came from over the hill. **Moo!**

*Moo, *moo*!*

The cows were going crazy. Something had really riled them up. Leaving the wheelbarrow where it was, he grabbed the shovel and made his way over the uneven terrain. One misstep could mean a broken or sprained ankle... or falling in excrement. Again.

He flopped to the side, narrowly avoiding a wide-eyed bull careening toward him. Getting up, Grant could see the silhouettes of the cows via a bright light radiating from a spot at the edge of the forest. By now, his itchiness had worn off. So, emboldened by his intoxication, he brandished the shovel and swiped left and right, clearing a path through the long grass. There were no threats in the region to deal with, not even dangerous animals. The worst thing that could happen, and almost had happened, was to be trampled by a herd of cattle.

His eye caught the glint of something in the distance. It looked like some sort of metallic object. "Stupid cows, scared of anything. It's probably a tool or piece of farm equipment."

Just as he reached the object, time stood still. The twilight was replaced by an intense aurora. Swirls of red, green, and purple light danced playfully in the heavens. Squinting up in awe, he gaped as the colors took the form of a sword thrusting, spinning, parrying, and deflecting. As the colossal cloud sword spun, it impacted phantom armor in a detonating shower of fireworks. Multicolored sparks rained down, and *still* the sword danced.

An insubstantial shadowy enemy fought back, but the sword of auroras deftly spun, perfectly timing parries and counterattacks. Thunder boomed as the spectral weapons collided, along with lightning and fireworks of weapon sliding against weapon. It was a spectacle the likes of which he could never imagine.

Entranced, Grant somehow managed to pull his eyes down toward the object. The aurora glimmered off its reflective surface. No... it was *coming* from this thing. He reflexively stepped back, his breath caught in his throat. Grant knew immediately what it was: a Wielded Weapon.

One of only three hundred and sixty-five Wielded Weapons in the entire *world*! Eyes darting from left to right, he glanced around to make sure no one had witnessed him even *looking* at the weapon. It was a crime, *treason* in fact, to take a Wielded

Weapon from the Noble houses. As he stepped backwards, his hand ventured forth seemingly with a mind of its own, grasping longingly toward the hilt.

On a normal day, the aurora would have alerted everyone for miles around. The hill would be swarming with activity as people investigated the source. In District January, Grant knew that people would be too busy partying, as they did day and night. They would assume that any lights in the sky were just part of the night's entertainment. Perhaps a gift from Lord January on his holy day.

The well of frustration in his heart overflowed. His life couldn't get any worse! It was the first day of the year, and he had been beaten, lost everything he owned, poisoned, forced to drink copious amounts of cider… the thought of which made his stomach turn. On the other hand, the booze altering his thoughts helped him make his choice.

"Why should only the Nobles have Wielded Weapons!" Grant declared as blood thundered through his veins. All of his effort over many years, completing countless low level quests, had amounted to *nothing*. Cultivation rewards from quests were denied to him, and adding insult to injury, he was once more Timeless, having been robbed by his so-called 'caretaker'. He strode forward, grasped the weapon, and pulled it out of the log it was embedded in.

Grant proudly thrust it into the air.

The aurora instantly dissipated, replaced by the darkness of night. A crescent moon shone weakly above, struggling to penetrate the menacing shadows of the forest. As the sword reflected the moonlight, Grant could make out the name of the weapon etched on the side: February Twenty… *Nine*? A three hundred and sixty-*sixth* Wielded Weapon? The sparkling sheen of the perfect weapon was replaced by a thick coating of brown rust.

Status update: name change.

"What have I *done*?" Grant frantically opened his full status sheet.

Name: Grant Monday (updated from Grant Leap)
(Intoxication: 3 hours remaining)
Rank: Wielder
Class: Foundation Cultivator
Cultivation Achievement Level: 0 -> 1
Cultivation Stage: Early Spring
Inherent Abilities: Swirling Seasons Cultivation
Health: 59/59
Mana: 1/1

Characteristics
Physical: 6
Mental: 2
Armor Proficiency: 3
Weapon Proficiency: 3

Wielded Weapon: "February 29"
Weapon Inherent abilities
1) Weapon Absorption: This sword has the ability to absorb the power of another Wielded Weapon, taking its ability into itself. Restriction: Only one weapon per Monthly series.
2) Locked
3) Locked
4) Locked

Weapon Absorbed abilities
1) None
2) None
...
12) None

Spells Known
1) Elemental: None.

Quests (2 active)

Grants snapped closed the status sheet. All he had read was that his name had changed to Grant Monday, of the *Noble House* Monday. He threw the sword down as if he had been bitten by a poisonous snake, and fell backwards into the grass. Hyperventilating, his mind spun at a thousand miles a minute.

"Curse of the Regent! Lord January preserve me!" He slapped the sides of his head. "Wake me from this nightmare!"

Grant squeezed his eyes closed, then took another peek at the status sheet. It boldly displayed *Grant Monday*. In a panic, not knowing what to do, he grabbed the weapon and flung it in the waiting wheelbarrow. With adrenaline-fueled urgency, he bounded over the rough terrain and skidded onto the dirt road. As he ran, he tried to think of how he would manage to hide his identity for the rest of his life… when anyone that could make out his features clearly could see his name boldly displayed above his head.

As he sprinted toward the comfort of the farm, he failed to notice a shining message in his status sheet.

Quest gained.

CHAPTER FIVE

Cock-a-doodle-do!

Grant jerked awake, startled by the rooster, and plucked pieces of hay from his hair. "Oh, man. A hangover two days in a row? I'm becoming a regular Januarian."

He extracted himself from the pile of hay he had flopped onto last night and stretched stiff joints. The soft glow of the sun peeked out from over the horizon. Orange shards of light filtered through the trees and fence posts, painting everything an orange hue. Sunrise was his favorite time of day. The world was still and peaceful. Most people were sleeping, and would be till noon after a night of partying hard.

"A new day, full of new opportunities." Grant'd had some crazy dreams. Something about cow pats and swords in the sky? He laughed at the thought, then glanced at a familiar object, the wheelbarrow at the side of the barn. His breath caught in his throat. "If that was real… what about the rest? The *sword*!"

He crept over to the wheelbarrow, then thought twice about looking inside. He had to do this. Peering over the rim, there lay February Twenty Nine, sitting half-buried in cow pats. "Oh. I'm dead. I'm a dead man."

He picked it up by his fingertips and ran into the barn, tossing the sword into the nearest hiding spot he could find: deep within the pile of hay. The sword was now literally a needle in a haystack! No one would find it there.

Cluck.

"I don't care if *you* find it, Frank. Drat, right. You must be hungry," Grant turned to a chicken pecking away at an apple core. "Apples… ugh."

After his run in with the cider, he never wanted to see another apple again. A quick splash of water to the face, and he was ready to face his day, completely putting the previous day's event out of his mind. The chores went quickly, and seemed much easier than normal, for some reason.

Grant had a spring in his step as he ran around the farm. He fed Daisy and the other cows, did the milking, and collected the eggs. All the usual activities of his morning routine. He even spent an hour gathering fruit: apples, oranges, and pears from the orchard. He was sweating lightly by the end and breathing hard, but he wasn't in the sweaty mess he was in yesterday. He dug into an orange, savoring the sweet flesh and trying not to let too much juice escape down his chin. He found his increased stamina rather strange, but he wasn't complaining.

"Status." The status sheet materialized.

Name: Grant Monday
Rank: Wielder
Class: Foundation Cultivator
Cultivation Achievement Level: 1
Cultivation Stage: Early Spring
Inherent Abilities: Swirling Seasons Cultivation
Health: 59/59
Mana: 1/1

Characteristics
Physical: 6
Mental: 2

Armor Proficiency: 3
Weapon Proficiency: 3

"Cultivation time!"

Cultivation Time: 2:24 Hours (Time to Next Level 997:34 Hours)

"Okay. I gained two hours and twenty-four minutes of cultivation... how? Inherent Abilities: Swirling Seasons Cultivation, what are you?" Grant read over the information that became available to him when he focused on the line in his status.

Inherent Abilities: Swirling Seasons Cultivation. Any physical or mental exertion that can be used for the cultivation of characteristics will be automatically applied as cultivation time. This cultivation manual is one of the slowest, at a one-to-one minute of effort to minute of cultivation conversion rate. Seek out other manuals or methods to achieve faster cultivation on any individual characteristic.

"This... I can *cultivate*! I don't know how, though? 'Automatically applied', I understand that, but what counts?" Grant struggled to do the math needed to understand how his cultivation time had changed him. His eyes glanced down at his status, then all the way up again. Something wasn't right. A lot of things weren't right. "Cultivation Achievement Level *one*? How in the name of the twelve Lords and Ladies did I get that?"

Grant peered closer at the status sheet. There were many more information fields than he was used to. Several times, his eyes glanced over the name Monday. "Monday. *Monday*... Grant Monday! Oh no... what have I done!"

Wielded Weapon: February 29.

As much as he wanted to get rid of the weapon, it was now bound to him, part of who he was. He glossed over the other information that he had no way of understanding. His characteristics had increased. That explained why everything was just a little bit easier today. Weapon absorption and weapon absorbed abilities...? None of that made any sense. He had no idea what a 'monthly series' was, and he didn't like the sound of it.

The final stat that caught his attention was 'Quests'. As far as he was aware, there should only be *one* active quest. He stared at the word, almost too afraid to look. The quest tab flipped open. There were pages upon pages of completed quests, each with a line through them. The great majority were easy grey common quests, with the odd uncommon green quest, like the quest 'Beat the Bully'.

Quests, like loot, had a 'color' assigned to them to help people sort easily and by color. This went from Common grey, Uncommon green, Rare blue, Epic purple, to the final *Legendary* gold. Every item, creature, and quest was impacted by ranking. Each rank respectively increased the difficulty of using, defeating, or completing them by twenty percent of the previous rank. Yet, the rewards from them… everyone always spoke of them with dreamy eyes. Ignoring the expired quests, he looked up at the active quests. The optional grey quest 'Cow Pat Collector' was there.

"It should have been mandatory," Grant scoffed at the thought. If he failed to deliver the quest to his caretaker, Randall, he'd get a whooping or worse. That left one quest. It was mandatory, and unlike the other one, it appeared in an ornate golden frame, with a pattern of golden dragons and interlocking swords. It had the title 'Heal the World'. He swallowed hard, wanting nothing more than to close the quest tab at that moment. But… the quest was both active and *mandatory*. Curiosity led him to open the tab and read further.

Quest: Heal the World (Lvl 100. Legendary.)

Grant Leap, by picking up the Wielded Weapon 'February 29', you will be henceforth known as Grant Monday and will gain one cultivation level automatically, no matter how much cultivation would otherwise be required.

Important Information: The Wielder of February 29, Grant Monday, has one year to gather the power of the Lords of the Month and return February 29 to the status of a completed Wielded Weapon.

Rewards: Completion of the quest 'Heal the World' will result in the reward of the title 'Calendar King' and all wealth and responsibilities associated with that position, along with the ability to wield the most powerful weapon in the world.

Failure Conditions: Failure to complete the mandatory quest 'Heal the World' within one year will result in the loss of all cultivation levels gained since the acquisition of February 29, plus the loss of an additional one level.

It was clear now why he was at Cultivation Achievement Level one. At the moment, his mind was blown. "Is anyone looking at me? Do I *really* have smoke coming out of my ears? Frank, anything?"

Normally, following completion of his chores, Grant would start practicing his sword forms, but not today. He didn't even want to *think* about February Twenty Nine hiding nearby. Instead, he made a plan to go to the market immediately. If he went as early as possible, there was less chance of running into people that he knew.

"Level one hundred mandatory legendary quest." Grant giggled with manic energy as he grabbed an old sack and ripped it into strips. Afterward, he bound his head, leaving only space for eyes to peer out. He grabbed another old torn sack, held his nose as best he could, and forced it over the bulk of his torso. This one stank of moldy cauliflower. His stomach heaved from the smell, but his disguise wasn't yet complete. Grant snatched up the broom handle and used it as a makeshift walking stick. It would do. He hoped. "That means a recommended level of one hundred and *eighty* to complete it? Haaa."

He trundled off to the market at his normal pace, leaving the cart behind. With the bandages covering his nose—mitigating the smell slightly—and chest constricted by the sack, he struggled to breathe. Even so, he couldn't let anyone see his face clearly. If he did, they would see his name. While Grant would rather avoid breathing the stench of rotting veggies… being smelly was infinitely better than being put to death for treason.

CHAPTER SIX

There was a hubbub at the market. It was packed with people from all walks of life; servants whispered excitedly, Aristocrats talked in overly loud voices, and merchants fell somewhere in between. Grant caught words like 'spectacle' and 'fireworks'. He tried squeezing past stealthily, but there was no way to hide his presence. Not looking and smelling like he did. Servants and well-to-do alike turned away in disgust from the wretched creature in their midst, glaring daggers at his cloth-coated form.

"It was *spectacular*!" a Noble gentleman mused.

"Lord January really outdid himself this year. I expected *some* fireworks, but not a full theatrical display," a feminine voice spoke haughtily.

"Indeed, Lady Wednesday." One of the men nodded vigorously in agreement. "I almost choked on a leg of lamb when the first clash resounded!"

"*Hoo, hoo, hoo*. It was quite something."

"No, no. I heard Lord January *wasn't* behind the festivities. Not beyond what we are used to, anyway."

"I've heard this as well! Apparently, a magigram was sent to thank Lord January. His court replied that there were *no* fireworks or magical theatrical events scheduled for that evening. Hold on… *what*," Noble noses wrinkled, and Lady Wednesday finished her statement by gagging, "is that *revolting* smell?"

"*Eeek*! A diseased monster!"

"Quick, Lord Tuesday! Throw some Time at it; maybe it will go away." The group of Nobles tossed handfuls of Time at Grant. The coins stung as they struck his unprotected arms and legs, but despite the pain and humiliation, he dropped to all fours to collect them. Grant told himself that it was all for the act, but he knew that he desperately needed the coin. He quickly shuffled off, leaving the Nobles to their discussion. He glanced around, finding that they had already forgotten he existed and were animatedly gossiping over last night's events. One Lord spread his arms, mimicking an explosion and laughing the whole time.

Grant squeezed through the masses. Most people gave him a wide berth; the rotten aroma proved a rather effective repellent. He froze as a familiar voice drifted over, "Anyone seen Leap today? I figure we could use the time while everyone's distracted to shove him in a hole and throw rocks at him."

Grant glanced up to see the group of bullies, led by Mo, searching through the crowd. "Nah. He usually gets here just before closing time."

"Be on the lookout, boys. After he knocked out my tooth, I *struggled* with eating dinner! I managed, but I couldn't eat as fast as the new plates were brought out! I even… I missed the fourth round of dessert," Mo whimpered pitifully.

There was a sharp intake of breath as his co-conspirators gasped at the unfortunate event. To be deprived of a *dessert*? Simply shocking. Grant, bent over and head down, hobbled with the cart to a familiar stall. "Sorry, dear. I don't have any spare Time. Can I offer you an egg in these tryin' times?"

Madame Mercredi presented the leper with a tasty-looking omelette. "Madame Mercredi, it's me, Grant."

"Eh? Granite?" She scratched at her head in confusion.

"Why are you playin' tricks on an old woman… and what in the name of Lord January are you *wearin'*?"

"I'm sorry… I was kicked in the face by a cow last night." Grant was ashamed to be lying to the kind old woman, but he had no choice. "My face is pretty messed up. After I'm done here, I'm going to the apothecary to get some ointment and fresh bandages. Here's today's milk."

"You're speakin' differently… is it really you in there?" Madame squinted at him suspiciously, and Grant realized that he had stopped speaking formally.

"It's me." Grant grinned under the bandages, not that she would have noticed anyway. "Even with the kick, I'm feeling more alive today than ever."

"Happy for you, dear. But… that doesn't explain the smell. Please have a wash, girl. Men don't like skinny girls, but they also aren't too keen on *smelly* ones, either!" She smiled up at him while holding her nose, then cackled to herself as she ran a hand down her side. "I speak from experience. Back in the day, I was known throughout the land for my *seductive* curves."

"Do you know why it's so busy in the market today?" With a shudder, he tried his best to put the picture of a more curvaceous Madame Mercredi firmly out of his mind. "I usually come later, but I'm pretty sure it's never like this?"

"Somethin' to do with swords and fireworks. I can't hear much with these old ears." She wiggled a droopy lobe to make her point. "All mornin', people have been comin', demandin' answers. Lords, Ladies, servants, even *Vassals*, if you believe it. I told them I was busy countin' sheep last night, hehe. After me cocoa, I go straight to bed. Here's your Time, dear."

Grant tried to remind her that she had already paid in full the day before, but she resolutely ignored him. She counted out one Hour and thirty Minutes and handed them over. "Go on, head over to the apothecary and get yourself fixed up."

"I will. Thank you, Madame Mercredi." She waved as if it was nothing. Now, Grant had no choice but to pass by the apothecary's stall. At least it would give him a chance to overhear more gossip. Bracing himself with his broom handle, he hobbled across the thronging market square. People were still excitedly discussing and debating the events of last night, but the tales were starting to become wilder.

"There was a sword, I tell ya! It was attacking *something*... something dangerous!"

"Where? I didn't see anything like that," a voice scoffed in return. "All I saw were some fireworks."

"Up in the sky, you dolt!" The Lord pointed up, shaking his finger vigorously.

"I don't know. Sounds a bit far-fetched. Swords and all. Sounds like someone had too much wine!" The group laughed haughtily.

"I know what I saw."

"Excuse me, sir." Grant ignored the voice coming from near his elbow and kept his head down as he crept through the masses; careful not to bring attention to himself. The crowd parted easily in an attempt to avoid the incoming stench. "*Hello.* I'm talking to you."

"Oh... hello, m'lord. I'll be on my way. Sorry." Grant's knuckles went white as his grip on his broom tightened.

The servant came uncomfortably close. The middle-aged man was wearing a tailored yellow shirt and pants, emblazoned with the coat of arms of House Wednesday: a monstrous clawed foot in the shape of a 'W', surrounded by a spiked circle. "Wait. I was wondering if you had news of the events of last night. People are saying there was an epic battle in the sky. That the twelve Lords and Ladies of the Months were fighting in the heavens, and the winner wielded a silver sword?"

"Um... sounds unlikely." Grant refused to meet the other man's eyes.

"I was working in the kitchens," the servant continued, uncaring of how uncomfortable Grant was. "After serving the sixth round of main courses, I stepped out to fetch another cask of wine. My lord would have my hide if it ran out... anyway, as I was saying... I saw bright lights in the sky. It seemed to be coming from over a field to the north. Please, sir. Did you see anything? I'll split the reward with you!"

"Reward?" That single word made Grant go cold.

"Yes. Lord Wednesday is offering a reward for any information. He even sent a magigram to the court of Lord January. Sir Monday the Thirty First is in the region and coming to investigate!"

"I-I'm sorry. I have to go and get these festering wounds looked at. My face might fall off if I don't hurry!" Grant's eyes darted around, like those of a caged animal looking for a way to escape. He pushed through the crowd, ignoring the sputtering servant and getting more than one angry stare and curse. He shook his head in bewilderment at his own words. "My *face* might fall off? Seriously? That's the best that I could come up with?"

Up ahead lay the apothecary's stall. He had no intention of buying anything; he had just earned a few small coins by appearing to be diseased, but that didn't mean he felt a burning need to spend them. Plus, there was little wrong with him that a bar of soap, hot water, and a good scrub couldn't fix. Still, it was nice to have an excuse to look over the wares.

Jars of all sizes lined the stall, and cages holding a variety of plants and chittering animals hung from beams. Every surface held one wonder or another. Mysterious potions and unguents piqued his curiosity. Some fizzed, others bubbled. Most remained inert, thick pastes in a multitude of colors. He picked one up, a fist-sized bottle with contents so dark, they absorbed all light. Writing he didn't understand was scrawled on the label. As a Leap child, schooling wasn't exactly *forbidden*, but it was just as likely that he would become the Lord of the Month as it was that he would learn a skilled trade that required actual education.

Despite that, he had managed to teach himself the basics of words over the years by reading quest descriptions in his status sheet and by deciphering signs. Working on the farm, he didn't need to know how to read, but it was important to him to strive to be better tomorrow than he was today. As the apothecary was busy serving a customer, he went to pop the lid on an interesting looking bottle and give it a good sniff.

"Hey! What are you *doing*?" A hand clasped over the lid and yanked the bottle out of his hands, just before he managed to break the seal. "Can't you read? If you'd opened that, half the market would be comatose for a week! The apothecary would lose her license at best, and be thrown in jail at worst! You'd be long dead by then, so *you* wouldn't exactly have to worry about it, but it seems unfair to the rest of us!"

"Oh… sorry. I didn't realize. I just wanted to sniff it." His cheeks burned in embarrassment at the stupidity of his words. "I thought it might smell nice."

"Sniff it? Wait… *Grant*? Is that you? What happened to you? You weren't hurt that badly when I left you yesterday!" Grant glanced up from the bottle to see Becky staring at him, her brow furrowed in worry.

He wasn't sure why he hadn't made the connection that Becky, as an herbalist, would work for the apothecary. Feeling even more stupid than when he almost put half the market to sleep, he blurted out, "Shhh. Not so loud! My head's throbbing. I… I was kicked in the face… by a cow."

"Let me have a look at it." She reached over to tug at the bandages, concern etched on her face. "I'm sure we have something here that can help."

He slapped her hands away from his cheeks. "No. Please. I can't. I don't have any Time."

"Don't worry. You can owe me one." She smiled at him and once again attempted to pull at the bandages.

"I said *no*!" He spat the words out rather forcefully as he pushed her hand away again.

She pulled her hands away as if stung. "I… I was only trying to help."

"No. I'm sorry, Becky. I just… I can't explain it right now…" Grant twisted away, but her soft hand landed on his shoulder and pulled him back. Grant had assumed the strong medicinal smells were covering up his rags, but at this distance?

"No problem. I can't say that I understand... but it's up to you. Here, take this for now." She replaced the bottle he previously held with a roll of medicated bandages. "It will help. You know where to find me, Grant. If you don't want a permanent disfigurement, come *soon*."

He flinched as she said his name, not wanting anyone to overhear it. Unlikely, considering the din of the market, but he was full of paranoia today. Becky continued in a soft tone, "If I'm not here, you will find me in the house next to the bakery across the square. The one with the red door. Take care of yourself."

Grant mumbled his thanks, face burning with shame. He took the opportunity to head back to the farm. If anything, the market was even *busier* by the time he escaped. People spoke excitedly, with a few even trying to leap into the air with their oversized bodies, mimicking explosions and thrusting imaginary swords. They soon stopped, sweating heavily and patting at their heads with lace cloths. If the hubbub hadn't been his fault, he would have stayed to watch; it was certainly a sight worth beholding.

But it *was* his fault. His heart pounded, threatening to escape his chest and burst through the rotten cauliflower sack. Apart from Becky and Madame Mercredi, who thought he was a girl called Granite... no one realized that Grant had visited the market.

Best of all, no one knew that he was now named Grant *Monday*. He grumbled at himself as he raced up the path, "So much for people being too busy partying and drinking to realize anything had happened. Lousy *sword*!"

CHAPTER SEVEN

Back at the farm, he quickly turned in the quest for Cow Pat Collector before he forgot, obtaining an hour of increased physical cultivation speed as a reward. "Only nine hundred and ninety-ish hours until I level up!"

After his whole life of not being able to level up or increase his cultivation, that huge number was *actually* exciting for him. He crept past the front of the estate, terrified that he might be heard and bring the wrath of the household down upon him. Yet, as he turned to leave, a small gust of wind whistled through a crack in the front door. With a **creak**, it slowly swung open. "Randall must have forgotten to lock it? Come to think of it… I think I saw his face in the market. The news of the light show must have *really* spread like wildfire."

"Where is everyone?" As he went to close the door, the onyx figurine on the mantle caught his attention again. He didn't know why, but he felt the overwhelming urge to investigate it. Against all good sense, he crossed the threshold and stood in the kitchen. The table was heavily laden with half-eaten plates of bacon, eggs, and sausages. Grant's mouth watered, threatening to leave a trail across the floor. Without another thought, he stuffed a sausage into his mouth, almost choking before forcing it down with a gulp of water from a nearby crystal decanter.

If Randall saw him now… Grant might literally be killed. The man would be within his rights to destroy a thief, yet even still, he couldn't help himself. All he'd had since yesterday was a few oranges he'd picked, cider, a stolen cake, four eggs, half a chicken, and some milk from Daisy. He was *starving.*

Rashers of bacon were shoveled into his awaiting mouth. His hunger was eventually satisfied by the salty treats and washed down with quality juices. It was only at that point that he remembered where he was, and came to his senses. Grant snatched the figurine and slammed the door behind him in a panic. He didn't know what had come over him. Never before had he been so disobedient or so reckless.

Now in his secondary—and much more basic—lean-to by the barn, he took the onyx figurine from his pocket. He didn't know why, but it was… *important.* He had a niggling feeling that he'd seen it before, but he couldn't place *where.* As he stared at the smooth stone surface, a notification popped up on his status sheet.

New Quest; for more information, see Status Sheet.

Quest: Ties that Bind (Lvl 50. Epic)

Important Information: Multi-tiered quest. Proceed to Mid-January for more information.

Rewards: Unknown

Failure Conditions: Unknown

"Well, that's mysterious… what will happen in mid-January? That's almost two weeks away. A level one hundred Legendary, and a level fifty Epic all within a day… Happy New Year, indeed." He pocketed the small humanoid stone figure. Grant eyed the broom handle and considered carrying out his sword forms. They were an important part of his daily routine and his personal quest to level up his cultivation. "Wait… I own an *actual* sword! Why in the twelve Districts would I train with an old broom handle?"

Curiosity about the sword led him to jump into the haystack in search of the needle. He found it almost instantly—causing a sudden rising concern about his lack of skill in hiding things—and thankfully only received a few small cuts to show for it, since the rusty blade had a mostly-dull edge. Sure, he'd knocked a couple of hit points off, but they'd regenerate over time. They always did.

In the noonday sun, Grant carefully examined the sword, February Twenty Nine, for the first time. He ran his fingers over the handle, feeling the contours and details. He looked down the length of the blade. It was straight and true, if extremely rusty. He could only imagine how spectacular it had looked when new, or would, once it was properly restored.

Due to the length of the handle, it could be wielded as either a one or two-handed weapon. The handle was separated from the blade by a circular guard, a ring of steel: upon closer inspection, it showcased two stylized dragons forever chasing one another's tails. He balanced the blade on his index finger. Most of the weight was in the ornate hilt, perfectly balanced. With a finger from his other hand, he nudged the end of the hilt. The sword spun effortlessly atop his finger.

He didn't know a great deal about swords, but it looked similar to a traditional katana, with the length from point to buttcap around a hand longer than his outstretched arm. The handle was dull, but Grant could almost imagine the two dragons breathing fire and clawing at one another. The ivory creatures were inlaid with gold, which would buff up nicely, but he didn't want to bring any more attention to the weapon than need be.

As if responding to his thoughts, the hilt and guard *shifted*, becoming dull, black leather around the hilt and a plain iron ring guard. It was all he could do not to throw the weapon when it shifted in his hand like a snake.

"How? Magic? I need to learn more about this thing." He closed his eyes and felt the weight of the blade in his hands. First, holding the sword in his left hand, he flicked his wrist. It made a soft whistle as it sliced through the air. After stretching and flexing the muscles in his wrist and forearm, he repeated the process with the other arm. Now limbered up, he held the weapon in a two-handed grip and thrust forward.

"*Ha*!" The chickens scattered with flapping wings and cries of alarm, startled by the announcement. For around an hour, he swung the sword in both a one and two-handed grip, thrusting, slicing, and parrying the weapons of imagined foes. After a quick water break, he was back on his feet, excited about the possibilities offered by the sword. He looked at the fence. "What are *you* looking at, huh? I'll show *you* who's a worthless Leap!"

Grant pictured Mo standing there, laughing at him, ready to torment him once again. Holding the sword in both hands, he sprinted toward the fence post. Clearly, it was frozen in fear, since it didn't even *attempt* to get out of the way. With a roar and downward thrust, he took aim at Mo's head. As the blade connected, the vibration reverberated up its length and the sword sprang out of his grip, landing several feet away. He rubbed numb hands and arms.

"That'll teach you!" In his mind, the sword was embedded in Mo's surprised skull, instead of gathering a fresh layer of mud. Grant picked up the sword, and—more carefully this time—hacked at the fence post. The last thing he wanted to do was break the blade on his first attempt! Over the next half hour, he switched between attacking the fence post and a series of imaginary foes that closed in from all sides. He sliced, swiped, and ducked until his arms gave out and he struggled to raise the tip of the blade off the ground.

After the sweat-induced training session, Grant put down the sword. Reality flooded back in. Mo was gone, replaced by a fence post covered in cuts and missing chunks. Thankfully, he hadn't decapitated or sliced any chickens or cows during practice, but the damage to the post wouldn't go even a day before being noticed.

Grant checked over the blade; somehow, the edge was pristine. He hadn't nicked or rolled the edge. Hesitating a moment, he finally decided that, rather than hide the sword in the hay and risk turning his fingers into kindling, he'd take the sword into his shelter. He could use the bandage Becky had kindly provided to wrap it behind a post in the back corner where even *he* could barely fit. No one else in January was going to look for it there, or even fit in there without tearing the entire structure apart.

Somehow he had lost nearly the entire day. He stunk of sweat and rotten cauliflower, but there was no help for that now. He needed to get some non-drunk sleep tonight, and turning in early would be for the best. Before stepping out of his 'house', he checked his status sheet to see what, if any, progress he had made.

Name: Grant Monday
Rank: Wielder
Class: Foundation Cultivator
Cultivation Achievement Level: 1
Cultivation Stage: Early Spring
Inherent Abilities: Swirling Seasons Cultivation
Health: 59/59
Mana: 1/1

Characteristics
Physical: 6
Mental: 2
Armor Proficiency: 3
Weapon Proficiency: 3

"Nothing changed? Regent's foot, I worked so *hard*!" Since he was looking at his status already, he hovered over 'February

Twenty Nine' to see if it would offer more information. To his surprise, it did.

Wielded Weapon: "February 29"

Weapon Type: One / two-handed Uchigatana

Description: The word uchigatana is formed from two words. 'Uchi' which means 'to strike' and 'gatana' (katana) meaning 'sword,' so that uchigatana means 'sword to strike with'. The uchigatana was originally used only by individuals of low status or rank, such as the ashigaru.

Well… as a Leap child, he certainly held a low status in society. It was fitting, then, that February Twenty Nine was an… uchigatana. He rolled his eyes, knowing that he was going to just call it a katana and be done with it. In the tiny shelter, Grant lit a candle, which instantly spluttered and threatened to go out. He left his ramshackle door ajar in an attempt to air the place out and let in some much-needed light, since the solitary candle did little to penetrate the oppressive gloom.

**Clop, clop, clop*.*

The sound of horses reached him, and he felt his heart constrict. He didn't recognize that gait, and there were a *lot* of hoofbeats quickly increasing in intensity. They soon thundered through the gate of the estate, the horses coming to a stop in the courtyard. The exceedingly well-fed beasts snorted and breathed heavily from exertion, their manes slick with sweat.

Grant pressed an eye to the gap in the door, curious but trying to remain unconcerned. Randall often had highborn guests over to entertain; it was only his nerves and the light treason he had committed that was making Grant uneasy.

Randall extracted himself unceremoniously from a large bay horse, which looked relieved to be rid of its bulky load. There were five other black horses—equally sturdy so they could deal with their loads—and a couple of ball-shaped hounds. An enormous fellow jumped down, the clang of his boots hitting stone startling the dogs and making them snarl.

Grant's caretaker looked like the 'dieter of the month' award winner compared to the new fellow. Dressed in a full suit of armor, the obese figure mopped frantically at his brow; looking *wildly* unhappy to be present. The other four individuals, slimmer than the one who was clearly the boss, dismounted and formed a ring of steel around him, lances and swords arranged in a loose defensive formation. They were clearly not expecting trouble, and from the way they were rubbing at their sore rears, it was unlikely they could handle any if they found it.

Though he couldn't hear much, a gust of wind brought the words 'Grant Leap' and a moment later, 'out collecting cow pats'. They were about to enter the house, but Randall waggled his hand in the direction of Grant's shelter. The four guards and their boss walked toward the lean-to, increasing Grant's confusion and nervousness. "Maybe they will go inside the house… what do they want with me? How could they know?"

Sweat beading his brow, he quickly snuffed the candle and prayed to the Lords of the Month for guidance. The footsteps were getting louder, heavy boots smacking off cobbles. Breathing heavily now, Grant made a decision. He grabbed February Twenty Nine, made sure it was tightly wrapped in the bandages, then strapped it across his back. It was too large to fit inside his shirt or down his pants, and an unfortunate slip with it down his pants risked turning him into a eunuch. He slipped out the crack in the back 'door', hoping they wouldn't see him-

"Stop, by the order and authority of Sir Thirty-First!" a Vassal bellowed at Grant's instantly-frozen form.

"Grant, come here, boy," Randall shouted over in a calm and loving tone. That, more than anything else, made Grant terrified. "Don't make this more difficult than it needs to be. Sir Thirty-First here just wants to ask you some questions, is all."

He had a friendly grin, but Grant knew that Randall couldn't be trusted. He only grinned like that when he punished Grant, relishing the pain and discomfort he inflicted. Grant bolted like a cornered deer, scrambling over the boundary wall in an instant.

"What's this, now?" a new voice shouted in surprise. "Why are you running? Why is he running? Stop him!"

Grant fell heavily, but was up and going right away. The physical barrier would only buy him a few moments; he needed to *move*. He slid down a steep ravine, tumbling as he lost his footing and landing in a heap at the bottom. He quickly flexed his arms and legs; thankfully, nothing appeared sprained or broken.

Toot, toot, toot, to~o~ot.

The hunting party was already closing in.

Woof!

The hounds! He hadn't thought about how he would outrun them. He pictured himself being ripped to pieces by gnashing teeth or speared by a stray lance before they had a chance to question him. Panicking, Grant had no time to think; he could only react. He looked around desperately and heard the burbling of water. Huffing, he stumbled over roots and boulders that appeared as if out of nowhere. They seemed to have something against him, always reaching for his legs and trying to trip him up. Grant couldn't let it happen; dog bites were nasty business, more often than not leading to long-term debuffs.

The rushing water was louder now. He had reached a stream.

Baying dogs were close, almost on him. Grant splashed along the bank, following the flow of the water while his feet sank into the mud or smacked painfully off rocks. He barely felt the health loss. Louder than the dogs was the sound of his heart hammering in his chest, and his breath as he tried to catch it and keep from sobbing in terror. The noise he was making was matched by the rush of water ahead as the stream abruptly ended. Grant found himself teetering at the top of a waterfall. His only options were jumping or waiting for the inevitable teeth closing in.

He chose to jump.

In mid-air, as his life flashed before his eyes, he wished he had taken the time to learn to swim. But why would a farm worker need to *swim*?

Splash!

He belly-flopped into the freezing water. It dawned on him as he sank, weighed down by his clothes and sword, that he should have taken a breath on the way down. His lungs burned, and his vision darkened. Grant longed to inhale, but the cool wetness of the water reminded him that it was a bad idea. Feet finally touched the bottom, and with a frantic kick, he propelled himself back up; breaking through the surface and choking giant gasps of air. The roar of the waterfall filled his ears as he was ironically forced to doggy-paddle to shore. He wrenched himself up onto the bank, soaked through but still alive.

After a moment of lying there, Grant got on all fours and stood unsteadily. The sword was somehow still strapped on by the bandages. If it had rested at the bottom of the waterfall, he didn't think he'd have the courage to go get it.

Ruff!

The hounds were still searching. He sighed and carried on, kneeling down first to spread the soft, silty mud over his face and exposed flesh. Hounds hunted by smell, or so he'd been threatened by Randall. The memory was particularly vivid because Randall had forced Grant to remain in a tree that night, his favorite hunting hound jumping and snarling at him whenever he had descended even a little.

Grant walked until his blisters had blisters of their own, and the yelping of the hounds and tooting of horns had long since faded away. A quest completion notification popped up. Breathing slowly now, he opened the page to see what was going on.

Quest: Who Let The Dogs Out?

Information: Outrun or outsmart a pack of hunting dogs.

Reward: Live to fight another day. +20% Physical Cultivation Bonus for 24 hours

His mind now on quests, Grant fumbled around in his pockets, searching for the strangely familiar lump of onyx. For some reason, it gave him comfort. He searched one pocket, then another. Both were empty. All he had with him were his soggy boots, clothes, and rusty sword.

"It's… I don't have it." He laughed in a manic rhythm as he realized what he was about to do. "I have to go back? I can't go *back*."

Grant remembered that he'd placed the figurine on the stool before lighting the candle. It was *important*. He wasn't overly bothered about the associated Epic-level quest, but he knew that the small statue was… it was important to him? He knew that what he was doing was risky, even dumb… but he doubted that Randall or Sir Thirty-First would expect him to go back to the shelter. By now, they would be digging into their nightly feast and waiting for a report from the people who were still searching.

Maybe he had finally had enough, or perhaps owning a Wielded Weapon had changed him, but Grant wasn't leaving without his statue.

CHAPTER EIGHT

Darkness had fallen hours ago, but Grant still hid in the bushes outside the estate, listening for movement. It was quiet.

Too quiet.

The cows should have been making some noise; certainly the *chickens* should have! He snuck around the perimeter, careful not to make too much racket. A couple of times, a twig snapped underfoot, and each time, he stood motionless. The only sound was that of his heart hammering in his chest, and an owl hooting as it hunted overhead. Finally satisfied that all was clear, he laboriously climbed over the wall.

His shelter door was ajar, just as he'd left it. Grant crept inside. Relieved, he found that the onyx figurine still sat where he'd left it. As Grant picked it up, the shelter door slammed closed. By picking up the figurine, he had tripped a trap of some sort, alerting his captors to his whereabouts with a cacophony of trumpeting alarms. Was this a spell? He pulled at the handle. It wouldn't budge. Grant was straining with everything he had left, his biceps and back protesting, but no matter what he tried, he couldn't open the door. He was sealed inside.

"Come out with your hands up!" A genteel voice, presumably that of Sir Thirty-First, broke the silence of the night a short while later.

"No?" Grant finally managed, after the moment had stretched too long.

"What… what do you *mean*, 'no'?" Sir Thirty-First bellowed at the closed lean-to, "First you make me chase after you, then you refuse my orders? Who are you to refuse a Wielder? We're here to *help* you."

Grant floundered for an answer to that, and came up with a plausible explanation for his refusal. "Well, Sir… whatever you said? I'm sealed in here. I can't get out."

"Oh. Yes. I forgot about that." Sir Thirty-First chuckled, and a snapping sound resounded through the area. "I've released the ropes. Now, come out with your hands where we can see them."

Taking a deep breath, he refused once more. "Still… no."

"What? Why not? The rope is gone." There was no fury, only confusion at the refusal this time.

"I haven't done anything wrong. Leave me alone!"

Sir Thirty-First wasn't sure how to respond to the demand, so he stamped his foot and huffed at the closed door. "If you are so innocent, why did you run? Why are you refusing to comply with a Noble of House Monday?"

"Good call, boss," answered one of the guards, pleased with his Lord's detective skills.

"I was scared and tired. I heard my name and panicked. I've had a terrible year so far and just want to be left alone." Grant's voice dropped off, then picked up for one last shout, "So go away!"

"Lad, I just want you to answer some questions. Come out!" The Noble was almost kind with his tone.

"No. What are you going to do? Throw me in prison? Look at how Randall makes me live; that would be an improvement!" Grant leaned against the wall, as far away from the door as he could get, just in case they smashed it.

"You little brat… if you don't come out, I'm coming in!"

the Noble declared with a threatening growl. The door swung open, and Sir Thirty-First had to duck and turn sideways to maneuver his bulk through the opening. Once inside, he wiggled enough that he could get the door closed. Immediately after catching a whiff of the foul air, he sprayed a perfume bottle around. "What a… delightful place you have here."

"What can I say? According to my status, I am only a child, which means this is how Randall treats the children in his care. See why I don't trust anything that he does? He brought you along with him. That means I can't trust *you*." Grant wasn't going to fall for any tricks; he was prepared to draw his weapon whenever he saw the Noble make a single threatening move.

Sir Thirty-First sprayed a silk handkerchief with more perfume and pressed it firmly against his nostrils, then used an outstretched finger to light the solitary candle. "A minor issue that I can easily address. Let's get down to business, shall we? Grant *Leap* was it…?"

He squinted up at the name tag above Grant's head, but couldn't quite read the name clearly. The candle provided little light at the best of times, and was wholly insufficient for the middle of the night, instead casting an ominous shadow against the multitude of chins and dainty hands holding the handkerchief. "Come closer so that I can see you better."

"No. I'm fine here." Grant tried to wiggle deeper into the shadows, but ran out of room.

"I've had enough of your games, young man." Sir Thirty-First stuffed the handkerchief back inside his armor, wrinkled his nose, and held his hands out before him. A nimbus of yellow light gathered from the shadows, spreading in arcs from the base of his fingers to the tips. Moments later, the shack was bathed in yellow light as he struck Grant with a minor lightning spell. "Now then, let's begin, Grant… *Monday*? Wha… no, you can't… he treated a *Monday* like this? I'll kill him myself!"

Damage taken: 3 lightning.

"Yes. Okay. Deal." Grant closed his eyes and took a deep

breath through his charred lungs. He twitched as feeling returned to his limbs. "You kill him; then we'll talk."

"*Randall!*" The bellow made dust fall from the unsteady roof of the lean-to.

"Yes, Sir Thirty-First! How can I be of assistance? I would be happy to punish the boy for you. Give him a thorough beating, take a few layers of skin-" Randall was cut off by an unexpected snarl.

"You *dare*?" The unexpected question brought Randall's words to a halt immediately. "I thought you said his name was Grant *Leap*?"

Trying to regain his steam, Randall nodded vigorously, even though the Aristocrat could not see him. "Yes. Of course. He was born on a leap year almost twenty solar years ago now. Four, *almost* five leap years old!"

"Well… why then am I staring at *Grant Monday* of the Noble House *Monday*?" Sir Thirty First's outburst was met with silence, and finally a sputtered reply.

"That… that can't be! It must have something to do with last night!" Another pause, and Randall latched onto the lifeline. "That must be it! He *stole* a name!"

"Stole a name? Are you braindead, Randall?" Sir Thirty-First's demand was greeted by total silence this time, so he turned cold eyes on Grant. "Hmm… very unusual. Care to explain, Grant *Monday*?"

"Not… not really." Grant was now on his feet, his hands clasped behind his back. "In fact, I'd love to just go."

"What do you have there behind your back?" The bulky man positioned himself so that there was no way Grant could slip past him. The huge man's face flushed to a dark purple. "Did you find… *something* last night?"

"Oh, no. It's nothing. I just stand like this when I'm nervous." Grant laughed nervously, fiddling with the bandages that were covering his sword.

"Enough of this farce! No Monday would live like this. Somehow… Randall must be right about you. This is what irritating a *true* Noble really means." Sir Thirty-First gathered a fresh charge into a swarm of lightning and slapped his hand against Grant's chest before the boy could move.

"*Ahhh*!" Pulse after pulse sizzled Grant's skin. Arcs of plasma formed between his limbs, lighting up the small space and causing the smell of cooked pork to overwhelm the stench of the shack.

"Are you going to talk, Leap? Or am I going to go report a *tragedy*?" The Noble's smile told Grant everything he needed to know: the 'tragedy' would be reported by the end of the night if he got his way.

"I…" Sparks connected from the bottom to the top of his teeth before Grant could get anything else out. Sir Thirty-First maintained the spell with a terrifying gleam in his eyes. Grant knew that this man just wanted to kill him at this point. The lightning suddenly cut off, and Grant sank to the floor. Sir Thirty-First dabbed his forehead, having finally tired from the strain of maintaining the spell.

"What did you find in the field last night? Tell me, and I'll let you go after only cutting out your tongue for your insolence." The arcing lightning finally broke Grant, and the young man gave up.

"Please! Don't… don't shock me again. I'll show you!" The yellow light cascading across Sir Thirty-First's hands faded, then dissipated completely; leaving only the light of the single guttering candle to illuminate the space. Grant rolled to the side when he could force his body to listen to him, and heaved his bulk off of the trapped sword. With a pull at the cloth, Grant presented February Twenty Nine to Sir Thirty-First, holding the sword with both shaking hands.

The member of the nobility leaned forward to read the description of the katana. His eyebrows rose higher and higher the further he read, and by the time he finished, his breathing was labored and ragged. He clutched at his chest and gasped for breath, falling forward and impaling himself on the unsheathed sword. Grant tried to scramble out of the way, but between the exertion of the day and the pain racking his muscles from the lightning spell, there was nothing he could do to dodge. A sound like tearing paper filled the room, and the new corpse finished its fall by landing on Grant and taking him to the ground.

Critical hit! Coup de grâce! You have landed a critical hit against a helpless target! Instant kill!

Grant's body was infused with a soft golden light that seemed to be coming from within him, and all aches, pains, and weariness instantly disappeared. Then the light was gone, and only the amazing feeling of sudden perfect health gave any indication that it had been real in the first place. He eventually managed to shove the limp body off of himself and scrambled backwards into the corner. He didn't have to go far, and his feet were still touching the body. "Oh, swords and calamities... what have I done? I'm sorry... I didn't mean it! Sir Thirty-First! Are you okay?"

The enormous bulk of the *clearly* dead Sir Thirty-First knelt before him, too thick to look like he was laying flat on the ground. The candle cast an eerie glow against the corpse, making it seem like he would rise at any moment. That wasn't likely, since February Twenty Nine was penetrating his neck, brainstem, and finally poking out the top of his head. Sir Thirty-First's armored cap teetered on the tip of the blade comically, like a flag over a conquered fortress.

"Son of a sweet bun." Grant covered his face and peeked out occasionally. Yes, the body was still there, and it was still dead. "I really, *really* am sorry. You... I... I need my sword back."

He crept forward and yanked on the sword.

Shlurp.

It exited with a spray of blood.

"I'm no killer. I'm not... a murderer." The armored cap fell to the floor, startling Grant. The candle went out, and the light finally faded from Sir Thirty-First's eyes. Grant's sword suddenly became weightless, and words that only he could see appeared in almost slow motion.

Do you, Grant Monday, wish to absorb the power of January 31: Sword Expertise? Accepting 'Sword Expertise' will override any previous Wielded Weapon power absorbed in the current monthly series. If not overridden by another weapon of the same month, this ability will return to its current Wielded Weapon at the end of the year, unless the quest 'Heal The World' has been successfully completed.

Accept / Decline.

"Sword Expertise… that sounds useful. I need something to… I need help." As a fringe benefit, he didn't have any previous weapon power to worry about overriding. "Accept!"

February 29 now has the ability 'Sword Expertise'. Further information can be found on the Status Sheet.

The sword, still bloody from its recent foray into never-before-explored depths, dropped back into his hands. Grant decided that now was a good time to check his status. Anything to get his mind off of the fact that a person voided their bowels after death, and Sir Thirty First had a *very* full colon.

Name: Grant Monday
Rank: Wielder
Class: Foundation Cultivator
Cultivation Achievement Level: 2
Cultivation Stage: Early Spring
Inherent Abilities: Swirling Seasons Cultivation
Health: 71/71
Mana: 1/1

Characteristics
Physical: 14
Mental: 4

Armor Proficiency: 5
Weapon Proficiency: 7

Wielded Weapon: "February 29"
Weapon Inherent abilities:
1) Weapon Absorption: This sword has the ability to absorb the power of another Wielded Weapon, taking its ability into itself. Restriction: Only one weapon per Monthly series.
2) Locked
3) Locked
4) Locked

Weapon Absorbed abilities:
1) Sword Expertise: Imbue your weapon with a Sword Spirit that creates a model that allows for physical, mental, and weapon cultivation. Restriction: the training plan must be followed, else the ability locks for 24 hours. There is only one warning given per day.

Quests (2 active)

Grant's eyes flashed as he saw the changes. "*That's* what the inner light was. I leveled up to Cultivation Achievement Level two! But… how?"

CHAPTER NINE

A piece of flapping white cloth exited the shelter. Grant had sliced off a piece of bandage and attached it to the end of the blade. It was followed immediately by Grant's sheepish face. He waved the flag in surrender, hoping not to be skewered on the spot.

The guards and Vassals looked at one another, then at Grant, then back at each other, and drew their weapons. "Where is Sir Thirty-First?"

Grant went with the best excuse he could think of, one with at least a little truth to it. "He… he needed to lie down. It's been a long day, said something about… asthma?"

"He *has* been struggling with his allergies." Another Vassal nodded along, unwittingly helping Grant's deception. "He hates it up here amongst nature, away from the city. He has the worst hayfever!"

"Maybe we should just let him sleep it off then." Grant nodded his head too vigorously, causing blood to dribble down the sword and splatter across the cobbles.

"Oi! What's that?" an eagle-eyed guard demanded. "Why

do you have a sword? A sword requires a permit, which you assuredly do not have."

"Jelly. It's jam and jelly. Sir Thirty-First had a jar of raspberry jam; no idea where it came from, but he used this to scoop it out." The armed men nodded and muttered amongst themselves.

"Does he have a spatial device? That lucky beast; he's been holding out on us! Well, he does like his jam…" As the Vassal trailed off, a slick of red liquid seeped out of the door and pooled around Grant's feet.

"There… um… there was a lot of jelly!" Grant laughed nervously. This time, no one believed him. They had seen too much blood to not recognize a pool of it.

"Sir Thirty-First has been slain! Get him! For Sir Thirty-First and Lord January!" The heavily armored Vassal lumbered toward him, plates of toughened leather bouncing off his body, a sword aimed directly at the young man's chest. Grant stood there dumbfounded, not knowing what to do. Maybe being still would be a good idea. If he held still it would hurt less, right?

<*Dodge*!>

"What? Who-?" Grant called out to the owner of the phantom voice.

<*Dodge*, if you don't want to be turned into a kebab, thickness!> Grant stepped to the side, narrowly avoiding the sword as it embedded itself deep into the door with a thunk. <Thrust forward!>

Rather than think twice about it, Grant followed the instruction that no one else seemed to hear, thrusting the sword directly forward and somehow managing to put the metal between the plates of armor and into the exposed midsection of the Vassal.

Damage Dealt: 4.5 penetrating. Critical! Multiple organs damaged, debuff added! -20 health per second as Bleeding/Poison/Acid damage!

The Vassal promptly collapsed in a heap, bleeding and groaning. Glassy eyes stared accusingly up at him. "I'm gonna miss… breakfast…"

<Goes to show that you can't ignore an attack from someone weaker than you. Good kill.>

"Wait. He… he *died*?" Grant's body internally glowed with a now-familiar soft light, indicating that he had leveled up. The three other men closed in on him, wary after witnessing the sudden demise of their colleague. "Wait, please don't kill me!"

<One out of four targets down,> the unknown, echoing voice stated jovially. <Only three more to go, and you're golden. Congrats on the level, by the way!>

"Who…"

<Duck!> Grant dropped down, narrowly missing a spear streaking in an arc overhead. A few stray hairs weren't so lucky. <Focus, maggot!>

The voice was hard now, its previous playfulness gone. Grant quickly took stock of his opponents and surroundings. He had his back to the door. A spear swiped at him from ahead, and two additional swordsmen were either side, blocking his escape and looking for an opening to quickly end the fight.

<Drop down and push forward with your right shoulder.>

"What?"

<Now!> Grant obeyed, slamming into the lancer and bowling him over. <Slice!>

"I don't want to do this!" Grant took February Twenty Nine and ran the edge along the exposed flesh of the prone figure's neck, who grasped at the clean cut before succumbing to his fatal wound.

Critical hit! Coup de grâce! You have landed a critical hit against a helpless target! Bleed damage tripled!

<Behind you!> The swordsman on the left spun his long sword in a figure eight and stepped carefully from side to side. Grant was too slow; as he spun to avoid the blade, he took the impact across his thigh. <Abyss it, boy, have you never fought before?>

"Ahh!" Hot fire spread through Grant's body. Blood drenched his trousers, and he felt like he was going to collapse from the pain… but adrenaline kept him upright. Breathing heavily, his white knuckles clenched the sword in a death grip.

<Defensive pose.>

"What's that?"

<Fecal matter. You haven't had any lessons yet, you worm? What kind of Noble are you? No wonder you're useless in a fight. Stop wagging the sword out in front of you and bring it close, in front of your body. Project your vulnerable trunk. What a *trunk* you have to protect! Ugh, you are such a large target that I'm surprised that you only took one hit so far.>

Grant did what he was told. The combatants frowned at each other in confusion, wondering who their opponent was talking with. <Following the death of their Lord, the Vassals lost the Lesser Sword Expertise ability. Despite this, they are a level above you and have *years* of experience to fall back on, and they are *still* Vassals until their statuses are revoked by the new Wielder!>

"Great. I feel much better now, knowing for *sure* that I'm going to die," Grant grumbled pedantically.

<Don't let them get behind you. Keep an eye on both sides at all costs.>

"I'm *trying*!"

<Try harder if you want to see tomorrow, cake-for-brains! Swing your sword up and left; it's called a parry!> Grant deflected the blow of a surprised swordsman. <Counter! Hit him!>

Grant pushed back against the blade and rammed the hilt into a proud-looking nose. It made a satisfying crunch, and the sound was followed by a spray of blood. The swordsman fell back, grasping at his face.

Damage dealt: 2 blunt. Bleed debuff (minor) added to opponent, -1 health per second!

<Improvise. You're on your own now.>

"What? Don't leave me now! I need your help." Grant cried out at the unfairness of it all.

<I'm already almost out of energy. There's a *reason* Sword Expertise is an out-of-combat *only* ability! If I tell you everything, you'll never learn, and I'll never wake up again. Step back.>

Grant stepped back, just in time for a wild swing to whistle past his throat. Ducking or parrying would have been a fatal mistake. "Okay… what should I do? Hey! *Hey*!"

The cogs in his brain spun as a sword streaked down toward his head. He dodged and attempted to counter like he had before, slicing across the armor and losing his grip on his sword. Somehow, he caught it in a one-handed grip before he fell. As he did, he managed to pull the sword back and slice the leather cords binding the plates of armor together. The swordsman's cuirass clattered to the ground, and Grant kicked it to the side. More determined than ever, the Vassal raised the sword and let out a bellowing battle cry before lunging at Grant.

Rather than dodge, the chubby young man stepped in to engage, getting under the weapon and slicing twice at the exposed skin of the sagging belly. Flesh parted like tissue paper, and the long sword clattered to the ground, the Vassal crying in agony as he held his stomach in an attempt to stop his guts from spilling out onto the cobbles. "I *yield*!"

Sword versus unprotected flesh… sword wins!

*Damage dealt: 8 (slashing * 2 attacks)! Major wound added to opponent, multiple debuffs!*

Fueled by rage and adrenaline, Grant spun. The blade whistled forward, eager to end the Vassal's life. He stopped himself just in time, confused by listening to a man that was trying to kill him. Still, the man was down and wasn't a threat. He had to deal with the other swordsman first. An inner light burst forth once again!

"*Another* level? This is awesome!" February Twenty Nine was raised in the… defensive posture? Grant ran like an avenging angel at the swordsman nursing his broken nose.

"Stop, *please*!" the man spluttered, spitting flecks of blood. Grant continued on, his rage clouding his judgement. "No!"

The cultivator's arm was raised in defense as he knelt on the ground. "I have a family. I just got this guard job to pay the bills! Little Billy loves cake and chocolate, and it costs so *much*!"

After hearing this random information, Grant stumbled to a halt, sword still raised and ready to strike. He looked around at the carnage. Sticky blood slicked the cobbles. The bodies of two people lay in oversized heaps, eyes staring blankly at the sky or ground. One swordsman struggled to hold in his guts and would likely die. The other's nose was destroyed, and he knelt here, a sniveling mess.

He did this. His sword clattered to the ground at the realization. "I... I *had* to do it! They were going to-"

<Stop. Calm yourself. Well done. There may be hope for you yet! We haven't been formally introduced. I am February Twenty Nine's current training program, obtained by the absorption of the skill Sword Expertise. You can call me 'Sarge'.>

"Y-you? You're the *sword*?" Grant's knees started to waver at all the new and terrible things that he was experiencing. He had *killed* people, and he had a voice in his head. He had heard that that was a sign of being truly sick. "Why are you talking again? I thought you were... out of energy or something?"

<Your cultivation level increased. I got enough back to tell you one last thing.> Sarge's words faded into silence as he finished his thoughts. <You *do* realize that defeating a Wielder or Vassal doesn't mean you need to kill them? You *can* kill them, but defeat comes in several forms. I'm off to sleep now.>

"What is that supposed to mean? Why does that matter?" Grant surveyed the courtyard. Randall was nowhere to be seen; he had probably taken the opportunity to escape at the first sign of bloodshed, the coward. Grant walked over to the defeated Vassal. "Here, take my hand."

"You're not going to kill me?" The surprised swordsman reached out instantly.

"I really don't want to do that. But I need your help." Grant assisted the man to his feet. "We need to save your friend."

He grabbed his sword, in case the Vassal decided to get ideas, darted back inside the shelter, and squeezed past the bulk of Sir Thirty-First to collect the remaining bandages Becky had given him. He sprinted back to the moaning cultivator that was trying to hold his guts in. Together, they managed to wrap the bandages several times around the fat stomach. A slick of blood spread across the white cotton, but it was the best he could do at the moment. "Help me load him onto a cart."

They huffed and puffed as they struggled with the protesting cultivator. "Let me… die! Sir Thirty-First is waiting for me in the afterlife. In the land of milk chocolate and… honeycakes…"

"Not today, if we can help it." Once the bleeding man had been secured onto the cart, and they had hooked the conveyance up to one of the bay horses, Grant set off out of the estate with the moaning cultivator in tow. Looking back, he could see the lone figure of the broken-nosed Vassal standing there, bewildered. His Lord was dead, he was out of a job… but maybe he could still go back to his family and feed little Billy those sweet treats he loved so much?

As Grant rushed to the apothecary, he took the opportunity to check the changes to his status sheet.

Name: Grant Monday
Class: Wielder
Cultivation Achievement Level: 4
Cultivation Stage: Early Spring
Inherent Abilities: Swirling Seasons Cultivation
Health: 82/82
Mana: 2/2

Characteristics
Physical: 21
Mental: 7
Armor Proficiency: 8
Weapon Proficiency: 14

"Is this *really* what it takes to become stronger?" Grant's eyes were dry as he rushed to town; he had shed all the tears he would for these men.

CHAPTER TEN

Bam, bam, bam.

"It's this house, right? Becky said it was the one with the red door." Grant didn't want to knock too loudly for fear of waking up the neighborhood. He winced and hoped for the best as he heard movement coming from within. "Sword Saints, I hope it was the red one."

The muffled voice that came out didn't help his anxiety. "Who's there?"

"Becky, I need your help!" Grant called out in a stage whisper. "It's Grant!"

The voice came closer, and he relaxed as he recognized it as Becky's. "Grant… who?"

Grant knew that there would be no disguising himself this time, so he went with a lie he had prepared. "A few days ago, I was Grant Leap. I got… adopted, and now I'm officially Grant Monday."

"What are you doing here at this time of night?" The door finally opened a crack, and Becky's face peeked out of the opening. She was able to see the state of the man on Grant's cart, and the door flew open the rest of the way. "*Celestials*, Grant! What happened to you? Who is this?"

"Long story. Too long to tell right now; he's dying. Help me! Help *him*; he's a cultivator in the service of a Noble!" They dragged the bulky character through the red door, leaving too large of a blood trail to be healthy. Just as worryingly, the man's moaning had stopped entirely.

"On the table. Quick now." The herbalist swept the dishes off the table in a single motion. The body landed with a thud, and the table creaked alarmingly even as Grant looked at her with a new respect: she had single-handedly moved the huge Vassal. "Get me alcohol and fresh bandages."

Grant looked around, trying to decipher the text on the various bottles. Becky saw his confusion and snapped, "The big clear one with the red 'X' symbol. Bandages are over there. Hurry!"

She took the bottle of spirits and took a swig before applying a generous amount to the gaping wound, holding it together with the other hand. "This isn't the best way to steril-ize… it's going to leave a nasty scar and maybe damage the tissue permanently. However, it is still going to be the fastest way to work on him without an infection setting in after I'm done. Grant, hold *here* while I sew up."

Grant hesitated; he didn't like being around blood. He steeled himself and pressed his hands on the torn flesh. He had *caused* this; if he wasn't willing to help heal it, if he was going to be sick at the sight of blood, he needed to give up on his dreams of being a fighter right now. The man didn't stir. Grant was glad. He didn't want to be reminded of the pain that he had inflicted upon the mutilated figure. After many deft strokes, Becky had sewn up the man's stomach and applied a fresh set of bandages.

"Will he live?" Grant was unable to hold back the question; he needed to know.

"You got here in time… I think. After I apply a poultice,

and with plenty of rest, he should be as good as new. The wound wasn't too deep, but the big danger is the risk of a massive infection debuff. People can even die from small cuts that are left untreated." She glanced down, her focus honing in on the bloody red bandage wrapped around his thigh. "*Grant*! Your leg! Let me have a look at it!"

"It's nothing." He assumed leveling up had healed the wound, just like it had removed his aches and pains after hitting level two.

"Nonsense. Didn't you hear what I just said? Even *small* cuts need to be treated." She unwound the bandage constricting his thigh and stammered, "Oh, don't-"

That was the last thing he remembered hearing before collapsing from the utter shock of the night.

Grant came around hours later, lying on a cot with fresh sheets. This beat his bed of hay any day. He snuggled into the pillow, trying not to remember where he was. No luck.

"You're finally up?" A beautiful woman looked down on him, and for a long moment Grant was lost in the ecstasy of waking up to a smiling face.

"Oh… hello." Recollection flooded back. The chase, waterfall, fight, and talking sword. The murder of Nobles. Grant sat bolt upright, wincing in pain. "Is he okay?"

"Yeah, surprisingly." She laughed and pushed him down as he tried to struggle to his feet. "You'll be okay after some rest, but I can't believe you managed to get here, dragging him in that condition. You're a *hero*, Grant!"

"Why did I pass out? Did you drug me?" He ignored her last comment. His body was stiff and a little sore, but nothing compared to the man in the next cot over. Grant reached out to touch the covering on the wound, and his hand was promptly slapped away.

"What *is* it with you wanting to touch or sniff things? I had to apply a poultice of Greater Healing to him." Her hand, used to slap at him, was now resting on his leg gently.

"Sounds… expensive." He'd never even seen a poultice, let

alone a greater one. Grant couldn't stop staring at her hand, yet she let it remain where it was, even as she noticed his stare.

"The ingredients are rather difficult to find… iridescent fungus, fire beetle larvae, turmeric, aloe vera, and some other odds and ends. Then lots and *lots* of mana. Iridescent fungus can only be collected at midnight and forms the base. Fire beetles are pretty common, but their mothers protect their larvae and spit flame at intruders. Crushed, blended, and titrated, the ingredients are soaked into a bandage, becoming the poultice you see before you."

"Sounds like a lot of work…" Grant gulped, wondering how he would ever find a way to pay this off.

"Oh, yes. At least eighty hours of work per poultice. We sell it for eight Days and eight Hours at the stall. Most people would rather hand over the Time than go out collecting. Especially when they are already wounded." Becky grinned as Grant blanched at the figures she was casually throwing around. He had seen Minutes and Hours, but Day coins were for skilled laborers or people that could afford to save up.

To him, eight full Day coins was a vast fortune. "I… I can't afford to pay for that. I only came to seek help for the cultivator."

"What are friends for?" She was grinning down at him. Friend? She considered him a friend? "Besides, you saved a cultivator in service to an actual *Wielder*. I'll add the charge onto his Lord's bill and they'll *thank* me for it."

"I don't know what to say… except thank you. I *will* repay your kindness," Grant promised both her, and himself.

"I have nothing better to do in the middle of the night than fix people up. Who needs sleep?" Becky's face drooped, and Grant noticed dark bags under her eyes for the first time. In his heart, he reinforced the promise he had just made.

"Wait. Becky, I need your advice." The smile faded from his face. Before he could say anything else, she pressed a firm, beefy hand against his chest.

"Rest first. I'll make breakfast."

She stood and turned to go, but he couldn't let her. She needed to know; she could be in danger. He would lose his resolve if he let her go right now. "No. This is serious. Becky… I… I killed Sir Thirty-First, a Vassal, and a cultivator last night."

There was a sharp intake of breath as she processed this news, and she stumbled away from him, fear of *him* showing on her face. "How? *Why?*"

"Technically, Sir Thirty-First killed himself. I was just standing there with my sword… and he just… *fell* on it." Grant's hands were shaking, and he couldn't stop seeing the blood that he knew had already been cleaned off.

"Okay… just let me go and get, um, breakfast. Yeah, breakfast. Not the Peacekeepers of House Tuesday. Just food." She started edging away, her eyes flicking to the sword that she had just… *left* next to the murderer in her house.

"Becky, I mean it. He had an asthma attack and collapsed right there. He was inspecting my sword, and he just had an allergic reaction and *fell*." Grant's voice broke on the last word, and Becky calmed down as she saw that Grant was being tormented by what he had gone through.

Then, a dark suspicion formed in her mind. Now she wasn't wondering if he was a bad person; she was wondering if he was full-on crazy. "Where did you get a sword, Grant? Yesterday you were being bullied by Mo and his gang, and now you're a Vassal and Wielder murderer? How does one go from not winning against bullies to killing trained cultivators?"

"It's been an interesting year." Grant laughed weakly, hoping she wouldn't run out of the room before he could finish what he had to say. Her stance became less guarded, and she took a step toward him.

"I got this sword…" He waved at February Twenty Nine, which was pretending to be all innocent, and his tone darkened. "When I picked it up, it changed everything. My personality, my confidence; it gave me a cultivation method that I just *know* somehow… and now I'm Grant *Monday*!"

"What advice do you want? Turn yourself in? Throw yourself at the mercy of Lord January? I'm not sure how I can help." Becky raised her hands in the air placatingly, paling as she realized she was chastising an actual *murderer*. "You committed treason, Grant. *Treason*. There's no way out of that. It doesn't matter how crazy you try to pretend to be."

"Becky. When I picked up the sword, I triggered the start of a mandatory quest. Let me explain it to you." He opened up his status sheet and started reading. "The quest is called 'Heal the World'. Here's the details: the Wielder of February Twenty Nine, Grant Monday, has one year to gather the power of the Lords of the Month and return February Twenty Nine to a completed weapon."

Grant took a deep breath, then finished explaining the rest of the quest. "The reward sounds pretty sweet. Completion of the quest, Heal the World, will result in the reward of the title 'Calendar King', and all wealth and responsibilities associated with that position. If I fail to complete this mandatory quest, it will result in the loss of all cultivation levels gained since the acquisition of February Twenty Nine, plus the loss of an additional one level."

She sat silently for a minute, contemplating all the information that he had dumped on her. Then she let out a scoff, "To complete the quest, you have to defeat the Lords of the Months? *All* of them? In one year? That's crazy! How can you possibly defeat the most powerful people in all the twelve Districts?"

"I… haven't figured that part out yet."

"Can you repeat the last part?" Becky's eyes lit up. "I think I might have found a loophole."

"Sure. It doesn't sound so bad, does it? I have always dreamed of leveling up, but I don't know what becoming the Calendar King means. You think I could be a king? I might like-"

"Grant!" Becky snapped her fingers in Grant's face. "This is *important*. Tell me again what happens if you fail."

"Okay. Sorry… failure to complete the mandatory quest, Heal the World, within one year, will result in the loss of all cultivation levels gained since the acquisition of February Twenty Nine, plus the loss of an additional one level," Grant recited once more.

"What were you so worried about?" Becky clapped, then swatted at him almost playfully before she remembered where they were. In her house. Alone. His weapon within reach. "So you lose a level; so what? What level were you when you picked up February Twenty Nine?"

"Zero. But, I'm level four now!" He shook his head at his sudden change in circumstances. "So, you think it wouldn't be so bad? I really thought it sounded like something terrible would happen."

Becky sat down, her head shaking to ward off his stumbling questions. "I hate to break it to you, but… if you fail to complete the quest, you will drop to level minus one. Which means you'll die. Instantly."

Grant froze for a moment, swallowing and trying to force out the words. "It… does? I'd hoped someone would know a better way. I don't want to do this quest… but I *really* don't want to die."

"I know what you should do, Grant." Becky nodded firmly and reached out a hand to brush his arm tenderly. "If I were you, I would take this opportunity to live like a Noble. Sell the sword to Lord January. Gorge yourself on delicious food, the likes of which we could never imagine. Party hard. Maybe bring a pretty girl along for the ride? Have the best year of your life, and leave a pretty corpse!"

He sank his head into his hands. "Maybe you're right, Becky."

"Of course I am, Grant. There is *no way* to complete that quest. Not only do you need to defeat all the Lords of the Month, but you would need to travel around the entire world in under a year. It'll be *way* easier if you just give up, Grant. The end result will be the same either way." Becky leaned in and gently traced his lips with a finger, then stood and turned to go.

"I'll be right back, with breakfast."

CHAPTER ELEVEN

The best breakfast he had ever had in his entire life finally complete, Grant left the house with the red door. Becky waved at him and reminded him to hurry back to her after selling off the sword. He considered taking the cart with him, but knew that the Vassal's personal equipment was too recognizable. "No. He's going to need the horse when he recovers. It'll take him two or three times as long to leave if I take that cart away. Maybe someone can go get his horse?"

Grant passed through the market. It was filled with the usual hustle and bustle, but notably, no one was talking about the sword and fireworks. Instead, as he passed clusters of people, he overheard the words 'murdered' and 'Thirty-First'. 'Manhunt' and 'Noble Houses' alerted him that he should keep his head down. In the center of the market was the town's notice board, something that Grant rarely paid any attention to; usually he was far too busy with his chores and delivering the day's produce.

Today was different. This morning, he was expecting to see his own face looking back at him. But… it wasn't. Instead, there was an advertisement.

. . .

The Grand January Caravan!

Today—and today only—the Grand January Caravan will be in town! Buy wondrous delights from across the land and sample luxuries straight from the capital city, Mid January. Hurry now. Calendar Sale. Prices marked down in honor of Lord January's month of power!

Beside this notice was a smaller, more drab one. This was a job offer.

Calling All Adventurers. Opportunity Awaits.

The Grand January Caravan is in need of a guard. Danger level: minimal. This opening is due to the death of a guard, but fear not! He died from choking on a strawberry pie. Your duties will include: scaring away cattle and turning away undesirables. Prerequisites: Can carry a weapon. Optional: the ability to swing a weapon.

Pay: 3 hours per day + simple rations.

Having wasted enough time, Grant continued on through the market, only to be stopped by Mo's far-too-familiar voice. "Hey, Loser Leap. Where have you been? We missed you yesterday!"

As Grant walked toward his tormentors, he considered unstrapping the sword from his back. His fingers twitched uncertainly, but the memory of holding a gut closed while it was getting stitched stayed his hand. They didn't deserve that. No one did, not really. "Loser, loser Le… huh?"

"Mo. Why's his name end as Monday, instead of Leap?"

"Strange, that, ain't it?" Mo shrugged at Curly and Larry, who stood staring at the tattered-robe-wearing young man like a pair of confused panda bears who had lost their bamboo, not knowing what to do. Mo hesitated for a long moment, then felt at his mouth where a clear gap reminded him of their last interactions. With a firm-set jaw, he ordered his lackeys, "Stop asking questions. I couldn't care less if his name was *January*. He's just a *Leap*. Get him!"

Larry and Curly loped toward Grant as fast as their bulky frames would allow. Just before they grabbed him with their meaty paws, Grant's newfound experience kicked in. The word *dodge* came into his mind; and he stepped backward, then took his left fist and slammed it into the gut of the boy on the right. Rolls of force rippled out as clear, gelatinous waves.

Ooof!

Damage dealt: 4 blunt.

Everyone had fifty health at a minimum, but numbers could not accurately represent how someone would react to pain; a surprised Curly went down. Larry took a swing at Grant and missed as the thinner man… *dodged*? Off balance, Larry staggered and tripped over the prone lump that was the sobbing Curly.

"Looks like I have to do things myself! What kind of *mortal* dodges? Everyone knows combatants that are properly fed just *take* the hit." Mo presented a gap toothed grin, cracked his knuckles and slowly closed the distance to Grant. "You appear to have leveled up somehow, Leap. That's good. There's different laws for cultivators, you know. Let's make things more… interesting."

Mo pulled a set of brass knuckles out of his back pocket and strapped them over his meatball-fists; then tapped them together with a **clink, clink**.

"I don't want to hurt you." Grant swallowed as he watched the brass knuckles dance closer to his face. He reached behind himself and gripped the hilt of his Weapon, barely stopping himself this time around. "The only reason you don't dodge is that you *can't* dodge. It's practically impossible to miss you if I want to land a hit. Check your teeth."

"*You're* giving *me* combat advice, Leap? Who do you think you are?" Mo's chuckle was cut off as Grant replied firmly.

"My name is Grant *Monday*."

"Shut your pie-hole, 'Monday'. I'm about to punch you into next *Tuesday*." Mo swung, narrowly missing Grant's left cheek-bone but opening a small cut on his cheek. Regaining his footing after the wild swing, he stalked toward Grant.

Still, Grant was holding himself back. "I don't want to hurt you, Mo. Even with everything you've done to me over the years… I just don't want that. I know you, and if my dreams last night were anything to go by, you'll haunt my dreams a lot longer than people I didn't know."

"You talk a lot, Leap. Why do you think you can hurt me? Let me show you how the law works in these parts." Mo struck again, frowning when Grant let the fist drift past him and he realized that he was unable to land a proper strike. "Hold still and take your beating! I know you're weak. You can't hurt anyone. Even when you hit me with that bottle, you nearly wet yourself."

"I killed two men last night. You force my hand, and I'll do it again." Grant stared Mo down, risking a glance at the area they were in, "I'll do it right here, Mo. Right in front of everyone."

Mo stopped in his tracks at Grant's cold tone. A chill went down his spine as he looked into Grant's eyes, and found that he didn't recognize the boy… no, the *man* that was looking back at him. "You… *you're* the murderer? I knew you were even worse than I thought you were! You'll hang for this!"

Grant just about slapped himself; why had he opened his giant, uneducated mouth? "I was defending myself."

"Wait till I tell my *dad*." With an expression that was half shock and half excitement, Mo started to waddle-run down the road, bellowing, "*Daddy*!"

"I should not have said that. By Lord January, what's wrong with me?" Grant watched Mo start to gain some distance and rubbed at his head with both hands. "Now what?"

<You should run after him and slice his wagging tongue off.> Sarge's voice reached Grant from within the wrapped

sword. <That will give you enough time to plan and make your escape.>

"What? No! He's a bully, a jerk, but I could never do that. I'm not a monster; I'm just a guy who doesn't want to die." Grant looked down, wondering when killing a man in self-defense morphed into something that was better than cutting off someone's tongue because he knew the guy lived to eat.

<A cultivator should always be ready for death. Their own, or their opponent's. Hmm. Okay, positive reinforcement mode: I was impressed last night. I knew you could do it!> Sarge paused for a long moment. <That's a lie. I thought you'd be dead by now, so I made sure to conserve as much of my energy as possible. You've got more grit in you than I imagined. By far. In fact, if you gained a point of health from every time I doubted you, you would have->

Grant cut off the sword before it could finish its home-brewed analogy. "I get the picture, Sarge! Can you leave me alone? Or better yet, offer a solution? I'm in a bind here!"

<Go and cut that man to pieces.> Sarge demanded without hesitation. Grant sighed and started moving out of the town as quickly as he could go with such a packed crowd. <Where are we off to now, trainee?>

"Back to the farm. I… I have chores to do." Grant's step faltered as he realized that Randall would know everything. He could never go back to the farm, the only place he had ever called home, and live as he used to do.

<*Chores*? We have training to do! Let's work on your blood-lust first. You still have time to catch up with the sweaty escapee over there. Turn him into samurai sushi!>

Grant ignored the voice and started walking up the path.

CHAPTER TWELVE

As Grant walked in a daze, trying to understand the rapid changes in his life, Sarge kept telling him that he was in shock. The young Wielder couldn't seem to focus on the voice. The excitement of the past few days seemed a distant memory, and he smiled and looked around with glazed eyes as he came within viewing distance of the entire estate. "I didn't have a bad life. I got to work and train in peace and quiet, and I had all the fruit that I could eat…?"

He looked at the orchard and smiled brightly. Today, despite the ache in his soul, he'd hardly broken a sweat, almost effortlessly walking along the sometimes-steep path. In the distance, he could see Daisy merrily munching away. A notification appeared, shaking him out of his current state.

<Alright, fine. This should get you out of your head. It's time for you to complete your daily training.> Grant didn't answer at first, so Sarge snarled, <This is your only warning.>

Sword Expertise—Daily Training

Warning: Failure to complete the built-in training plan will lock the ability for 24 hours!

"Training plan… what training plan? Hey. What am I doing?" Grant remembered something about a training plan being one of the sword's absorbed abilities, but he had no idea what that meant. He got the 'training program' for… killing Sir Thirty-First. He stared wistfully back at the orchard and muttered, "I could always ignore it…"

Sarge's voice rammed into his head, loud enough to make Grant wince, <Look here, *maggot.* I put a lot of effort into developing this training plan. The least you could do is drop your mental pitchfork and pick up the sword you've always dreamed of having. I'm here *now.* Put some effort in. Unless… are you *happy* with your current level? Maybe we should go find someone else who can make better use of February Twenty Nine, huh? Take that girl's advice and just give up now if you are going to fall out! Go stuff your face. Knowing the exact day you die will make you *really* live it up. Just give up on everything forever.>

"Wait! that's not fair!" Grant scowled at the sword that had appeared in his hand. "I've been working my butt off by going all over these paths! I *never* walk this fast over such a long distance!"

<You call *that* work? Ha! That wasn't even a warm up.> Grant could practically feel Sarge glaring holes into him. Confusing, as the sword didn't have eyes. <You either get to work now, or I won't just lock for twenty-four hours. We're *done.*>

"Fine. Just… how?" He tried to access it by saying 'training plan', 'begin', and a few other choice words. The weapon lay silently on the bench, and he felt like a fool for talking to the inanimate object.

<Look…> Sarge sounded irritated, likely because it needed to explain itself. <I can't give you all the answers! You need to

start thinking for yourself. I get it. I really do. Stuck on the farm and downtrodden, you don't get many opportunities to challenge the ol' grey matter. Why don't you start by opening up your status sheet? There's a good lad. Now, you have been given plenty of hints; figure it out.>

Grant didn't respond to the patronizing tone. Sarge was right; hand-feeding chickens and cows, picking fruit, and completing low-level grey quests like 'Cow Pat Collector' weren't exactly intellectually challenging. "Status."

There it was, something that he hadn't seen since, well, ever: a new tab. 'Training'. He flicked across to it, opening it up and reading the information.

To start your daily training, say or think 'I want to become the very best, most powerful, prettiest Sword Expert there ever will have been. Ever.'

"Sarge, I swear to Regent December that I will chuck you in a lake. I don't care if I stop existing after a year, I'm not saying that." The text changed to 'say become a Sword Expert' in the next instant. "That's better. Become a Sword Expert!"

As Grant spoke the phrase, the familiar barn and farm in the distance faded, becoming insubstantial and grey.

Sword Expert—Training Program—Level 1 (The Heavy Man's Introduction to Swordplay.)

<Attack.>

Training dummies faded into existence around him, and Grant tensed up, ready to be swarmed by the strange scarecrow-like creatures… yet they didn't move. It appeared that they were waiting for *him* to attack. He felt proud that he had figured that out by himself without asking for help. "Attack? Here goes."

Using February Twenty Nine in a one-handed grip, he thrust the sword forward, penetrating through the chest of the straw man. As he did, out of the corner of his eye he glimpsed a straw arm swiping at his head. He ducked and sliced the weapon in a circular arc, cutting down the remaining assailants. "This was easy? Ooh. I like this program."

The odd scarecrows appeared again, apparently no worse for wear. The word *Dodge* appeared, and Grant paused to consider it. "So I need to learn to-?"

One of the straw men slammed into his chest, knocking him over and forcing the air out of his lungs. He rolled over and rose up on shaky legs as fast as he could manage. "By Lord January, Sarge! That hurt! Take it easy!"

Damage taken: 5 blunt damage.

Current health: 54/82

<I thought after last night's adventure, that lesson would have been self explanatory?> Sarge commented breezily. <Better start paying attention. You'll end up dead if you're killed by these things. Surprise! Dying kills you.>

Dodge.

This time, Grant leapt to the side, narrowly avoiding the dummy's three-clawed hand. A terrible pain shot through his chest, and he found the tip of a sword protruding from it before the world turned to black.

Attacks can come from any direction. Be ready at all times. You died due to negligence. Attacks survived: 4. New high score!

An unknown length of time later, he was back in the training arena, blinking in the grey light of the illusory world. "Wait. I died? Like... actually dead?"

Dodge.

He yelped and threw himself to the side, actually dodging and retaining awareness of his surroundings. The training dummy leered at him, and Grant started to get *mad.*

Counter.

He thrust at the enemy, skewering it through where a heart would be on a human. It disappeared in a puff of smoke, but then he was surrounded once again.

Thrust. Dodge. Repeat x3.

He followed the instructions, thrusting then dodging attacks from the side. He almost completed the routine, only forgetting the final dodge and taking eight piercing damage. His arm was made of lead. Since he clearly lacked the strength to wield his weapon one-handed for a prolonged length of time, he switched to a two-handed grip. Strangely, this made the lesson shift slightly and start over. He took it to mean that there were different forms he needed to learn for each stance, and he would be forced to repeat the lesson until he proved that he understood what he was supposed to be doing.

<There are three basic poses,> Sarge gruffly chimed in, disrupting Grant's concentration and causing him to take four points of blunt damage. <Defensive. Balanced. Offensive. Poses can be switched at any time. The pose you use can greatly influence the outcome of a battle.>

The words for the poses appeared in the air, and under them stood three training dummies. Each was wielding a replica of February Twenty Nine, their respective postures and sword positions perfectly demonstrated. Even to Grant, who knew little about sword fighting, it was evident that with the sword held high in a two-handed grip, it could be swung down powerfully, potentially slicing a victim in half.

A negative aspect was that the body was exposed and open to attack. On the other hand, with the defensive pose, the sword was once again held in a two-handed position but braced lengthwise across the body. The Wielder of the sword could carry out a weaker slashing attack while also protecting their vulnerable midsection at the same time.

<This lesson would have been handy last night, huh?> Sarge laughed sharply, cutting off his humor as though flipping a switch, <Select the appropriate pose and fight. Do it wrong, and you'll die again.>

Targets ran at Grant from all sides. Instinctively, he drew the blade close to his body. A sword slashed down. He brought his blade up. The other blade slid down it in a ring of steel. <No! Protect your-!>

Blood sprayed into the air, and Grant screamed in pain while Sarge *tsked* in frustration. Another sword slashed across his side while his arms were raised. His hand pressed against the wound, and he glanced down, expecting to see his river of life streaming from it… but he was fine. There was no wound? But the pain was real. The fight reset, and Sarge lovingly informed him that he had died again.

Attacks survived: 24. New high score!

Grant staggered around to face the second of three attackers swinging at him. He parried the blade and thrust forward. February Twenty Nine sank deep into the dummy's gut; poof. Gone. Two remained. They all circled each other and took turns finding a weak spot. While he was focused on Lefty, pain lanced through his shoulder as Righty got in a clean shot. In a real battle, the fight would be over; he'd have lost the use of his arm. As it was his dominant arm, he'd be completely at their mercy.

The pain was excruciating.

<Hurts, don't it? Hurts Donut, the least popular treat on the planet. Grant, to make the fight as realistic as possible, I made sure that the pain simulation was *top* notch. Also, each time you die, just know that *is* what it feels like. The tunnel vision, everything going dark and numb? Get used to it, and learn to fight on. It's the only way you'll learn. Unfortunately, we can't *really* make you bleed, but blood spray and making you feel like it's in your eyes is the next best thing.>

"I'm… a bit too busy to chat right now!" Grant snapped at the snarky sword, sucking wind as he struggled to breathe through the pain.

<Shame we don't have any roasted nuts, I do love a good show.> Sarge's words had the unintended effect of making

Grant's stomach rumble. <Don't even *think* about it. You aren't getting out of here till we're all done.>

Grant solidified the names of the dummies in his mind so that he could focus on them individually—and not his hunger—and Lefty took advantage of Grant's distraction to swipe in an arc. Though he was in pain, he was ready. He half-rolled, half-belly flopped to the ground. As he passed under the blade, he slashed up and sliced deeply across the back of Lefty's legs. In a puff, the dummy was gone. That left only Righty. Grant's vision darkened. The pain simulation was *way* too accurate.

In a real battle, he would be suffering from major blood loss by now. He knelt in the dirt, breathing heavily. On his right, Righty stalked closer and brought its sword down to end him. From somewhere, he found a hidden reserve of energy, bringing his sword up with a roar. At this angle, rather than parry, the sword tip whistled through the dummy's upper arm. Its sword disappeared, and a stunned Righty stood for a moment, waving its stump of an arm before joining its sword in a puff of smoke.

End of Lesson. Free Fighting Mode Unlocked.

<Bravo. I did not expect… *that*! I might hang around after all. We are going to have a lot of *fun*, me and you. I may even up the pain next time, so you can *really* fight through it! That was what, about… thirty percent of what real sword wounds feel like. Overall, I give you a… C plus. Acceptable for a first lesson, like any common person could do, so a 'C' for 'common'. Could also be a *lot* better. The plus is purely for the entertainment value you provided.>

The pain immediately ceased, and Grant's health showed only what he had been missing while his leg continued to heal; all the damage from training had vanished. "Sarge, you're right. Beyond the pain, this was… fun? Is that a good word for this? I hated it, but want to do it again soon? It was definitely more effective than spinning around with a broom handle or a sword-shaped wooden lump."

Filled with adrenaline and enjoying the novelty of the new training system, Grant reactivated the training program and carried on fighting the dummies, focusing on thrusts and dodge attacks. In the end, he completed two hours of intense Weapon Cultivation.

He had been introduced to poses, but he'd assumed the system would provide further training at a later date. The dummies were pretty, well, *dumb*, and didn't put up much of a fight. Multiple dumb enemies attacking together, on the other hand, were far more of a challenge, and he was looking forward to seeing what else was available. "Time to check my status."

Name: Grant Monday
Rank: Wielder
Class: Foundation Cultivator
Cultivation Achievement Level: 4
Cultivation Stage: Early Spring
Inherent Abilities: Swirling Seasons Cultivation
Health: 71/82
Mana: 2/2

Characteristics
Physical: 21
Mental: 7
Armor Proficiency: 8
Weapon Proficiency: 14

Grant had leveled up four times in the past two days, and he didn't really understand *how*. It was supposed to take a long time to level up via cultivation, and he was determined to do so; yet the hours needed had not changed at all, and he had still somehow increased in level.

Looking up, the sun was directly overhead. "Midday already, and I still haven't taken the produce to market? Wait… nevermind. I don't get to do that anymore, do I?"

<You *don't*. I'm glad you woke up. Why are you even thinking about that, Grant? There is no way that turning yourself into Randall can help you, and you'd just be putting your-

self in a position to be tossed in jail or killed for treason.> Sarge's assertion made him nod, though he remembered loading up the cart oddly fondly. <You realize that you can only die and come back in my training simulations. You fail the quest by getting tossed in jail? You know what happens. There are no do-overs.>

"After mouthing off to Mo, I'll need to watch my back. The Peacekeepers may be after me." Grant swallowed and turned away from the farm, heading back toward the town for his second visit of the day. "Okay. I have a plan. I'm gonna join the caravan as a guard and get to the capital."

<Grant, if I had feet, I would be kicking you. If I had hands, I'd be slapping sense into you. Stop! You have no experience making plans, and you're terrible at it.> He wrapped the sword in the by-now tattered bandages and felt the familiar shape of the lump of onyx in his pocket, wondering once more what it was for.

He ignored everything the sword was spewing at him and started his journey to the Grand Caravan.

CHAPTER THIRTEEN

Grant gazed around the market as if for the first time. It was all so familiar, yet so alien. As a Leap, he had never fit in, but as a Monday he could dine and mingle with any Noble, party all night, *every* night… and people would lavish attention on him to gain favor with 'his' Noble House.

The fluttering job notice on the post caught his attention once again, and the Grand January Caravan it referenced had arrived and was in full swing. There was a buzz around it, a vibe that tantalized him with objects and information that he had never before known existed. People scrambled to buy all manner of goods, from exotic spices to kitchen utensils. Pots and pans flew off the shelves—an essential purchase for the numerous chefs in the region. How else would they prepare the daily banquets? Cooking products were *always* in high demand. Quality cookware was a rarity out here, so far from 'proper' civilization.

"Maybe I could just… no. I can't stop to shop. I have to figure out how to get the abyss out of here." He strolled up to Madame Mercredi and simply watched her for a long moment. He wanted to say good-bye but found that he couldn't muster up the energy. He eventually turned away, trying to find something else to focus on, and the crowd obliged. The buzz around the caravan still hadn't died down, and in fact, two chefs were squabbling in the dirt. As the combat progressed, each pulled on a deep-dish frying pan.

"It's *mine,* I tell ya!"

"I saw it first, you two-bit Sous chef!"

"Why would a second-rate *line cook* like you need a marvelous pan like this?" The woman spat the insult at the shocked man, who was clearly horrified to be called a *cook*.

"How *dare* you…!"

Grant passed the squabbling pair, drawn like a moth to a flame toward anything that could distract him. The crowd parted for a moment, and he noticed the largest man he had ever seen, seated on a wagon seat. Size was power and respect, which meant this man was *powerful* and must be someone important. He walked toward the huge man and was greeted with, "How may I help you, young man?"

The jolly man's grin split his prodigious face. He towered over Grant, who certainly couldn't be called *short*. A patchwork of colorful material in a multitude of textures enrobed the gentleman, swirling as his arms made a 'tada' motion toward the train of carriages. "Don't be shy! We have all manner of wonders at the Grand January Caravan. I am the owner of the Grand January Caravan and merchant extraordinaire, Joviality Thursday. You can call me Jo, young friend Monday!"

Grant nodded at the showmanship, impressed despite himself. "Hello, Sir Thursday. This insignificant one saw your notice, and was thinking about signing on as a caravan guard."

"Looking for adventure, young buck?" Jo deflated slightly, realizing that Grant wasn't a potential customer. He considered the young man's clothing, wincing as he realized that a *Monday* had such low-quality garb. Also… he was so *thin*! What had happened to this poor thing's family? "Or… perhaps trying to get to civilization?"

"You could say that." Grant knew that there had been a

misunderstanding, but he didn't mind; it was in his favor. "Is the space still available?"

"We *do* happen to have a position open for Random Guard Number Four! Work hard, and in a few years my boy, you may even make Random Guard Number Three, with the respect and recognition that such a lofty position entails!" Jo smiled brightly around him, ensuring that everyone could see that he was a happy Caravan master.

At first, Grant thought the preposterous man was joking about the name of the position, but judging by the look on his face, he was deadly serious. "I'll take it, though I only plan to stay on for a short while."

"I understand, but not so fast!" Jo roared in laughter at Grant's enthusiasm. "Pay is two Hours per day. We don't have spare kits, and guards have to supply their own gear. Take this list."

He presented Grant with a scroll of paper, but Grant refused to take it. "*Two* Hours per day? The notice said three!"

"A sudden recession has hit January. The sugar market has taken a dive, quite unexpected… we are *all* having to tighten our belts!" The large man patted his vast frame in sadness. "We leave in one hour. If you are not back within the allotted time, you will have to wait three months until the Grand January Caravan passes by this… quaint backwater again. We leave for Mid January!"

"Thank you. It's been a long day. I accept your terms." Grant bowed forward, showing proper respect for the caravan master.

"Fifty-*eight* minutes, Monday." Jo tapped on his wagon and motioned for Grant to get out of the way. He had sales to make! As soon as Grant stepped aside, Jo's trademark grin beamed across his face once more. Grant turned and ran around the market, hunting for the supplies he would need for such a long trip. As a fringe benefit, since his name was now 'Monday', the people that didn't recognize him were willing to trade with him and not spit… or worse.

"Mid January… the quest 'Ties that Bind' said to proceed to Mid January. The *place*, not the time." Grant had originally assumed that the quest meant to wait till the middle of the month, when in fact, it meant the *city*. "What had I been thinking? I need to find a teacher."

He found a general goods stall and picked up a small backpack to store the other gear he planned to purchase. It was thin and poorly constructed, but it was the best his limited budget could stretch to afford. He quickly ticked off the other items: bedroll, boots, a length of hemp rope, bar of soap, waterskin, whetstone, and the most expensive item of all—which wasn't on the list—a scabbard for February Twenty Nine, costing an entire two Hours!

Then he remembered another issue: coins. Grant had given up at first, setting down everything he had gathered—to the disappointment of the merchant that had been watching him like a hawk—but at the last moment, he remembered the coins that the Nobles had thrown at him yesterday which he had managed to scoop up. He had hidden them in a tight, hand-stitched pocket near his belt, and was so used to being broke that he had forgotten them until this point.

Grant felt that he should run back to Becky and pay her for the care she had given him, but the scabbard was a necessity. He could hardly go on a grand adventure with a Wielded Weapon wrapped in tattered bandages… he could picture it already.

'Give me a minute, bandits. I just have to remove these bandages from my sword before we can fight. That okay? Eat this pie while you wait, *so* sorry for your trouble!' Grant laughed to himself at the inane thought. He passed by the apothecary's stall just then, and he contemplated the small amount of Time he had remaining. "Becky, are you there?"

She popped her head up from amongst a collection of ferns, "Hey there, Grant. Everything alright? You look pleased with yourself. How's the sale?"

"I made a decision." He paused, then placed every coin he had on the wood between them.

"Great. I'm busy at the moment. Don't have much time to chat right now. Can I catch up with you later?" Becky saw the coins just then, and a sour expression crossed her face.

"I'm off to Mid January, with the Grand January Caravan. We leave in under an hour." He smiled at her, but his grin faded as her face darkened further.

"I told you to *sell* the sword. You were supposed to..." She slammed her hands on the table, then waved at the coins. "What's this, then?"

"Payment. Everything I have, for what you did for me." Grant's voice was softer; he had wanted this to be a happy parting.

"Just wait here," she snorted, then ducked into the back and returned holding an item wrapped in a protective film. "I'm not going to swindle you. The Vassal paid in full for both of you, and then some. Take this."

"What... is it?"

"It's a Healer's kit. Contains a poultice like the one we used on your Vassal friend, and some other essential items for the aspiring *Adventurer*!" She spat the last word and shoved the package into his hands, then turned away to try and draw in customers.

Grant stared at the package and lightly set it down on the counter. "Becky... you've done too much for me already."

"Nonsense. I also don't agree with your decision. I'd be off partying like there's no tomorrow, and you would be paying for it. *That's* the repayment I wanted." She laughed darkly, still looking away. "But it's your decision to make. Frankly, it's pretty terrible of me to want you to die so that I can have a fun year. I'm... I'm sorry I've been so cold about this. Come back one day, and tell me all your tales and adventures."

He hesitated for a moment, unsure how to handle the abrupt shifts the conversation had taken. "I will. I promise."

"Don't die." She leaned over the counter and embraced him

in a light hug, then shoved him. "Look. Go. The caravan has started rolling."

With a wave, Grant was off. The only time he glanced back, he thought he saw a tear in her eye. A strange woman, that. He darted through the stalls toward the caravan that was slowly making a getaway, inching its bulk forward. A familiar voice made him slow once more. "*Granite*!"

"Madame Mercredi, I don't have time to stop. I'm off to Mid January-!"

"Not without one of ma' delicious pies, you're not!" Bony arms darted out in front of him as she presented him with a succulent chicken and leek pie. "Go on now, girl. Remember… eat regularly and wash. For the love of the Lords and Ladies of the Months, *wash*. The state you were in yesterday!"

"Don't worry. I own soap now." With a wave and an eye roll, he ran to catch the caravan that was making its leisurely escape.

The final carriage had snaked out of the market when he easily caught up to it and hopped on the front carriage, sitting beside a chuckling Jo. "I thought you weren't going to make it, young Lord Monday."

"Wouldn't miss it, Sir Thursday." Grant was heaving deep breaths from the run, and sweat was pouring down his face. "That was harder than I thought it would be."

"I assume you got everything you need?" Jo handed over a waterskin to the wheezing young man.

"Yes. It's all here." Grant patted his new backpack, almost poking a hole through the thin material.

Jovality waved toward the horizon and let out a deep belly laugh. "Then let the travels begin, Grant Monday! Destination… adventure! Wealth! Hedonism forever!"

The caravan creaked its way ponderously out of the town, past shacks, small houses, then vast villas and estates. As the sun set, Grant could hear the sound of distant laughter and music as people dug into one of their many banquets.

Grant was happy to leave most of these people behind; his

only worry was the animals he had abandoned. His life had been turned upside down these past three days, but he had made his choice. He was determined to *Heal the World*.

At the minimum… he would die trying.

CHAPTER FOURTEEN

Without a single Minute in his pocket, and a two week walk until the caravan reached the capital city of Mid January, Grant gazed out at the rolling fields with butterflies in his stomach.

<Quick!> The young man jumped at the words that sounded directly in his mind. <Someone call the circus, a clown has escaped!>

"That's not funny," Grant grumbled, careful not to wake Jo or the other caravan members, who were snoring loudly off to his left. As the newbie, he got the oddest clothing to mark him as a guard; the multicolored robe made him look ridiculous, but it served its purpose well. Everyone could see where the guards were with a single glance.

<It is funny; you just don't understand humor, you uneducated peasant. Well, the adventure begins. Where are we off to, my adipose adventurer?> Sarge's caustic words were becoming commonplace to Grant, though he was confused by a few of the things the sword was implying as negatives.

"I'm on my way to Mid January," He ignored Sarge's strange insult for the moment, unsure what 'adipose' actually meant, but it didn't sound good. "That's where I intend to defeat Lord January in a duel."

<How? What are you gonna do? Sit on him? Crush him to death? Asphyxiate him with your body odor?> Sarge paused for a moment as he thought about his last comment. <Didn't I hear you mention that you have soap? Why not just… use it? You do realize that I'm *strapped* to your sweaty self, yes?>

Grant tried hard to ignore the assault on his hygiene. "Lord January… I haven't worked that part out yet. I won't asphy… axe fix… I'm not gonna sit on anyone! The soap? Why would I use that already? I don't smell and it isn't bath week. Just… tell me, Sarge. Do *you* know what I should be doing?"

<For starters, you have to train every day. Hard. Secondly, you need to stop shoveling food into that gob of yours! What's that you're eating now? You're always *eating*.> Sarge scoffed at that fact and snarled, <Why is everyone always *eating*? You're killing yourself and hampering your physical cultivation all in one go.>

"This pie was a gift from Madame Mercredi, though? Besides, what are you talking about, Sarge? I don't always eat; I'm *way* too poor for that! Abyss, I'm actually thinner than literally anyone I've ever met! People look at me and see a beggar!" As the caravan rumbled along, Grant started nibbling at the pie again. He blinked as he looked down, surprised to find that only half of the delicious pie and a few crumbs remained; so he licked his fingers and mumbled, "I'm still a growing boy. I need the energy-"

<Growing *outwards*. You're nearly twenty solar years old; you aren't getting taller. Stop that. If you stop hunching like someone is about to hit you at all times, you're nearly six and a half feet tall. We're getting you on a proper cultivation path, starting now. First thing that we're doing is making a lifestyle change. You're *going* to follow the nutrition plan I lay out for you.> Sarge waited for acknowledgement, but Grant didn't answer. <That means *now*, kid. Put that food down.>

Grant guiltily put the pie-half back in his backpack, and the conversation between the two of them devolved into what amount of food was necessary. <Right now, all I can do for you is improve your weapon cultivation, but I can at least *help* with the others. The Swirling Seasons cultivation manual you got is considered the weakest of all four-method manuals, but it has the impressive benefit of increasing everything evenly. With me to guide your sword training, you currently get a double weapon cultivation benefit, but everything else is a one-to-one ratio. Another benefit is that the speed of the manual doesn't matter if you walk the martial path and hunt Vassals and Wielders. You'll see.>

The ominous, bloodthirsty tone gave Grant pause, but not as much as the other things Sarge had said.

"What's a ratio?" His query gave the sword pause for a short description of mathematical concepts. Once the human understood the basics, Sarge got right back into the swing of his explanation.

<Actively working to enhance your body will kickstart your physical cultivation. You'll benefit somewhat from working with me to improve your weapon cultivation, but until we find a better way to do it, you're stuck with the basic version. Better than nothing. Barely.> Grant tried to interject, but Sarge wasn't having any of it. <The impurities you've built up will start melting away, starting with all the *extra* you have stored on your frame. Now, I can't do anything about your mind and armor cultivation. Yet. You need armor for the second, and enhanced ways of thinking for the first. On the other hand, I am certain that all of the new ways of thinking and new experiences will be enough to increase your mental cultivation in the short-term.>

"Wait… are you saying I'm going to get even *thinner*? I thought physical cultivation would help me bulk up! It does for everyone else!" Grant was aghast at the idea that he would start losing even *more* status if he followed Sarge's instructions. "I've also been gaining points in my mental cultivation when I increase my cultivation level. Is that normal?"

<It is. Each cultivation level increases your characteristic

points a random amount between an upper and lower bound. As to physical cultivation… you *will* bulk up. As you train, and as you lose the bonus weight, you'll start gaining size rather quickly. Specifically, *muscle.*> Sarge's words cut directly to the heart of the matter. <For some reason, this District seems to have thrown away actual, productive, physical cultivation methodologies in favor of deviant cultivation. I don't understand it, but I'm sure you will find the reason as you continue your quest. Enough questions for now… let's go train.>

"What are we training?" Grant eagerly quizzed the sword.

<For weapon cultivation, we'll take time each day to practice with the simulations I can create in your mind. You'll move in real life, of course, but I can't kill you over and over against real enemies.> Grant winced as Sarge cheerfully let him know he'd be in lots of pain soon. <To boost physical cultivation, you're gonna be learning a movement technique.>

"That sounds fun…?" Grant cautiously ventured. "I've heard tales of people that traveled a mile with each step; is it something like that?"

<No, this is called 'running'. But we'll work our way up to that. First, you'll just walk next to the caravan each day until I think your body can handle more. About the other two cultivations, there's nothing… oh! I know! I'll teach you human anatomy, so you can more efficiently kill people and know where to aim for better critical hits.>

Grant paled at that thought. "Sarge… isn't *defeating* people way better for gaining cultivation achievement levels?"

<It is. *Way* better. Twice as fast. Yet it's far harder than just killin'. You need to make them *submit*, or put them in a state where they can't fight back.> Sarge let Grant think about that for a moment. <If it makes you feel better, knowing the best way to kill means you also know where *not* to hit if you want them to live.>

"I… I suppose." Grant muttered as the caravan started coming to life around him.

<Good. I prepared a song for you while you were thinking that though.> Of all the things Grant had been expecting, the sword bursting into song wasn't it. <*Ohhhh*, the arteries of the head and neck are a great way to kill; you hit em' here and get a thrill! The common carotid artery is a great target; open it up, they feel regret! The external carotid artery will make them bleed free; slice and dice until they flee!>

The song that was now playing constantly in his head made no sense to him until they stopped later in the day, when Sarge made him attack eerily anatomically perfect dummies in specific spots while he sang along. Three days of training, 'songs' in his head, *walking*, and forced starvation later, Grant plucked up the courage to have an actual conversation with the group of guards responsible for looking after the rear of the caravan train.

He wasn't shy, but he had more experience talking with farm animals than with people. Life as a 'Monday' was still new to him. He had to constantly remind himself that he was no longer a Leap, and the looks he got for cringing away because he was still expecting to be tormented at any moment were starting to get murmurs of concern. For the last few days, as he went through what Sarge called 'sugar withdrawals', he had just kept to himself and trained when told. It really helped the terrible headaches to *sweat,* for some reason.

Now that he had a feel for the 'lifestyle'—if you called denying yourself every pleasure *living*—Grant decided that he needed to get out there and practice talking to people. Since Jo had told him to talk to 'Red' if he needed anything—as Red was a higher ranked 'Random Guard' and his superior—he did just that. "Pardon this one's intrusion, senior guardsman… when do we get to fight some bandits?"

"What in the seventh layer of the sword? *Senior*?" The guards turned wide eyes on Grant, wondering if he was pulling their leg. Realizing he wasn't, the small group simultaneously burst into laughter. The ferret-faced guard that had spoken kept at it, "What kinda upbringing did you have, that you'd use such old-fashioned terminology?"

"We'ren't *mercenaries*, newbie. Ain't no bandits 'round these parts, lad. People are more likely to suffer an attack of indigestion," the mammoth guard, Red—apparently named after his tangled mass of red hair—replied in amusement and disbelief. To prove his point, he brandished a pair of shiny hand axes. "These things are only for show. You can tell when someone is an actual fighter, because their weapons have been *used*. Perfect weapons, shiny armor... those are things used by people that don't fight. Us as guards are just part of the theater and spectacle that is the Grand January Caravan. At four Hours a day, I'm not paid to fight!"

"Oh." Grant's heart sank. He had assumed the trip would give him ample opportunity to hone his new-found fighting skills against real fighters, and not just during training with Sarge. "As a guard, I thought I'd have some fighting, or... at least some guarding to do? Hey, wait. Four Hours per day? I'm only getting two!"

"Ah, to be young. When I started, the notice said six Hours of pay! But due to a sugar market crash or some such nonsense, we were forced to take a pay cut." Red's words made the entire group chuckle knowingly. "There's *always* a sugar market crash when it comes time to bring on a newbie, newbie."

Understanding dawned on Grant. "Still... why do I only get two?"

"You're a Random Guard Number *Four*. That's why." Grant decided not to push the confusing matter as Red pressed on, "If you're lucky, you'll get a chance to shoo away some cattle in the next few days. Make sure you do it where either Jo or some of the other higher-ups can see you, and you'll get a bonus. Cattle's a right pain in the fourth chin, if you know what I mean! When the caravan stops, it takes an age to get it up and running again. So, apart from pre-planned stops, such as this one or at a village, the caravan must not stop. At all costs. So, move right quick when we tell you."

The ferret-faced man with a scar above and below his left eye decided to join the conversation. "The closest thing we get to a bandit round these parts are those calendar freaks!"

"Calendar freaks?" Grant inquired more out of curiosity than actually wanting to know. He'd heard them mentioned more than once, and they were never talked about in positive terms.

"Yeah," replied a wildly obese guard, showcasing his wealth further by strumming an actual lute by the campfire. "If you're lucky—or should I say, unlucky enough—to come across one, take that chunk of metal at your hip… and stick them with the pointy end! Also, I don't think we've met. The name's Skinny."

"Grant Lea… um, Grant Lee Monday. What's a calendar freak? How will I recognize one?" He allowed his concern and enthusiasm to seep into his voice. He was both nervous and excited about the prospect of dealing with such a deplorable character.

"Oh, that's easy!" The ferret-faced man leaned forward and stared deeply into Grant's eyes. "Above his head will be the name… *Leap*!"

He spat the last word out in an attempt to cleanse his mouth of such a filthy name. Grant shrank back in horror. He was glad that the evening was giving way to true darkness, and they hopefully couldn't see his features clearly. He had known that he'd had it rough, but he couldn't believe Leap children were so… despised. This was new information; he had thought he was a special case.

"Ugh… Fergus. I wish you didn't say that name out loud. Makes me blood run cold and sends shivers up me spine, it does." Skinny put the lute down by the fire and sighed, releasing his pent-up tension. He'd looked ready to smash the instrument after the conversation turned to the 'calendar freaks', likely not for the first time, judging by his reaction.

"Sometimes," Red added to the mix, "the odd one will try to steal goods from the caravan. In the dark, if we can't read their name, they can always still be recognized by their build.

They're almost always as thin as rakes. They have to scavenge for food to get by, you see. They won't be well-built like most of us."

Skinny patted his huge belly and grinned. "That's one of the reasons Jo hires guards, to stop the thieving vermin!"

"Ya know, Grant…" Fergus leaned in, the firelight reflecting in his eyes. "We heard there was one in New Dawn, that town you signed up in. I swear! They kept it alive; probably as a pet. If it was me, I would have gutted it and listened to it *squeal.*"

Red alone didn't laugh. "You're one sick man, Fergus. It could have been you. Can you imagine being tossed aside just because you were a Leap? They're still people, you skinny fool. If they didn't try to steal from us every time we met one, I wouldn't care at all."

Grant flinched again at the word 'Leap'.

"Actually… Me maw did try to get ridda me. She didn't want a tenth mouth to feed. One night, she tossed me into the woods." Fergus was trying to hold back laughter as he went on. "Too bad for her; even as a babe I had an appetite! I bit a tree as I was sailing past it, chewed through the trunk, and knocked it over. Ever since then, she would put me to work getting the firewood for the week!"

The assembled guards around the fire roared in laughter as Red put his head down and made sputtering noises before coming back up for air with a lopsided grin. Grant broke the good mood of the group a moment later. "I didn't get a chance to meet him. The Leap, I mean. I did hear that he was a hard worker, and well thought of in the village."

The troop laughed twice as hard at such an absurd statement. Skinny rolled around in hysterics, unable to contain himself, and almost crushed his lute in the process. "Good one, Monday. Good one."

"Listen. While I were there, I heard a rumor. His caretaker, a guy called Randall," Red waved his hand to get attention and quiet the others down, "had placed a contract on the Leap… a contract with House *Saturday*."

Red tapped the side of his nose and nodded knowingly at the others. Grant looked around at the involuntary gasps that the others had let out. "What? What does that even mean?"

"Oh, lad, you're a hundred years too early to be wandering about on your own if you don't even know that much." Red shook his head gravely, looking around before speaking again. "I know you're from a backwater town, but you're a member of the Noble House Monday! How do you not know about…?"

Fergus swooped in during the pause, explaining with a low voice, "House Saturday, you young fool. The *assassins' guild*."

"Fergus, you know as well as we all do that there's no *evidence*! If even House Tuesday can't pin anything on them, you can't be making claims like that. Don't go saying something that will get us killed for no good reason!" Skinny chided him, chucking a small rock at the other guard.

"Every House of the Week has its specialty, and we *all* know the abyssal truth about House Saturday!" Fergus snarled at Skinny before making a sweeping motion at Grant, "Only reason that Leap is still eatin' is… well, fact of the matter is that no one wanted to come all the way out here, this far from civilization, to deal with one little Leap! It was too menial a task. I heard they just told Randall to put down some poison and let nature take its course, like it does for all the rats… but he couldn't do that. House Tuesday has decreed that all kids under sixteen have to be looked after till they come of age, if they were assigned a caretaker ."

Skinny spat into the fire, "I don't understand it. Everyone knows that the Lords and Ladies made the world have three hundred and sixty-five days. Every four years there's an extra day to remind us that we *need* the Lords and Ladies. Leap children are *abominations*!"

"You're still going on about that prophecy?" Red shook his head and rolled his eyes. "Nothing keeps you up at night quite like a thousand-year old prophecy claiming that, 'if February Twenty Ninth lives, it will become the Calendar King and break time and the world itself'. I bet you're still afraid of the tooth fairy, aren't you?"

"No, I'm afraid of their larger and much more dangerous cousins, the carnivorous bone fairies!" Fergus's furious reply made the group howl with laughter.

CHAPTER FIFTEEN

Grant dashed forward to strike down imaginary enemies. To the nonplussed onlookers, it even appeared that the invisible foes fought back, making Grant collapse to the ground after a particularly vicious blow.

"Did he lose his mind?" Red was watching Grant with a critical eye.

Fergus shrugged and went back to chewing on a drumstick. "Maybe it was something he ate?"

"Huh?" Red scratched his head. "He has barely eaten anything in the last few days, and that's at quarter rations!"

"Then maybe it is something he *didn't* eat? Forget it. He's clearly insane. Not only is he fighting something that isn't there, they're winning!" Fergus lounged on top of the final carriage next to Red and made a few more off-the-wall comments.

"The piece that gives it away to me..." Red lazily waved a chicken wing in Grant's general direction. "Who in their right mind would walk beside the caravan when there are fried fowl to enjoy?"

"Crazy, I told you!" Fergus shook his head in wonder. "He's

an odd one. Talks about 'bettering' himself, can you believe that? He says he's doing physical cultivation."

"Haha. Cultivation with any method beyond what Lord January shared with the District is so slow that it's virtually pointless. Doesn't he know that?" Red chuckled at the thought as he tore a chunk from his meal. "Even then, if it wasn't so easy, it just flat out wouldn't be worth it. You get an hour of physical cultivation for every five that you spend on it, ya know? Basically just two hours a day."

"What are you two doing? Work? Unlikely." Lady Vivian, the daughter of Joviality Thursday, started clambering laboriously up the stairs to stand beside the lounging guards. "You're doing what you're always doing; eating all my father's food."

"Part of the contract, my lady. Jo, er, I mean, Lord Thursday, doesn't mind. In fact, he encourages it. We're entitled to all the rations we can eat to properly cultivate, which is why our pay is… the way it is. Fergus has a fast metaba… metab… wotsit called? Look at how *skinny* he is! Plus, we need the energy to be able to fight off intruders."

"I don't *see* any intruders." Lady Vivian pointedly scanned the empty landscape.

"Exactly! See? Our strategy is working. As long as we keep eating, no foe will dare attack the caravan," Red chortled around a mouthful of chicken.

"All I know is that you're literally eating into our profits. Hmm. Also, the word is 'metabolism'. I've no idea why we employ people with such low mental characteristics." Sudden and rapid movement near the carriage caught her eye and made her flinch away. "Oh, *my*. Who is that, and what in the twelve Districts is he *doing*?"

"That," Red shook his head sadly and pointed with a fresh greasy drumstick, "is Grant Monday."

"Monday…? As a Noble house, they *are* well respected for their combat proficiency. Born leaders, they say." She mused softly as she watched blood start to pour from Grant's nose.

"But… what is he doing, jumping around like that? He's using a rusty sword; is that… helpful?"

"Says he's 'training'," Fergus answered, spitting half-chewed food with every word. "The lad joined us about a week ago now. Trying to better himself through training and cultivation; what we were just talking about, matter of fact. Poor fool is a few sandwiches and a lemonade short of a picnic, if you know what I mean!"

All three of them laughed while they observed Grant from the comfort of the loungers atop the carriage. Red's eyes gleamed as he had a dark thought. He could mess with Grant, and laugh at Vivian at the same time. "Lady Vivian?"

"Hmm. What is it, guard dog?"

"Grant was saying, the other day-like, after one of his training sessions, that he has a thing for strong, dominant women." Red pinched Fergus before he could comment and ruin his joke.

"*Really*?" She perked up, focusing on what he had to say, even though she was clearly uncertain if he was telling the truth.

Red nodded heavily. "Oh, yes. Now, I shouldn't be spreading rumors… but I believe he may have a thing for *you*. Not only are you the princess of his employer, but you have the reputation he desires to partake in."

"Oh. Do *behave*! You naughty, naughty man. What utter nonsense!" She fanned herself furiously as her cheeks flushed. "That you think you can talk to me like this and get away with it…!"

"Fergus?" Red turned his head fully to the side so that Vivian couldn't see his wicked grin. "Is it my imagination, or is Grant *thinner* than he was about a week ago?"

Both guards turned a critical eye on Grant and frowned. It had been meant as a joke, but Red actually had a point. Fergus lifted his chicken bone, then lowered it with a frown. "Can't be because of the training. Everyone knows you don't lose size through physical cultivation; you get *bigger*. Probably just skipped his meals? What do you think, Vivian?"

"Muscles… I see broad shoulders and taut *muscles*? He did smile at me the other day…" she mumbled as her fan fluttered even faster. "I'm sure of it. I had thought he was just being friendly, as we've never met… but perhaps he has simply been admiring me from afar? That would make sense…?"

"He *is* a friendly chap. Smiles at everyone." Fergus got a backhand to the side from Red for the idle comment. "Though, yes, who doesn't admire you?"

"I… I suddenly feel faint. I think I need to lie down… I've been in the sun too long." Vivian gazed down at the shirtless, sweat-soaked Grant, who was resting after his intense session. She abruptly left the two men to their spread of food and retired to her carriage.

"That was a mean thing to do." Fergus shook his head. "That wasn't like you, Red."

"How so?"

"Telling porkies and playing tricks. Saying Grant has a thing for how she acts?" The guard turned a level stare on Red. "We both know he barely speaks to anyone, let alone meet the eye of the lowliest of us. Being bold enough to announce his feelings just isn't something that would happen."

"But he *does*!" Red claimed with a look of false astonishment.

Fergus gave him a hard glare. "No, he doesn't! It was *me* that said I can't say no to strong, dominant women. You've met my wife, haven't you?"

"Oh… huh. Now that you mention it…" Red took a bite of poultry to hide his grin.

That didn't stop Fergus from shuddering at the thought of Lady Vivian coming after him. "But even *I* wouldn't cross paths with Lady Vivian. She scares the cake right outta me!"

"Oh, no… what *have* I done?" Red grasped at his chest in false panic, then waved uncaringly. "Please, Fergus, I'm sure she's forgotten about it already. We were just having a bit of fun."

"I wouldn't be so sure. She'll eat him alive, Red. Afterwards, she'll crack his bones and suck out the marrow." Fergus's eyes widened as Red started laughing and couldn't stop, joining in after a moment. They took deep swigs from the wine jug, quickly forgetting the conversation.

Grant sucked heaving breaths of air into tired lungs. His fitness was improving, but the training sessions took *everything* out of him. He glanced up and noticed that Red and Fergus were spectating atop the Grand January Caravan. They had the 'important responsibility' of protecting the rear against attack. In his mind, all they were protecting was their right to be as close to the food wagon and eat all the rations they could get their grease-stained hands on.

As someone with a deep knowledge of hunger, it pained him to witness *everyone*, not just those two, constantly gorging themselves. He sighed and started daydreaming about cake. "When is it going to be *my* turn to live well?"

He had noticed a stout-looking woman wearing a frilly dress joining the guards, but when he looked up after his training session, she was already gone. He ignored that and tried to rid his mind of dancing sugar plums; he didn't have time to daydream. Sarge snapped him out of his thoughts with a sharp, <*Grant.* Can I finally have your attention again? There will be plenty of time to booze and feast with your band of merry men *after* you're a Sword Expert.>

"I was just catching my breath, Sarge!" Grant heaved himself to his feet, swaying slightly in the process.

<Hmm. Almost a week of training, and you've mastered the most basic of the basic poses, and learned some feeble attacks. Sword Saints, I'm even starting to believe that there's a slightly lower chance that you'll trip over your own feet or impale your-

self during your next battle. Let's see how much you'll disappoint me. The next lesson begins!> As the caravan trundled along, a straw man ran toward Grant, sword raised high. As it swung, he easily parried the blade before slicing across its stomach.

"The descending thoracic aorta is too deep to know it; a heavy chop is the only way to show it…!" Grant mumbled as 'blood' sprayed out of the dummy. Another straw man followed, sword held low. He parried the blade as before, then thrust deeply at its heart and ended the training dummy in a puff of smoke. "This is too easy!"

A third dummy ran at him, sword held high. The grin was wiped off his face as a boot connected with his chest. Grant flew backwards and hit the ground with a thud. Lying there with his back hurting and his chest bruising, he fought to get air into his lungs.

<In a real fight, that kick would have been followed up by a sword through the heart, custard brain. Don't get complacent just because you can do *one thing* over and over again.>

"I thought…"

<You didn't think, you *reacted*! Reacting in combat allows a more intelligent opponent to deceive you. The point of this lesson is to learn about deception and avoiding repetition. As you can see, falling into predictable or repetitive patterns of movement can result in unfortunate consequences. You can't just parry, thrust, and dodge in every encounter and expect to live to fight another day! You may get lucky against some low-level Vassals, but that's about it.>

<Before you charge in, you must study your opponent and continue to monitor their movements throughout the fight. Do *they* move in predictable ways? As you study them, disciplined fighters will also be studying *you*, looking for a weakness to fatally exploit. The best fighter and victor isn't necessarily the strongest or highest level. Randomize your methods of attack. Now, I'm sure that info dump has already passed through the

mass of pudding between your ears and exited the other side. Isn't that right?>

"Yes. I mean no! I was listening! Deception. Study my opponent and move in unpredictable ways." Groaning, he got to his feet and prepared for the next foe.

<My, my. Maybe you aren't quite as dense as I thought. Good. Let's follow up with a little test. I've prepared a scenario for you. Deal with the attack, and the lesson will be complete for the day.> There was the noise of fingers clicking, and reality faded away once again, the caravan was now as insubstantial as early morning mist.

Grant found himself on a wooden pier. Ahead lay a massive body of water stretching into the distance. He assumed it was the sea or a large lake; he'd overheard people talking about the sea at the market. Nobles had villas along the coast and would summer there during the warmer months.

An eruption of water, followed by the crash of an object landing on the end of the pier, brought him back to the semi-reality of the training scenario. He backpedaled in terror as a monstrous *thing* pulled the rest of its bloated body onto the pier. Angry tentacles, each twice the length of a grown man, smacked the planks. The impacts reverberated up his shins and through his teeth. Grant wanted to run but was pinned in place by fear; knowing that it was only a test didn't make him feel any better.

<That, my newly-minted maritime-monster-murdering martialist, is a baby Kraken.>

"A *baby*...?" He didn't want to meet an adult. Regent's glare, he didn't want to meet *this*! "Okay, so just imagine it like I'm facing eight opponents, and deal with them one at a time?"

<If you think that's the way to handle it.>

Grant stepped forward, closely examining the movement of the purple tentacles. There was no easy way to target the Kraken; too many limbs were moving erratically. He stopped, forcing the creature to grope its way along the planks toward him. A ropy tentacle swiped at him from the left. He pretended to dodge, but instead swiped upwards. A length of gelatinous arm was cleanly cut off and landed on the deck. It flopped around with a mind of its own before falling over the edge and into the dark water.

Rather than retreat, he took the opportunity to dart closer while the creature flailed around in pain. He jumped over a tentacle, taking a retaliatory swipe, and managed to hack off two more flailing limbs before rolling back to safety.

Another whipped at him from the right. He assumed that it wouldn't fall for the same attack, but he managed to sidestep as the arm battered the planks into kindling. A cartwheel-sized eye, filled with hate and what appeared to be slimy tears, focused on him. The baby Kraken opened its beak and let out a shriek. Grant stepped back, but where he expected planks, he was met with air. With the memory of jumping over the waterfall fresh in his mind, he managed to take a breath before submerging. His head bashed against the underside of the pier as he attempted to find a way back to the surface, and panic set in. Training simulation or reality, this felt painfully real.

A thickly muscled tentacle wrapped around his waist and squeezed, forcing out any air remaining in his lungs. His body broke the surface, but he was unable to inhale. The rubbery arm continued holding on tightly to its prize. Grant's vision began to darken through lack of oxygen, and yet, the Kraken hadn't finished playing with its toy. It pummeled his broken body repeatedly into the deck, and the last thing he remembered before passing out was the multiple rows of undulating, gnashing teeth and a foul fishy breath… just before his body made its way toward the gaping razor-lined maw.

He awoke from the nightmare on familiar grass. The Grand January Caravan was already a speck in the distance. Sarge cheerily called, <Well, *that* was fun, wasn't it? I bet you can't *wait* to visit the seaside now. Maybe do a spot of fishing? Build a sandcastle?>

"Ugh…" The horror and pain had left Grant a quivering mess. "So… many… teeth."

Sarge seemed to decide that it was time to test Grant's knowledge. <What lesson did you learn? You failed to kill the Kraken, but did you *learn* anything?>

"Stay away from the water?"

<For you… that may be a good idea. But you fail. The lesson was one in deception.>

"But how could I have-?"

<*It* deceived *you* by sacrificing its limbs. You were lulled into a false sense of security and blithely hacked away at the limbs that it was practically *giving* you. The Kraken had smashed the pier on purpose, knowing that you would fall into the water: *its* domain.>

Grant shook his head furiously, unable to believe what Sarge was telling him. "Why would it sacrifice its arms? That seems… unrealistic."

<No, not really. They grow back. Not for you, but for it. Now, about this lesson: I know it wasn't fair. But… it was fun to watch! In all seriousness, Grant… no combat is *ever* fair. There's almost no one who will start a fight with someone when they *know* that they are going to lose. In a fight between two people, both of them believe that they will win, for one reason or another. However, only one of them can be correct. You must learn all you can about your enemy in order to give yourself the greatest chance of victory. If you don't do this, you *will* die. Never pity your enemies. Take every advantage you can get. Learn your failings and fix them. Learn *their* failings and *use* them. From now on…>

<Ignorance is not an excuse.>

CHAPTER SIXTEEN

As he hurried after the slow-moving caravan, it dawned on Grant that he hadn't checked his stats in days. Now was as good a time as any. "Status."

Name: Grant Monday
Rank: Wielder
Class: Foundation Cultivator
Cultivation Achievement Level: 4
Cultivation Stage: Early Spring
Inherent Abilities: Swirling Seasons Cultivation
Health: 83/83
Mana: 2/2

Characteristics
Physical: 22
Mental: 7
Armor Proficiency: 8
Weapon Proficiency: 15

"My characteristics have increased. I… I'm so *happy*."

Hours of training every day with Sarge, running around the carriages, helping out with physical tasks other people were too lazy to do; all of this came together to let him *progress*. Despite Sarge's consistent sarcasm, he felt *amazing*. He had even been paid for his work, for the first time in his life! Ambling along, he paused beside an old oak tree. At its base, in the damp shadows, grew a clump of mushrooms. He plucked one to have a closer look, twirling it in his fingers. It was a vibrant blue with white spots, a pretty-

You have plucked your first Rare herbal ingredient, a blue cap mushroom. To learn more about herbalism and the wonderful world of plants, visit your nearest herbalism trainer.

Skill gained: Plant Insight (1/5).

Tier one effect: It is 10% easier to spot plants with medicinal effects within a ten-yard radius.

<You've gotta be kidding me. You found a random mushroom and met the prerequisites for an herbalism skill with no training because it's *rare*? If this doesn't show that your luck has been improving recently, I don't know what will.>

"Interesting… *why* is my first skill this, and not a sword skill?" He sauntered along, examining the mushroom as he walked and trying to figure out how to use the skill. As it was his inaugural skill, he wasn't sure how to use it, or if it was a good one to have. By the time the caravan was in hearing range, he had *almost* forgotten the horrific experience against the Kraken.

<Getting any new skill is one of the hardest things to do if you don't know what's required.> Sarge snorted and called Grant's attention to the mushroom. <Getting a sword skill requires either ten *thousand* hours of training, *or* you could->

"Why… *hello*, there." An imposing woman stepped out from

behind a tree. One hand was braced against her hip, the other holding a wicker hamper. "I was wondering when you were going to turn up, Grant Mond*a~a~ay*!"

"I… hello?" He stumbled to a halt and stuffed the mushroom in his pocket. The way she had drawn out his name to an uncomfortable degree reminded him of dragging a plow over rocks. "I don't think we've met?"

"Don't play coy, my little *Granty-moo*!" She held out her hand, apparently waiting for something. "I am Lady Vivian Thursday, daughter of *Joviality* Thursday, but you can call me *anytime*!"

"It's a… pleasure? Yes, I see the familial resemblance. I think I saw you on top of the carriage earlier, chatting with Red and Fergus?" He wiped his hand, awkwardly grasping the fingers presented, then shook her hand.

"*Granty*! So you *were* watching me. I couldn't help but notice *you*." She gazed down at his bare chest. His sweaty shirt was slung over a shoulder, and February Twenty Nine rested in the scabbard at his hip. "The appropriate way to greet a lady, such as I, is to *kiss* my hand!"

"Oh! Of course, my lady." Grant pecked her hand with a quick kiss, then looked for a way past Vivian… but there was no obvious means of escape. She towered over and to either side of him, sharing the high-class build of her father.

"Come along *now*." Her sharp tone demanded obedience, so rather than argue, Grant followed behind as she started walking. She handed over the hamper, a pleased smile on her face as if she had just confirmed something. "Take this."

He followed her to a clearing in the trees. Light filtered through leaves that gently swayed in the breeze. The smell of grass and spring wildflowers lingered in the air. In the center of the clearing lay a colorful woolen blanket, which could have been the double of Jo's multicolored coat, where he was directed to set the hamper down.

"Granty, sit here and pour me the lemonade." He did as he was told, pouring with uncertain motions. Because of this, lemonade flowed over the rim of the glass and spilled on the blanket. He was in for it now, and winced as he waited for a rebuke. "Don't worry about the spilt lemonade, little Granty."

She wiggled herself onto the spread blanket, aware that he was staring at the basket. "Eat; enjoy *all* of the pleasures before you!"

He didn't have to be told twice. Grant was famished from his grueling training session. Vivian giggled as his stomach grumbled, and watched as he devoured a tower of tiny sandwiches, dinky pork pies, and a thick wedge of cake; washing it all down with tangy, freshly squeezed lemonade. "That was delicious. Thank you, Lady-"

Meaty hands gripped his shoulders, kneading his taut muscles as he reflexively clenched up. While he had been devouring the plates of miniature food, he hadn't noticed her getting up and scooting behind him.

"Re*lax*," she cooed into his ear. Heavy perfume filled his nostrils, and her fingers drove into his muscles *far* too hard to be comforting. Relaxing would be difficult, as her powerful grip appeared to be trying to tear his tired muscles from the bone. He tried to relax anyway, since she might beat him to a pulp if he refused, and he certainly didn't want to draw February Twenty Nine on his employer's daughter to defend himself. After several agonizing minutes, his mangled body slumped to the blanket out of sheer exhaustion.

"My turn!" She declared excitedly. Vivian removed a knee-high boot and presented a swollen calf that neatly hid her ankle and almost half her pedicured foot. Painted toes wiggled excitedly as she thought about the incoming foot massage. Grant gulped, then tentatively reached out and prodded the prodigious foot.

"Ooh. That's it, Granty, rub my poor sore feet!" Grant couldn't take it anymore. Overwhelmed by the sun, the sheer quantity of rich food that he was unused to, the smelly oversized foot dangling nearby—or perhaps all of it—he turned his head and vomited onto the grass.

"I... I'm *so* sorry." In a panic, he got up and grabbed his sword and shirt and bolted toward the caravan. "I've got to go!"

"Granty, it's okay. Don't be embarrassed!" He made a beeline for the caravan, ignoring the confused voice calling out behind him. "Granty? Grant. *Grant*! I demand that you come back here this *instant*!"

His legs had a mind of their own, and luckily there was no way they would obey her wishes. "Better escaping now than enduring the foot rub and whatever else she comes up with. I've no idea why she was punishing me, but I'd almost rather face the Kraken again."

<I'll put it in my notes,> the previously silent Sarge chuckled.

"Come on, you lot. Get a move on!" Joviality motioned to the assembled guards. The caravan had rolled to a halt at the base of a windmill. Up on the hill, past endless fields of wheat, lay a colossal structure; its turbine blades motionless despite the stiff breeze from the north. Its shadow engulfed the entirety of the Grand January Caravan, where Jo shouted in a thunderous tone, "It's time you earned your keep! Get in there and start loading the sacks of flour!"

"What *is* that?" Grant's jaw fell slack and his eyes went as wide as teacups. The structure, made of white limestone, was unlike any he had seen before. He'd seen windmills, yes. Small, *normal*-sized buildings that the village used to grind grain, but this was on another level.

"Boy. Close that mouth of yours, or you'll catch flies!" Jo snapped at him, aiming a boot at his rear for interrupting. "The purpose of the Royal January Mill is to supply flour for the entire *city* of Mid January. This structure alone supplies over two-thirds of all the flour required by a thousand bakeries across the District."

"Wow..." was all Grant could think of saying. As he looked

at Jo, he couldn't help but shiver as he recalled the... *incident.* Vivian shared a striking similarity with her father, which was probably why he had gone out of his way to avoid her since then. He risked a glance back at the caravan and met her penetrating gaze. It seemed that he could never look in her direction without seeing her furious face. How did she always know when he was going to peek over? Or was it... was she *always* staring at him? "Yeesh."

Now that everyone was moving the way that they were supposed to, Joviality started to relax, and turned to face Grant directly. "Stopping here is an important part of our trip, and a profitable one. Our job as the Grand Caravan is not just selling pots and pans to *peasants*; our business license is approved by Lord January himself! While we're here, we will earn another three months of operating expenses by picking up enough bags of flour to fill half of our wagons to the brim."

The caravan contained dozens of gigantic carriages, each the size of a small house. Grant hadn't even considered what was in them, or what they were carrying, apart from cookware and the carriages that housed passengers.

"You know what? You're a Monday... there shouldn't be an issue with letting you see what goes on behind the scenes. Come with me, and I'll introduce you to Head Grinder Godfrey." Jo's cloak billowed in the powerful wind as he strode forward. If it wasn't for his bulk, he'd likely sail away over the horizon. Grant could see why the windmill was in this particular location.

As they walked in the shade, approaching towering oaken doors, the other guards filtered off toward the warehouses. They had apparently carried out this task many times before, but it appeared none of them had accompanied Jo where he was leading Grant now; if the glares were anything to go by.

They passed through the doors, and he felt somewhat let down. He had been expecting some kind of grand secret, but it was just a normal mill—if larger than usual. Inside, workers moved frantically around the center of the edifice, where a towering tree trunk encased in bands of steel soared up, and up, seemingly forever. The top of the tree faded into the darkness, and the bottom appeared to sink into the floor, where machinery was hidden in a basement or cellar.

A lone figure sat forlornly in a chair, his head buried in his hands. As the two newcomers walked up, he didn't stir—apparently tormented by something.

"Hey, Godfrey. How are you, fella?" Jo boomed, clapping a porterhouse-sized hand to the man's hunched back.

"Oh, Jo… it's you." Godfrey didn't even flinch at the surprise slap. "I've had better days, I can tell you that."

"Why? What's wrong?" Joviality eyed the center of the mill. "Hmm. I see the shaft isn't spinning. You know, I thought it *never* stopped? What-"

"It's not *meant* to stop, is it?" Godfrey snapped out the retort, then hung his head contritely. "Sorry, my friend. It looks like we'll be short a few… *thousand* sacks this time around."

"What!" Jo roared loud enough to cause almost the entire mill to come to a standstill. "Lord January will have my *hide* for this! Not yours, far away and protected in your windmill! Get it working; get it working right *now*!"

Godfrey stood upright in a fury, causing his oversized chair to fall to the ground with a thunderous boom. "What do you want me to do, huh? We have an *infestation*."

"That doesn't explain why the shaft isn't spinning!"

"We think something got stuck in the… mechanism. We're trying to fix it right now. A load of poison was left in the cellar specifically to deal with the rodent population. A new recipe imported all the way from District February, and guaranteed to work… eventually. It's at least ten times more potent than the regular-"

Jo cut off the rambling with a bellow. "You believe this was caused by *rats*? Just go down and unblock the mechanism!"

Godfrey slowly shook his head, bending slightly to grab the long arm of his chair and set it back up. He sank down into it with a sigh, then looked up sharply to meet Joviality's eyes.

"Two teams were already sent. We haven't heard from them since."

"Come now, Godfrey. We can... let's... look! We have a strapping lad here." Jo swiped his arm across Grant's back, then gazed at Grant pleadingly as he almost face-planted from the force. "Random Guard Number Four here needs to break in his sword! He's always complaining about the lack of adventure and looking for a challenge. Training constantly, this one. He'll take a look!"

Godfrey hadn't missed the silent entreaty, and slowly shook his head. "I... I don't think that's wise, Jo."

"Nonsense. You'll do it, *won't you*, boy?" Jo's words were light, but his deadly stare made Grant's skin crawl.

"I'm... I'm sure I could deal with a few rats. I've killed rats before." Grant tried to keep his tone light, already being directed forward by Jo before the words were fully out of his mouth.

"That's the spirit." Jo loosened his death grip on the young man's shoulder, leaving behind a red mark that Grant was *sure* would turn into a bruise.

Godfrey looked Grant over and shrugged, calling, "I'll give you one Hour per giant rat tail, and an additional five Days if you manage to free the mechanism."

Quest gained: A Bouquet of Flours! (Lvl 5. Uncommon.)

Information: Kill the poisoned rats in the Royal January Mill and collect their tails. Optional: Free the grinding mechanism to restore the Royal January Mill to operation. The Lords and Ladies must have their wheat!

Reward: One Hour per giant rat tail collected. Five Days for freeing the mechanism.

Accept / Decline.

"I accept!" Grant blurted out. How could he not accept the challenge and the potential reward? It would take *months* working on the caravan to earn such a sum. Plus, he might as well be paid for what he was about to be forced to do anyway.

Jo clapped him on the shoulder and shoved him roughly toward the cellar door. "Hurry, lad; we're already going to be so far *behind*...!"

Godfrey was unable to look either of them in the eye. He motioned to a few workers and pointed at the cellar door. They grunted with effort as they rolled back the heavy grinding stone holding it closed. Grant gulped, suddenly unsure of his decision. Jo wouldn't force him to go *alone*, right?

"I'll prepare a feast for your return!" Jo grabbed a torch and practically tossed it *and* Grant into the unknown. "Ring the bell when you free the mechanism, and we'll celebrate together while we let the other workers load the sacks!"

"Hold on, he can't take a *torch* down-" Godfrey's panicked voice was cut off as the stone rolled back into position behind Grant, oppressive darkness swallowing him in an instant.

CHAPTER SEVENTEEN

Grant could feel his heart hammering as he stood at the bottom of a long flight of steps. He slowed his breathing by taking deep inhalations, forcing his racing heart to calm down. It was so dark that, even with the torch, it took a while for his eyes to adjust to the gloom. Squinting, he drew his sword and steeled his heart. This was the perfect opportunity to prove what he was capable of, both to Jo and himself. "Come on. I'm sure I can deal with a few *rats*!"

Using the torch to light the sconces, he glimpsed a small brown rat scurrying between his feet and almost jumped out of his skin. With the torch in one hand and February Twenty Nine in the other, he swiped at the rat and almost cut his own leg off. He got it as it headed back between his legs; it acted like it had been trying to escape the cellar.

"*Gotcha*! Ha! I expected a 'giant rat' to be bigger!" Grant cut the tail off the large rat and stored it in his pack. As he gloated, pairs of green points of light appeared in the darkness. First one set, then another… and another. He took a step back. The lights slowly grew in size as they approached. He couldn't be certain but they resembled streetlamps. Or, perhaps… glowing eyes the size of a small chicken.

<*That* wasn't a giant rat. *Those* are giant rats.> Sarge sighed as oversized teeth began to glint in the firelight. <They don't look too pleased that you killed one of their litter.>

"Did you know what these were? You could have warned me earlier… you know, *before* I accepted the quest?" Grant waved the torch, trying to shoo away the rats.

<Look, *Wielder of a Weapon of Power*, I'm not here to wipe your rear after you mess yourself! I've better things to do than listen to the inane banter of humans. It *bores* me.>

"Literally *what* else do you have to do?" Grant stopped trying to argue, growing serious and slightly fearful. "Sarge… I need a plan. What should I do?"

<Survive, Grant. Survive.> This was the first time in days that Sarge had spoken to him kindly, and it made Grant twice as nervous about the rats. <I'll help as best I can, but the odds aren't in your favor, and I can't help you in combat for more than a few seconds after combat starts. Those are the *rules*, and I cannot ignore them. A Wielder must remain calm at all times, especially times of great danger. Stay calm, stay alive, heal later.>

The rats screeched and charged; instantly transforming into a multitude of gnashing teeth and glowing eyes as they scampered through the darkness.

<Throw down the torch in front of you!> Grant obeyed, and the torch clattered off the ground. It almost guttered out, but a few pieces of hay caught fire… and the flames spread fast. Too fast. The rats—rats with poison coursing through them, if their gigantic, pustule covered bodies were any indication—charged on undeterred. Moments later, the greasy and furry rats running at him were replaced with giant rat *fireballs* that were running at him. Their hairy hides were mere tinder to the flames, and the fire caused their boils to rupture and **pop**, spilling poison across the floor. It was *potent,* judging by the way the flagstones were hissing and melting.

<Don't let the poison touch you. It appears to be corrosive.>

"Save your precious few seconds of help for things that I don't already know!" Grant practically screamed at the sword as a flaming rat leaped at him.

<Not the time to whine!> Sarge barked a command, <*Thrust*!>

Grant followed instructions, and February Twenty Nine sank deeply into the first hungry creature.

Damage dealt: 2 piercing! (5 mitigated.)

Target is on fire: -4 health per 5 seconds! Target is poisoned: -1 health per second!

"*Two* damage? Are you kidding me? I stabbed it in the face and did *two* damage?" Grant grunted as his sword practically bounced off the rat. "This thing has armor? What?"

<It is an actual *monster*, trainee! It too has characteristics and its own cultivation. If you survive, it appears we'll need to have a discussion on what your characteristics actually *do*, yes?> Sarge pulled his attention back to the issue at hand. <Still, to see a rat reach this level of armor cultivation? Even in only one characteristic? The level of lazy in this District…!>

Still, between the poison, fire, and Grant stabbing at the monster enough to keep it off him, the rat died. The familiar inner light bathed him, taking away his weariness as he obtained cultivation level five. For a brief instant, the light of the fire penetrated deeply into the cellar… illuminating a sea of burning, squirming bodies closing in. One leaped through the air with a screech a tiger would be proud of, and Grant didn't have time to consider the swarm as a whole.

<There's your last easy level. All uphill from now on.>

Grant lost his concentration from Sarge saying something so out of place. "What?"

<Pay attention, maggot! Spin, then slice! *Now*!> The attacking rat bounced off the sword without taking any further damage, the weight of it causing the human to spin. <That's… that's all I got. Rules are…>

Sarge went silent as another fiery rat flew directly at Grant, who ducked and *lifted*, drawing his sword across its belly in a shimmering arc. The blade sliced through the thick meat of the rat's flabby belly, and Grant was notified of a critical hit. The gnashing teeth of the fallen rat reached out in one last attempt to nibble his flesh, so Grant let the sword turn at the end of its sweep, coming down and impaling the head moments before it would have torn into his ankle.

The heat in the confinement of the cellar was becoming unbearable. He panted, struggling for breath as he mopped at his brow. Around him, the fire's intensity was taking a toll on the rats. Bloated bodies burst as the poison evaporated in their blood, causing half-digested flour and poison to drift in the air and coat their fellows—resulting in inhuman screams as the increased exposure to the poison and heat forced them to share the same fate. More and more rats started to *pop*, yet the swarm continued their relentless advance. New troops replaced the twitching, burnt bodies. Teeth and claws marched over fallen comrades. The air smelled of charred fur, roasted meat, and *hate*.

"D-defensive pose." Grant changed to a defensive posture, terrified as the tsunami of teeth and flaming green bodies bore down on him. "Good-bye, Sarge. I don't know if you can hear me, but thanks for being the nicest person I ever-"

Thump.

The air *shook*, and a numbness came over Grant as he was blasted away from the tide of vermin. Fire roared through the confined area, and a guttural scream rose from somewhere deep below. As he watched his death approaching, he also took note of the fact that the rats were being destroyed by the same explosion.

Half a dozen rats were airborne, focused on his legs, head and torso. Time slowed to a crawl, and Grant watched in terror as razor-sharp teeth and claws groped toward him in slow motion, illuminated from behind by the fire. Grant lifted February Twenty Nine and held on tight as the explosion propelled the meaty rockets at him. They collided, pinning him to the wall… but also protecting him from the scorching flames that they had ridden in on. Numbers flashed in front of his face, and Grant woozily realized that his health must have increased with his level up.

Health: 41/95

Suffocating. Time remaining before asphyxiation damage is taken: Approximately 35 seconds!

Grant started to choke. He couldn't breathe! Shoving his way out of the pile of smoldering bodies, he forced his way into open air and tried to inhale. He figured that it would hurt to breathe in the hot air, a risk he was willing to bear… but *nothing* came in. No charred soot, but also no fresh air of any kind. Where had the fire… it was out? He stumbled around, trying to figure out what was going on. The *air* was gone! How was the *air* gone?

Around him, the few rats that had survived the strange and unexpected explosion began to die. He hadn't killed them; he hadn't done *anything* to them. Frankly, they should be up and attacking him at this point. But they weren't? They were just… dying. Grant managed to take a few more steps, but he was dying too. How? *Why*? His wounds weren't even that bad! Or… were they?

Health: 40/95

Poisoned. -1 health per second!

He looked down. Amongst the gore and blood spatters coating his body were droplets of green, eating away at the cotton shirt and pants. Grant's flesh sizzled silently where poison splashes had connected with exposed skin. He felt good in the knowledge that not even the greatest swordsman could have avoided all of the poison in the air and on the ground. He dropped to the bloody floor and worked his mouth, doing anything to pull in one last gasp. Nothing.

The room started to darken, differently than just not having light. Had he been in a tunnel? That was strange, he thought he had been…?

Just before he suffocated completely, a blast of air *sucked* through the room, rolling him along the floor and reigniting a few small fires. Grant pulled in a lungful of *amazing*, smoky air… and started coughing. After a long moment, he got to his feet and rolled a few of the smaller rats onto the fires to put them out completely. He looked back at the exit, which was only a few dozen paces away. He wanted to leave.

But if he did leave, he would miss out on the reward of five Days. After everything he and Sarge had just been through, not collecting the reward seemed silly—considering the central shaft was just on the other side of the long, long room. All but one of the fires had all died out, and he got that one after he used it to reignite his torch.

Trudging along, he soon came upon the shaft. It was clear why it failed to turn: at its base, the twisted bodies of both a giant rat and a mill worker were lodged into the great gears. He looked around for something to help pry the corpses away so he could leave this place as quickly as possible. A short search revealed a metal rod beneath a pile of equipment in the corner.

A vibration shook the stone floor, coming more frequently the closer he got to the shaft. He started running; he needed to do this fast! The fine hairs on his arms stood to attention, and he had the feeling that he was being watched. "Raging Regent, the giant rats are back!"

No, it *wasn't* the rats, he discovered. It was a single *gargantuan* rat with teeth the size of gravestones. It was barely scorched, and clearly furious. Grant made a move to dart past it, but it slammed to the side, crushing bodies of its smaller fallen brethren and popping a few sacks of grain not already destroyed. As the grain spilled out, the beast lost focus on Grant and scooped the kernels toward its gaping maw, greedily devouring the tasty treat.

Grant winced as he saw an extensive health bar explode into being and become proudly displayed above its head. Just like that, he got to learn the name of this filthy beast: Rabid Rodent Rat-a-Louie. A red skull pulsed beside the floating name tag, indicating that the enemy wasn't hiding its power, and was a *much* higher level than he was.

"Creatures can have *names*?" Louie was distracted by the grain, so Grant took a chance and darted under its other paw. From behind, he sliced open a huge boil on the enormous rodent's back. Poison pumped out of the open wound, and he thrust February Twenty Nine through it, entirely coating the blade in the corrosive substance.

The monster roared in anger at the unexpected pain, and a swipe from its arm caught Grant and launched him into the corner. The first attack was immediately followed by foot-long razor-tipped claws. Grant, dazed from the impact, managed to parry and deflect the weapons, then thrust deep into the flesh of its wrist. Checking the monster's health bar, he saw that it had barely registered the impact, with only a tiny sliver knocked off the end. Conversely, *he* was only standing because his legs hadn't got the message that it was time to collapse.

Health: 32/95

"This isn't going to work. *Ahh*! Claws!" As Rat-a-Louie swiped in a frenzy, Grant screamed and flopped under the arm, rolling behind the mill shaft as fast as he could. Looking up at the mechanism, the answer to his current problem came to him. He scrambled over to the base of it and ducked behind just as a pustule-coated limb swiped through the space he had first rolled into. "Just a bit further, you freaky beast."

He thrust his weapon at the monster's palm, drawing a bead of blood. It hissed at him and crept a bit closer; he knew that it was now trying to make sure that it could kill him with a single hit. As the claw whipped toward him, Grant dodged… and the oversized paw smacked the twisted bodies stuck in the mechanism. The force of the impact shifted the corpses *just* enough to free the gears, and the shaft sprang to life with a rumbling noise. The remnants of the bodies were flung out of the way as the shaft of the Royal January Mill was free to spin once again.

Rat-a-Louie flinched at the sound, scurrying backward with a deep hiss. Now that the shaft was spinning, grain spilled into the awaiting chamber and was ground into flour by the relentless wheel. Grant took the opportunity to make a run for it, knowing that the oversized rat would be distracted by all of the free food.

It still took a half-hearted swipe at him and missed, then grumbled and returned to investigate the incoming deluge of grain. Shovel-like paws scooped up the crops that seemingly endlessly spilled into the chamber below. Grant nearly started sobbing when he realized that his plan had worked: it would rather gorge itself on grain than deal with a nuisance such as him.

"Let's get the *abyss* out of here!"

CHAPTER EIGHTEEN

Grant burst through the open hole, startling the throng of guards and workers that had been trying to work up the motivation to investigate the noises and smoke. A range of weapons—lances, swords, even pitchforks—were pointed directly at the terror that appeared from the depths.

"Get these poison-covered clothes off me!" he howled as he stripped in front of the group without a hint of shame.

"Grant?" Jo's mouth opened and closed repeatedly. For once he couldn't speak, and with no food in his mouth to blame! "You're alive! I think… you're not an undead, are you?"

The young cultivator glared at the man that had forced him into that terrible position, practically spitting his next words. "No, Jo. I need a healer!"

"I don't know how you did it, but you saved the Royal January Mill! The shaft spins once again!" Tears of joy streamed down Godfrey's face. "Tell me your name again, so that I can sing its praises!"

"I… wouldn't get too excited. There's a Rabid Rodent Rat-a-Louie down there, munching on the grain. You need a small army to come out here and deal with that, 'cause I'm never going back in there."

"Really? He's there now?" Godfrey's nonchalant tone made Grant narrow his eyes in fury. "I thought he was still hibernating. That isn't a problem. When he's awake, he helps keep the vermin at bay. The noise of your fighting must have woken him up."

Grant drew an inch of his blade and took a threatening step toward the man. "You didn't tell me there were giant *poisonous* rats down there!"

"They weren't poisoned until we left the special dosage down there. It should have killed them!" Godfrey stumbled backward as Grant advanced, though the guards closed ranks around him to stop the furious young man.

"It did nothing but turn them into a plague swarm!" Grant slammed his weapon back into his makeshift sheath, "Whoever sold that poison to you was a liar, a cheat, and trying to destroy this place."

"How… *exactly*…" Joviality's eyes glittered in excitement as he contemplated the singed cultivator before him, "did you survive?"

"To tell you the truth, I've absolutely no idea. Godfrey, my reward please?" Grant was snarling in pain and didn't care one *whit* for how respectful he was supposed to be to his employer. He thrust out his hand filled with rat tails, on the verge of passing out. He didn't like all the attention he was getting, so tried to divert them. "A question for you. Why would this flour and 'poison' explode?"

"Yes. Of course. The reward… you deserve every last Minute!" The guards watched in wonder as Hour after Hour was poured into Grant's cupped hands. "As to an explosion? Well, there's a reason the torches down there are never lit if the mill is in *operation*. When flour is in the air, in a contained space, it will explode if exposed to an open flame. That couldn't have been what happened down there, correct? Otherwise, this entire place would be in flames by now!"

Grant decided to keep that to himself, sweating over the fact that he could have destroyed the building that produced most of the flour for the capital city. He wasn't exactly sure why the place hadn't been destroyed, or why the fires hadn't raged out of control, but he assumed that it had something to do with the strange phenomenon of all of the air vanishing from the mill-wheel room.

"I nearly forgot! Five Days for restarting the mill." The crowd gasped upon hearing the amount Godfrey quoted.

"I'll take that and hold onto it for you." Jo's hand shot out and clasped the pile of Time, making it vanish into his pockets nearly instantly. "This kind of wealth must be stowed in the safe. You can't just walk around with jingling pockets!"

Grant, in his delirium, went to draw steel on the multicolored Jo… before promptly passing out. Just before he did so, a quest complete notification popped up.

Quest Complete: A Bouquet Of Flours! (Rare).

Information: You killed the poisoned rats and collected their tails. By freeing the grinding mechanism, the Royal January Mill is once again fully operational. The Lords and Ladies shall eat cake once more!

Reward: Five Days and twenty-two Hours. (5 Days for freeing the mechanism. One Hour per rat tail collected.)

The first thing Grant noticed as he came back to himself was the intense smell of incense, followed by the acrid tang of medicinal herbs. It reminded him of Becky's poultices, and he smiled at the thought. "It was all a dream. I'm with Becky now, tucked up safely in bed."

"*Granty*! You're *awake*! By Lord January, I was so worried." Grant's heart sank at the familiar high-pitched voice. No, he wasn't back in New Dawn. He clenched his eyes shut, wishing Vivian away. The last thing he remembered before losing consciousness was *pain*; the unendurable pain of a million nerve cells screaming in agony.

"Oh, my little *Grantykins*." Coolness spread across his brow as a damp cloth tenderly mopped his brow. "You poor *thing*! You must still be in so much pain… they had to cut the remainder of your clothes off of you to tend to your wounds!"

"Vivian…" His eyes opened as narrow slits. "Where am I?"

"Call me *Vivi*, silly! We're past dealing with formalities, you and I. After everything we've been through together?" Vivian brushed his forehead a little too vigorously for his liking.

"We… what are you talking about…? Vivi? Where are my clothes?" Grant abruptly realized that he was barely covered by a blanket; apparently, whoever had undressed him hadn't bothered to put new clothes on.

Vivian clasped his hand and squeezed it tightly. "I thought I was going to lose you! When I learned you had collapsed after bravely fighting off the rodent horde, I *ran* to be by your side. I had you taken to my carriage, where you would have my undivided attention."

"Really? You… *ran*?" Of all the parts of the story, that was the most unbelievable for Grant.

"Oh, *yes*, Grantymoo. I've watched after you day and night. Day. And. *Night*! It was a rough few hours, but I've hardly ever left your side."

"Thanks… I guess. I'm fine now. Can you help me up and hand me my clothes?" He went to move but found his wrists and ankles bound tightly to the bed posts. As calmly as possible, he questioned his current captor, "*Why* am I tied down?"

"I didn't want you to hurt yourself. You were flailing in your sleep. Mumbling incoherently about a cracker with tentacles eating you on a pier… I did this for your own good."

"You can let me go now." Grant swallowed back his anger when he realized that Vivian wasn't making a move to help him.

"Do you have a preferred date?" She leaned heavily on the

plush bed and rubbed her nose against his. "I was thinking February fourteenth, Valentine's Day."

"Valentine's Day-?"

"Oooh, *perfect*! I'm so happy you agree. That's what I was thinking. We're one mind and one heart, joined as one! On Valentine's Day, we'll get *married*! I've so many things to arrange. Flowers, bridesmaids, and most importantly… the feast! Wait till Daddy hears-!"

"Vivian, let me go." When she did not move, still lost in her own fantasy, Grant let his voice get dark and serious. "I'm *not* marrying you!"

She pulled away as if he had slapped her, and her chest heaved as she tried to fathom what he was saying. Tears fell onto the sheets. "Wh-what are you saying, Grantymoo, my love?"

"Look. It's not you, it's me." Grant knew that he needed to be careful with what he said. Her gigantic fists could pummel his face into dust, and right now, he could do nothing to defend himself. "I'm not ready for such a commitment. I've a mission, and if I don't succeed, I'll be dead by the end of the year!"

Her eyes lit up at that, exactly the opposite that he had been going for. "All the more reason to get married *now*! Declare our love to the world, and we will-"

"No! The only feelings I have for you are ones of *disgust*!" Grant rocked back and forth to get her away from him. "Leave. Me. *Alone*!"

Each word struck like a hammer to the heart, and Vivian collapsed backward hard enough to make the entire wagon rattle. Grant watched her cry in silence for a long moment, then thought, 'That wasn't so bad… it could have gone much worse, actually.'

Lady Vivian slowly stood up, her puffy face a blank slate, her emotions unreadable. She heaved in a deep breath, and with the full force of her massive lungs, screamed:

"*Daddy*!"

"*Precious*! I'm coming!" The enormous bulk of a flustered Jo burst into the carriage, and a strange light surrounded him as he prepared to do battle. "Vivi, is everything all right?"

Vivian thrust a meaty finger at Grant. "This beast was trying to attack me! I want him skinned alive and fed to the dogs!"

Jo looked down at the barely-covered, clearly tied-up, half-dead Grant. "Um… how did he get tied up? What's going on here?"

"*What?*" Grant squirmed against the bindings, and thought of a plan as quickly as he could. "I just woke up, and she is telling me that I need to give up my life and serve her! My family will not stand for this! I *order* you to release me, on the authority of House Monday!"

"Daddy! You *believe* me, don't you?" Vivian's fists were clenched, her face beet red as Grant struggled weakly for freedom.

Joviality's eyes hardened as he regarded Grant, and the young man could easily see the choice that had been made. "Of course, my dearest. Please, calm down. Let me deal with this monster."

"Well… alright, then." She visibly deflated, the pressure cooker of her temper momentarily decreased.

"Go on, now." Jo hugged his child and stroked her hair. "You look famished. Head to the dining carriage and make yourself feel better. They have a tower of cupcakes with your name on them."

"Well…" she huffed. "I do enjoy cupcakes. Are there any with frosting?"

"*All* your favorite toppings, and they literally spell out your name. If there's anything else your heart desires, tell the chef, and he'll whip it right up!" Joviality promised her with a smile. "Run along now, princess."

As she went to leave, she turned and blew a kiss at Grant, pleased that he would be punished for humiliating her. Finally alone in the carriage, Jo let out a sigh. "Just what am I meant to do with you, boy? This past week or so, you've done more work than a dozen guards combined, and I quite enjoyed having you around."

"For starters, you can remove these bindings. I can go back to work, and we will never speak of this again." Jo sighed at Grant's words and cut the bindings, letting the young man rub at his wrists. The rope had dug in deeply, leaving angry red rings around the joints.

Grant went to stand up, but Jo dropped a hand and firmly kept him on the bed. "I'm sorry, but you *do* have to be punished."

The young man slapped at the hand that was on his chest, blinking in shock when the flesh didn't even jiggle at the blow. "What? On what grounds? You *know* I didn't do anything. You literally just cut me free! She was arranging our *marriage,* and I said no. Now you're telling me that I should be punished? I'll get House Monday involved."

"Oh… now I understand. No one *ever* says no to my little Vivi when her mind is set. It's best to give her what she wants." Jo nodded as he spoke, ignoring the rest of Grant's words. "Listen, dog. You have nothing to threaten me with, so stop barking. Either you're a runaway, or something equally disparaged. No member of House Monday would be caught wearing what you were dressed in when I found you. I know you don't have any political pull, and I do not fear your supposed 'family' for that very reason. You're likely a bastard, completely unknown to the Noble House."

"So, what? You're going to put me down like a giant rat?" Grant fumbled around, searching for February Twenty Nine. He wasn't willing to go down without a fight.

"Not quite, lad." Jo held his hands up in an attempt to calm Grant down and diffuse the situation. "I'll give you a choice. You can marry my daughter-"

"No."

"-or you will be punished with a bounty on your head. I'll release you, and put out an unspecified bounty for punishment, not a death warrant. Anyone with the Time to spend can put a bounty out for something like that, and whoever doles out thirty lashes to you with a cat-o-nine tails gets the reward. Take your time to think about it."

"*Punishment.* I'd rather be caught and crippled by that many lashes than marry your disgusting daughter," Grant snarled at the man who had only ever underpaid him and thrown him into terrible situations. He found February Twenty Nine next to the bed and grabbed it right away. Luckily for Jo, it had been tied down with a peace knot by someone. It would take at least a few minutes to undo the knot, but at least he had his sword again.

"We're close to Mid January. Here's your second week's wage. Now, I know the week isn't over yet… but you *have* worked hard." Jo threw down a small pouch. Coins spilled out onto the bed.

Grant counted out fourteen Hours and shook his head in confusion. "What about the rest? I'm owed five Days and twenty-two Hours from completing the quest at the Royal January Mill."

Joviality laughed in his face as he tossed the young man out of the carriage. "Ha! Bounty hunters aren't cheap, boy. Those funds will be the payment for the price on your head! I'll be generous. Leave now, and I'll give you a day's head start. After that… House Friday will begin their hunt."

Still nude and unsure how to fix that, Grant slunk out and around the wagons until he found someone that he recognized. "*Psst.* Red."

"Huh? Who goes there? Show yourself!" Red clinked his axes together menacingly.

"It's Grant. Listen, I-"

Red interrupted him with a shout of joy, "Grant! You're up and at em', boy? Excellent! What are you doing out there in the darkness? Join us in the dining car; the buffet will begin soon. They have delightful little cupcakes, Vivian's favorite."

"I can't join you. I've been fired from the Grand January Caravan." Grant told him darkly.

Grant's words shocked Red to his core. "What? *Why*?"

"I refused Vivian. She wanted me to marry her."

Unexpectedly, Red started to laugh. "You? *Her*? I never thought the joke would go that far! Sad to hear about your fate, but I'm not going to associate with someone who's not a part of the caravan. I'd lose dining privileges!"

"Stop thinking about your stomach for one *minute*! I don't know why, but Vivian thought that I liked her. I turned down her advances, and I'm now being punished." Grant noticed that Red wouldn't meet his eyes after his explanation, but he didn't know why.

"Oh… is, uh, that so?"

Grant nodded and came a little closer, his bare flesh shining in the twilight. "Yes. Can you help me?"

"What do you need?" Red finally gave in, knowing that he had a hand in the situation. He figured it would be easier to just help the boy instead of explaining his role.

"I need your help breaking into Jo's safe in his private carriage."

Red almost dropped his axes in surprise and had to fight to keep his voice down. "Why in the *twelve Districts* would you want to do that?"

Righteous indignation filled Grant's face, and he stepped fully into view. "He's withholding my reward from saving the mill! He's even going to use it to pay for my bounty. He is going to use *my* Time to get *me* flogged! Can you believe that?"

"I'm sorry, Grant. I can't help you." Red backed away, shaking his head and holding up his hands. "Nope, *nope*, not doing it."

"Why not? I thought we were friends?" Grant practically sagged into himself. This was the farm all over again.

"Yeah, but if we do this, House Tuesday, Friday, or… *Saturday* will be after us both. I've known you for like... ten days? Just take your beating. It's far better to suffer a little, maybe get a few broken bones at House Friday's hands, then suffer the wrath of Tuesday or Saturday." Red turned away, refusing to look at Grant directly. "Just make sure to take the beating on your *own*, got it? Leave me out of this."

"You… you at least *believe* me, right?"

"Sure, kid." Red tried to get away, but Grant's next complaint made him stop and sigh heavily.

"I've no idea why Vivian thought I had a 'thing' for her! The other day, she was waiting near the caravan with a hamper, forced me on a picnic, and made me rub her feet till I vomited!"

Red pulled off his outer robe, and tossed it to Grant; still without looking at him. "It's a… mystery. Maybe one of the other guards knows what is going on? Just… no, this is our fault, we can't let this happen to you. We're only a day from Mid January. You know what…? I've had enough of Vivian. She's a spoiled brat, and you're not the first guard to lose his job at her hands."

"Thank you." Grant's hope was rekindled in an instant, and he tossed the cloak over his bare shoulders. It was far too big for him, but in that moment, that fact was comforting instead of insulting.

"I'll be right back. Stay there." Red walked away, and Grant crept beside the caravan to hide in the darkness. The Grand January Caravan's gaudy colors had once promised excitement and adventure, but now all he wanted was to get as far away from it as he could. A rustle reached his ears, and Grant pulled on the hilt of February Twenty Nine, exposing a length of rusty blade. He had managed to remove the peace knot before wandering around in the dark.

"Stand down, Grant. It's Red." Three guards came forward: Red, Fergus, and Skinny, all with packs on their backs.

"We could just hand him over to House Friday. Split the bounty! We all heard what Vivian is telling everyone she can see! Every time I hear her story, it is twice as bad as it was before. There's no smoke without fire, I say! If we leave now, I'll miss the buffet… and worse, breakfast!" Skinny appeared to be rather unhappy with whatever Red had told him the plan was.

"Skinny, Grant is innocent. Why should he be punished for

Vivian's lies, huh?" Red was staring at the ground, a strange air of guilt surrounding him.

"I guess…"

"*I* believe him." Fergus spoke up quickly, cutting off anything else that Skinny might have said. "I wonder how Vivian got that *crazy idea* into her head that Grant wanted to get involved with her. Huh, Red?"

"Complete mystery…" Red mumbled unconvincingly.

Fergus spat to the side and started walking. "Okay, then. Let's go. We can hide out at my home for a bit. The wife will be *pleased* to see me. What with being jobless and whatnot."

The four men walked off into the darkness, following the beacon of bright lights on the horizon to Mid January.

CHAPTER NINETEEN

The group rested in a public lounge just inside the gates of Mid January, breathing heavily and fanning themselves. They had walked through the entire night, getting into the city just after the typical breakfast time. Even still… someone on horseback must have arrived and set a bounty. There was no way anyone had gotten here faster than them otherwise.

"So much for a day's leniency. I saw a wanted poster at the city gates. Said that I was wanted by House Friday for punishment? I keep hearing you mention the Houses; what can you tell me about them?" Grant watched the area around them, paranoia filling him. "How worried should I be?"

"Don't look at me," Red shrugged and bit into a buttery loaf of bread. "I struggle to remember what day of the *week* it is."

"Grant," Skinny puffed his cheeks out and closed his eyes against the bright morning light, "how can you *not* know about the Noble Houses? You're a Monday!"

For a moment, Grant considered sharing the knowledge of discovering February Twenty Nine in the field, his surname changing from Leap to Monday… but then he remembered the discussion around the campfire and their opinion of 'calendar freaks'. As much as he wanted to, he couldn't bring himself to fully trust these men, especially with a bounty on his head. If he spilled the beans now, he risked getting a knife in the back.

Grant tried to think of a plausible reason, but luckily, he did not have to stretch the truth very far. He had heard his caretaker discuss how little he'd wanted to focus on politics, or the District in general. "It's just that, in New Dawn, we were so far from the big city. Everyone was so focused on feasting and partying that no one ever got around to discussing the Noble houses, or their role in the District."

"Makes sense. I couldn't believe what I saw when we went out there." Skinny eyed Grant strangely. "Abyss, they even had a pet *Leap*! I guess it isn't too surprising that they didn't keep up with the rest of us."

"Let me give you the *skinny* on the Noble Houses, Grant." Fergus sent a cheeky wink toward a nonplussed Skinny. "Don't worry, Skinny. I sent a messenger to my wife. She should be bringing the carriage around sometime soon. No more walking for you."

"The blessings of Lord January upon you," Skinny nearly sobbed.

"Grant, there are seven Noble houses, as I'm sure you're aware: Monday, Tuesday, Wednesday, Thursday, Friday, Saturday, and Sunday. Let's start with the one that *you* should be the most familiar with: House Monday. Your house, ruled by Lord January in this District, is typically considered to be the bureaucracy of the Houses of the Week. They focus on proficiency in combat and leadership, and are known to be well-versed in fighting, administration, and governance. They do not tolerate fools, and have disdain for people that do not try to improve their own circumstances. They won't go out of their way to help others, but they appreciate the effort that people put in."

"Maybe that's why I'm so focused on bettering myself through training cultivation?" Grant offered, meeting their eyes awkwardly. "My… parents *were* always pushing me to improve."

"Nah, mate, your personal family is just weird, in that case." Fergus shut down the easy explanation that Grant was trying to put together. "The few Mondays I've met have been lazy sods when it comes to cultivation, but they could swing a weapon. You've got that going for you, at least. Let's see… Tuesday!"

"House Tuesday are the Peacekeepers. They focus on proficiency in combat, as well as the rule of law. This makes them slow to act, but *incredibly* powerful foes if they find that they are justified in their actions. They're practically unstoppable." Fergus swallowed as some memory hit him. "Point in fact, they're the harshest toward themselves, but I would say this makes them the most well-trusted and respected House that exists. If a member of House Tuesday is found to be breaking the law, the punishment can be anything up to and including the loss of a Wielded Weapon, which means expulsion from the Noble House for themselves and their inheritors."

"There was a bully in New Dawn, his father was a Peacekeeper…" Grant trailed off as he thought about Mo's chubby face. He wanted to knock a few more teeth out.

"Be glad, Grant, that House *Friday* is after you, and not Tuesday," interjected Skinny. "Luckily, House Tuesday wouldn't come after you for a simple punishment bounty. Since anyone can put those out, it means that there's no proof that you have done anything criminal. In fact, you could probably seek shelter from them if people try to claim that bounty."

"Don't want Saturday after you, most of all!" Red butted in. "They're assassins!"

"*Red.*" Fergus growled at him with one eye twitching, "Shut your pie hole, or at least lower your abyssal *voice*!"

Grant remembered that they had mentioned that his caretaker, Randall, had tried to place a contract with House Saturday. He gulped and tried to refocus on the situation at hand.

"As I was *saying*… I'm on Wednesday, right?" Fergus glared at Skinny and Red. "House Wednesday focuses on logistics and planning. They tend to have the best combat gear of all the Houses, and focus typically on taking down monsters and accumulating components for the creation of weapons and armor. Not that there are *monsters* in January!"

"I beg to differ," Grant broke in harshly. "I killed *dozens* of giant plague rats under the Royal January Mill!"

"You *personally* killed them?" Fergus grinned as Grant looked away.

"I killed one directly; the rest kinda just… died."

"Interesting. I know that *I* never saw them, and I heard you'd get paid per kill. Now, I know you say that Jo stole that money… but how do we know for sure that there were even monsters down there?" Fergus waved off the indignant retort. "I know you fought down there, lad. I'm just giving you a clear picture of how other people are going to react if you start telling tales. Doesn't matter how *true* the tales are. Now, back to the matter at hand, House Wednesday is very proficient at combat with monsters, but rarely takes the field against other people."

Red jumped in when Fergus pulled out a flask to moisten his lips, "I know the next one. House Thursday is a merchant organization. You have already met at least two: Joviality Thursday and his *delightful* daughter. They, like every member of House Thursday, focus entirely on profit, and are usually the only House that is allowed passage to different Districts."

"Really?" Skinny's eyes were wide and *hungry*. "I didn't know that *anyone* was allowed passage to February or beyond! Or that they *could* go beyond the boundary of January!"

Fergus picked up where Red had left off, as the other two devolved into arguments. "Rarely will Thursday fight, but if they need to *defend* themselves… well. That's a different story altogether. Thursdays tend to have the most well-fortified and dangerous fortresses. Typically, they also have lots of expendable items that they use to defend themselves. In truth... I think even Lord January *himself* would think twice before going up against House Thursday in their own territory."

"How in the twelve Districts do you know so much about

the Houses?" Skinny turned back to the conversation with a hint of disbelief in his eyes.

"It's a long story... one that I'm not gonna get into. Next is House Friday, the House most *pertinent* to your current situation, Grant." Fergus paused for Grant to perk up, knowing that it was important that he listened carefully. "House Friday is filled with bounty hunters. They could care less about the *law*; they only care about combat proficiency against other people. They hone their skills by taking on more and more dangerous contracts; contracts to hunt down the most dangerous criminals."

"Criminals like you." Red pointed at Grant. "I saw that bounty. The most exciting thing about it wasn't how much they would be paid, it was that you were labeled as a serious threat. A well-trained, armed individual."

Fergus continued unabated, blowing right through the interruption. "Typically, they don't care at all about Nobility or commonality. They only care about taking down their targets. However, they *almost* exclusively use non-lethal techniques. They desire to hone their technique, not become massacre artists. Also, they are often in contention with House Tuesday, as they will take less-than-legal contracts on the regular."

"As for House Saturday..." Fergus leaned forward, and everyone else leaned in to hear his whispered description. "Rumor, and *only* rumor, has it that House Saturday is an assassin organization. They take the contracts that even house Friday will not touch. They often work in conjunction with House Monday and House Thursday, pretending to follow the law, while in fact slaying dozens of people a day. They do not hold back. They do not surrender. They do not take prisoners."

Everyone leaned back as Fergus finished his short lecture, and the man himself took another swig from his flask before feeling confident enough to continue speaking. "Of course, publicly, they create wonders of alchemy. This gives them a logical reason to be *anywhere*, searching for potent herbs and hidden resources."

"Finally, House Sunday is full of people with a more *technical* calling. They often fill the role of armor and weapon creators, as well as being able to *repair* weapons and armor. A good chunk of them are Healers, but their services are mostly reserved for the Nobility. Almost all of their Wielded Weapons grant the ability to heal instead of hurt, meaning that even the Vassals can moderately restore people or items."

Skinny grinned at Grant, then slapped him on the arm to remove the slightly glazed look in his eyes. "So, Grant, that is a run-down of the seven Houses of the Week. Get all that?"

"Um… not really." Grant admitted sheepishly. "I'll do my best to remember."

"Don't worry. You'll figure it out eventually. Just remember that the ability of a Wielded Weapon, whether it is a Wielder or a Vassal, is generally determined by the House they belong in. Same deal with combat power. House Monday is typically the strongest in direct combat, House Sunday the weakest. For the moment, all you need to know is that your situation would be far worse if either House Tuesday–the Peacekeepers–or House Saturday–the alleged Assassins–were after you."

"Fergus, you still haven't explained how you know so much about the Houses?" Skinny pressed the issue, much to Fergus's disgruntlement.

"I wasn't *always* a guard on the Grand January Caravan," Fergus snapped, giving Skinny a look that warned him not to push further.

"Fergus, dearest! Breakfast is ready. I've prepared a grand meal on behalf of our honored guest!" A very welcome voice called out of a carriage that had pulled up next to the public lounge.

"Come on, Grant. Let's get back to my place and eat." Fergus heaved himself to his feet, followed by the others. "Welcome to Mid January. I know you've had a rough few days, but just remember, it ain't all bad!"

CHAPTER TWENTY

Skinny patted his stomach, belched, and drifted off to sleep in his chair at the end of breakfast. The meal had been as grand as it had been advertised, and everyone had laden Fergus's wife with the compliments she deserved. Just as Grant had planned to stand and help clear the mess, someone banged on the door; waking Skinny up with a snort.

"We have reason to believe you're harboring a fugitive. Open up!" The group of overly-large men at the table looked at each other grimly, realizing who was at the door.

Red turned to Grant and mouthed the word, '*Hide*'.

Grant gazed furtively around the open concept home, finding not a single place where he could hide even half of his body. "Where?"

All he got in return was a shrug, and Grant nearly pulled his hair out in frustration. The knocking was persistent. "In the name of *House Friday*, we have a warrant to search any building in Mid January!"

"A warrant my *tush*, this isn't legal!" Fergus bellowed at the door.

"Over here," Anna—Fergus's wife—whispered to Grant, who latched onto her words and ran to do as she bade him.

Red went to answer the door before it was kicked in, grabbing a small cake to pretend that he had been stalling only due to eating. "How can I help you, m'lords?"

Two men in the garb of House Friday shoved Red out of the way, making just enough room for them to get past him and into the house proper. They glared around at the small crowd before presenting a sketch that looked vaguely like Grant. "Have you seen this man? His name is Grant Monday."

"Can't say that I have." Red's eyes darted around as he looked for where Grant was hiding. Though he didn't know where Grant had gone, exactly, he'd been in this house before. The fact of the matter was, it wouldn't be long till the man was found.

"We *will* be checking the premises. Stay out of the way if you know what is good for you." The men scattered throughout the house before anyone could say anything to stop them.

Their aggression spurred an irate Anna to step forward and snap, "How *dare* you barge into my house? You know that breakfast is a sacred time of day!"

"Norman, I've checked upstairs," one of the other bounty hunters shouted down after a few minutes. "No sign of Grant Monday. Just a gaggle of kids, and one that was peeing on the walls! Hah!"

"Timmy!" Fergus shouted as he scrambled to get up from the table. "I *showed* you, boy. Do. It. In. The. *Toilet*!"

"Sorry to bother you. We'll be on our way. We have instructions to check everywhere. You can't be too careful. Especially when there's a convict on the loose! If you see him, do not—under any circumstances—approach that beast in man's clothing! Contact House Friday immediately, and we will deal with the reprobate!"

The men left and could be heard banging on doors along the street, though they were clearly confused by not finding Grant in this house. They'd had it on good authority that he *should* have been there. Anna directed Fergus to lift one of their lounge chairs, where a series of dirty plates and empty dishes had been stacked. Grant's face came into view, red from the heat, lack of air, and concern. Sweat was pouring from his body, but he started to calm down as he looked around and only saw familiar people. "Is it safe to come out?"

Fergus looked at Anna sharply. "Do I *want* to know why you have a smugglers' couch in my house?"

"Doesn't *sound* like you want to know." Anna smiled demurely and rubbed Fergus's belly. "Just think about what you *want* to think about, and enjoy the benefits."

"We need to go." Skinny stood up and sidled toward the door, intentionally not looking at the mess left in the dining room. Anna noticed him *not* noticing, and had to school her expression as he made his escape.

"Maybe we should stay at Fergus's for a while?" Grant looked at the others in confusion. "What's the rush? They're out there right now; we'll need to get past them if we leave!"

"No." Red stopped him before he could say more. "I agree with Skinny on this one; they *will* be back to do a second or third sweep of the area. I have a place where you can hide out until the heat dies down."

"They're right, boy," Fergus announced, giving his wife a peck on the cheek and grabbing his cloak. "You'll hide in plain sight. I know the place Red is talking about; the workers in the Crafting Quarter despise the Noble Houses, especially Friday. You'll be safe there. *Safer*, at least."

The robust Red, stout Skinny, flabby Fergus, and greasy Grant wove their way through the alleyways all the way to the Crafting Quarter. Hammers clanged off anvils and black smoke billowed out of chimney stacks from furnaces that never seemed to quiet for even a moment. Grant couldn't help but ogle the selection of wares on display. Razor-sharp, gleaming knives were stacked high; ready to grace the kitchen and prepare feasts for Nobles throughout Mid January.

"Those knives," Fergus pointed out when he noticed Grant's

interest, "will be used not only by chefs in Mid January, but across all of the Spring Districts. January is well-known for its love of food, and the ability to produce the grandest of banquets requires the highest quality knives and utensils. Thursday's merchants will travel far and wide to reap the maximum profit."

"Can we stop talking about food for now? I'm *hungry*!" Skinny grumbled as he thought about all the delicacies those knives would get to touch that he never would.

"You're *always* hungry! You'll have to wait," Red placated him without looking in his direction. "Breakfast ended less than an hour ago, and we still have at least thirty minutes until mid-morning snacks."

"I'm *starving*. I. *Need*. To. Eat! When I go for an hour without food, my energy… fades. I'm… feeling dizzy." Skinny melodramatically wiped his brow and stumbled.

<Probably massive fluctuations in blood sugar. Three-quarters of the people of this city are going to be losing their feet in the next few years, I bet.> Sarge's caustic voice made its way into Grant's head, and Grant perked up immediately. He hadn't heard from the sword since the battle at the Mill.

"Here." Grant fumbled around in his pack and brought out the remaining half of Madame Mercredi's pie. He had been saving it, and despite roughly two weeks in his pack, it still *appeared* fresh.

<You've gotta be kidding me. That's rancid by now. You aren't actually going to let him put that mess in his…> Sarge trailed off as Skinny grabbed the pie and started to scarf it down. For the first time ever, the sword's mental voice was shaky. <The people of this District need outside intervention.>

"Oh, thank you, Grant! I owe you one." Skinny had instantly cheered up, his momentary dizziness forgotten. The pie hadn't lasted for even a full thirty seconds. "Aww… so good."

<If you *ever* do *anything* like that, every single training session is going to be Krakens and Vivians.>

"We're here." Red drew up in front of a massive metal door. He rolled the barrier to the side, releasing a wave of heat that blasted Grant's hair back. They all had to shield their eyes from the torridity and sheer *glare*. "You will not find a more impressive refinery in all of January! Look there: molten metal being poured into molds for mass manufacturing knives and other equipment. Steel ingots stacked up, ready to be sent to blacksmiths and armorers! Those will be further refined and turned into high-quality Early-to-Mid-Spring weapons and armor!"

Red continued talking, but Grant was distracted by a notification that appeared in front of his face.

Warning: At risk of getting locked out. The training plan must be followed, or else the ability will be locked for 24 hours.

"Sarge, you *just* woke up!" Grant complained as quietly as he possibly could. "Come on, give me a break. I've been kind of busy!"

<No.> Sarge went quiet after the denial, refusing to back down.

"Red, I need somewhere to train," Grant shouted over the din of mechanical presses and the banging of tools. His request immediately caused eyes to roll and disparaging comments to be muttered.

"You want to train in *this*? You're going to die! The heat alone will make you melt like the butter on my flaky biscuits! You're serious? I… follow me." Red waved them over toward a soot-covered man, who was wearing a black apron and thick gloves. "Derek. Hey, *Derek*!"

"Red, my old friend! What brings you to these parts?" The two performed a strange handshake that Grant had never seen before. For some unknown reason, the smith completely relaxed after the handshake was complete.

"Just passing through. Is it okay if my *friend* here," Red

nodded toward Grant, "stays a while? He's in a spot of trouble with the Nobles. House Friday is on his tail."

"Friday?" Derek spat and uttered an unrepeatable curse. "Red, any friend of yours is a friend of mine."

"Red, I *need* to train," Grant was watching a timer that had appeared in his vision. He didn't want to lose Sarge again so soon after his sword woke up.

"What? You need to… train? Oh!" Derek snapped his fingers in realization, "There's a well-stocked dining hall just down the road there. You can go there to practice for any eating competition, though you might have to fight for a spot. With all of the upcoming events, anyone thinking of impressing the aristocracy is training their jaw muscles. I *am* surprised that a *friend* of Red's would want to do that…?"

"That's not the type of training he has in mind," Fergus stepped in hastily as Derek gave Red the evil eye. "The lad wants somewhere to swing his rusty sword around. He's actually doing weapon cultivation, if you can believe anyone would be so foolish!"

Derek scratched his head in confusion; just like the others, he was unable to comprehend why Grant would want to waste his time. A delighted Skinny immediately left the group in the direction of the food hall. "Perfect! I'll be off training my intake!"

"See?" Derek waved his hands at the oddly-focused Skinny, "*That's* normal behavior, though I hope he is not actually trying to join the eating competitions. Boy, how do you ever intend to gain a glorious gut like that guy? Training with a sword won't give you status! It takes a *lot* of effort to put on so much weight. Working here all day, I struggle to keep up. Luckily, the work I do allows me to get the highest quality foods! Otherwise, I would start to look like… well, you."

Grant stared forlornly down at his body; he had perhaps only thirty-five percent body fat. It was shameful, he *knew* it was, but he also knew that comparing himself to people at eighty percent should no longer be his goal. His goal was *living*, and to do that… he needed to do his training. "I know you're only trying to help, but the fact of the matter is that I don't intend to put on weight. I don't have the kind of money needed to compare sizes, so I've decided that the only way forward is bettering myself through training and cultivation."

"Haha. Is this guy for real?" Derek let loose a deep belly laugh, eyeing the others, who watched the show stoically. He slowly lost his good humor as they nodded seriously in response.

Fergus shrugged and waved at the much younger man. "Grant's a bit *special*, is all. I'm sure he'll grow out of it… I think he's going through a phase."

"Derek. Is there somewhere I can train in peace? Alone? Please?" By now, Grant was irritated. No matter where he went, people were mocking him and trying to control his actions. No one got to tell him what to do anymore! That is… *Sarge* could, but that was different! No *human* could tell him what to do!

"Feel free to waste your time, if that's what you want to do." Derek couldn't hide his smirk as he waved at a door down the hall. "Go over there. No one will bother you, and they certainly won't *join* you!"

"We'll be in the dining hall attached to this building if you need us, Grant." Fergus caught a glance from Derek and amended the statement, "Just check the normal eatery, not the Noble-sponsored one."

"I'll join you when my shift ends, Red." Derek and Red clasped arms before parting ways. "It's good to see you again."

They had more to say to each other, but Grant didn't bother to stick around to listen. The countdown was almost complete, and he wasn't about to go another day without hearing the only voice he could trust.

CHAPTER TWENTY-ONE

Grant tried to turn himself inward, to get into the state that Sarge had told him would benefit his training the most. It was hard, and the heat of the furnaces was almost unbearable, but at least he had somewhere to train. Suspended walkways littered this section of the steelworks, and liquid metal was being poured into crucibles by sweaty, hard-working men. They didn't pay any notice to Grant, focusing entirely on their demanding tasks.

He opened up his character sheet, intending to study the training tab. While he was there, he glanced at his stats.

Name: Grant Monday
Rank: Wielder
Class: Foundation Cultivator
Cultivation Achievement Level: 5
Cultivation Stage: Mid Spring
Inherent Abilities: Swirling Seasons Cultivation
Health: 95/95
Mana: 3/3

Characteristics
Physical: 30
Mental: 9
Armor Proficiency: 12
Weapon Proficiency: 23

"Leveled up to cultivation achievement level five after killing a giant rat, and… oh! I got all the way to Mid Spring cultivation? How...?" Grant flicked to the training tab and read over the waiting information.

Training Session: Physical and Weapon Cultivation – Timed Assault Course Challenge.

Information: Use your newly forged weapon skills and fitness to beat the course in under 5 minutes to finish today's training. Next training session is locked until the assault course challenge is successfully completed.

Reward: Complete the challenge in 4 minutes or less to obtain a 20% bonus to Physical and Weapon Cultivation for 10 hours.

"Five minutes, four if I want to get the bonus? I can do that. Good to know that this will be a fast session." Unlike his previous training, the background didn't fade away into mist. Instead, additional platforms, walls, obstacles, and combatants appeared to block his path. They held a variety of weapons, *sharpness* being the only thing they had in common. The countdown began, and he tensed up.

3… 2… 1… Go!

A five-minute timer started counting down, then flew off to float in midair; visible whenever he looked up. February Twenty Nine freed from the leather scabbard, Grant dodged past the first dummy, narrowly avoiding its sword. He didn't have time to waste if he wanted to complete the course in under five minutes. He planned to avoid every enemy he couldn't kill quickly, but he'd have to watch his back much more closely.

His plans fell to shambles in an instant. The path ahead was blocked by a knight holding a tower shield. The immense shield was around five feet tall, and completely blocked the way forward. He attacked the knight hiding behind the shield, but every swing was intercepted and turned to the side by the sheet of metal. A polearm poked out in an attempt to skewer him, and he barely dodged the unexpected attack by throwing himself back.

Tick, tick, tick.

The timer was quickly and loudly counting down. Grant had already wasted thirty seconds trying to get past a single enemy, and he still had many obstacles remaining. Looking around wildly, a chain swaying to his left caught his attention. It dawned on him that he could use it to climb past the tower shield and knight, in fact skipping nearly half of the trial!

He jumped at the hanging metal, using it to pull himself slowly and painfully higher and higher. Grant's physical training was finally showing its worth as he heaved his bulk up the thick chain. It took a full minute to reach the top, and he was breathing as loudly as the bellows at the front of the workshop—but at least he was almost at the end. He checked the timer, grinning as he realized that there were over two full minutes remaining!

As he started to pull himself over the edge, a dummy leaned over and showed a scarecrow grin to him. The dummy faces usually had only clumsy caricatures of features, but this one was apparently intentionally endowed with a cruel smile. Try as he might, Grant couldn't both swing at the dummy and hold on to the chain at the same time. It took its time, reaching over to the side before pulling a lever. A loud **thunk** sounded, and a bucket tipped over.

"By Lord January-!" Grant only had a moment to see the

searing liquid before molten iron engulfed him. The excruciating pain was thankfully brief; his nerve endings were incinerated almost instantly. Sight returned shortly thereafter, and he found himself flat on his back at the start of the course once again. A brief and panicked test confirmed that all his fingers and limbs were fully functioning, if sore and tired from the intense exercise he had just done. Even so, he leaned to the side and puked at the memory of his phantom demise. "Got it. I'll not be taking the shortcut. Just… just give me time to-."

The most important time to train is when you don't want to do it!
3… 2… 1… Go!

"Oh, come on." With no time to waste, Grant sprinted forward, sword in hand. His body was whole, but fatigue was already starting to accumulate. He dodged the first enemy and attempted to squeeze past the right of the tower shield. The massive shield scraped along the ground, blocking his path. Anticipating this move, he deftly sidestepped and twirled left before darting forward; slicing a backhand swipe at the dummy knight as he got through.

The knight wasn't able to reverse course with the heavy shield in time, but the attack was more to vent his anger than it was to deal any damage; he needed to continue running. The timer ticked down–in fact, he could have *sworn* that he saw it speed up–but he did his best to ignore it. The Wielder ran up the steps and along a suspended walkway, and found a wide gap blocking his path. Difficult footing, even at the best of times, but here… molten metal sluiced between the platforms every ten seconds. This was a waterfall that Grant didn't intend to jump into, through, or even *near*. Not after his last experience with liquid metal.

He was breathing heavily, and sweat was pouring off him. Grant's eyes stung from the heat of the furnaces as he watched the pattern a couple of times to make sure that it repeated exactly the same each time. Confidence built, he sprinted forward and took a leap of faith. He could see the bubbling metal far below, and above him hung the telltale sign of the swinging bucket ready to pour out its fiery contents. He reached the other side and stumbled; almost losing his balance and falling backward into the stream of death.

Grant's heart hammered and his panting became gasping… but he couldn't rest. Three dummies were waiting for him, their swords glowing in the reflected light of the molten metal. He ran with his sword held high in an offensive pose, screaming at his foe; who raised its sword in defense. Feinting with his blade, he brought his knee into its middle. The dummy bent over in apparent pain, disappearing when he ran February Twenty Nine through its torso.

"Two to go, and one platform to jump before the end." The other dummies wouldn't fall for the same trick. They held their blades in a defensive posture, waiting for Grant to come to them. February Twenty Nine flashed through the air to engage the left target. Blade bounced off blade, sparks joining the inferno below.

Forty-five seconds remaining.

Grant started to panic; he had to hurry up. He fought furiously against the left dummy, making no progress apart from further tiring his already screaming muscles. The right target—slightly behind the left on the narrow platform—tried to get a hit in, managing to score a glancing strike against his shin. He winced at the pain but remained focused.

Pretending that he was about to retreat, he turned around. The left dummy stepped forward to chase after him, and was greeted by Grant's blade through its chest as he reversed his grip on February Twenty Nine. "Twenty-five seconds!"

He turned and shuffled at the remaining target. It swung its blade, expecting Grant to meet it head on. It was in for a surprise. He dropped onto his butt and slid past the surprised dummy, swinging up and eviscerating it on his way past. "All targets down and… fifteen seconds remaining. Go!"

Using the last of his energy to hobble run toward the glowing green checkered flag, he muttered, "Just one… last jump… to go!"

At this point, he couldn't care less about the cultivation bonus. He just wanted to finish the course and collapse. He leapt into the air. There was no molten metal to worry about, meaning he was going to make it across the line with five seconds to spare!

Grant didn't see the volley of arrows that skewered him in the back; he could only focus on the bloody arrowhead that penetrated through his neck. The timer ticked to zero, and the welcoming goal flashed red.

His eyes closed in defeat as the world faded to black… then flashed open only to be greeted by the now-familiar and somewhat hated timer. It started right away, not even giving his screaming muscles a second's rest from the torture.

Grant's sword-wielding antics were drawing an ever-larger crowd that pointed and laughed at the crazy guy wildly jumping and swinging a rusty blade. The steelworkers had stopped their tasks and were watching his crazy training session. They gossiped like fishwives, unable to understand what he was doing and—more importantly—why he wasn't giving up. Each time he failed, he would get a blank look on his face and walk like a golem back to the starting point, lay down, then sigh dramatically before standing and starting again.

He *wished* he could give up. Grant wanted nothing more, but he would be unable to progress in his training until he had passed this grueling test. Despite bone-tired muscles, his times were improving. He was down to just under a minute remaining before he was peppered with arrows. It didn't matter how fast he ran, or if he tried swatting them away with February Twenty Nine, at least one *always* got him.

Dying once more, Grant found a hidden well of anger and determination deep within. He would *not* give up. On his previous run, he saw the dummy that fired the volley of arrows and had learned that it fired three simultaneously. As angry as it made him to have to find a way to get past it, Grant tried to find a way to look at the situation positively. "It could be worse, there could have been *three* archers. Wait… that's the answer!"

The timer began, and he efficiently dodged and dispatched targets, then vaulted the fountain of fiery death. Rather than killing the final dummy like he had on previous attempts, he chopped off the hand wielding its sword. The handless body disappeared, leaving behind its weapon.

Quickly thrusting February Twenty Nine into its scabbard, he took a deep breath and aimed. He had the archer in his sights. Releasing all his pent-up rage, Grant launched the sword at the final archer.

It missed.

Wait! No! It bounced off the ceiling, falling and impaling the surprised archer as it awaited its opportunity to procedurally generate holes in his body. The Wielder didn't want to risk throwing February Twenty Nine, either for fear of his sword dropping into a vat of bubbling metal, or worse, losing his progress on the course.

He vaulted the final gap and hobbled through the gate marking the end of the course. The timer stopped at one minute… and two seconds! Not only had he completed the trial, but he'd achieved the optional cultivation bonus, coming in under *four* minutes!

Training Session Challenge Complete: Congratulations. 1:02 remaining. Future training sessions unlocked. For completing the course in under 4 minutes, a 20% cultivation bonus will apply to both Physical and Weapon cultivation for the next 10 hours!

Grant was laughing and crying as he dropped his limp body onto the suspended platform. It was only then that he became aware of the churning mass of cheering people below. He thought a few had been watching him train, but a glance down revealed that every inch of the floor between the red-hot furnaces held a steelworker excitedly discussing the spectacle they had witnessed. No one was laughing at Grant. Instead, he found that he was the center of attention for his efforts... and he was being praised.

For the first time in his life, he beheld a crowd of people that were regarding him with envy and admiration. It was *amazing*, and fed a part of him that he'd had no idea needed sustenance.

Grant was going to chase this feeling.

CHAPTER TWENTY-TWO

"You're one crazy son of a goat!" A soot-covered steelworker slapped Grant on the back as he came down to walk among them.

"Is *that* what exercise is?" another asked with awe in his voice. "I often wondered, but it seemed like too much effort... you looked like you were having a *blast*! I was told that it was the worst thing ever!"

Grant smiled at all of the people that strangely wanted to talk to him. He tried to answer seriously, "No... that wasn't about fun. I was training."

Collective sighs and oohs came from the group, who were hanging on his every word. A ridiculously massive, soot-streaked, hirsute steel worker barged through the crowd, coming to a stop only when he towered in front of Grant. He was holding the bounty order, and this one had a too-accurate depiction of him on it.

All of the excitement that Grant had been feeling, all the happiness and strange sensations in his chest vanished in an instant, leaving only exhaustion and resignation. "So... this is it, then. You're going to take me to House Friday and get the reward. Can't say I blame-"

"Mr. Monday. Sir." The man held out the notice with both of his heavily muscled arms. "Can I… umm, have your autograph? Just from what I saw there, I know that you're going to be famous someday."

For a moment, Grant was completely unable to utter a sound. The only time he had been more shocked in his life was when Sir Thirty-First had impaled himself on the sword he had been holding. People admired *him*? They actually wanted *his* autograph? Trying his very best to appear like writing was simple for him, he scribbled his chicken scratch onto the notice. It took every ounce of schooling he had ever stolen to write the word 'Monday' passably. Grant beamed, reveling in his new-found celebrity. "There you go. Would anyone be willing to show me the way to the dining hall? Also, if anyone else wants a signature… please go tear down any bounty order you can find and bring it to me?"

That got a roar of laughter and approval.

"This way!" The mountainous man twisted and used his bulk to clear a way through the masses. People were starting to drift back to work, but this time, they were wearing smiles as they got to it. Only a few minutes later, Grant sat heavily on the bench next to the ex-guards and Red's friend, Derek. Grant was confused at first by the looks that they were giving him, until he realized that his new-found fan club had joined him.

He coughed awkwardly and reached for some food. "Well, I'm starved. How're you all doing?"

"*You* lot!" Derek got to his feet, shocking the people that had surrounded the table. None of them had noticed that their boss was sitting at the table they had crowded. Even before he got out another word, the horde of huge men were scrambling away as quickly as they could. "Back to work, on the double! If you don't hit today's quota, your wages will be docked four Hours! I recognize *all* of you!"

He received various shouts and curses in response, but the

steelworkers were already headed back to work. A frustrated Red slapped the table, "*Sword Saints*, Grant! The point of coming here was to blend in; stay incognito! Thin chance of that now, isn't there?"

"They won't tell…" Grant looked around at the firm faces. "Will they? I was just training. I didn't expect such a large crowd to-"

"Training?" Fergus almost choked on the bundt cake that he had just bitten into. "I came back to check on you! You've been swinging and jumping around like a madman for the past four hours!"

"You missed *lunch.*" Skinny shook his head sadly at that thought. "We *all* went to see what you were up to, then came back for second lunch and pre-dinner."

Grant was utterly ravenous. He reached for a cake, only to have Sarge's voice pop into his head. <Don't. You. *Dare.* The next thing you reach for had better be that lean chicken meat on the left-hand side of this table.>

Feeling very put-upon, Grant did as he was told. Every once in a while, Sarge would chime in with a new thing that he should eat, or to tell him to stop eating what he was. The only thing he was allowed to drink was water, which was very hard to do with all of the tantalizing chocolate drinks and ale that were available at the table. A whistle blew, and Derek stood and winked. "That's the end of my shift. Come back to my place and share your adventures; I've plenty of appetizers that we can snack on until dinner!"

<Stay here; we need to talk.> Sarge's command made Grant freeze. He had been hoping for this, but for some reason the powerful voice made him nervous.

"Don't mind if we do," Red answered for the group as a whole. Everyone except for Grant stood, earning him some confused looks as well as a glare.

"Not coming with us, Grant *Monday*?" Skinny spat out the surname. "Too good for us, now that you've got a fan club?"

"Nothing like that. If it's fine with you, I'll stay here for a bit. There's a few more dishes I'd like to try… and I'm not sure I can walk right now." Grant was clearly circling around what was really on his mind, but the others–sans Skinny–didn't mind giving him some alone time.

Derek leaned forward, clasping his shoulder and nodding. "Not a problem at all, Grant. You'll find us a five-minute walk from here. Twelve Iron Circle. Take the first left after Candlestick Lane. You can't miss it. Number's on the door. Make sure you try the stew before you leave!"

"Thanks. I'll catch up with you later." Grant waved at them wearily as they walked away. Once he was alone, he let his left-hand drift down to the handle of his sword. "What's going on, Sarge?"

<First off, my apologies for the lack of responsiveness over the last… however long it's been. I just regained enough energy to come back to my senses.> Of all the things that Sarge could have said, an apology wasn't what Grant had expected. Before he could assure the sword that everything was fine, it continued blathering on. <When you killed that monstrous rat, I told you that your last easy level had been gained. It is time to fill in the gaps of your knowledge. Frankly, it's getting embarrassing.>

"I'm sorry to hear that my lack of education as an abandoned and practically-enslaved orphan is embarrassing for you." Grant kept his tone very bland as he responded. The sword had a habit of punishing him by making him respond physically to combatants that weren't actually there; there was no need to make others further doubt his sanity.

<Acceptable. There are going to be three points to our conversation: what cultivation does for you, how you can increase in cultivation achievement level, and what the different stages mean.> Sarge's pronouncement made Grant's eyes widen in excitement. The secrets of cultivation that he had yearned for his entire life were about to be… *given* to him? <First of all, let's discuss what your cultivation numbers—also known as stats or characteristics—actually *mean*.>

"Thank you; I've been wondering-"

Sarge barreled forward without taking note of the interruption. <As I'm sure you know, from even how little *you* understood or were taught of this... system... an adult with no cultivation at all will still have fifty points of health. This can only be increased by physical cultivation. Now, I'm sure it's obvious that, until a certain point in your cultivation journey or before you gain certain skills, being stabbed in the heart is going to kill you no matter how many points of health you have. Getting your head chopped off is the same. That's where armor comes in, as well as armor cultivation. We'll get to that in a moment. First, just understand that each point you have in physical cultivation gives you one and a half points of health on top of that base of fifty.>

Grant was following along on his status sheet, and he instinctively raised a hand to ask a question. "But... if it doesn't matter how much health I have, why is that tracked?"

<When did I say that it didn't *matter*?> Before Grant could say another word, Sarge exploded, <Fatal blows are *fatal blows*. Ask *Sir Thirty-First* how his physical cultivation worked out for him. However, an increase in your pool of health allows you to take many times more non-fatal blows and survive. When your side is sliced open by a serrated blade, and you're bleeding out at ten health per second, you've gained *ten* additional seconds to get healed up, simply by having an additional one hundred health! How would that *not* matter?>

Grant had nothing to say to that, so Sarge pressed forward.

<Physical cultivation and armor cultivation have a synergistic effect. That means they *help* each other. Armor cultivation makes it harder for weapons to damage you, even when you're *not* wearing armor. Combine a large health pool with skin, bones, tendons, and organs that simply refuse to be damaged, and you have a 'body cultivator', or a walking wall. They are a person who can take hits from all over the place and continue moving forward with their head held high.>

"Are there... *numbers* involved with physical cultivation?" Grant winced as he said the word 'numbers'; he could barely tally his Time coins. To be fair, Time was never something that he had large quantities of, or needed to keep track of for more than a few days at a time.

<But of course.> Sarge's casual acknowledgement made Grant sigh. <Now, while you're in the 'Spring' stage of armor cultivation, your body will automatically decrease the amount of damage you take by your cultivation number, divided by four. At Summer stage, divided by three. I'm sure you see a pattern here. When you reach the winter stages, your body is so tough and durable that it is a one-to-one damage mitigation.>

Grant tried to put the message into a form that he could understand. "That's… I don't really understand the stages, but that means that if I hit someone with a sword directly in the throat, it could just… bounce off? Like what happened with the rats?"

<Very similar, the main difference being that a standard sword would also probably be dulled by the impact. In fact, you might even *take* damage for hitting something so solid.> Sarge's affirmation wasn't something that made Grant happy to hear.

"How am I supposed to defeat the Lords of the Months? Their cultivation has to be *way* higher than the damage I can put out!"

<We'll get to that right now.> Sarge paused while Grant collected himself. <Weapon cultivation. It uses the same system that armor cultivation does. When a weapon hits someone that has an equal amount of armor cultivation, no damage is done to either party. This is where gear comes into play, because the fact of the matter is that no one is going to be attacking you bare-handed if they're a weapon cultivator. We can talk about mental cultivation another time, because while most people with high scores are able to think faster, that's only because they are used to using their mind in exotic ways. All the characteristic does *directly* is allow for mana regeneration and spell damage. You have no spells. If you get one, we'll have that talk immediately.>

<There are thirty-six ranks of gear, but they can easily be

broken into three categories. Each type will have a prefix, and there are only three prefixes: Early, Middle, and Late. The middle word of each type of weapon or armor will be either Spring, Summer, Autumn, or Winter. If you put some thought into this, you could see that a prefix and a middle word could be comparable to one of the months each. Early Spring? January. Late summer? June.> Sarge paused to let Grant catch up, knowing that his mental cultivation was fairly low.

<The reason for this division is that the materials to make those weapons or armor are typically only found in each of those Districts. You might find Mid Spring equipment starting in January, but that is going to be *highly* sought-after, and it's very unlikely that you'll be able to attain it with the resources you have, especially when compared to a member of the aristocracy.>

"I think my brain is melting," Grant whimpered as he frantically wished he had a way to take notes. He knew this information was important, and he really wanted to be able to understand it fully.

<Here's the big difference between cultivation stages and gear.> Barely a hint of a pause this time. <There are only twelve cultivation stages. Gear has a third designation, a suffix. The three suffixes are light, medium, and heavy. As I'm sure you could guess, heavy weapons will do more damage than light weapons, but are slower to attack and are heavier. However, an Early Spring Heavy sword combined with weapon cultivation would be able to deal damage through an opponent's Early Spring Medium armor and armor cultivation. That is why proper cultivation of *all of your characteristics* is incredibly important. So that you do more damage, *take* less damage, and can survive a fight.>

"But Sarge, all I've got is February Twenty Nine. I don't have any other weapons! I certainly don't have *armor*!" Grant was starting to panic. Never before had his task seemed quite as impossible as it did now, after barely understanding exactly how large of a difference in combat potential both cultivation and gear provided.

<It is all going to be okay, Grant. Here's a fun fact to make you feel better: there's a good chance that your Wielded Weapon will transform into a more powerful version of itself in the near future. The ability is locked, but I feel like that will change soon.>

There was a long pause, and Grant looked at the rusty sword strapped to his side.

"What?"

CHAPTER TWENTY-THREE

A whistle blew, and Grant rubbed at his tired eyes. "Must be closing time?"

<You should get going. While you walk, I'll explain to you how you can increase in cultivation achievement level.> Sarge chuckled as he recalled their previous conversation. <There's a reason that the different cultivation methods are complicated, but most of them are at least a little intertwined. Sorry if I blew you away with too much information at once, but it was the minimum that I could impart to give you a basic understanding.>

"It's... it's fine." Outside, Grant patted February Twenty Nine at his hip for reassurance. He had too many memories of being jumped and beaten or robbed, but this wasn't New Dawn. Grant felt safer here amongst the warehouses and cobbled streets, particularly after the reception he'd received from the steelworkers. He arrived at the junction of Candlestick Lane. "Take a left at Candlestick Lane... or... was it a right?"

He couldn't remember. "Left or right, either way, I'll probably come across Iron Circle soon."

Grant took the right path, heading toward the center of

Mid January. He walked until his feet were sore. "That must be more than five minutes… I better head back."

"Halt! Who goes there?" A bulky guard came jingling down the road toward him, poorly-fitting armor and barely-strapped-on weapons creating a cacophony every time he took a step.

"Um…" Grant tried to think of a good excuse. "Just a steel-worker heading home after my shift."

"Come over here and let us have a look at you. No one is meant to be out after curfew!" Grant hadn't seen the second guardsman behind the first, but since the first took up most of the path; that wasn't overly surprising.

What *was* surprising were their words. "What's a curfew?"

The first guard responded with dark suspicion in his voice, "*Curfew*. A stay-at-home order. There's a criminal on the loose, and House Friday is in hot pursuit. A curfew has been enforced to protect the citizens."

"You're not… House Tuesday?" Grant was told to be wary of the Peacekeepers, as they didn't mess around. If they were after him, he was in serious trouble.

"No. We're with House *Friday*, good sir. Come here, so we can get a better look at you." The second man spoke up with a much more friendly tone than the first.

"Ah, not guardsmen as I had thought. Bounty hunters. So a curfew isn't a *legal* thing." Grant mimicked Fergus's words from earlier, even as he found that his feet were glued to the ground with fear. He didn't know what to do, but there were really only two options available to him. He could turn and head back in the other direction, but he looked and found another two men–probably more bounty hunters–headed his way. That left only one way out of the situation, because he wasn't going to let himself get flogged.

"Regent's shaky knees." Grant slowly started to draw his weapon. "I'm too tired for this."

"What was that?" demanded the closest man. "What did you say?"

"I said... feast. I'm, uh, starved."

"You and me both!" The cheery bounty hunter held his lamp high to get a better look at Grant, then his face hardened immediately. The two bounty hunters shared a swift look. One immediately went for his weapon, while the other reached for a steel whistle. Grant freed February Twenty Nine in the moment it took the man to blow three high-pitched notes, though he couldn't stop him from shouting at the top of his lungs.

"It's him! The *murderer*, Grant Monday is *here*!" He took a deep breath and glared at Grant. "Make it easy on yourself, son. Obviously, there's not enough proof that you're a murderer, or House Tuesday would be after you, as you feared. Come in for punishment of your own accord, and we'll go easy on you."

"I doubt that." Grant brandished his sword like it was a flaming torch keeping the night at bay. There was a faint whistling noise, but before Grant thought to react to it, he found himself tangled in a net and dragged to the ground.

The angry bounty hunter slammed his weapon into its scabbard, then came and gave Grant a kick in the side. "Aww. That was too easy, Norman. I wanted to play with him for a bit first!"

"There will be plenty of time to play with him when we get back to headquarters. My whip has been freshly oiled and awaits a bare back to cut its teeth on." The bounty hunters that had been coming down the path behind him had finally shown up, and they brought a nasty surprise with them. They laughed as they slowly closed in on the squirming Grant.

"Calm yourself. You're just making it worse." The previously cheerful man tried to stop him. The more Grant struggled, the tighter the net became. Finally, he managed to maneuver the edge of February Twenty Nine against it, getting the point in between the holes in the mesh. It made a ripping sound as it tore open, and he managed to free himself after a brief struggle.

"He's getting away!" Grant heard another faint whistle and managed to dodge a second net before it closed over him. A large man cracked his knuckles and approached from the rear.

None of them were wielding edged weapons, instead relying on fists or clubs. Grant ducked under an incoming arm as its huge fist swung out ponderously, yet powerfully. It met only air, and Grant slapped the flat of his blade against the man's back.

Damage dealt: 6 blunt.

The huge bounty hunter stumbled forward, and the three others laughed at the insulting attack. Grant looked around, then carefully put February Twenty Nine away. They weren't brandishing weapons, and he didn't want to seriously hurt or kill one of them accidentally. That would only bring more wrath upon him.

"Putting away your little pig sticker, Monday? We were looking for a challenge," Mr. Angry Man taunted him.

Grant shook his head slowly. "I don't want to hurt you. I don't care what that bounty says, I *didn't* hurt anyone. This is literally a case of a rich man not wanting to pay me the money that I am owed, instead using it to punish me for refusing to marry his daughter!"

"How sad. Good to know you're single. I've got a new lady to introduce you to: meet Jackie." Norman pointed to the remaining man behind Grant. "Well… he considers his left hand a lady, at least."

"Hw*aaah*." Jackie's hand weaved in a variety of patterns, and his legs jiggled oddly as he changed stances. Grant had heard about the martial arts of serious cultivators, but he had never seen them performed before. Jackie attacked, leaping forward with a chopping motion. Grant managed to sidestep the attack, but Jackie spun around and planted his right foot in Grant's middle.

Damage taken: 1 (Blunt).

Grant bent over, more in surprise than the force of impact, and responded by springing upright and punching Jackie square on the nose.

Damage dealt: 5 (Blunt).

Debuff added: Bleeding (very minor). -1 health per 15 seconds!

<I don't know if you knew this, but right now, February

Twenty Nine only gives you a single point of bonus damage, but it does transform every strike into slashing, blunt, or piercing damage, based on what you attack with. Those types of damage have a much higher chance of inflicting secondary effects, also known as debuffs: such as bleeding, broken bones, or punctured organs. Even so… nice hit.>

"Middle of combat, Sarge." Grant grunted at the sword as he lifted his fists.

"Ouch, that hurt!" Jackie held his nose, blood trickling down onto his House Friday uniform. "I'll be docked thirty Minutes to pay for cleaning my uniform! Oh… we're gonna make you pay, *bounty*. You won't be able to kill a *keg* when we're done with you!"

"Get him! Ali, box his ears in. Jackie, do a flying kick or something!" Norman was making clearly ridiculous demands at this point. None of these men could get more than an inch off of the ground when jumping. Three of the four moved in with deadly intent, the fun and games apparently over. Grant easily dodged the huge fists of the boxer, and Jackie managed to get another kick in, but it bounced relatively harmlessly off Grant's leg.

"Archie, you too!" The remaining man, previously known to Grant as 'cheerful bounty hunter,' took out a small truncheon. Something sharp was embedded in it, reflecting the light of the lanterns. Archie swung and missed, giving Grant a too-close look at the black metal shards embedded in the wooden club as he ducked.

Something smacked the top of his thigh as he was distracted by worrying about the deadly weapon that was in the mix. Grant let out an involuntary yelp, once more of surprise instead of pain, though he did take three points of damage. As he limped forward, his entire right gluteus went numb, and little feeling was left in the leg overall. A glance revealed that Norman was *also* carrying one of the bladed truncheons.

<This has gone on far too long; bring me into the fight!> The bloodlust was practically *pouring* out of the weapon.

"Not yet!" Grant still didn't want to risk taking out February Twenty Nine. "I can handle this much without needing to seriously damage them."

The big boxer guy had given up, panting heavily as he leaned against the wall of one of the terraced buildings. Jackie kept his distance, not keen on taking any more damage than a bloody nose. Archie swung again and again, but he kept missing the more agile form of Grant, even though his numb leg was slowing him.

"How..." Norman puffed as his weapon missed as well, "are you *doing* this? Who *dodges*?"

"Why does everyone I fight ask that same stupid question? Why *wouldn't* I dodge? Who wants to get punched?" Grant dodged yet another attack, punctuating his point. "As to *how* I am doing it? Exercise and training."

"Enough of this nonsense!" As Norman made a halfhearted swing, Grant elbowed him in the arm. The truncheon slipped out of the large man's grip and clattered to the cobbles. Grant picked it up and before either Archie or Norman could react, he smacked it against Norman's jaw before holding the bladed edge to his throat.

"Ugh! I *sull*endah," Norman slurred as the truncheon's power turned on him and made it a struggle to speak. "I *sull*endah!"

Norman motioned for the others to stop and for Archie to put away his weapon. The panting bounty hunters were more than happy to take a break. Grant took both truncheons, but he only glanced at them—even though he was curious about the power they contained. Archie shook his head at Grant and took a moment to threaten him, "Sir Friday Twenty-Ninth won't stand for this! He'll come after you himself."

"He can try," Grant smirked as he turned and fled with his new weapons.

<Well, would you look at that.> Sarge's voice was warm and excited. <You just defeated four whole Vassals and even

disarmed two of them! Good on you, kid! You know, that leads us right into our discussion on cultivation achievement levels.>

Grant sighed as Sarge moved straight into a lecture. "Sarge, I've really been looking forward to gloating for a little bit."

<But this is a teachable moment!> Sarge pleaded as Grant hightailed it out of the area. <You know what? You can't escape my lessons. So, as I was saying…>

CHAPTER TWENTY-FOUR

<Cultivation achievement level has multiple factors, and each level gained will give you bonus points in each characteristic. Before you ask, I'll tell you that the amount earned varies. We'll talk about the specifics later, but just assume it is based on cultivation stage.> Sarge launched further into his explanation in spite of Grant's sigh. <For a regular cultivator, they can only achieve higher levels by directly cultivating.>

<Every forty hours spent cultivating a single aspect—whether it is weapon, armor, physical, or mental—will give them a single characteristic point in that category. If you ever look at your status and see a number with a little plus next to it, it is because you gained a point there directly from *cultivating*, not increasing your total cultivation achievement level. Now, a thousand hours of total cultivating, even if spread between all four of the different aspects, increases their cultivation achievement level by one.>

"Well then this just doesn't make sense," Grant complained as he hustled around the empty streets looking for Derek's house. "I already reached cultivation achievement level *five*, and I'm nowhere *near* having a thousand hours of-"

<Listen when I talk! I said that was for a *regular* cultivator. *You* are a Wielder of a Weapon of Power.> Sarge knew that Grant had no idea what the difference would be, so he decided not to keep him waiting. <A Wielder has *eight* total ways that they can increase in cultivation achievement level. Standard cultivation is one of them, but the easiest ways are killing or—as a separate option—*defeating* other Wielders. Most of the time, Wielders or Vassals cannot take advantage of this option. You cannot go into a playacting fight and 'defeat' someone; you have to *earn* the win with your life on the line. Easy for you: *every* fight from here till the end of the year could cost you your life. For most people, it is also illegal to kill other Wielders, as they tend to be members of the Nobility.>

"But I've defeated a bunch of Vassals, and I haven't gained any levels recently. Regent's crooked nose, I just beat *four* of them and took their weapons, and I *still* didn't level up!" Grant finally found the street that he was supposed to be on, and with great relief started looking for the correct house.

<The first time you *kill* either a Lord or Lady of the Month, Wielder, Vassal, or Monster, you will gain a level. You have done all of those, except the Lord or Lady bits. The first time you *defeat* one of those same options, whether they surrender or you simply completely overpower them and render them helpless, you gain a level. You have done this as well. Good work on that.> The sudden compliment from Sarge made Grant pause, blink owlishly, and refocus on the conversation. <I told you that your easy levels were already achieved. Killing or defeating a Lord or Lady cannot be considered *easy*.>

<Luckily, you have a few more options..> A hint of bloodlust crept into Sarge's voice as he recounted, <After *killing* four total Wielders, you will gain a level the *next* time you kill one. You can do that over and over again. However, if you *defeat* just two Wielders, the third one will give you a level.>

"But... by your logic, I've not yet defeated a Wielder," Grant chimed in, excited to make that connection. "So if I defeat just one, will I gain a level?"

<I…> Sarge hesitated and Grant felt a strange energy enter him. <Yes. Here. You cannot access this without me, but I can show you the 'gain sheet' that you have achieved currently. I don't want to show this to you very often, since I want you to focus on perfecting *yourself,* rather than seeking just to gain levels for the sake of leveling.>

Lords/Ladies Killed: 0
Lords/Ladies Defeated: 0
Wielders Killed: 1
Wielders defeated: 0
Vassals Killed: 1
Vassals defeated: 5
Monsters Killed: 1
Cultivation: 1

"Hey! I killed way more than *one* monstrous rat!" Grant argued instantly.

<No, the poison and explosion did. You, *personally*, only killed one *monster* rat. Regular rats, even if large, might not count as a monster. Just so you know, traps and such do not count toward your gains.> Sarge considered the kill sheet contentedly. <You are correct, you have not yet *defeated* a Wielder. Also, if you defeat just two more Vassals, you will reach another cultivation achievement level.>

"So… every six Vassals defeated counts for one level; how many do I need to *kill* for a level?" The excitement in Grant's voice was something that Sarge had been hoping to hear.

<Let me give it to you in a direct breakdown: every two Lords or Ladies killed will give you one level. You gain one level for each of those that you *defeat*, though. Every two Wielders that you defeat, or every four that you *kill*, will give you a level.> Sarge highlighted each area as he explained so that Grant could see what he was talking about as he referenced it. <Every six Vassals defeated, or every twelve killed. Finally, every fifty monsters killed will bump you up, too. Of course, you can

always increase your cultivation level by actually *cultivating*, which is what most people need to do, but it does take quite a long time.>

"It seems that..." Grant applied every mathematical trick he knew to work out his next words, "*defeating* them is the fastest path toward a high-level? I would only have to defeat *half* as many as I needed to kill, to reach the same level?"

Sarge's response was slightly mystifying, <What is a Calendar King without subjects to rule? Oh, last note. Killing cultivators does nothing for your personal level. Might help with skills?>

"Look who it is!" Fergus's drunken shout caught Grant off guard, making him flinch away from the large man. "I've been out looking for you, lad! Come on, this is the right house!"

Grant was dragged into Derek's home, and Red looked him over with a frown. "You said you wouldn't be long. What happened?"

"I fell asleep in the dining hall, then took a wrong turn trying to get here." Grant's answer was plausible, and would have been accepted... yet there was *one* tiny detail he had forgotten.

"That doesn't explain your leg!" Skinny pointed at the bloody limb as he dug into a late night snack, dipping a large sausage into a jar of mayonnaise, followed by ketchup and mustard. He ate the 'snack' in two bites, then reached for another.

"Well..." Though he hadn't wanted to get into it, Grant reluctantly told them what actually happened. "After the wrong turn, I ran into a group of Vassals serving Sir Friday Twenty-Ninth."

"You ran away and only got that little cut?" Red leaned forward in his chair to get a better look. "Remarkable."

"I was nicked by a... I think it is called a truncheon? A club with a blade on it. It hardly touched me, but I still can't feel my thigh. My right leg is pins and needles, but I'm at least starting to get feeling back in that. Now, as you can see, Sir Friday

Twenty-Ninth will be after me, since I've got a couple of his toys." Grant pulled out the small wooden truncheons and dropped them on the table. They continued to glow with a faint inner light.

"Grant…" Fergus pointed at the glowing truncheons with wide eyes and a shaking finger. "That's *Wielder* magic. Do you not understand? Vassals are people that have been granted a weaker version of the power that infuses their Lord's Wielded Weapon. I think… I'm pretty sure they can track those down."

"You need to get rid of these. You should get over to see Bob Sunrise; he can probably even tell you how to fix your leg, if it isn't better by then." Derek looked pleased to add something to the conversation that he'd been left out of until this point. "Across the river where the upper classes hobnob. He'll be able to help you out. You'll see a sign at the corner of the plaza that says 'Bob's Armor Emporium'."

Grant looked around the room for confirmation, but everyone else just shrugged. Since this was the only lead he had toward figuring out what he was up against, he nodded at Derek. "Many thanks. I'll head there first thing in the morning."

Exhausted from his training and the fight, the night passed in a blur for him. Getting up before dawn, he slipped out of the house. With a bounce in his step, even though his leg was still a little sore, he left the Crafting District behind. The mega bakeries were already churning out bread and pastries for the nobility across the river, making the air smell *glorious*. "I can't imagine what would have happened if I hadn't been able to fix the mill. Actually, I can… there would probably have been riots in the streets."

Thinking of the mill brought back sour memories, but he tried to ignore the fury and just do his best to enjoy his morning. As he walked along the path sandwiched between the river, known as 'The Trickle', and a towering bakery wall, he was careful not to breathe too deeply. The bread smell was just too *tempting*… and the river smell was disgusting. Such a dichotomy made his empty stomach churn.

As pretty as the river appeared in the morning light, on closer inspection, Grant could detect discharge pumping into it from the south, and raw sewage from the wealthy townhouses to the north. He picked up his step and held his nose tightly against the miasmic stench. Hurrying along, he almost missed the city changing dramatically as he strode across one of the many bridges. The view was suddenly akin to a many-tiered wedding cake; but here, each layer contained a myriad of fine buildings.

Grant soon passed the Imperial School of Cookery. An obese guard yawned by a filigreed gate, paying Grant no attention; his focus remained on a box of donuts while trying to figure out which one to nibble on next. The other thing Grant noticed as he walked up steps toward the next layer of the Noble quarter was how quiet it was. Back in the south of the city, the sound of industry was constant, with laborers hard at work to meet the multitudinous needs of the Nobility and the major city at large. Here in the north, there was silence. "People are hungover from their night of feasting and partying? That has to be it."

A central plaza opened up in front of him, and he walked past an oversized statue of an absolute *ball* of a man. The plaque at its base read, 'Lord January provides for all'. The statue's huge arms were spread wide, and around the base sprawled the figures of peasants and Nobles alike with their faces turned up to admire their ruler's benevolence; eating the feast supplied by Lord January.

From the corner of his eye, Grant noticed the freshly painted sign of 'Bob's Armor Emporium'. His destination in sight, he picked up his pace; but his heart sank as he reached the door and noticed a closed sign hung behind the glass. "Maybe I'm just too early?"

The streets were still deserted, and it was starting to feel creepy instead of normal. The sun was just starting to rise when he crossed the river, but that didn't stop him from looking through the window. His face pressed against the shop window, Grant attempted to peer into the darkness within. He could see the outline of breastplates, gauntlets, and sturdy leather boots. In the depths, there appeared to be full suits of armor, but squinting didn't help.

"Get away from my window, *peasant*, or I'll call for the Peacekeepers!"

CHAPTER TWENTY-FIVE

Grant swung around as the commanding tone reached his ears. Waddling toward him briskly was a bulky figure wearing a pleated suit and half-moon eyeglasses draped on the end of a pointy nose. Grant could just barely make out the name 'Bob Sunrise' above his head. "Shoo. Go on. I need to open up!"

"I'm a customer." Grant stepped forward and gave a sketchy bow. "I'm here to buy a suit of armor."

"Huh. No chance. Look at the size of you! If you can't afford a proper meal, you certainly can't afford…" Bob paused, wiped his eyeglasses, and peered through them. "Oh. *Oh*! I do apologize, Sir Monday. Dressed like that, and so *thin*, I assumed…"

"I know that-"

Grant's words were cut off as Bob pressed forward. "You must have been to a masquerade party, of course! How silly of me. For a moment there, I thought you a lowly peasant that somehow snuck into the Noble shopping quarter!"

"Yes. A party," Grant deadpanned, seeing only benefit in going along with Bob's interpretation of the situation.

"Give me a moment, sir, while I open up the shop." The full

figure of Bob Sunrise entered the premises. The door was twice as wide as needed even for him; this shop clearly catered to the aristocracy above all else. Grant's excitement was building; soon he would own a suit of armor that would protect him from Sir Friday Twenty-Ninth's Wielded Weapon, *and* he would be able to begin armor cultivation.

Across the plaza, obese individuals approached various shops, and the unease that Grant had been feeling by being in such an empty area began to fade. The slimmer silhouettes of normal people were starting to trundle around, bearing heavily laden carts on their way up the hill. Bob's sign flipped around, and Grant didn't waste a moment before entering. Bells tinkled merrily as he crossed the threshold, and Bob boomed, "*Welcome*! To Bob's Armor Emporium! We have wonders from all across the Spring Districts, fulfilling the armor needs of the aspiring adventurer, monster slayer, or dungeon crawler!"

"Wonderful. I need a suit of armor." Grant walked up to the counter and took a seat on a plush cushioned chair, as though he shopped at places like this regularly.

Bob laughed and wiggled a finger at him. "You have to be a little more *specific*, sir."

"I need protection from impacts and cuts." Once more, Grant was interrupted by the garrulous man.

"Ho *ho*! All armor here will protect you from cuts; everything from Early Spring to Early Summer armor can be found in this wondrous shop! Perhaps I can be of some small service for milord's selection? Do you need protection from slashing, or piercing attacks?"

"I… I'm not sure. Slashing, I think? I'm going to be going through rough areas, so I require protection from a… a weapon. Think of a… peasant weapon; a club that has metal nails embedded within it." Grant tried to be as vague as possible, but he thought he had described what he had fought against.

"Hmm… in that case…" Bob tapped his chins, deep in thought, "Leather armor will probably suffice. It is light, you'll be able to move much more easily than in chainmail, or full plate armor."

"That sounds-"

"Of course, we *do* have special suits of armor for our more… *discerning* clients." Bob pulled a sheet off a mannequin, presenting Grant with a gleaming suit of obsidian-colored armor. The gleaming black metal was stunning and appeared to absorb the light. Grant realized he'd seen a suit of armor like it before, worn by the magnificent Wielder in the market of New Dawn long ago. "I'll *take* it!"

Bob swooped in front of Grant, showing nothing but a smile as he stopped the young man's outstretched hand from touching the gleaming surface. "*Everything* is available, for a price. This beautiful armor is a stealth enhanced plate, and contains *many* unique properties. It is an Early Summer Heavy suit of armor, providing *maximum* protection while allowing you to be as agile as wearing a thin suit of leather armor. Now, if you look closely, you can see that the plates don't actually touch."

Grant bent over for a closer look. There were *tiny* gaps between the obsidian metal plates. They were perfectly aligned, but something stopped them from touching and making a noise.

"The ore was mined in the depths of the darkest pits in March. Many adventurers died extracting this coveted mineral, and it is said that the armorer who made the set," Bob whispered, leaning in closely to draw Grant's full attention, "sacrificed himself upon its completion. His life force is embodied within each and every metal plate, and that force provides its enhanced stealth abilities. These properties are highly prized by assassins, such as House Sss—well, let's not give in to supposition, shall we? Ha! It's also sought by adventurers that brave the deep mines and dungeons across the lands."

"Sounds awesome, Bob! I'll take it!" Grant pictured himself slaying dragons, cutting the head off Krakens, and leading vast armies to victory in war. This was *his* armor. Lords and Ladies of the Months would tremble at the sight of such a warrior… they would be so intimidated that they'd surrender at first sight!

<What's the point of looking at this junk? You can't wear it.> Sarge's non-sequitur gave Grant pause, but not so much as Bob's next words.

"Excellent. A fine choice, sir! We take coin or cart. Unfortunately, we don't accept credit anymore… not after that adventurer made a run for February!"

"Ah… cart?" Grant had never heard anyone ask for a cart as payment before.

Bob nodded gravely. "Yes, indeed; that *is* the most popular option. A member of your household can bring over a cartful of small Time, and once payment has been received; your armor will be available. Free delivery is available throughout January.

"Cart… full of Time." Grant coughed and blinked a few times.. "Let me, um… check my family finances for approval."

"For you, sir, today only, I can let it go for the low low price of… fifteen Years. Do be quick, as armor of this caliber *will* be snapped up. I can only keep the price this low until tomorrow!" Bob smiled cheerfully at the thought of making such a *wonderful* sale.

"A *Year* is a unit of currency? I thought Days were as high as they went…" Luckily, Grant's mumble didn't reach Bob's distracted ears. The young man narrowed his eyes; he suddenly didn't buy the hard sell sales pitch. It may be an expensive suit of armor, but merchants across January were all the same when it came to money. It didn't matter if it was a snot-covered loaf of bread, or a suit of the finest armor.

Grant brought up the money tab of his status sheet.

Time

28 Hours, 10 Minutes

"Twenty-eight Hours and ten Minutes suddenly doesn't sound like the huge amount I had thought it was..." Grant opened his backpack and spilled the contents out onto the counter, including the small pile of coins. The onyx idol Grant had forgotten about rolled onto the table as well, though he grabbed it and shoved it back in instantly. Still, it hadn't been fast enough to keep Bob from seeing it.

"I… I'll have to… visit the bank." The embarrassed Grant didn't want Bob to laugh at him, but the talkative Bob was oddly silent, staring longingly at the closed backpack..

"Can… can I have a closer look? Please?" Bob begged in a strangely quiet voice.

"That's a… no." At Grant's denial, Bob sank to his knees and held his hands in a pleading motion.

"*Please*, Sir Monday!" Bob waited desperately, and Grant finally relented out of sheer discomfort. The Wielder pulled the idol out of his bag and set it on the table. Bob's eyes couldn't shift away from it. He reached out and picked it up tenderly, as if it were a priceless work of art. "I've never seen one in the flesh before. Relics of the Wielder Wars are hard to come by… and they *never* come up for sale. It is said that Regent December holds the world's greatest collection, and only a few pieces are passed down the generations by powerful Houses… such as House Monday, apparently."

"Is it… is it for sale?" The merchant clasped his hands together once more, and his eyes were *shining*. His fat fingers trembled at the thought of possessing such an item. "You can have the suit of armor, and I'll even throw in a Bottomless Bag!"

"I… um." Grant seriously considered it. He *could* hand over the idol. It wasn't actually worth anything to him, and if it were this valuable it would certainly bring him endless trouble in the future. Especially now that someone knew he had it. He popped the idol out from Bob's sweaty palms and stared at it intently, mulling over his decision. He glanced over at the armor, dark as the dead of night. He'd never need another set… but it niggled at him how easily Bob would swap the insanely expensive set of armor for a lump of onyx. He put it in his bag with a deep sigh.

"I'm sorry, Bob… it's not for sale. My… my *family* would never forgive me."

Bob looked crushed. Tears streamed down his chubby cheeks. "I can throw in a set of Dragon Armor? List price of one Century and four Decades! The plates are taken from *live* Greater Dragons in District September! One hundred percent fireproof, guaranteed!"

<This is becoming dangerous, Grant. Get some armor, and get out. Early Spring, up to medium armor, is going to be the only thing that works for you properly, anyway.>

The offer was tempting, but Sarge's warning raised Grant's hackles. It was time to leave. Grant stood up and took a step toward the door. "No, sorry, Bob. I can't part with it. In fact, I'm leaving right now to get it back to the vault. I should never have brought it out for the… party."

"No, no. I understand… I wouldn't trade it either." Bob wiped away his tears and wiped his fogged up eyeglasses. "What *are* you doing, walking about with such a priceless artifact?"

Ignoring the comment, Grant slipped the idol back in his pack just as an announcement popped up.

Quest Update: Ties that Bind (Epic Level)

Information: You have discovered that the onyx idol is an ancient relic from the Wielder Wars. Proceed to Valentine to learn more.

Reward: Unknown.

"Bob, I think a suit of Early Spring Medium armor would be suitable at the moment." Seeing that the huge man wasn't trying to mug him, Grant forced himself to calm down and get what he came here for.

"Of… course." Bob composed himself and went away to collect the armor. He came back with a suit of flimsy brown leather armor. "Here you go! A full set of Medium armor: head, torso, and legs. It may not look like much, but each piece will mitigate two damage if you are hit. You do need at *least* ten points of armor cultivation to see it's benefits, of course…"

Grant quickly checked his stats again. "Twelve armor proficiency… it's appropriate for my level."

<*Why* would you tell someone your *characteristics*!> Sarge's roar nearly knocked Grant over. <That is the same as telling them *exactly* who they need to send to kill you off!>

"*Twelve*?" Bob's face was quivering in delight. "That's *incredibly* impressive for someone your age! You must focus all of your efforts into armor cultivation? Well… at that great height, the armor will mitigate a full *five* points of damage in total!"

Not wanting to get another earful from Sarge, Grant quickly agreed. "I'll take it."

Bob nodded hurriedly, "*Excellent*. For delighting me with your wonderful relic, it is yours for only… six Days!"

Grant stopped short at the price. That was almost as much as Jo had stolen from him. His mouth worked, and another idea appeared in his head. "My friend *Derek* said to mention his name? That you might be able to offer a better deal?"

"I've to say, Mr. Monday… you're an odd one. Walking around with a priceless artifact, and then haggling over the price of a suit of Early Spring armor?" Bob sighed dramatically, then waved his hand. "I *do* owe Derek for a job he completed for me. If you come back today, you can have it for five Days."

Grant opened his mouth to argue, but Bob cut him off harshly. "*Sir*, that really is the lowest I can go. I take a loss at that price, but I will be repaying Derek's debt."

"Okay. I will be back later. I just have to visit the, um… bank." The bells tinkled as Grant left the shop. His initial enthusiasm was long gone. "How in the twelve Districts am I going to come up with *five Days*?"

With sixty Minutes in an Hour, and twenty-four Hours in a Day… unless he got a job and worked for almost two whole weeks—since he could only provide unskilled labor—Grant wasn't going to be getting his armor anytime soon. He entered the Noble shopping plaza in a daze, unsure where to turn.

CHAPTER TWENTY-SIX

A pavilion was being raised in the center of the plaza, and something about it reached a part of him that was still lost in childish things. With nowhere better to go, Grant wandered over to take a look. An entire crew was busy pulling on cables and erecting a tent that resembled a fairytale castle, its walls bright vertical stripes of yellow and pink-dyed cloth.

He waved at a worker, who was puffing and attempting to erect a wide banquet table. "What's going on here?"

The busy man ignored him at first, but after realizing Grant wasn't going away, he turned around and cast a wary eye. "I'm pretty *busy*, as you can see… sir. M'lord. Regent's left b-"

He bit off the last curse after noticing that he was talking to a Noble of House Monday. Grant only smiled calmly. "You hiring help?"

The words made the laborer blink and sputter. It was *audacious* to think that a Noble needed to do such menial tasks. Nobles were the ruling class; they didn't *help* anyone. "I'll get a *beating* if my Lord discovers a Noble such as yourself helping me."

"I… understand." Grant didn't really understand, and he

didn't want to. The class structure and the divide between rich and poor confused him. The Lords and Ladies of the Houses bled just like the lowest peasant—he knew that for a fact. In January, due to the overwhelming abundance of food, no one starved, not even the poorest of the poor. Why all this pageantry? "Could you at least explain to me what's going on? I just got into town."

A small bit of recognition appeared in the man's expression, and he hastily turned his eyes away from Grant's very ordinary clothing. "This afternoon, there will be a contest right here in the plaza. Every week this month, we hold a culinary contest."

"Culinary?"

"Cooking related." The worker eyed him oddly, confused that Grant didn't understand the common term. "Last week, there was a bacon eating contest, and this week is ice cream."

"Ice cream. Cool." Grant chuckled, though the worker wasn't amused.

"I really have to get on with this, sir. If you want to take part, the competition starts at four this afternoon, and will go on until the last participant remains. If you don't mind me saying… you're a bit on the skinny side to *really* compete. The competition will be fierce; peasants and Nobles alike participate from all across January. Everyone is equal during the competition. Entry fee is one Day."

"One *Day*? Then… is there a prize?"

The man nodded, slipping into his normal customer-service mode. "But of course! Ten Days, plus a quarter of the total entrance fees. This week's competition is sponsored by House Friday, so come early if you want a seat. The spectacle always draws a crowd!"

The men nodded at each other and parted ways. Grant decided to head back to Derek's, his mind whirling with all of the new information he had gained in the last few short hours. "Ten Days… more than enough to get a set of armor."

He shook his head in frustration. The fact of the matter was that he was no closer to coming up with the Days. "It's a shame I don't have a… bigger appetite. Hmm."

Grant finished his long walk and rejoined his new friends. He sat down with a light sigh beside his heavy companions, who nodded, greeting him through mouthfuls of bacon and eggs. Breakfast was the most important meal of the day, so they didn't bother speaking. Once they were done, Red wiped his mouth with the back of his hand, then deposited the residue onto his pants. "So, did you get what you were looking for? Armor, wasn't it?"

"No. Turns out, proper armor is too expensive for my meager budget." Grant looked over at Skinny, who had cleared his plate and was eagerly shoveling a second, or perhaps tenth, helping into his bottomless stomach. Grant stared for longer than he cared to admit; it was hypnotizing and impressive in equal measures. He decided that now was his chance, so he cleared his throat and poked the other man. "Hey, Skinny. *Skinny*!"

"Hmm," Skinny growled mid-bite. He was completely focused on devouring the heaping plate of food in the most efficient manner. "I'm busy, Grant. What?"

Grant gave him a moment to clear his plate before continuing. "I've a proposition for you-"

"Sorry, Grant. Not my type. Need more cushion-"

Red and Fergus couldn't contain their laughter, spitting out lumps of scrambled egg as Grant furiously backpedaled. "*Skinny*! That's not what I meant! I-!"

"Say it in simple words then! I've no extra room in my head. If I did, I would fill it with this bacon! What is this brand? Dean?"

"*Turkey* bacon?" Fergus looked down in disgust. "Can't be Thorn brand if it's turkey bacon. Must be Dean."

Grant ignored the strange conversation on branding and pressed forward with Skinny. "Do you like ice cream?"

Skinny paused to think it over, "Ice cream aids the digestion, clearing the old digestive tract. I could go for some ice cream.

Why did you have to bring it up? Now I'm going to be thinking about it all day! Speaking of clearing the system…"

"Time to make some room." There was a rumble like a miniature earthquake, followed by a noxious smell. "I've just demonstrated the impressive workings of my digestive system."

A few conversational backfires later, Grant gave up on decorum and simply spat out what he wanted to say. "This afternoon there is a competition, all-you-can-eat ice cream! Do you want to participate? I'll pay the entrance fee."

Skinny stared at him in confusion. "I'm up for it, but what's in it for you? What's the catch?"

Grant leaned forward with gleaming eyes."No catch. I'll foot the entry fee, you just make sure to win. We split the prize money. I need the Time to buy a set of armor, and you can do what you want with your share."

"Hmm…"

"I need your talents, Skinny. There's no one better suited to winning this competition than you!" Grant pleaded with the obstinate man.

"Well… when you put it that way…" Skinny allowed a grin to spread across his face, and his chest puffed out in pride. "I'm in! Since you've publicly announced how impressed you are with my talents, I'll do you a solid. When I win, you can even keep the prize money. I eat for love, not money!"

Breakfast was finished in a flash, and the rest of the morning was spent strategizing for the big event of the day. Skinny skipped snack time, high tea, pre-lunch, lunch, after lunch snacks, and even early afternoon tea in preparation for the competition. By the time they were walking to the stage, he was nearly falling over from lightheadedness.

Grant, Red, and Fergus got Skinny into his seat, paid the fees—bringing Grant down to a total of only four Hours and eighteen Minutes—and found a seat on the packed benches lining the square. Grant had managed to squeeze in his daily training session; his fanclub at the steelworks had left him in peace to train after a stern warning from their boss. Even so, he had enjoyed their cheering and clamoring as he performed feats of physicality that they had never seen before. It was a strange, *strange* confidence boost. Grant shook himself out of his reverie; the competition was about to begin, and it was time to learn if he had thrown his Time onto the table or had bet on a winner.

"Have I missed anything?" Derek squeezed in alongside them, still sooty from the smeltery.

"Nothing." Red slapped him on the side. "Glad you could make it."

"I never miss it. These events are the highlight of the week, here in Mid January. Food warriors battling it out? Nail-biting stuff. You might think the biggest guy will always win, but that isn't always the case. This is the one place where *anyone* can truly showcase the talents that they have!" Derek warmly stated.

"Look, there he is!" Fergus elbowed Grant excitedly. The huge bulk of Skinny walked onto the stage, pumping his fists. The crowd went wild, cheering and shouting from their seated positions at the newcomer, as getting up posed a challenge for the spectators and tended to be frowned upon. At a glance, everyone could see that the incumbent champion was in for some serious competition.

The eaters lined up behind a massive bench. Peasants wearing stained clothes sat next to nearly perfectly-round Nobles in voluminous silk shirts and stretchy pants. There was even a soot-covered steelworker, who must have come straight here after his shift. Grant pointed him out, causing Derek to narrow his eyes and mutter something savagely.

"Ladies and gentlemen," the announcer on stage screamed into an amplifying horn so that all could hear, "sit tight and enjoy this afternoon's entertainment. Ample refreshments will, of course, be provided, courtesy of this week's sponsors: House Friday. Remember, folks, if you need a man hunted, a villain punished, a *scoundrel* brought to justice… go no further than House Friday! House Friday: *Promised and Delivered*."

He paused for the obligatory cheering. "Porta potties are located under your bench. Remember, all you have to do is *flip the switch* to use the facilities! You won't miss any of the exciting developments, but remember: *flip* the *switch.*"

The crowd laughed and cheered, sharing knowing glances. Not everyone remembered to flip the switch… at least not in time. There was always one, and it made for almost as good of entertainment as the competition itself. Grant flipped the switch on the side of his seat out of curiosity. The bottom of the bench swung open, and he had to grab on to Red and Fergus to avoid joining the fecal matter already churning below. "That is *disgusting.*"

<Yes.> Sarge's and Grant's thoughts were in perfect alignment for the first time ever.

"Don't knock it till you try it. This is the latest technological advancement! No one ever wants to miss out on the entertainment, after all," Derek called to the struggling Grant. "Also, be careful. The seats are made for the *average* Mid January frame, not a small tush like yours."

"I didn't know what would happen when I flipped the switch!" Seat closed and crisis averted, the group waited for the event to begin.

"You could have *asked*, you know." Red chortled as Grant blushed in shame.

"Mohawk is in for a real challenge today!" the announcer shouted, dragging their attention back to the competition itself. "These twenty brave competitors will be challenging Mohawk for the weekly crown! Three to one odds are on the newcomer, *Skinny;* make sure your bets are placed!"

The crowd tittered upon hearing his ironic name. As soon as they calmed down, the announcer dropped his hand theatrically. "*Begin*!"

Huge tubs of ice cream opened at the gesture, and the contestants eagerly dug into theirs. Grant could hear Skinny moan as his day-long starvation was alleviated. Up and down the silver spoons flashed, and the seconds turned into long minutes. It didn't take long before some started to struggle with lifting their spoons, and ice cream of all flavors dribbled down rough cotton shirts and silk alike.

"*Brain freeze*! Ha! This is what sets the Nobles apart from the rest of those contestants; they know how to pace themselves properly!" There was an exclamation from the crowd as a contestant passed out and slumped forward into the ice cream tub. The helpers rushed forward, and it took several workers to save and drag the fallen man off the stage.

"One valiant food warrior down! Who will be *next*, ladies and gentlemen?" Tub after tub of fresh ice cream replaced empty containers.

<Can a sword vomit? I want to vomit.> Sarge muttered a stream of consciousness into Grant's mind.

"*Look* at Skinny," Grant whispered to Fergus, awe filling his voice. "How does he manage it?"

"Skinny is a professional. Food is his life!" Fergus didn't bother to whisper; he was proud of his friend at this moment. After two hours of entertainment, the contest had worn down to two finalists: unsurprisingly, Skinny and the equally imposing Mohawk. Neither contestant looked ready to give in; though Mohawk had sweat beading on his brow as he glanced over at Skinny.

Skinny, who had brought his own wooden spoon, was oblivious to the staring. For him, there was nothing else, only the ice cream. He methodically took scoop after scoop. Vanilla, chocolate, strawberry… it didn't matter to Skinny, and each was equally delicious and deserving of his attention. The only time he paused the entire competition was to 'flip the switch', getting a roar of approval every time he did so.

"Ugh! Brain freeze!" Mohawk held his head and moaned in agony before finally conceding defeat by throwing his spoon in a half empty tub.

<There is no *brain* involved in this. No thinking person would ever do this to themselves intentionally.> Sarge's words, normally caustic, were practically despondent. <Would they?>

Skinny kept eating, and had to have his hand grabbed to

stop him, though his spoon-wielding hand continued to mechanically scoop through the air. "We have a *winner*, folks!"

<Does anyone *win* when this is how you show prowess?>

"Oh, hush, Sarge." Grant was cheering as loudly as anyone else in the stands.

It finally dawned on Skinny that it was over. "I won?"

"Yes! Additionally, our sponsor was so impressed by your ice cream-eating skills that you have been awarded a bonus prize! All the ice cream you can eat... for the next *year*!"

Skinny's jaw dropped, and he couldn't find the words to speak as he teared up with pure joy. The announcer noticed, and smiled kindly at him. "Do you have any words for the crowd who has been cheering you on, Skinny?"

"Thank you, everyone. Uh... hunger is the loss of a meal, and a missed opportunity to eat. If you want to be able to compete on my same level, remember these words!" The crowd *oohed* and *ahhed*, glad that Skinny was imparting this important lesson, one that would help them perhaps one day reach his heady heights.

Mohawk, having recovered from his brain freeze, waddled over to Skinny and shook his hand to show his very real respect. Grant was attempting to figure out how he should react in the situation. On one hand, he had spent his entire life learning that eating enormously vast quantities was the highest privilege. On the other hand, by following Sarge's words, he had never felt better in his entire life, and he wanted to share that with other people. Even with his mind not yet made up about how he would react in the future, Grant couldn't hold back his admiration for the present. "That... was oddly amazing!"

CHAPTER TWENTY-SEVEN

**Ding*.

The small bell above the door rang brightly, completely the reverse of Bob's attitude as he looked up from his ledger. It took him a moment, but then his face brightened into a professional smile. "I didn't expect to see you again today, Sir Monday! I was closing up."

"I've got the money. Sorry about the wait. The… bank manager was busy." Grant cringed inwardly at the lie, but it was better than the truth: that he was a Noble in name only, and that his friend had won the Time for Grant's desperately-needed armor in an ice cream eating competition. There was not a single member of the nobility that wouldn't be completely humiliated.

Bob looked out at the twilight, and grimaced at the thought of even doing a *speck* more work today. "You can come back tomorrow if you like? I will honor the deal."

"No, sir. I need it now." Grant kept his expression blank, simply going quiet after he insisted on service.

Bob stared at him, remaining quiet as well. However, the store owner broke first. At least he would gain some money off of this transaction. "Of course; what was I thinking? I'll go and get it for you."

It only took a moment for him to come back laden with the suit of Early Spring medium armor. A full set consisted of three armor pieces: head, torso, and legs. From the time the system was implemented until now, anything else that was worn simply wouldn't count toward armor rating. Things like armored boots or gauntlets were simply given the same overall armor rating as the main pieces for that position, which had caused a huge shift in fashion and armor trends ever since the barriers had gone up. It was equally impressive and confusing to see silk gloves block a sword, or obsidian gloves get cut through like butter.

"It looks even better than before," Grant stated approvingly. Light from Bob's lanterns gleamed off the surface, making the extremely basic armor look like something almost impressive to wear.

"I had one of my workers oil it for you. Can't have a Noble of House Monday wearing dull armor, now, can we?" Bob let his smile shine through. It was always nice to have their extra effort appreciated.

"Payment." Grant eagerly placed five Day coins in Bob's palm. "Can I put it on now?"

Bob laughed and gently shoved the armor into Grant's eager hands. "You can do what you want, sir. It's *your* armor!"

Grant stuffed his old shirt and pants into his backpack. Standing in his undergarments, he pulled on the gear first the leather legs, then the bulky torso, followed by the helm, and lastly, matching boots that Bob had thrown in after Grant had made him smile. The torso and leggings were a bit big, but Bob pulled on the leather straps until everything fit like a glove, taking a moment to teach him how to properly care for them.

The young man stood before the full-length mirror that had been set up in the shop, admiring his reflection. Yes, the helm was a simple leather skullcap, and he struggled to wiggle his toes in the tight leather boots, but he almost didn't even recognize the dangerous champion he saw before him. Bob continued to fuss over the straps, mumbling small platitudes as he finished up. "Don't worry. The leather will loosen up over time, with use. When you—*by Lord January*!"

Grant had pulled February Twenty Nine out of the scabbard, and Bob's hands shot up. His face was contorted both in anger and resignation. "After all this, you intend to *rob* me? You scoundrel!"

It took a moment for Grant to realize that Bob was speaking to him, "What? *No*! Of course not! I just wanted to see what I'd look like in the mirror with my sword in hand!"

"A little warning next time please, Mr. Monday. You'll give this old merchant a coronary!" Bob put his hands down, reaching for a handkerchief to wipe the sweat off his brow.

"Right. My apologies." Grant turned to the full-length mirror and popped off the leather skull cap, watching how his hair fell as he removed the protection. "Not bad, if I do say so myself."

"Ready for adventure *or* your next masquerade party, sir," Bob winked at him. As Grant stood there examining himself, considering how far he'd come since his days on the farm, something strange occurred. The flakes of rust coating February Twenty Nine fell off, and he was left holding a dull, but no longer corroded, sword.

"Oh my, Sir Monday!" Bob moved closer to inspect the strange sword that didn't need to be scrubbed to remove rust. "You are *full* of surprises. A Wielded Weapon! I thought that you were simply a second or third child of a Wielder, not the Wielder himself!"

"This old thing? It's just a family heirloom," he lied, disturbed by how smoothly the lies were slipping out of his mouth lately, and how easily he was stepping into the role of a Noble after a lifetime of practically living as a hated abomination. Still, he was excited by this new and unexpected development. Grant checked his status sheet to see if it would offer any insight into the shift.

Name: Grant Monday
Rank: Wielder
Class: Foundation Cultivator
Cultivation Achievement Level: 5
Cultivation Stage: Mid Spring
Inherent Abilities: Swirling Seasons Cultivation
Health: 95/95
Mana: 3/3

Characteristics
Physical: 30
Mental: 9
Armor Proficiency: 12
Weapon Proficiency: 23

Wielded Weapon: "February 29"

Weapon Inherent abilities:
1) Weapon Absorption: This sword has the ability to absorb another Wielded Weapon's power, taking its ability into itself. Restriction: Only one weapon per Monthly series.
2) NEW! Weapon/Armor Synergy: When the Wielder is equipped with armor, this sword increases in potency and gains power. Increase is capped at the Wielder's cultivation stage, or average armor stage, whichever is lower. February 29 is now considered an 'Early Spring Medium' sword. Current maximum damage is: 8 (5.5 from weapon cultivation, 2 from weapon stage, rounded up.) Damage type is 'piercing', 'slashing', or 'blunt', depending on how February 29 is used.

"Synergy… what does that mean? I unlocked that just by putting on armor? Sarge, any hints at how I can get the other ones unlocked?" Grant was mostly muttering to himself, but he paused in the hope that Sarge would speak up. Nothing. "Wearing better armor will increase the power of February Twenty Nine. I've got a new goal, it seems. Get my average cultivation stage higher, then get better armor every single time that it increases. With how expensive this set was... I can't imagine what it's going to take to get my sword to Late Winter…"

He glanced over at the obsidian armor that he could have traded the small statue for, wincing as he realized that he actually *did* know what it would take. That still didn't explain what had happened to his sword. Sure, it would do more damage, but what was up with the rust falling off of it? He remembered that focusing on the weapon had revealed more in the past. He did so again, but there was no new information. Not giving up, he broadened his search on the status sheet itself and found a new tab, next to training. It said 'Weapons and Armor'.

Clicking on that revealed an image of his body. There were three armor slots, and they were filled with the corresponding pieces of Early Spring Medium armor. On the left was what he was looking for: February Twenty Nine. He stared at that until he was rewarded with further information.

February 29 (One or two-handed Uchigatana)

Condition: Dull (Updated from Dull and *Rusty. Next stage: Polished)*

"Sir? I really have to close up. Remember, Bob Sunrise is here for all your armor needs, starting daily at sunrise! Tell *all* your Noble friends, and… if you are ever looking to part with your Relic of the Wielder Wars, think of old Bob."

"I shall do so, Bob. Though I left it at the bank this time around." Grant grinned at his reflection once more, pleased with the way light glinted off his now only *dull* weapon. "I won't forget your kindness. I hope you do well in the future."

CHAPTER TWENTY-EIGHT

Grant had a skip in his step as he left the armor emporium. The competition finally over, the plaza had been cleared of all people with extremely… impressive stature. Workers in protective suits were clearing up the devastation left behind: litter piled high. Biscuits, snacks, and greasy bones coated the cobbles. Grant felt bad for the workers; it was one thing clearing up the roadway, but quite another emptying the tubs containing vast quantities of sloshing waste. "It will all end up floating in The Trickle, no doubt…"

As he was watching the workers and thinking about his new set of armor, he didn't notice a carriage roll onto the plaza. He *did* hear the yelps of surprise as waste-wielding workers wobbled westward, wary of wayward wheels. Too bad for them, the rapid movements required to avoid being crushed meant that foul flotsam frequently flew.

"What now?" Grant wondered to himself, searching for a way to get out of sight as the carriage door swung open. Two men in the livery of House Friday rushed to place steps in front of the door. Without missing a moment, the regal figure of Sir Friday Twenty-Ninth walked down the steps. An aide, probably a Vassal, held onto the end of his purple cape, ensuring that it wasn't soiled by the filthy cobbles.

"Grant Monday, there you are! I've been looking all over for you!" The Noble boomed, loud enough to draw the eyes of everyone in the area. Grant froze like a cornered rat, slowly turning to face the person who had sent people to hunt him since he had arrived in Mid January.

"I don't think we've... had the pleasure of meeting?" Grant made sure there was no one behind him; he wasn't going to get netted again.

"Enough! No backtalk from you!" The huge man stamped his foot in frustration. "Give me back my *weapons*!"

"I don't know what you mean." Grant faced the Nobleman directly, a hand resting lightly on the hilt of his own Wielded Weapon.

"You *stole* my Vassal's truncheons. They are imbued with the power of my Wielded Weapon, and I would rather not have to go through the ritual required for re-imbuements of weapons. It is long, and it is exhausting. Just give them back, or I will *take* them." He shook a large wooden truncheon warningly. It looked identical to the smaller versions, though it was somewhat more ornate.

"Oh, those things. Tell you what." Grant fished the small truncheons out of his bag and smacked them together playfully. "If you cancel the bounty on my head, I'll give them to you."

"What, what, *what*?" Sir Friday Twenty-Ninth's face was turning a darker shade of red by the moment, and he looked ready to explode. Maybe Grant would get another accidental kill by having yet another Wielder have a heart attack in front of him? "You are accused of the attempted murder of Lady *Vivian Thursday*! Your crime will *not* go unpunished, you scoundrel!"

"Now it's all the way up to *murder*? Her accusation is a blatant lie, and she is a despicable person for propagating such a foul, libelous story!" Grant couldn't believe the words that were coming out of his mouth. He had heard all of them before, he was *sure* of it, but since when was this his standard vocabulary?

Sarge filled the gap in his knowledge with an explanation that made Grant's eyes sparkle. <If you're confused, it's no longer because you have a terrible mental cultivation. You're able to learn at a much higher rate, and your memory has become impressive… at least compared to a non-cultivator. Also, sword out!>

"*En garde*!" Sir Friday brought up his cudgel, holding it like a swordsman about to duel. He pranced forward on his tiny feet. With a ringing of steel, Grant unsheathed the dull blade of February Twenty Nine.

Sir Friday stumbled to a halt, his wobbling body indicating his sudden uncertainty. "My Vassals told me your blade was rusty? Did you get a new… oh! You just stepped out of Bob's… it matters not! Prepare to defend yourself, Grant Monday. Or you can save yourself the humiliation of being publicly thrashed, and we can go straight to House Friday's headquarters, where punishment will be swiftly meted!"

"I'd rather fight." Grant moved into a defensive pose, and he felt comfortable with himself for the first time that day. This was what he trained every day to do; this was what he *wanted* to do. Fighting had become his passion, and winning here would increase his popularity. He craved that. He craved it *deeply*.

"So *be* it." Something flew from Sir Friday's fingers. Before Grant had a chance to react, a cloud of smoke enveloped him. He coughed and swung wildly, unable to see even his sword arm.

Debuff added: reduced sight! Duration: smoke dissipation.

Smack.

An object collided with Grant's back, dealing a glancing blow but no damage. He spun to face his attacker, and saw the cudgel just before it thudded against his leather-clad torso.

Damage taken: 5 blunt (5 mitigated.)

The impact knocked the wind out of him, but apart from that, he was practically unscathed. The embedded glowing shards of metal had barely left a mark on the oiled leather, and his limbs were *not* paralyzed. A wolfish grin appeared on his face, and he switched to an offensive pose.

The smoke cleared, and the knowing smile fell from Sir Friday's robust face when he realized that Grant wasn't crippled and lying on the ground. It was Grant's turn now. He jumped forward in an attack posture and brought February Twenty Nine down on Sir Friday's raised cudgel. Sir Friday reacted by planting a meaty fist into Grant's stomach, failing to deal damage past Grant's damage mitigation, but still pushing the young man back a foot. "Ready to give up yet, brat?"

"Never!" replied a winded Grant. There was a too-familiar faint whistle, and Grant dodged the net flying at him at the last moment. It was quickly followed by a second and third whistle. Unsure where to move, he sliced the air frantically. A shower of threads fell to the ground, but he did not.

"My Vassals warned me about you. Don't think I didn't come prepared!" Before Grant could react, Sir Friday blew a cloud of red dust in his face.

Grant's mouth snapped shut, since he didn't want to breathe in the powder. He failed to close his eyes in time, and barbs of pain lanced into his brain. Within moments he was effectively blind.

Smack.

Damage taken: 4 blunt!

The cudgel hit his leg and was followed up with a bop to Grant's new skullcap helmet. He couldn't see, but he could hear Sir Friday panting heavily with the effort of the sustained attacks. Grant's heart hammered… there was no way he could win the fight if he couldn't see. As the Noble paused to catch his breath, Grant also took a moment to calm himself. As he did so, he became aware of the noises as Sir Friday continued prancing around him. Metal plates of his suit of armor scraped against one another, and his heavy footfalls announced his every movement.

"You should have invested in a set of stealth armor!" Grant

coughed around the searing pepper that now clogged his mouth. He heard the weapon as Sir Friday lazily swung it through the air. Rather than let it collide with his leather armor, Grant parried the weapon. The impacts didn't cut through, but they certainly *hurt*, and would leave bruises all over his body.

Blow after blow was parried or dodged, and try as he might, Sir Friday couldn't get another hit in against the blinded Grant. The fatiguing Lord puffed, "How. Are. You. *Doing* this?"

Grant remained silent, focused on anticipating the next attack. When it came from behind, he was ready. He smacked his elbow against Sir Friday's wrist, and the Wielded Weapon fell to the ground.

"Ouch!" Sir Friday ponderously grasped for it as it rolled away. Grant, without missing a step, grabbed hold of the bulky fellow and pressed the edge of February Twenty Nine against the many folds of Sir Friday's neck. "I yield! I *yield*! Don't kill me!"

Inner light bathed Grant, who was delighted with his recent rapid progress. Cultivation level six. "Sir Friday, as I've already explained, that charge was *bogus*. I've no intention of killing you, nor anyone, unless *forced*."

Grant slowly withdrew his blade from Sir Friday's neck, wary of trickery. He blinked rapidly. As his vision returned, he was confronted by the panting, sweaty form of Sir Friday kneeling on the ground. A notification appeared, and Grant was able to see it clearly, though the rest of the world was still hazy.

Do you, Grant Monday, wish to absorb the power of January 29: Paralyzation? Accepting Paralyzation will override any previous Wielded Weapon power absorbed in the current monthly series. If not overridden by another weapon of the same month, this ability will return to its current Wielded Weapon at the end of the year, unless the quest 'Heal The World' has been successfully completed.

. . .

Accept / Decline

"Hmm. Paralyzation would certainly come in handy, but I'd lose Sarge's help with training. I can't let that happen… or should I-?"

<Don't even *think* about it! You're not getting rid of me that easily. I've almost fully recovered from bending the rules as far as I did, but going forward… no help in combat. None.> Sarge went silent, and Grant thought the conversation was over, but the sword spoke up once more. <Nicely done, by the way. I like how you dealt with that greaseball. Go on, put him out of his misery. That will send a message to the Lords and Ladies of the Houses. Let them know that Grant Monday is not to be trifled with!>

"That's… he already surrendered." Grant was happy to hear that Sarge was feeling better, but he didn't intend to follow his advice though.

<Double dip! Get a defeat *and* a kill!>

"You're pretty dark for a *sword*."

<I'm literally made for killing!>

Grant ignored the bloodthirst of his weapon and returned to the notification. It wasn't a difficult decision; he chose 'Decline'. He hoped he didn't live to regret it, but he wasn't confident enough in his abilities to lose access to Sarge or Sword Expertise's built-in training program. It was more beneficial to learn how to use his sword properly than to numb someone that was cut by his weapon. Sir Friday's eyes were squeezed shut as he mumbled a prayer. Grant shoved the quivering man to get his attention. "I *said* I won't kill you. Relax."

"Huh?" Sir Friday peeled an eye open. "Really? You're not going to poke me full of holes and dump my beautiful body in The Trickle?"

"That's a no."

"Well, that's just jolly nice of you, sir!" a delighted Sir Friday Twenty-Ninth beamed. He scrambled to his feet, and made a shooing motion at someone that Grant couldn't see, then a beckoning motion in a different direction. "Henry! Fetch me a clean cloak."

<You pass. I'm glad to see that you have honor. Honor may not win power, but it wins *respect*. Respect *does* win power.>

Sir Friday's servant scuttled over, quickly gathered up the soiled cloak, then fastened a fresh one in its place. "Ah, I feel better already. I can't stand the filth here in the city. I'm intrigued, Grant. Interesting… you don't *behave* like a scoundrel."

"As I told you, I've no interest in murdering anyone, much less 'Lady' Vivian!" Grant shuddered at the thought of the woman, but that didn't mean she needed to die.

"I've met the little minx; she *is* a little intimidating, isn't she?" Sir Friday chuckled and became contemplative. "I met her at a dinner party, where Joviality was actively trying to marry her off to some sap."

"I mean… the entire reason I've a bounty on my head is that she wanted to marry me next month, on Valentine's Day, and I *declined*." The emphatic tone of Grant's words made Sir Friday's eyes lock onto him.

There was a complex look on his face as he asked, "Had you been courting long?"

"I'd only just *met* the crazy merchant, and his daughter tried to marry me! When I said no, he *robbed* me and used the stolen Time to put the bounty on my head."

"I had wondered why someone would bother to post such a small bounty. At least you are as dangerous as advertised." Sir Friday let out a hearty laugh even as Grant grumbled about his stolen sum being 'small'. "It sounds like you had a lucky escape. Say, Grant… I could use a man like you. Someone who can *really* fight."

"What for?" Grant glared at the man that had just tried to beat him into submission. "Also, why would I believe that you wanted to help *me*?"

"Perhaps you just listen to my offer?" The Noble shrugged

and continued, "I can't *make* you trust me. All I can do is be enticing. At the end of the month, there will be an exhibition held in Lord January's honor, where Wielders and Vassals will fight for honor and glory! It will take place at January's End, the trading city near the January-February border barrier; the capital of January."

"That... sounds interesting..." The opportunity would certainly catapult Grant closer to his goals of defeating Lord January and crossing the border wall. "What would you need from me, and why would I work for you?

"Oh, it's interesting. With your stamina and ability to fight for an extended period of time... you may actually *win*. Not only that, but the winner of the tournament will be presented with a set of Mid Spring Heavy armor. I don't know if that's something you'd like, but you are the first person outside of matches that I've seen wearing armor, so... maybe?" Sir Friday looked him over again and again before continuing with his proposition.

"Beyond the armor, I will personally pay for your housing and anything you need to prepare yourself; such as food and trainers." Sir Friday's offer was tempting, and when Grant recalled the effect of the rust falling off February Twenty Nine... he was intrigued by the possibilities that better armor would offer. Sir Friday cautiously reached out a hand and clapped it on Grant's arm. "So, Grant Monday, what do you say? Will you be my champion?"

A quest notification window appeared.

New Quest: King of the Castle (Rare).

Information: Be a champion, representing Sir Friday Twenty-Ninth in the exhibition tournament at Castle January in honor of Lord January. Bring honor and glory to House Friday, and personal honor upon yourself.

Reward: A unique set of Mid Spring Heavy armor upon winning the tournament.

Accept / Decline.

. . .

Grant took a shuddering breath and clasped his new patron's hand. "Sign me up; I accept!"

Sir Friday beamed at him, "Excellent. We must hurry. There are many preparations to make."

"Okay. I can meet you-?" Grant took a step, but Sir Friday shook his head and didn't release his hand. "Sir, I've got to tell my friends where I'm going. They'll think I abandoned them, or been captured."

"There's no time, and *no one* must know about my secret weapon."

Grant still hesitated. "But… I can't just *leave*."

"You can stay here and go about your business, bounty lifted, *or* you can take part in Lord January's tournament with me." Sir Friday let go, turned, and entered the carriage that waited for him. The horses neighed, eager to be on their way. As he stepped in, he turned back one last time. "The choice is yours."

Grant stood stock-still for a moment as his head and heart battled for supremacy. He gazed past The Trickle. The comforting glow of lights filled windows in the Crafting District, and smoke billowed relentlessly into the sky. When the wind picked up, he could even faintly hear the pounding of machinery.

"If I leave now, my friends, who have gone out of their way to support me, will assume I'm dead, or that I've abandoned them." He looked back at the carriage door, its door open invitingly. "There lies the doorway to February. All I've gotta do, somehow, is defeat Lord January."

<When you are attempting to save yourself, better yourself, or move forward in life… the people that have no interest in progressing need to be left behind.> Sarge interjected kindly.

With a last look down at the smoke and lights, where his friends were probably eating and awaiting his return, Grant made his choice with a sigh. "It needs to be done… but it still hurts. They were the first people that were good to me."

Sir Friday made room as Grant entered the carriage. Easing back onto the luxuriously upholstered cushions, Sir Friday Twenty-Ninth nodded, and the carriage started to roll toward his estate. Grant closed the curtain and kept his head down, not wanting to be reminded of the new friends that he was already leaving behind.

CHAPTER TWENTY-NINE

The door to his private suite closed with a **thunk**, and Grant stood alone in the luxuriously appointed room. He couldn't help gawking, almost *scandalized* by the sheer wealth on display. "It's just like the one in my dream, only without the beauty bearing donuts."

To be fair, there *were* donuts on the sideboard, along with a dazzling array of sweets and desserts; everything a Noble would need to tide him or her over between meals. Surrounded by the luxury… he felt more alone than he had since living on the farm. He couldn't help but think of his friends, despite trying to put them out of his mind. Up until recently, his only friends had been Daisy the dairy cow and the other farm animals, but he'd doubted they would hang around if he'd stopped feeding them. That… that *might* be true of Skinny as well, but maybe not Fergus or Red.

With a sigh, Grant jumped onto the bed, sinking into the thickly padded mattress. He instantly fell into a deep slumber, the sweet aroma of pastries and other treats lingering in the air and influencing his dreams.

A tinkling bell awoke him from a troubled sleep. He pulled back the drapes and was greeted by the bright light of mid-morning streaming in, and the immaculately manicured gardens stretching into the distance.

After freshening up, he left his suite and almost collided with a servant hurrying through the halls, heavily laden with dishes. "Sir! Pardon my clumsiness! Good morning. The dining hall is this way. Please follow me. Second breakfast has already commenced; I fear they could not wait for you."

Grant followed the scurrying servant, almost offering to carry the plates, but remembering how the worker in front of the pavilion had responded. It wasn't his 'place', as a Monday, to carry dishes. Double doors swung open, and his mouth dropped at the sight awaiting him. He was trying to play it cool, to dance along the strings required of a Noble gentleman, but… crystal chandeliers containing hundreds of candles lit the room, and the massive table was at least fifty feet long. Every *inch* was covered by rich food, most of which he didn't recognize. Trestles had been stacked on top, each containing an assortment of exotic fruit of every color imaginable. In fairness, the perfectly stacked fruit looked like it hadn't been touched, and a good amount of it was on the verge of becoming over-ripe.

Dozens of sleepy Nobles and Vassals sat around the table, yawning and chatting away. Grant walked toward the only free seat he could find, which just happened to be beside Sir Friday Twenty-Ninth. An army of servants scurried around, refilling half-full platters and topping up crystal glasses. Sir Friday waved for him to sit. "I'm so pleased you could join us. You missed last night's feast, but as you had fallen asleep in the carriage… I thought it best not to disturb you."

"Thank you, sir. I've had a challenging few… days. Decades, almost. I don't even recall falling asleep." Grant's stomach rumbled. Nearby Ladies laughed at the sound, and—from the way their eyes washed over his body—his armor and lack of girth.

His face reddened in shame. Sir Friday noticed and tried to quickly move past the poor behavior of his guests. "Dig in, Grant; sample our wonderful delights from as far away as District *March*! Those chocolates, specifically; they have a delightful tendency to be a gamble to eat. They may be *delicious*, or they might be a chocolate-covered mouse! You never know for certain. First, though, let me announce your arrival to the group, who should remember that their actions reflect on their *host*."

Grant nodded as the room went silent, wondering how the assembled members of House Friday would react to having a Monday in their midst. Sir Friday stood and clinked his glass. "Please friends, welcome my cousin, *Grant Friday*. He has had an arduous journey, traveling all the way from *February* to be with us today! Make him feel at home, and *do* remember that customs are different across the barrier."

"Grant *Friday*... what?" Grant opened up his status sheet, deeply confused by yet another name change. The guests lifted a glass in welcome before quickly shifting to stuffing their faces once again.

Name: Grant Friday (Updated from Grant Monday)

(Identity hidden. Potion effect will remain active until it is dispelled. Click here to end potion effect: Hidden Identity)

"Sorry about that subterfuge, old chap," Sir Friday whispered with a wink. "I had to hide your identity on the way here. It's a simple, if *expensive*, potion. We don't want idle gossip spilling the beans on our arrangement, do we?"

"I suppose not." Grant inspected his name once more and smiled wryly. If only he had been able to afford that potion as a Leap!

"Don't worry, it can be dispelled at any time, but I strongly suggest you *don't*. If you do, uncomfortable questions will be asked. Please, eat!" A starving Grant couldn't hold back, and dove into the food, filling his watering mouth and aching gut. He tried not to eat too much of any particular dish, instead sampling as many delights as he could. At first, he felt guilty for eating and wasting so much, but he just couldn't... *help* himself. Luckily, he wasn't alone.

<Portion control module activated.> Sarge spat into his mind, the first words he had spoken today.

Warning: Daily calorie limit intake exceeded.

"C'mon Sarge. Just one more eclair..." He ignored Sarge again, taking one more bite into his gullet. His hunger well and truly satisfied, Grant slumped down in his chair beside the other Nobles. By now, most were practically sleeping in their seats, though a few continued to slowly shovel in mouthful after mouthful. Grant reached for another dish, but a spasm of pain from his swollen stomach stopped him.

<You're not going to listen? Then suffer the consequences.>

Training program locked until current caloric intake is offset.

"S-Sarge!" Grant stared at the message in horror. "What's a 'caloric'?"

"I'm glad to see you have a strong appetite, Grant," Sir Friday commented from his slumped position. "Strong appetite, strong contender."

Grant could only nod. Talking required too much effort at the moment.

"Train hard, lad. In two days, we leave for Castle January. Even now, my servants are making the final preparations. Hmmm. The training yard is at your disposal." Sir Friday hesitated and looked out at his guests. "I didn't want to mention it, but while you are at the dining table, it is appropriate to wear more... formal attire. A clean suit has been pressed and left in your room."

Grant groaned at the thought of training with a full stomach. He decided to wait, and instead joined the others in a food-induced sleep. An unknown amount of time later, he awoke with a start. From the position of the sun streaming through the glass ceiling high up, it was already early afternoon. He groaned and considered going straight to bed, but instead got up, collected February Twenty Nine from his suite, and headed out to train.

"Sarge? Let's get to training!" Nothing happened, and there was no response from his Wielded Weapon. After waiting a few moments, he opened the training Tab and attempted to start the training manually.

Training is locked until caloric overage is balanced. Caloric overage: 800. Recommended actions: Running, weight training. Weight training is optimal for fastest usage of calories.

"What does this mean?" The only 'weight training' that he had ever heard about was sitting at a table and trying to increase your weight. Yet, somehow, he did not think that was what this message was telling him to do. Since he only understood one of them, Grant started to run laps around the training yard. Once, twice around, and Grant nearly stopped. The only thing that kept him motivated was the notification that appeared.

Current weight: 330 pounds.

At current walking speed: 60 minutes for a 786 calorie reduction.

"I'm not *walking*, I'm running." Grant grumpily told the notification. It didn't answer him, so he assumed that it took his complaint under advisement. Half an hour passed, forty-five minutes, an hour. At an hour and twenty minutes he heard a chime, and Sarge began speaking to him again.

<I hope you learned your lesson. It will become harder and harder to reach a goal like this as you become healthier. At a hundred and eighty pounds, you would need to walk for nearly two hours for the same benefits. This is the first time that your lack of health and weight is actually *beneficial* for you.> Sarge paused, then growled at Grant. <My goal is to make you the most effective warrior I possibly can. I am *not* going to allow you to disregard my training. You want to become deadly? You want to survive the year? Do *not* try me again.>

The regular training module was now unlocked, and Grant

was forced to throw himself into it. Bells tinkled at regular intervals throughout the day, signifying the next mealtime. Since breakfast, he'd counted at least four bells. He practiced the moves that Sarge thought were the most important, focusing on dodging blows rather than parrying them. He'd discovered that each parry used a large chunk of stamina; once all his stamina was depleted, the dummy targets could easily land a painful hit.

"The energy from the food was *needed*," he informed Sarge with a groan. "How else could I train hour after hour?"

Sarge ignored him, though the next dummy tackling him looked *suspiciously* like Lady Vivian. At the end of the session, the sun was low in the sky, and delicious aromas were wafting from the kitchens. A bell signified the next meal would be served soon.

<Grant… you need *very little* food right now. I can monitor your body. You can have your dinner, but you *will* eat what I tell you to eat.> Grant took that as permission and raced to his suite to freshen up. After washing, he donned the suit that was waiting for him and admired himself in the mirror. The tailored outfit fit perfectly, and it appeared to be made from a highly stretchy fabric; a necessity when attending a Noble banquet!

After rushing to his previous position in the dining hall by Sir Friday Twenty-Ninth's side, he ogled the sheer abundance of food. All manner of succulent meat was stacked on the banquet table, from wild boar, to pheasant, and steaks the size of small children. Half-jokingly he muttered, "I hope they weren't really children."

An overeager guest was tearing directly into the side of a roast pig with his teeth. Despite Grant's shock over the matter, no one else seemed to care. No one stopped him, and everyone else was focused on either piling their plates high or stuffing their faces. Grant took a bite of a rich looking sausage, its smoky smell intoxicating. As he bit into it, the soft meat melted in his mouth. Grant finished the oversized meat and rubbed his stomach. "Ugh… so good!"

<You should have waited and eaten what I told you to eat. Could have filled your stomach instead of just tasting a rich food. Too bad. That's enough. Get up and leave.>

"Are you *kidding* me, Sarge? What will they think of me?" Grant was horrified at the thought of leaving at the *start* of the meal.

<Does it *matter* what they think of you? These people have no goals in life beyond filling themselves just *one* more time. They lead empty lives, with no virtue or redeeming characteristics. They help no one without looking for profit; they laugh at others for being healthy; they eat themselves to death. I ask you again, are *these* the people that you want to impress?>

"Sarge…" Grant scanned the hall, feeling dozens of eyes on him. How was it that someone could tear into the side of a cooked pig without using their hands, but the only thing they noticed was someone *not* eating? He reached for another plate, and just as his fingers brushed it, a notification appeared.

Warning: Daily recommended calorie intake exceeded (2nd and final warning)

With everyone looking at him, Grant ignored the warning and eagerly dug in, devouring as much as his protesting stomach could handle. Sarge didn't say a word, no matter how much he ate. A Noble guest slouched at the table paused in his feasting to talk to the young man. "So Grant, what brings you to January all the way from the District of February?"

"I want to take part in Lord January's tournament. The prize is a set of Mid Spring Heavy armor." Grant began to sweat, and not from eating all the meat. He realized that he and Sir Friday had not gotten their story straight.

"You came all this way for a lowly set of armor?" another Noble asked him quizzically.

"I… of course not. I come to bring honor and glory to House M… Friday." Monday almost slipped out. He wasn't used to his new identity. The guest was apparently satisfied with his answer and went back to eating. At the end of the meal—after *hours* of ingesting—Grant went to lie down, but his heart… hurt.

CHAPTER THIRTY

The following day, he was forced to skip breakfast. The rich food he was not used to, combined with a strange pain in his gut had kept him up all night. Grant hobbled over to the training yard, preparing to smack a wooden dummy in the yard to take his frustration and grumpiness out on it. Attempting to activate his training module resulted in a similar message to the one he had gotten yesterday.

Sword Expertise disabled until further notice! Eat small portions of healthy food to regain access to skill. Training is locked until caloric overage is balanced. Caloric overage: 9,400. Recommended actions: Running, weight training. Weight training is optimal for fastest usage of calories.

"It's over nine *thousand*?" Grant glared at the message. He hated being told off or punished; it reminded him of being back in New Dawn. "*Everyone* stuffed their faces, so why shouldn't I…! It took an hour of running to burn *almost* eight hundred calories! This… almost *eleven* hours of running?"

"Everything alright, Grant?" Sir Friday's voice pulled Grant back to the present.

Grant slid his sword into his scabbard and turned to face his benefactor. "I don't feel well. Had a bit too much to eat."

Sir Friday laughed. "The food is rather rich, but you get used to it after a while. Make sure to get an early night, as tomorrow, we set off for January's End, and Castle January!"

Despite the lack of a training module, Grant still managed to get in an hour, split between weapon and physical cultivation. Then, panting and exhausted, he knew there was nothing else to do but start working off his debt. Grant started running around the training yard, trying to pace himself so that he could go as long as possible.

After a long, grueling two hours, he collapsed to the ground and stared up at the sky. He quickly checked his status sheet, since watching the numbers increase was highly addictive.

Name: Grant Friday (Updated from Grant Monday)
(Identity hidden. Potion effect will remain active until it is dispelled. Click here to end potion effect: Hidden Identity.)
Rank: Wielder
Class: Foundation Cultivator
Cultivation Achievement Level: 6
Cultivation Stage: Mid Spring
Inherent Abilities: Four Seasons Cultivation
Health: 125/125
Mana: 3/3
Characteristics
Physical: 49 -> 50
Mental: 12
Armor Proficiency: 15
Weapon Proficiency: 29

"That's a big jump in health and physical cultivation! Really, though… the gains seem all over the place… Is there a breakdown of where my individual cultivation is at? System? Sarge? No answer? So I just don't know… there may be a keyword to access that. I'll need to ask around. Hmm… at least the time spent training is also slowly increasing all of my overall cultivation." Grant really wanted to ask Sarge about the seemingly random increases in his characteristics, but no matter how he asked, Sarge refused to talk to him.

Finally, extremely hungry from his long morning workout, Grant went to the dining area and tried to get some food. However, a message kept appearing whenever he went to pick up a piece of food; especially a greasy sausage or pudding.

Warning: This food contains a high level of fat and cholesterol. Eating this will increase your caloric balance, which will need to be repaid before Sword Expertise unlocks.

He didn't know what cholesterol was, but it seemed to be in most of the delicious cooked dishes before him. The only time Sword Expertise appeared to be happy—that is, it remained silent—was when he selected a 'strange' option, such as a small piece of toast or fruit. Wanting to be able to use his sword properly again, Grant grumpily acquiesced and ate only a tiny amount of food; restricting himself to things that did not increase his debt.

After the frustratingly dissatisfying meal, he returned to training: running, slowing, and finally walking when he could run no more. It took until just after midnight, but the caloric debt was finally paid. He collapsed into his bed, only to be shaken awake what felt like mere moments later by the household servants. At that point, he was too afraid to eat another thing—at least until he had heard from Sarge one more time.

As he climbed aboard the carriage, he was in a foul mood. His stomach was pleading to be filled, everything was loud, and his body *hurt* like it had never hurt before. He waited in the carriage for almost an hour before other people began to join him. Luckily, he had the chance to take a short nap, which helped a small amount. The four enormous carriages rolled out of the estate shortly after breakfast. Sir Friday Twenty-Ninth, Grant, and Sir Friday's entourage of Noble Lords and Ladies went in one house-sized carriage.

Another held staff, Vassals, and personal effects, such as clothing, armor, and weaponry. The third was a mobile kitchen, containing ovens and a smattering of chefs already hard at work. Grant could smell lunch being prepared as the carriages trundled along, and he almost puked from the painful reaction of his empty body.

The final carriage contained all manner of food stores, ranging from live animals ready for the slaughter, dry goods, and finally smoked and salted meats. Clearly, Sir Friday didn't intend to starve himself on the long trip to the castle. Grant felt that he was completely alone now, even sitting amongst the painted faces of the Nobility. Sarge had apparently had enough of him and was still punishing him, even though he had paid his debt. Sword Expertise didn't approve of his dietary choices and was still refusing to let him train until the full twenty-four hours had passed—and worst of all—his friends would think he was either dead or had abandoned them.

It was too much. He couldn't handle it anymore.

"Sir Friday," Grant shouted over the din of the wheels rumbling along the rough road. "I'm sorry, but I can't go with you."

Sir Friday spat out the mid-morning snack that he was nibbling. A Noble lady shrieked at being sprayed with a fountain of crumbs, but kept her mouth shut after realizing it was Sir Friday that had done the spraying. "What, what, *what*? Grant?"

His face went completely red as he spluttered. "It's too late, *brat*! I've already sent a magigram and *substantial* fee, enrolling you in the tournament. You *will* fight, young man!"

"Stop the carriage. I can't do this. This isn't what I want. I'll live out my final days free," Grant ended cryptically. He stood and walked unsteadily to the door of the still-moving carriage.

Sir Friday slapped his hand on a pillow. "We have *everything* here! The finest wine and food from all across the land. You are amongst Nobles… what more could you want? Do you want *pay*?"

"I miss my friends. They'll think I abandoned them." Grant put his hand on the doorknob.

"*Friends*? I will buy you all the friends that you want!" Sir

Friday was shouting now; he refused to believe that Grant would give all of this up. "Tell me what you want, and we will do it!"

The young man paused. "There is only one thing I want, Sir Friday. Pass by Twelve Iron Circle in the Crafting District, and give my friends the option of joining us. Their names are Red, Fergus, and Skinny. I suppose we could invite Derek as well?"

"You're *killing* me, Grant! We are already late-"

"No, Sir Friday." Grant spoke just loudly enough to be heard over the clamor of the wheels. "I'm specifically *not* killing you. That is the reason I'm here."

"Ha! You insolent *whelp*! How *dare* you talk to me like that? Everyone," Sir Friday bellowed, "clear the room! I need to have a word with our friend here, in *private*!"

The carriage ground to a halt, and Lords and Ladies couldn't move fast enough, not wanting to be the focus of Sir Friday's wrath. When the room in the carriage was clear, the man himself spoke softly to Grant. "Do *not* disrespect me like that ever again, Grant Monday. I am a patient and generous man, but I will not lose face in front of my Nobles. I don't know what issues you are facing, and to be honest, I don't care. If it will get us past this, I will do as you ask. We will travel by the South Gate of Mid January, and from there, I will have my Vassals collect your friends. After that, I will suffer no more of your insolence. *Agreed*?"

"Yes… Sir Friday Twenty-Ninth. Thank you. I'm sorry…" Grant felt small and weak in front of the simmering bulk of Sir Friday, whose anger was barely held in check.

The large man deflated. "Splendid. I'm sorry, too."

"Huh? For…?" Sir Friday's Wielded Weapon smacked into his jaw. Grant couldn't even feel the impact of his paralyzed head connecting with the floor of the carriage. Sir Friday bent over and brought his smiling face close to Grant's. The upside-down visage hung over Grant, who was slobbering helplessly on the floor. "Sorry about that, brat. I had to punish you for your disobedient tone. The Nobles would have seen me as weak otherwise. I hope you understand."

The Lords and Ladies came back into the carriage soon after, tittering at the slumped figure laid out in front of Sir Friday. Most of them gave him an approving nod, and soon, the small caravan was on the trail again. A short while later, there was a knock on the door, and a Vassal stepped through.

"Sir Friday, there was a little trouble at Twelve Iron Circle, but we managed to collect all the residents, as ordered." Grant, still unable to speak properly, and with spittle dribbling freely from his slack jaw, stared on in horror as a cart rolled up containing several bound, writhing bodies.

"This wasn't what I…!" Sir Friday growled in frustration and put his head in his hands. He snuck an apologetic glance at Grant and motioned for the Vassel to move out of the way, then for the Vassals to remove the gags and untie the wriggling men.

"Grant!" Red lumbered over to the still-paralyzed young Wielder. "You're alive! I was worried sick, and then this lot showed up, demanding we came with them. We put up a fight even *you'd* be impressed with, but the bounty hunters used their tricks on us. Blinded and bound, we were carted off here, fearing the worst."

"I missed breakfast," a distraught Skinny announced with tears streaming down his face.

"My *good* man," Sir Friday replied with a hand over his mouth at the scandalous declaration, "I am so sorry that my men interrupted so badly that you were kept from a meal! If you *choose* to join us on our trip to Castle January in January's End, you will feast like a true Noble! Fine specimens such as yourself are hard to come by, and should be held up as an example for others to aspire to become."

"I'm in," Skinny nodded vigorously, only hearing the word 'feast'.

"Castle January?" Fergus slowly nodded his head. "Yeah, why not. I've come this far. It will keep me out of the family's hair for a while. I'm in."

Red shook his head. "I was going to head back to the Grand January Caravan. Jo would take me back as Random Guard Number Two, and the pay is decent…"

"We just so *happen* to have an opening for a guard position," Sir Friday declared when he saw Grant's anguished look. "Your job will be to look after Grant Friday here, and make sure he doesn't get into too much trouble!"

"Friday?" Red's confused question was cut off with a sharp gesture.

"I may as well come along." The muscular Derek came into view. "I tried to explain that I wasn't with this lot, but the bounty hunters wouldn't listen! Anyway… this works just fine. I've been looking for a reason to get away from Mid January; needed a vacation. Enough people saw me getting dragged away that I will probably be able to get my position back when I return."

The small group boarded the staff carriage, as there wasn't enough room for the party in the Noble's carriage. Grant went with them and was bombarded with questions. He responded by slobbering enthusiastically, saliva flying in all directions since his face was still too numb to properly control.

It wasn't long before the carriages were rolling again, and Grant was finally on his way to defeat Lord January.

CHAPTER THIRTY-ONE

Fields and days blended together as the carriage train trundled toward Castle January. Yellow and blue spring flowers jostled amongst the hedgerows that lined vast, never-ending fields. The promise of new life was in the air as winter lost its dominion, the harsh cold replaced by crisp mornings and mild days.

Grant had lost count of the number of corn and wheat fields they'd passed. There was a reason January had once been known as the *world's* bread basket. Lord January had once been a genius engineer that bettered the lives of his people—making January the most technologically advanced District—and had brought his District everything from windmills to bread ovens. That had been before the barriers went up. Apparently, a restriction had come into effect after that. According to common knowledge, raw material could now only move a maximum of three Districts, and worked goods could only make it one more, and only with *great* effort.

Now that food from January couldn't make it past March, the District that had been supplying the world could now only supply, at *most* three Districts. Try as they might, the Januarians just couldn't consume all of the vast quantities of food grown, so merchants of House Thursday grew fatter and obscenely richer from the profits of cross-boundary trade. Sarge told Grant that this was probably why 'physical cultivation' took on a new form in January.

The only incident during the long trip was a broken wheel, but it almost ended the entire trip in disaster: a pothole had put the kitchen carriage out of action. Under *no* circumstances could the carriage be left behind. The Nobles couldn't be expected to eat *dry goods* from the pantry carriage! An unlikely hero came to the rescue: Derek stepped up and used his wide range of ironworking and carpentry skills to fix the wheel in a rush. This made him the most beloved man in the entire caravan for the remainder of the trip.

Near the end of January—both in terms of the terrain and the month—the land abruptly changed from endless fields of swaying corn, to a more rugged landscape. The horses whinnied as they struggled to pull their heavy loads up the hills. In the distance, the sky seemed to sparkle from the horizon to as high as Grant's vision could focus. "What in the Twelve Districts is *that*?"

"That," Fergus answered with a theatrical wave, "is the boundary between January and February."

Grant looked upon the barrier with awe. "I never thought it would look so… sparkly."

"What did you expect a rift in time and space itself to look like?" Derek scoffed at him incredulously. "Just wait until you see it up close. The view's not so bad here, but I hear that in March, you can vaguely see through the shimmering surface to April, where there are camps set up."

"Camps?" Grant turned his attention to the giant of a man.

Derek nodded solemnly. "Yes. Camps full of refugees, wanting to pass into March. They hammer fruitlessly on the barrier, attempting to find a way across. Their end goal is January, of course."

That was downright confusing. Grant wanted nothing more than to be *away* from here; why did other people want to cross a chunk of the world to get to this District? "But why would they want to come *here*?"

"Grant, the question you should be asking is, why *wouldn't* they? Nobles and peasants alike are fat and happy here. Life is easy! It isn't the *same* in other Districts." Fergus spoke up disparagingly. "They don't do things *properly*."

"I had… I had no idea." Grant was stunned by the revelation. "I knew that there was an abundance of food here, but I assumed the other Districts were just, you know… more of the same?"

"Lord January is the reason. He brought the entire District to heights that we never imagined possible, hundreds upon hundreds of years ago. Then he kept the bar for excellence high." As they rounded a corner, castle January appeared on the horizon. Skinny continued mumbling between swallowing a bread roll whole, "Look there! That looks like the pavilion from the plaza in Mid January! Only… much bigger."

"Lord January is there?" Grant's sparkling eyes turned sharp and hard.

He barely heard Derek answer, "Him, and *thousands* of workers, Vassals, and Nobles."

"Thousands of Vassals?" Grant asked his large friend. "How could that possibly…?"

"No, not thousands of *Vassals*." Red rolled his eyes and grumbled. "Thousands of people in *total*. It is a well-known fact that the nobility, specifically Wielders, have a limited amount of Vassals that they can make. It is the number of days in a month, minus their position, then doubled. For instance, Count Tuesday the Second could have… um. Thirty-one days, minus two… double that… *fifty-eight* Vassals!"

"So Lord January can have… sixty Vassals? All of them with a part of his power?" Grant was uncertain how he was going to fight his way through that, but the days of January were coming to an end; he needed to make a plan. The carriage rolled closer to the monstrous building, and he could now make out details on flags snapping in the wind. The flag itself was red with a stylized 'M' made of two sword-wielding warriors shaking hands, all surrounded by a jagged circle. A stylized silver numeral 'one' stood out, seemingly a separate addition to the standard flag.

"The banner of House… *Wednesday*, yes?" Grant quietly tested his knowledge with his friends.

"No. All of it but the 'one' is the flag of House Monday," Red grunted, by now used to Grant not having basic knowledge. "That one in particular is the flag of Lord January. You know, the head of House Monday that rules over January?"

Grant shamefacedly sank back into the plush bench in the staff carriage, wishing that he had managed to get in more training time. So far, he had managed only the required training of around ten hours during the trip. The swiftly moving carriages didn't provide many opportunities to catch up if he got left behind, unlike the ponderous Grand January Caravan. In fact, half of the training that Sarge's written programming had made him complete was simply running circles around the caravan for an hour or two each day while swinging his sword at various intervals.

Finally, the journey was at an end as the carriage rolled under the raised portcullis and through the gate. Inside, Grant's ears were assaulted by the familiar sounds of a bustling market. It wasn't so different from New Dawn or Mid January. Sellers hawked their wares to passers by, workers scurried around, and yet the Nobility were conspicuously absent, perhaps holed up in the castle.

The carriage train proceeded on through the next gate. Dogs snapped at its wheels and children squealed in delight as they played ball toss or leapt under the conveyances in search of adventure at the risk of being crushed. The fairytale castle and its multitude of towering spires loomed before them, growing closer by the minute. When they finally stopped, Grant jumped out, butterflies in his stomach. He rubbed at his neck, which hurt after craning it upwards for so long.

He didn't get much time to admire the fortress up close and

personal. In no time flat, he was bustled off to the secretive House Wednesday training area, so that he could prepare for the upcoming event and be in top shape. Fighting against targets in the training arena, near where the exhibition tournament would be held, Grant was interrupted by a *very* welcome voice. <Hey, wait a second? Who are you? Is that actually *Grant*? Where did all that excess go? You look downright *skinny*… comparatively.>

"Sarge! Hello, and I *hope* I don't look like Skinny. Much as I like the guy, we are definitely going for different things in our lives now." Grant laughed as the world around him faded into the standard training module. The edges of his vision were hidden by fog, and he felt like he was the only person in the entire world.

<You're starting to have your own actual goals in life…? Well, then. Let's both work to put the past behind us. How about we start a proper training session? See what I have to work with?> Sarge didn't bother to elaborate further, only giving Grant a pithy warning of, <Remember: do stupid things, win stupid prizes.>

The training session commenced and targets faded into existence, running at him from all directions. His dodge and parry skills were sloppy, and his reactions were noticeably slower from his recent lack of focused training. More than once, he was skewered by so many lances that he ended up feeling more like a porcupine than an aspiring cultivation warrior.

<Are you even *trying* to stay alive?> Sarge screamed into his mind as even more illusionary enemies approached. <You wanna stay alive, you kill them faster! Let's sing about the arteries of the lower extremity! Ohhhh…! The femoral artery is very well known, slice through the sartorius muscle, and the blood'll shoot out full-blown! The popliteal artery is *less* well known-!>

Even with the caustic remarks and off-tune singing, Grant felt like he was finally starting to understand what he needed to do. Over the next hour, his parries became better, his dodging more timely, and his attacks wasted less movement. Just as he felt like he was having an epiphany, the training came to a sudden and unexpected ending.

<Well, would you look. At. *That.*> Sarge sounded mildly impressed in Grant's head. <You did it. You *actually* earned a combat skill.>

"What do you mean?" Grant's chest was heaving, and Sarge wasn't making sense.

<Open up your skill menu and take a look for yourself, my Wielder.> Grant followed the instructions hesitantly, unsure what to think of this strange and respectful new tone Sarge was taking. It took but a single glance to notice that he had a second skill besides 'Plant Insight'.

Skill gained: Kenjutsu (1/10). You have taken the first true steps on the path that your Wielded Weapon has set for you, a path not of the sword, but of the Uchigatana. Masters of this skill can cleave the earth; Saints can part the heavens.

Tier one effect: All damage dealt when wielding a sword is increased by 10%.

<Congratulations, Grant. With that, I have nothing more to teach you.>

"*What?*" Grant screeched and fell to the ground in shock, sending Sarge into a fit of laughter.

<You should have seen your face! Ha! You *just* became a Novice of the sword; you think I can't whip you into shape better than *this*?> Sarge was laughing too hard to continue for a few moments, but he finally got around to his next point. <Novice, Beginner, Apprentice, Student, Journeyman, Expert, Master, Grandmaster, Saint, and finally Deity. Those are all of the possible ranks. Most people will never see that final one, and *most* skills can only be brought up to… let's say Expert. It takes a special someone to push past that and become a true Master.

My training can bring you up to Expert, but you will need to figure out something else after that point.>

"How long will that take?" Grant's body ached, his muscles protesting at the brutal session. The pain lingered from the many fatal wounds inflicted upon his sluggish body. He put away February Twenty Nine and limped in a daze toward one of the many exits surrounding the training arena as he waited for an answer. "Also, I thought you said it would take ten thousand hours to get a sword skill?"

<Reaching the highest heights all depends on you… but you only have a year. Get as good as you can; you don't have any more time to waste. As for the prerequisite… it takes ten thousand training hours to create a sword intent, or you can kill again and again while also training to form the same intent. There is no *one* true path to power.> Grant nodded at Sarge's words as he staggered out of the closed training area. He was more exhausted than he could remember ever being, making him wonder if there was a personal energy cost to gaining skills. As he tried to find his way back to his room, his rolling gait and slack-jawed expression caused people to whisper when they saw him, and some didn't even bother to whisper.

"Look at *him*," a child pointed at Grant. "Look how *thin* he is, momma! Is *that* what a beggar looks like? Can I give him some candy?"

An adult, presumably his mother, scolded the child. "How many times have I told you, Anthony? Stay *away* from thin strangers! As for a beggar, if you feed or give them money, it only encourages them!"

"He doesn't look very well… just a cake or… or *two*?"

The mother hesitated, then let a doting glance shine through. "Oh… go on, then. Throw a sweet cake at the funny-looking man. Or… is it a child? It's hard to tell at that size. Don't go near it, though; it's *clearly* sick," the adult warned severely. "You may catch a disease that makes it hard to eat!"

A sweet cake flew through the air and hit Grant squarely on the cheek. He ignored it and stumbled off along the vaulted corridors, his head fuzzy from overwhelming fatigue. He ignored laughter as he passed Nobles, and barely registered the glint of Time, imprinted with the bust of Lord January, landing at his feet as they threw coins to him. The strange pity granted him access through a restricted area, and he stumbled into the center of a small pit in an attempt to get away from the terrible people throwing things at him. "This must be the exhibition ground itself… I probably shouldn't be here."

Surrounding the sunken pit in the center of the room were terraced tables. It appeared as though every table had direct access to a kitchen. That made sense, due to the importance placed on feasting as an integral form of entertainment. It was essentially a food hall with a built-in fighting pit. At the edge—clear from the size of chair and ornamentation—was where Lord January would be sitting. The placement gave an unrestricted view of the bouts, and there were no steps from the Lord's seat to the exit. <Wouldn't want him to haveta go to the effort of walking up stairs, now would we? Grant, you'll just let this District burn, right? We can rebuild it better->

"Who goes there?" A deep voice boomed through the empty arena. "Halt in the name of House Tuesday!"

Grant, who had been examining the fighting pit, stopped in his tracks and slowly turned to face the figure striding toward him with footfalls that shook the stage. He remained frozen once he realized exactly who it was; he knew that he was in a restricted area, but it wasn't his fault! He'd taken a wrong turn somewhere!

"Are you *deaf* as well as ill, boy?" The grand figure striding toward him questioned solemnly. Grant shook his head and swallowed, and the giant in the yellow garb of House Tuesday spoke again. "Do you know who I am?"

"Count Tuesday the Second." Grant pointed a shaky finger at the name above the intimidating figure's head, not saying the quiet part out loud: this was the most powerful Noble in House Tuesday; the leader of the Peacekeepers for the entire District of January and the head of House Tuesday.

"I *demand* to know how you got access to the tournament grounds." Barely restrained rage bubbled beneath the Count's taut muscles and rippling body.

"Um... I just... walked in." Grant waved his hands helplessly, not sure what else he could say.

Count Tuesday wasn't buying it. "You don't just *walk* into the Mooredoor arena! This entire section of the castle is a restricted area, containing the kitchens and arena floors dedicated to Lord January. The Mooredoor wing is under heavy guard and has *stringent* entry requirements. There is a guard at each and every door!"

"I got a bit lost and ended up here, sir. Count." Grant gulped and looked around for anything that he could use to prove his story.

"I understand that you are *hungry*," Count Tuesday spoke slowly, as if to a simpleton, "but sick people are not *allowed* in the food hall, nor the arena, and you should stay out of the Noble quarter entirely. Run along. If you go out of the Castle January area, there is a workhouse on the left that provides care to the sick and needy."

The young man nodded and made to leave, but Count Tuesday wasn't finished. "If you are found here again, without a valid *reason* to be in the area... your next meal will be behind prison bars. Sick beggar or sick *Noble*, the law applies to everyone! Do I make myself *clear*, child?

Grant bowed, then scampered for the exit without another word.

CHAPTER THIRTY-TWO

As Grant left the area and entered more familiar grounds, he cursed himself for being such a fool. Sarge piled on to make him feel worse, <Ha*ha*, you really showed him! I think the real reason the second most powerful person in this entire District let us leave is that he was afraid of you. Perhaps he went to change his pants instead of throwing you into prison?>

"Sarge… you could help, rather than just being so… *edgy* all the time!" Grant snarled at his sword, fumbling as he tried to think of a way to express his thoughts clearly. Cursing at his sword didn't go unnoticed, but the people around him couldn't have a lower opinion of him anyway.

<Oooh… *edgy*? I'm a *sword*. I'm at least one-third edge! Someone's a little *touchy* today. Did I hurt those farm boy feelings?> Sarge's voice was a razor's edge against his tired mind. <You don't *get* to be sad, you don't *get* to be hurt by words. You can only be awesome at all times, getting stronger without exception… or you *die*, Grant. My job is to make sure that you are getting stronger, faster, and more *powerful* every single moment of every single day. Sometimes I need to remind you that I'm *not* your friend, I'm your trainer. Get strong enough;

then I'll become your friend. Today is *not* that day. You understand me, maggot?>

"Yes," Grant answered quietly, deeply hurt that the sword spirit didn't consider him a friend and trying not to show it. He was in no mood to be baited by Sarge today; the tournament was due to start tomorrow, and he had just shown weakness to one of the most powerful figures in all of January.

<I can't hear you!>

"*Yes*! I won't forget who I am or what I need to do!" Grant startled a few people with the sudden outburst as he yelled at the sky. They looked at the crazy beggar with a mixture of fear and pity.

<That's more like it! Go on, then. Prove it to *everyone*. Show them that you will not be looked down on! Get back in the training arena. I want to see you complete another session. You will repeat the drills until the moves are a *part* of you, Grant!>

"Someday… someday soon…" The previous session's fatigue was already a distant memory. Grant gripped the hilt of February Twenty Nine tightly and strode back toward the training yard with renewed purpose. "No one will *dare* make the mistake of threatening me or telling me that I'm nothing but a sick beggar!"

Training passed in a blur, and he was so numb afterward that the night was gone in a flash. He had needed to be *shaken* awake for his first match, two maids had helped him don his armor, and he had needed to *run* to get to the fighting pit in time.

Just before the match was called due to him not being present, Grant stepped into the circle. His eyes connected with those of his first opponent, Sir Saturday Twenty-Third. Sir Saturday stood across from him in the arena, and the dining hall seating area surrounding the fighting pit was almost completely deserted. Only a few spectators had bothered to attend; even they seemed more interested in the provided snacks than watching the early rounds of the tournament.

Lord January was probably sound asleep in one of his many

towers or digging into breakfast alongside his Nobles. Grant, nervous as he was, preferred the slow start to the tournament, rather than having the additional pressure of a bloodthirsty crowd jeering for entertainment. There was something to be said for learning to fight in front of a few more people at a time, and the minimal distractions allowed Grant to focus on exactly what was coming at him.

The powerfully-built giant of a man, Sir Saturday, pulled his shiny visor down over his grinning face and clunked his way toward Grant. He was a walking fortress coated in full plate armor. His Wielded Weapon was a spiked flail, a thick chain and spiked metal ball that hung down far enough that it almost touched the ground.

Grant was glad to be wearing the set of Early Spring Medium armor, but he didn't know if it would be enough. As Sir Saturday swung, Grant ducked, easily avoiding the spiked ball flying overhead. As he did, he unsheathed February Twenty Nine and struck at the plated wall of a stomach before him. Sparks flew as the blade's edge scraped harmlessly off the metal, leaving little more than a scratch. He looked at the tiny mark unbelievingly. "This might be a bit more challenging than expected."

Sir Saturday swung a heavy gauntleted fist and missed the darting form of Grant. The heavy armor, while offering great protection, made his opponent cumbersome and slow. The pair sparred back and forth, neither able to gain an advantage. Grant's blade slid off the metal plate, while Sir Saturday's ponderous attacks were easily dodged or sidestepped. Grant was careful not to try parrying the flail: doing so could result in his blade getting ripped out of his hands, and then he would be quickly beaten down.

"This isn't working… I have to try something else to break the deadlock." Grant switched stances, planning to go all-out.

Sir Saturday was slowing down, the heavy armor and long fight quickly tiring him. "Let's end this, Grant Friday! I'm getting bored, and if we don't hurry up, I'll miss second breakfast!"

"Bring it on then, sir." Grant replied with a flourish of his sword. Sir Saturday grunted, and his weapon started to *change*. Points of darkness spread between the metal spikes on the head of the mace, and moments later, only the wickedly sharp points remained visible amongst the murky substance surrounding the weapon. Grant slightly deflated at losing sight of his opponent's weapon. "Okay, I'll be honest that I didn't expect-"

"A riddle for you!" Sir Saturday closed in. As he hefted the spiked metal ball, it spun, slowly at first, but increasing in pace until it was a spinning black mass. Its points acted like a circular saw, ready to slice him to ribbons. Grant dodged to the side, but the spinning blades still managed to lightly connect with his shoulder. The force of the flail spun him around and threw him into the arena wall, while Sir Saturday's mass held him firmly in place. "Saturday and Friday get into a fight… who wins?"

Damage taken: 12 slashing. (6 mitigated)

"*I* will win." Grant hissed through clenched teeth as he stood up and wiped a dribble of blood off his hand. No reason to lose his grip.

"Saturday wins," Sir Saturday lumbered closer, "because no matter what anyone else says, Friday is a *weak day*."

"That joke hurt more than your attack did." Grant leveled his sword and got ready.

"That was a *warning* shot. The next one won't go so well for you. Concede and go on your way, boy." Sir Saturday shook his head. "You're a decade too early to challenge me."

Grant's shoulder throbbed, luckily his off-hand, so he could still grip his weapon correctly.

Health: 113/125
Mana: 3/3

Characteristics
Physical: 50

Mental: 12
Armor Proficiency: 15
Weapon Proficiency: 30

The impact had hurt, but his armor had kept him from getting any debuffs. Yet, that was merely a *glancing* blow; he didn't want to experience a direct hit. He darted under the swinging disc of death. Sir Saturday roared at him, "Stand still so I can beat you *down*, Grant! Let me end this quickly. I said I don't want to miss second *breakfast*!"

Grant scrambled across the sand and slipped, barely keeping his blade up. Sir Saturday had been waiting for this. The spinning blade came down, and Grant had no choice but to deflect with February Twenty Nine. Sparks flew as the circular saw hammered against his sword. The force of the impact brought the spinning blade closer by the second; if Grant didn't do something, he'd end up decapitated.

He rolled to the side and brought his sword up against Sir Saturday's mace-wielding wrist. On an unarmored opponent, the hand would have been severed. Happily, the impact did knock the difficult-to-control spinning flail out of his grip. It flew away and into the wall, cutting a deep groove as it continued to spin before coming to a halt.

The dazed Sir Saturday stood weaponless, not knowing what to do but unwilling to surrender. Even without a weapon, he was decked out in plate armor. He started lumbering toward his fallen mace, and Grant realized there was a way to end the fight quickly. He ran over to the wall before Sir Saturday could even make it halfway, and tugged against the mace's handle. It wouldn't budge. Grant braced both feet against the wall and pulled. It didn't look like anything was happening at first, but it unexpectedly popped out.

Immediately, the metal head of the mace became a blur again. The weight and momentum of the spinning ball of metal tore at his muscles, and it took all of his strength to stop it flying out of his fingers. Sir Saturday was closing in, and reached out a hand. "My weapon! Give it back!"

"Sure. Take it!" Grant grinned and walked toward his target. The spinning saw would make quick work against the plate armor. Sir Saturday didn't move, and Grant tried to threaten him. "I don't know if I can hold on much longer, Sir Saturday!"

Grant held up the mace to Sir Saturday's torso armor. Sparks flew in all directions. "Do you yield?"

"You think a Wielded Weapon would turn against its Wielder?" The head of the mace stopped moving, dropping to the ground as the black fog surrounding it faded away. Sir Saturday lunged at Grant, but the young man moved faster. He dodged to the side and around, wrapping the chain of the weapon around Sir Saturday's left foot and pulling it taut, taking him to the ground. In an instant, the point of Grant's sword was pressed against the nape of Sir Saturday's neck.

"Do you *yield*?"

"Yes. Yeesh. You take this too seriously. Get off me, I already can't breathe in all this gear." Sir Saturday removed his helm, revealing sweat dripping from his brow and off his nose. Grant awaited the familiar glow that he had associated with leveling up after defeating a Wielder, but nothing happened. The other normal announcement did appear.

Do you, Grant Monday, wish to absorb the power of Sir Saturday 28th's weapon, Accelerated Mass? Accepting Accelerated Mass will override any previous Wielded Weapon power absorbed in the current monthly series. If not overridden by another weapon of the same month, this ability will return to its current Wielded Weapon at the end of the year, unless the quest 'Heal The World' has been successfully completed.

Accept / Decline

. . .

"Decline. I lack the strength to handle such a power. Plus, this is more suited to weapon's such as a mace than a sword." Grant realized that if he applied the power to February Twenty Nine, there was practically an equal chance of decapitating either himself or an enemy. Grant walked away from his first bout as the victor. He turned around to Sir Saturday, who was sitting on the sand, attempting to untangle himself from his mace. "Sir... there's still time to catch breakfast!"

The red-lined eyes of Sir Saturday glared at him as he left the arena. Grant didn't notice, too deep in his strategy for the upcoming bouts.

"If Sarge is correct about how this works, I will need to defeat one more Wielder in order to level up. I should be able to make that happen either today, or tomorrow. I'm close... *so* close to getting stronger."

CHAPTER THIRTY-THREE

The competitor's dining hall—of course separate from the exhibition dining hall—was packed with Vassals and Wielders gathering their energy before or between fights. The dining hall was open throughout the day, so luckily there wasn't any risk of missing a meal during the tournament. Grant took his breakfast-laden tray and squeezed in between some of the Nobility. He had picked healthy options, careful not to upset Sword Expertise. He smiled at the other competitors, but they ignored him, focused on their meals.

"Can I ask you something?" The majority continued to ignore him, though his pestering earned him at least a few glares. "Excuse me?"

"You don't need *permission* to eat. Just do it, and stop bothering us!" A Wielder snapped, annoyed at having to clear his mouth enough to tell this *child* off.

"That's not what I wanted to ask..." Grant cleared his throat and continued. "Do you know much about cultivation levels? Specifically how the characteristic points are assigned?"

The man had reached his limit for being conversational. "Everyone knows that leveling up is a random occurrence. I'm level four and my Vassal Charly here is level three. I can't say *why* my level is higher. Quiet down. We have eating to do, and we need energy to last the fights to come!"

The Wielder turned and continued eating, but Grant didn't give in that easily. He turned to Charly. "What about your characteristics?"

"What about them?" Charly took over and spat out a mouthful of corn accidentally. "Look, we really don't have time to talk."

Grant tried one last time. "When you leveled up, did you experience increased damage output or weapon proficiency? What does each characteristic actually do-"

Charly shook his head and cut Grant off. "As we said, it's all *random*. Don't waste your time thinking about such nonsense. Focus on what's *important* in life, or you'll miss the best part of living!"

"What might that be?" Grant sat on the edge of his seat, eager to finally hear a fresh insight.

"Here is the secret to getting ahead in life: eat regularly. Don't allow yourself to get hungry. Food is life, and it supplies the energy needed to fight and win battles." Charly's words made anyone within earshot nod. All but one.

"Oh… thanks." Grant was disappointed, but it was the answer he had mostly expected. "I've lost my appetite. I guess I'm off to train some more."

All eyes at the table turned in shock as Grant got up, having hardly picked at his plate. *No one* skipped a meal. As he walked out of the hall, he passed a cloaked figure sitting in the corner, who whispered, "You ask too many questions, Grant Monday."

Grant stopped and turned to face the figure, who had their face hidden deep within the folds of a cowl. In such a strange turn of events, he fell back on his archaic upbringing. "Pardon this one's faulty memory; do we know each other?"

"No." The figure pointed to the name above Grant's head. "But *I* know *you* better than that. You need to stop your flapping lips."

"Oh. Yeah. I don't understand why no *one* understands levels. I'm just trying to figure-"

"Keep your voice down," the man ordered before pulling back the cowl to reveal a head of long sable hair and eyes almost completely pitch black. The *thin* face didn't match the body below it. Still, not enough was revealed to allow Grant to learn his name. "Knowledge is power. Most Vassals and Wielders, particularly low-level ones, are simply absorbing quintessence that has no will behind it. That means that, although they become higher level, all increases are applied exactly as they think it is: randomly."

"I didn't… that's… they're *right*?" Grant was more shocked by this fact than he should have been.

"After watching you fight earlier, you appeared to fight with some level of skill." The unknown man looked Grant over. "I'm surprised."

"I follow a training plan. I've noticed that focusing on weapon skills has increased my weapon proficiency, and therefore damage output when I level up. I just wanted to see what others had to say on the matter." Grant shrugged helplessly, "I can't be the *only* person who has questions."

"Training, and specifically following a training plan, isn't usual behavior here in January, Grant. In February and beyond, it is more common. However, Vassals and Wielders in January are mostly fat and lazy. They have no need to learn how to fight effectively." The mysterious man stood from his table.

"You've traveled beyond the boundary?" Grant had never met a boundary traveler before. "What's it like?"

"I have a feeling you will find out for yourself one day, young Wielder. As you travel east, life gets progressively more challenging, and to survive, you'll need your wits about you!" The man started walking toward the door. "That means you need to take care to whom you reveal your lack of knowledge."

"How do I…" Grant's words stopped as the man shook his head.

"I've said too much already. Knowledge is power, Grant.

Hold on to it. Seek it out and hoard it. You will need it in order to survive the many challenges ahead of you."

Grant reached out, "Wait… I have so many questions."

"You will have to discover the answers for yourself!" The cowled figure walked along the dark corridor and clicked his fingers. Just before Grant managed to touch the figure on the shoulder, he vanished around the corner. By the time Grant followed him around the bend, the man was gone—leaving Grant with many more questions than answers. His voice whispered down the halls, "We'll see each other soon, young master *Leap*."

Panicking now, Grant went back to the dining hall and tried to gather clues about the vanished man. The only thing he noticed was that the plate the man had been eating from was still full of food; another confusing thing to add to the day. Grant didn't have very much time to seek his answers. Discouraged but determined, within the hour, he was back in the arena.

He had several more matches before the finals, where he would finally be able to stand before Lord January. A Vassal of House Sunday was his current opponent, and he was sneering at Grant. "My Lord *died* today facing off against one of you scum Fridays!"

"How terrible! I'm sorry to hear that." Grant genuinely offered his condolences. "Was there no healer available?"

"Don't mock me, *Friday*! I will get my revenge. Meet my boom sticks!" The Vassal shook a pair of small warhammers barely larger than his own meaty hands. One side of each hammer's head was flat, meant for bashing. The other was pointed, clearly designed for penetrating armor.

"Yes. How… I feel so much fear.." Grant chuckled at the dinky hammers. After the last fight against the spinning mace, he looked forward to a more well-matched fight. The enraged Vassal came at Grant, who easily ducked under the attack and followed it up by a knee to the man's crotch. Most of the force was caught by the man's stomach, but he still staggered back, coughing and trying to reach over his stomach and comfort himself.

"I... I don't understand. How can you *move* like that? Why was my hammer so slow?"

"Were..." Grant squinted at the Vassal, knowing where this conversation was going. He had to take a deep breath before continuing, "were you expecting me *not* to dodge?"

"I won't go down without a fight. I don't care what dirty tricks you use against me!"

"Dodging isn't a *trick*. I didn't do anything to you except *not* letting you hit me!" The Vassal charged as Grant yelled at him, but Grant spun and slapped his blade against the back of the enraged Vassal's head. The man fell and slid across the arena, spitting out sand as he got up unsteadily and charged.

Damage dealt: 4 blunt. Debuff added: concussed (mild).

Grant stuck a foot out and tripped the angry—yet dizzy—man. As the Vassal collapsed to the ground, Grant calmly walked over and placed the point of February Twenty Nine against his neck. "I suggest you yield. I have no issue with you. I *am* genuinely sorry for the loss of your Lord."

The fight went out of the Vassal at Grant's firm, calm tone. He slumped to the ground in a sweaty heap. "I yield."

"Listen. If you want the power back in your weapon, make sure to serve under whoever becomes the new Wielder of that weapon." Grant told the Vassal, whose eyes widened in realization. Grant grasped the man's hand and acted as a support to help the man up. It took a while, but they managed.

He did not have time for a long break. As the Vassal was taken away, the next competitor entered the arena. This one looked like more of a challenge. A Wielder, another Saturday, stood before him. He was wearing a set of black leather armor, similar to Grant's, and gripping two long daggers. The blades came to a triangular point that looked wickedly sharp, but that wasn't what worried Grant: he feared the fact that they pulsed a sickly green.

<Grant, try not to get poked by one of those.> Sarge told

him unnecessarily. <Pretty sure we're about to experience our first poison user.>

"Oh, yeah, so glad you warned me," Grant mocked his sword as sweat broke out on his forehead. "First of all, I don't intend to be stabbed by *any* weapon. But yeah. Those are poisonous for sure."

<*Grant.*>

"Yeah, yeah. I'm paying attention."

Sir Saturday smirked at the crazy person talking to himself and crept toward his opponent. The Wielder cautiously circled Grant with one dagger held close—protecting his middle—and the other trained on Grant.

Grant attempted a clean strike, meeting only air as his foe nimbly sidestepped. He returned at a blistering speed, the dagger whistling forward lightning fast. Grant barely avoided it by stumbling backward. A green dot remained where the point of the knife had barely nicked his armor, and light pulsed once before fading away. He had to be careful. "Another Saturday? I can't believe the weekend came so soon."

"Shh… no more speaking." The Wielder whispered just before noisily licking his lips, creeping Grant out with his high-pitched voice. The pair danced together, and Grant found that he was having a *very* hard time. His opponent was agile, skilled, and clearly experienced.

Grant remembered his lessons and looked for a way to quickly end the fight. He had another two competitors to face before the semi-finals in front of not only the Nobility, but his target: Lord January.

An idea came to him in a flash.

Sir Saturday always struck using his left dagger first, then the right. There was a pattern, and he could exploit it. Grant waited for the inevitable attack to come. The Wielder lunged, his pulsing dagger coming dangerously close to skewering Grant. Before the inevitable follow up by the right blade, Grant reversed his grip and slammed February Twenty Nine into his opponent's chin. A dirty, yet effective trick; Sir Saturday dropped like a sack of potatoes.

Grant loomed over the fallen Wielder, who groaned in pain, his face filled with hate. He pointed February Twenty Nine toward his victim. "Do you yield?"

"Do you have no honor?" Sir Saturday spat as Grant leaned forward and drew blood. "Let me get to my feet."

"I do what I have to do."

"As do I." Sir Saturday slapped away Grant's blade, and with his other dagger scored a slice against the exposed flesh of Grant's wrist. It felt like a bee sting, and he jerked his arm back in pain. He leaned forward to skewer the man, barely stopping as the Wielder spoke again. "I yield!"

Grant was flooded by golden light: he had achieved a new cultivation level. Then poison flooded through his healing wound.

Damage taken: 3 slashing.

Debuff added: Lesser Lingering Death.

"Regent's cold heart! *Lingering Death*?" Grant paled as he stared at the wound on his arm.

<I did warn you, Grant. You never listen!> Sarge's next order was as sharp as the Swords edge. <Kill him, kill him *now*!>

Grant swung, but Sir Saturday had already rolled away and was surrounded by Vassals. He turned and looked at Grant as he swaggered away. "*I* did what *I* had to do. No one disrespects House Saturday and lives to talk about it!"

"What do I do?" Grant slumped to his knees as another pain raced up his arm. "What does this mean?"

<Well, the 'lingering' part, which means slow and painful, is followed by the little nuance of 'death'.> Sarge explained caustically. <Guess you'll die. You shoulda listened to me.>

"*Sarge*! What should I do?"

<Only thing you can do. Find a way to negate the power before you die. I estimate that you have around two hours left to live.>

Grant pulled open his stats to see the impact of the minor wound.

Name: Grant Friday (Updated from Grant Monday)
(Identity hidden. Potion effect will remain active until it is dispelled. Click here to end potion effect: Hidden Identity.)
Rank: Wielder
Class: Foundation Cultivator
Cultivation Achievement Level: 7
Cultivation Stage: Mid Spring
Inherent Abilities: Swirling Seasons Cultivation
Health: 138/139
Mana: 4/4

Debuff detected: Lesser Lingering Death. 1 health point lost per minute until death. Lingering Death can be dispelled by killing the Wielder who granted this ability, using a spell or Wielded Weapon ability to dispel the effect, or leveling up after poison has been diluted over time.

Characteristics
Physical: 59 (Cultivation Stage Maximized. Gains will be retroactively applied when all stages are aligned.)
Mental: 16
Armor Proficiency: 17
Weapon Proficiency: 32

Grant had no choice; he had to leave the arena and find a cure before it was too late! One hundred and eleven health points gave him just shy of two hours of life. He went to leave the fighting pit, but an announcer boomed, "A small reminder! Any competitor leaving the arena before completing all bouts leading up to the semi-finals will forfeit their place in the competition!"

"You've *got* to be kidding me." He stood at the edge of the arena, not knowing what to do. He could see Sir Saturday grinning, watching him from the shadows.

Sarge spoke in a softer growl than usual, <Grant, if you leave now… it's all over. You won't get the opportunity to face Lord January or cross the barrier. Also, something was wrong-"

"If I don't leave now, I'll *die* in two hours!" Grant snapped at the sword.

<Listen. Defeat the last two competitors quickly, and you might stand a chance! *Might.*> Sarge bull-rushed onward, <As I was saying: something is *wrong*. That *wasn't* a Wielder! If it was, you wouldn't be in this current predicament. I think it was someone using a hidden identity potion, like you are. If that had *actually* been a Wielder, you would have been given the option to take the power of their weapon for yourself. Instead, your counter of defeated enemies shows an additional *Vassal* defeated. You're slated to fight another *Wielder*, and when you defeat them, problem solved! You'll reach cultivation level eight!>

"That's…" Grant sighed and turned back to the arena, "a good point. Drat you."

He walked to the center of the fighting pit and awaited the next contender. He idly scratched his sore wrist, then pulled back the armor to examine the spot where he had taken the glancing blow. Green tendrils pulsed along his veins as the poisonous power made its way slowly toward his heart.

A Wielder of House Monday, Sir Monday the something or other—Grant wasn't listening very well right now—entered the arena. It felt strange coming up against a member of his own House, even though Sir Monday thought he faced a Friday. Grant started mumbling all the information he could think of. "House Monday, highly proficient with weapons, like I am… this may be a challenge."

The chainmail-wearing Wielder strode toward him,

broadsword held defensively, before giving a short bow in greeting and respect. The broadsword's edge looked incredibly fine… and razor-sharp. Grant wondered what power imbued this Wielded Weapon. "We only have this day. May you die well, my fellow warrior."

"Let's *not* have me die?" stammered Grant at the ominous greeting. "I like living. It's got its ups and downs, and I think I want to see more of those ups."

Grant sucked in a breath as the Wielder shot forward. He ducked and dived, narrowly avoiding slice after slice. He got in his own attacks, but February Twenty Nine simply slid off the chain ring mail. Realizing his attacks were doing nothing, Grant went back to the only plan that was working today. Dodge, duck, and dodge some more.

After ten minutes, Sir Monday hadn't managed to land a blow and was breathing heavily with the effort. His armor was a medium weight set, like Grant's, but the sword was clearly heavy. It took all of his strength to swing it at the more agile Grant. Sir Monday went all in, swinging wildly and using the little energy he had left to force Grant toward the wall, closing him in.

Grant was aware of Sir Monday's plan. As he reached the wall, he scrambled up a dangling rope and pushed off to the side, swinging around and behind Sir Monday. The Wielder's head darted around in confusion, but he didn't have time to respond as a kick to the back of the knees left him lying on his back with February Twenty Nine bearing down on his aorta. "I yield! Well fought, Sir Friday. I am truly impressed."

The panting youngster stood back and nodded at Sir Monday, who got back to his feet and walked unsteadily toward the edge of the arena. Light filled Grant as he reached cultivation level eight, and he took a deep breath of relief as he felt the debuff of *Lesser Lingering Death* fade away and his wounds heal. He checked to be sure.

Health: 139/139

Mana: 5/5

Characteristics
Physical: 59 (Cultivation Stage Maximized. Gains will be retroactively applied when all stages are aligned.)
Mental: 18
Armor Proficiency: 20
Weapon Proficiency: 36

A notification appeared, offering him yet another power, but Grant ignored it after seeing that it only increased the sharpness of his weapon based on his cultivation level. Sir Monday left the arena, not even realizing that he'd almost lost his Wielded Weapon's power. To be fair, as far as Grant knew, no known weapon held the power to absorb that of another Wielded Weapon. He turned to taunt 'Sir Saturday,' who was watching from the sidelines, to show that he had recovered.

Sarge stopped him as soon as he realized what Grant was planning to do. <Wait, nope, *no*. Hear me out, Grant. I think you should still pretend that the poison is impacting you. We need to figure out if this was as easily explainable as that assassin pretended it was. That is, was he *really* just after revenge for dishonor… or was there a more insidious plot against you?>

CHAPTER THIRTY-FOUR

Another Wielder entered the arena, this time a Sir Thursday. The final pre-semifinal combatant was holding a curved sabre —a falchion—that had a filigreed guard sweeping around and protecting his hand. Grant nodded at the man, who inclined his head gently. "House Thursday, a merchant. Shouldn't be a problem."

<*Never* underestimate your opponent! Think lightly of yourself, and deeply of the world!>

Sir Thursday pulled out a vial and applied oil to his blade. Upon making contact, liquid fire spread across and engulfed the blade. Simultaneously, the lights in the arena dimmed, leaving the only light that of the flaming sword in the now-dark fighting pit.

Thanks to Sarge's warning, Grant was now looking for a plot against him, and this fit too well. He shouted to the surroundings, "How is *this* a fair bout? You're putting him at a clear advantage!"

No one bothered to answer him, so Grant had no choice but to grumble to himself. "At least I know where he'll be."

Sir Thursday closed in like a boulder rolling downhill,

clearly wanting to end this fight as quickly as possible. He swung the sword in seemingly random patterns, leaving a trail of light on Grant's retinas and temporarily blinding him. Grant narrowly managed to bring up February Twenty Nine, parrying the blade as it came from his blinded left side. The smoldering fire on the edge reflected in his opponent's eyes as he leaned forward to threaten Grant.

"Yield now before your smoking corpse is served for *lunch*!" Sir Thursday was whispering, and the blade scraping against Grant's masked his words from any onlookers.

"Nice to meet you as well." Grant shoved Sir Thursday away, following up with a kick that landed on his opponent's knee and dealt two blunt damage. "I hope my 'smoking corpse' at least gives you indigestion!"

<Grant, a little tip,> Sarge whispered, even though only Grant could hear him. <Focus on his left leg. He has a limp he's trying to hide, and your little kick did more damage than it should have. A wound from a previous battle, perhaps?>

He spun and thrust his blade into the leather of Sir Thursday's leg, and the huge Noble yelped in pain as the blade pierced through the armor into the soft flesh below. Blood pumped out of the wound onto the sand, which had turned a shade of reddish-brown after the morning's deadly bouts.

Sir Thursday limped away and pressed the flat of his flaming blade against the wound. Flesh sizzled, and the smell of barbecued meat wafted across the arena as he cauterized the wound. Grant was sickened when his stomach rumbled in response to the scent of cooking meat, but managed to quip, "It looked like *you'll* be served for lunch, not me!"

"We'll *see*...!" Focused on the burning blade, Grant didn't notice the objects that spun in the darkness toward him. He did *hear* them, though, and managed to dodge at the last moment. He wasn't *quite* quick enough, and a blade embedded itself deeply in his right thigh. He could feel blood trickling down his leg. A quick check revealed that the impact had knocked five points off his health, but he was doing fine. Yet, if this was truly a conspiracy against him, the Noble would be expecting that Grant's health was almost fully drained. "That makes us even in the leg department!"

The flaming blade struck against February Twenty Nine, and the limping pair of Wielders danced around the blood-soaked sand of the fighting pit. Grant had to end this quickly, or someone would notice that he was too healthy. The comparatively thin young man launched a furious offensive attack, giving everything he had against his opponent.

Sir Thursday backed off, his flaming blade attempting to ward off the wrathful Grant. In doing so, he'd left the other leg exposed, and February Twenty Nine found an opening; stabbing deeply into the Wielder. Grant remembered his training and opened the femoral artery, and instantly, Sir Thursday fell to his knees on the sand and dropped his sabre. Through gritted teeth, he stopped the follow-up attack by saying, "I yield."

Grant couldn't believe it. He had fought and beat multiple Vassals and Wielders in a single day. In two days, he should be facing off against competitors in front of Lord January… if he managed to live long enough. A notification appeared, asking if he wanted to absorb the Wielded Weapon's power, but Grant waved it away without bothering to look.

"On to the semifinals. On to Lord January." Grant clenched his fist, but before he could get too excited, someone interrupted his thoughts.

"Halt," boomed the announcer. "This bout has been declared invalid due to a technicality. The competitor, Grant Friday, left the surface of the arena for an extended period."

"What technicality? Are you trying to tell me that *jumping* is against the rules?" Grant shouted as guards came forward to escort him away. He pulled the dagger out of his leg and tossed it to the side to show his fury. "I won fair and square!"

The announcer ignored him and droned on. "Even so, as Grant Friday didn't leave the boundary of the arena, the judges have graciously allowed competitors Grant Friday and Sir

Thursday the Twenty-First to rematch against alternative opponents."

"Oh, come on-" Grant hissed, slamming his mouth shut when the announcer stated:

"Any further debate will lead to disqualification. Grant Friday will now fight competitor *Roderick*, Second Vassal of Lord January himself!"

Roderick entered the arena and smirked in contempt at Grant. "Come on, thin-boy. Let's get this over with."

"Who are you calling *thin*?" Grant demanded indignantly, then looked down at himself consideringly. "Wait, no. Thanks?"

<There you go!> Sarge was quick to add positive reinforcement, <That's a *good* thing. Getting healthy has brought you *this* far; imagine what actually being in *proper* form would do for you!>

Before the announcer even called to start, Roderick pointed a rapier forward and immediately launched his attack. He managed to twist his blade just as it collided with Grant's parry, throwing him off balance. Grant sprawled onto the sand and rolled over before the rapier's piercing attack could hit home. The tip of the rapier whistled through the air, pausing only once as Roderick offered one last chance to escape. "Give up now. I *will* be taking part in the exhibition tournament."

"No chance!" Grant's harsh retort only made Roderick nod in appreciation at his dedication. The Vassal launched a brutal attack, a series of complex moves. This opponent was clearly more skilled than previous competitors, causing Grant to briefly wonder *how* he had become so skilled. Each attack that landed on his sword or armor resulted in him stumbling backwards; he had no idea how such a thin blade could carry so much force.

He darted out of the way of the rapier and got inside Roderick's guard, slashing his leather armor. The lucky cut sliced through the armor and bit into flesh below. The Vassal winced in pain and grasped at his side.

Damage dealt: 6 slashing damage. (5 mitigated) Debuff added: Bleeding (medium).

Rather than retreat, Roderick retaliated by whipping around and driving his rapier into Grant's leg. The point hit true, sliding deep and only stopping when it hit his bone.

Critical!

Damage taken: 7 piercing (7 mitigated) Debuff added: muscle damaged! Move speed -30%. Bleeding (minor).

"Ahh!" Grant tore his body off the rapier in a spray of blood. The puncture wound was deeper than any previous real wound he had ever suffered, and the bleeding was dropping two points of health per ten seconds.

Roderick reset his position and grinned, swinging his rapier in artistic patterns. "I will sign my name in your flesh for refusing to give up when I gave you the chance. You will learn to respect your elders."

<Grant,> whispered Sarge. <I can't help you… just remember your training. What would you have done in *training*? >

"I'd keep my… center of gravity low, then take his hand off when he overextends." Grant subvocalized his thoughts, and decided to act on them. He squatted down slightly and prepared for the next attack. Blade struck blade. Roderick held his wounded side with his free hand while launching attack after blistering attack. Each time the rapier connected, Grant slid back through the sand, buffeted by the strength of the man… but he didn't lose his balance. "It's a start. I can *do* this."

"Let's end this, *boy*!" The Vassal leapt toward Grant, rapier outstretched and aimed at his heart. Without a moment to spare, Grant sidestepped and swung with all his might using a two handed grip. There was a metal-shearing blast as February Twenty Nine connected with the rapier near its hilt… followed only by silence.

Roderick tumbled onto the sand and got up with a look of shock and bewilderment, staring at the rapier's dented hilt, the blade lying in the sand alongside his sliced-off hand. "This… wasn't meant to happen! I'm *supposed* to compete in the exhibition!"

Grant leveled the point of February Twenty Nine at the Vassal's throat. Roderick put his hand and stump up in surrender. "I am satisfied, sir…"

They stepped away from each other, and Grant went to leave the arena as a healer was called forward to reattach Roderick's hand. The announcer stopped him and pressed something cold into his palm, though the feel wasn't *nearly* as cold as the look he was given. Inspecting what he had been handed, Grant found that it was a golden token, a strip of metal embossed with the bust of Lord January. An entry token to the semi-final stage of the exhibition tournament! He wanted to shout for joy, but halted himself as he glanced back at his opponent.

The defeated Vassal was currently sobbing inconsolably on the sand as a Wielder held his severed hand and forced it onto the bleeding stump. Grant didn't know what the issue was; had the man never lost before, or did the healing hurt *that* much? The man hadn't even whimpered when Grant had cut him! He stepped out of the arena, then hesitated. He peered around the corner once more, just in time to see the healer flee as a large man loomed behind the Vassal.

A knife came down, and blood sprayed up in an arc. "How *dare* you dishonor Lord January? I will help you *repent* of this shame."

Grant *knew* that voice but couldn't place it. He drew an inch of his sword from his scabbard, but before he could challenge the killer… the man was gone. Grant scanned around the empty room and slowly backed away. He wasn't going to allow himself to be caught with a corpse; he could already imagine how happy they would be to get rid of him.

After creeping through his exit, Grant started to run.

CHAPTER THIRTY-FIVE

"What in the twelve Districts happened to *you*?" Red was so concerned that he actually got out of his lounge chair as Grant limped into one of the guest suites that had been taken over by Sir Friday Twenty-Ninth and his party. Grant only managed a grunt in reply as he started peeling off his blood-soaked leather armor.

"Here, sit down and get that looked at!" Fergus pulled out a chair and fetched a towel stitched with the bust of Lord January. Grant winced as he sat, and Fergus hurried to tie the towel about the wound to stymie the blood loss.

"You a medic now, too?" Skinny commented as he took a bite out of a ham shank.

Fergus glared over at Skinny but continued treating the wound. After applying a poultice, he shrugged. "Best I can do for ya, but it should at least stop the bleeding. You should stay off the leg for a few days, Grant."

The young Wielder shook his head and forced a weak smile. "I don't have a few days. I won. The day after tomorrow, I'll be taking part in the semi-final of the exhibition tournament."

"I *knew* you could do it!" Derek roared at the announcement, coming over to slap him on the back. "What does this mean for you? For Sir Friday? I assume he's sponsoring you? Actually… don't take this the wrong way, I just can't understand what your motive for participating is. If you don't mind me asking? It's a long way to travel, and a lot of hardship, for the mere chance of winning a set of Mid Spring armor."

Grant opened his mouth. He was going to tell them about fighting for honor, for the glory of House Friday… but he couldn't lie to his friends. He started over after taking a deep breath. "I'm on a quest… by the end of the year, I have to heal the world. Also, *no*, I don't know what that means."

The assembled company sat and waited for him to continue, clearly unsatisfied with his answer. "If I don't defeat all twelve Lords of the Month by the end of the year, I will revert to the cultivation level I was when accepting the quest, minus an additional one level."

"So?" Red pushed him gently to continue. "That's not so bad, is it?"

"I'll go negative," Grant whispered.

His friends stared at him with great concern, until Red was the one to finally say it. "But if you're negative, you're dead!"

<Grant.> Sarge cautioned him darkly. <Be *careful* what information you share.>

The young man didn't want to hold back the truth from his friends. He felt that he owed them the truth after they were bundled into a cart and basically forced to come on the trip. He steeled his heart, needing to know if this friendship only went one way. "There is one more thing… I wasn't always known as Grant Monday."

The party looked even more confused, and Grant forced the words out. "Before I picked up this sword… my name was Grant *Leap*."

A lump of ham was jettisoned from Skinny's mouth and sailed across the room. Red and Fergus grinned at the prank; calendar freaks were always the butt of jokes and sources of derision. They looked over to Derek, who wasn't smiling. The powerful man slowly stated, "I don't think he's teasing."

Skinny had turned white and fumbled around for something. He grasped the handle of his bread knife, his knuckles white. "A *Leap*! Help me hold it down; I'll put it out of its misery!"

"Skinny! Come on, I was joking! My delivery is a bit off, that's all." Cold sweat was dripping down Grant's back. It was clear that he had found his answer: these men would turn on him in an instant. "I was going to use that line against my next opponent; put them off and confuse them! You know, get a quick victory while they stand there trying to figure out what's going on. I'm here to bring honor to my family name and get more resources devoted to our estates. C'mon, Skinny, put that down. Are you going to *butter* me to death?"

Grant laughed, diffusing the tension that had suddenly escalated in the room. Skinny slowly lowered his knife and shook his head, returning to his food. "Don't *do* that to me, Grant. Lost a perfectly good piece of ham!"

Silence fell over the group. The silence was only broken when the bulk of Sir Friday Twenty-Ninth entered the suite. "Why all the sour faces?"

"I told a joke that wasn't stomached very well." Grant answered calmly, not looking over at his 'friends'.

"Well, *enough* jokes!" Sir Friday waddled in front of Grant and clapped both his hands onto Grant's shoulders. "There is no time to rest. We have a problem!"

"Problem? What problem?" Grant pulled out his golden token. "Take a look. I won. I'm in."

"That *is* the problem. I just discovered that the tournament was rigged. Roderick, the Vassal of Lord January, was supposed to be the fourth contender of the exhibition. The Nobles and Lord January are *not* happy. Not only was he defeated by you, but the Vassal seems to have had some kind of accident. No one has seen him since your fight, and Lord January is furious."

Grant remained silent. He wasn't about to expose what he

knew. Sir Friday waited a long moment before continuing awkwardly. "Well… you have caused quite the kerfuffle amongst the top brass in Lord January's court. Their men will be on the lookout for you, wanting to question you on recent events. Look… token recipients are a secret. I need you to stay hidden until the exhibition tournament the day after tomorrow. *Can you do that?*"

"I have no choice, do I? Back to running and hiding." Grant took a deep breath and met his benefactor's eyes. "I'll need somewhere to train."

"Good lad." Sir Friday patted his shoulder and handed him a potion. "This should fix you right up; drink it down. I can't help you with a training space, as my suites will be pulled apart while they look for you. You'll have to find somewhere on your own. Tell *no one*."

"I… I have somewhere in mind." Grant studied the ground and nodded thoughtfully.

"Good. Remember… tell no one. Not me, not a horse, nor a cow that's on the way to slaughter. Hide away, and stay there until trumpets announce the commencement of the exhibition tournament. I must leave. I will be taken for questioning over the incident. Lord January's men know that you are with me, and we've messed up their plans. Unlike you, there is nowhere *I* can hide!" Grant nodded and watched the bulky figure of Sir Friday hurry from the suite.

Heaving himself clumsily to his feet, he grabbed his backpack, careful not to put weight on his leg. The blood had stopped, but jolts of pain shot up his leg with every step. He popped open the bottle and guzzled it down, hoping it would work quickly.

Fergus came up to him as he was about to leave, and spoke softly. "Don't worry, Grant. Your secret is safe with us."

Grant hesitated. "What? Oh… that. Fergus, I was only joking."

"Despite what was said around the campfire, I don't have anything against Leaps." He whispered the word 'Leap'. "It was just talk. Red, despite his size, is a big softy. Same for Derek there. Skinny… he forgot it happened by now."

"I appreciate it, Fergus. I really do." Grant clasped the hand of his… friend? He couldn't tell for certain, but all trust had fled. "I better go."

"Be careful. House Tuesday will have eyes everywhere." Fergus watched Grant leave, a shadow crossing his face.

"Get a good seat at the tournament. There may be an unexpected competitor." Grant gave a half-smile to the group. They waved, all but Skinny, who was busy devouring another ham shank. The door closed with a thunk, and Grant was on his own once again.

Sounds of the bustling market rushed in, assaulting his ears as he exited the sanctuary of Sir Friday's suites. He was on high alert. Too high, since he jumped as a dog barked. The previously exciting hustle and bustle of the market was now menacing. In his mind, House Tuesday goons lurked around every corner, ready to pounce as soon as his attention wavered.

Grant wandered around aimlessly in the afternoon sun, trying his best to blend in with the locals. It *was* hard to seem like he belonged, considering how thin he was compared to everyone else, let alone the dried blood crusting his armor. The only thing saving him from getting reported was that armor was a familiar sight during tournaments, and blood was common today. The market and surrounding areas were packed with competitors, both Vassals and Wielders taking part in the initial stages of the competition.

He passed a stall where the owner was busy bartering over the price of a scarf, pausing as he realized he needed to hide his face. "Excuse me-"

The merchant cut him off with a gentle wave, "Be with you in a minute, sir."

Grant waited patiently, his heart jumping when he saw a bright yellow shirt coming his way. Turning around, another House Tuesday Peacekeeper was heading toward him. He was surrounded on all sides. There was no escape, he needed to hide immediately.

"How can I help you?" The rotund salesman turned to Grant with a greasy smile.

"A scarf. I need one. Now. How much for that one?" He pointed at a black scarf with an embroidered motif of Lord January.

The salesman sauntered over to the scarf. "This one, boy?"

"Yes." Grant snapped as he noticed the Peacekeepers closing in, looking around and scanning the names of the people they saw..

"This is two…" the salesman saw the desperation on Grant's face, and amended his words. "That is… *ten* Minutes."

"Ten! I'll take it!" He threw over two five Minute coins, and scowled at the smiling shopkeeper. He was frustrated at overpaying, but now wasn't the time to haggle. Grant ducked and wrapped the scarf around his head, hiding his identity just as the Peacekeepers met up with each other and clasped hands.

"Heya, Joe."

"Bob. Want to grab some dinner? My watch is coming to an end."

"Don't mind if I do. Regent's rumbling tummy, that's why I was coming to see ya!" Bob chuckled as they started to chat. Grant squinted out a gap in the scarf at the Peacekeepers chatting beside him. They weren't after him? They seemed more concerned about the state of their stomachs. "Come on. The feast is crazy. Lord January is going all out to impress his guests this year!"

"Let's go, Joe. I'm starved. By the way, new orders: be on the lookout for someone called 'Grant Friday'. He needs to be taken in for questioning."

Grant coughed involuntarily. As the Peacekeepers looked at him, he wanted to disappear; sure his cover was blown. The man called Joe aimed a kick at Grant. "Get away, you filthy beggar. You should be in the workhouse, where they can keep an eye on you."

"Come on, Joe. Let's go before I lose my appetite!" Bob spat at Grant as they turned to walk off.

Grant could hear them laughing as they headed toward the dining hall. The salesman looked at him with a smirk. "Were you worried about *them*? They're after a Grant *Friday*; you must have heard that they were after 'Grant' and got worried?"

He pulled up his status sheet and noticed that his name had reverted to Grant Monday. The potion had worn off? When? Had Sir Friday deactivated it somehow? He let out an involuntary sigh, and the salesman waved him away with a laugh at his expense. Grant went in the opposite direction to the Peacekeepers.There *was* somewhere he could go; the workhouse. Count Tuesday had mentioned it previously, and these Peacekeepers had just reminded him. Disguised and making a good job of looking like a beggar, he approached a stone building on the left side of the castle's keep. The sign above the double doors read 'Kane's Poor House'.

He gulped, then entered, hoping that he'd be allowed a quiet place to hide until the semifinals of the tournament began.

CHAPTER THIRTY-SIX

Long shadows stretched between the crates that Grant had been allowed to sleep on overnight. There had been little fuss when he arrived; a single look at his thin, blood-speckled form, and Corporal Kane had ordered a vat of soup for Grant and sent him to sleep until the following morning. Which, from the glow of the soft orange light, was now. Grant could see that it was just after sunrise, and he needed to make a plan. "Just one more day to hide out, then I can sneak into the exhibition tournament."

Up and awake and with nothing better to do, Grant decided to do a practice training session before breakfast. He felt confident in his growing sword skills. Two uneventful hours passed, and he was covered in sweat but feeling strong. His leg had fully healed over the night as well, thanks to the potion he had drunk before making his escape.

He could feel the recent improvements to both sword skills and stamina. Halfway through his session, Grant lunged, attacking an imaginary foe. Distracted by his thoughts, he overbalanced and fell over, the tip of his sword just barely touching against the handle of a frying pan.

The frying pan swung around in slow motion. Grant watched as it fell onto another pot, which hit another, then another. He stood in horror as the precariously stacked tower of various stored goods rumbled, then came down like dominos. There was an almighty crash as the pots and pans collided with one another and the floor. Grant coughed, enveloped in a cloud of dust.

"Maybe… no one noticed?" A moment later, heavy footsteps thundered through the halls of the poor house, and two orange-uniformed Peacekeepers kicked open the door to the storage room that Grant had been sent to the night before. Another, more familiar, face appeared at the same time.

"My *door*!" The elderly figure of Corporal Kane attempted to squeeze past the Peacekeepers. "I was right here; you *saw* me coming! Why did you kick in my door? I'm sure whatever fell was only an accident."

"Get out my way, old man." The obese Vassal of House Tuesday pushed Corporal Kane, who landed heavily amongst the scattered kitchenware. As Grant rushed over to help the frail figure, his scarf caught on one of the towers and was pulled off. "Are you okay?"

Corporal Kane nodded. "I… I'll be fine. Thank you, sonny."

Grant turned on the Peacekeepers. "How *dare* you treat an old man like that? Do you have no respect for your elders?"

"Hey, it's him!" The thinner Vassal nudged his obese buddy. "Grant Friday!"

"Grant Friday, you are charged with disturbing the peace. We are Peacekeepers; it's our job to keep the peace. You are also charged," added the other man, "with *rigging* the tournament, and with the death of one of Lord January's personal Vassals!"

"Hold up, his name isn't Friday-" The first Peacekeeper muttered as he got a good look at Grant.

The second Peacekeeper wasn't listening. "You will have plenty of time to respond to the charges. If you are found innocent, the process shouldn't take more than… oh, a couple of days to sort out."

Grant immediately saw the trap that had been placed for him. "Two days? But I'll miss the tournament!"

"Heh. Seems he *is* the one we are after, even if his name is incorrect." The fatter of the two relaxed after deciding he had found the right man. He walked forward and held out a pair of manacles. "We'll get things sorted as quickly as possible. If you're lucky, you'll be able to watch the final match. Put these on and follow us."

Up until now, Grant had been trying to do everything as legally as possible. The Vassals back at Randall's estate had been killed in self-defense and he felt terrible about it; Sir Monday the Thirty-First had impaled himself on February Twenty Nine, and anyone else that had died had been trying to kill *him*. Grant had spared everyone he could. Now it was time to take a step into a darker space. He was going to die if he listened to these men, and he wasn't about to let that happen. "If I don't fight now and kill members of House Tuesday… but I don't want to hurt anyone. I *earned* the right to be in the semi-finals."

Ignoring the proffered manacles, Grant unsheathed February Twenty Nine with a ringing of steel. "Please leave. I will not be going quietly."

"That's how you want to play this?" The fatter man responded with a scowl. "Billy, go get some backup. I'm going to need someone to help drag him back to a cell after I put him down."

"Right, boss." As Billy hurried out of the room, his boss dropped the manacles and unclasped a club from his belt, a common weapon wielded by the Peacekeepers. The wooden club changed color before Grant's eyes, rotating through a spectrum of hues: that *wasn't* common. After his run in with Sir Friday Twenty-Ninth's cudgel, Grant was more wary. He didn't know what power the clubs contained, but didn't want to find out.

"You're a Vassal?" Grant questioned the man, who nodded seriously.

"I am. *All* of us are. Are you ready to come with us now that you know?" Rather than run in, the Peacekeeper stood there, waiting for backup. It arrived soon after; a full ten Peacekeepers, including Billy and his boss, squeezed into the entrance to the cramped storage room.

"Not a chance." Grant shook his head. "I am sorry about this. I can't let you take me."

He stood at the intersection of four stacks of towers. He had to be careful; with a modicum of effort, they'd be able to circle behind him and take him by surprise. A Vassal ran toward him, club raised, hoping to quickly dispatch Grant. All he got was a hilt to the chin. He collapsed moaning to the ground, holding his dislocated jaw, and had to be dragged out of the way by his colleagues.

Critical!

Damage dealt: 11 blunt damage. Debuff added: unconscious.

Using the distraction, another Vassal lunged from the side and grabbed Grant in a bear hug, immobilizing his arms. The obese boss walked forward with a smug grin, and brought the multicolored club down. As it swung, even as pinned as he was, Grant raised his feet in an attempt to kick the obese Vassal in the gut. The shift in weight forced his captor to bend over, and the club struck him squarely on the top of his head. The man screamed as his hair ignited upon impact, and he went running back into the depths of the storage room, attempting to put out the flames.

Since the nearest opponent was distracted by his colleague's flaming hair, Grant planted a fist in the wobbly stomach of the Peacekeeper boss, who promptly collapsed like a bag of potatoes. The storage room was mayhem as Vassals attacked recklessly. They missed, tripped on a pot, or struck one of their buddies as Grant dodged the blows. One Vassal gasped as a club hit his leg, and Grant could feel a chill coming from the immobilized limb.

Grant was able to hold back from killing, since the Vassals were doing more to damage themselves than he could to them in the confined space. A few times, he had to duck or sidestep, but mostly, he was able to simply stay out of the sluggish men's way. His hand came off of February Twenty Nine. He could have quickly ended the fight, but he was still hesitant about becoming a wanton murderer.

Dodging and darting around, it wasn't long before all ten of his opponents were down, either collapsed in a heap due to overwhelming fatigue or with limbs incapacitated by the power from other clubs. Grant used his fists, pounding pudgy middles and soft faces until he was certain they were unconscious. Light filled him, and he coughed blood. This… this was too much! He bent over, heaving in a breath. In this position, he could clearly see his wounds heal, the flesh flowing together in an itchy instant.

<Cultivation level nine, and your highest characteristic broke through a cultivation stage,> Sarge confirmed in a pleased tone. <What you're feeling right now are all the increases that have been held back by the restrictions. Your physical cultivation is already maxed out, unable to go any higher until your lowest stage breaks through. Physical cultivation reached Early Summer, Mental and Armor Proficiency reached Mid Spring, and Weapon Proficiency got to Late Spring. Congratulations.>

Grant dusted off his hands as he stood. He was glad the fight was over, but it was time to go. He went to gather his belongings; he clearly needed to find another place to hide. When he picked up his backpack, he froze as he glimpsed a silhouette blocking his escape route. The towering bulk resolved into Count Tuesday as he entered the storage room. The Wielder did *not* look pleased. "We meet again, Grant Friday… or, should that be Grant *Monday*, hmm?"

"You are mistaken." Grant's cover had been blown, and the next words confirmed that it was not just because they had run into each other here.

"We had a word with your sponsor, Sir Friday Twenty-Ninth. He told us about your 'arrangement'. I will be taking you in for questioning while we sort this out." Count Tuesday looked around at all of his fallen men. "I'm glad to see that your will is weak. I look forward to breaking you."

CHAPTER THIRTY-SEVEN

"No." Grant puffed out his chest in defiance, despite resembling a child in front of the immense form of Count Tuesday.

"Have it your way. The *law* is on my side." Without wasting a single second, Count Tuesday flowed forward and swung his multicolored club into Grant's stomach. The colors on this Wielded Weapon, the source of his Vassal's weapons, was so much more potent than Grant had expected. His speed and form were impeccable, and Grant had become complacent due to dealing with the weak subordinates.

Damage taken: 10 blunt damage. (11 mitigated)

Grant gasped and toppled backward, winded from the hit, but also shocked at how much damage had just been blocked. He managed to refocus in time to dodge the second attack; the green glow had made him *very* nervous as it passed a whisker from his face. Green—from previous experience—meant poison. He'd rather be burned or frozen that have his health bar deplete over time; although the other options weren't particularly appealing. As he scrambled back on all fours, Count Tuesday lunged forward and clipped Grant on the chin.

Damage taken: 12 blunt damage. (9 mitigated) Debuff added: Paralyzed (2 seconds remain).

"You have a tough chin! That would have broken a bone for most people!" Count Tuesday laughed at the sight of Grant's body convulsing as if struck by lightning as he lightly tapped him again. "Do you focus on armor cultivation, then? I hit you directly, and that weak gear you wear can't be doing much to help."

The young man couldn't answer. He *felt* the lightning that was coursing through him, and he just didn't have the speed required to dodge the club. He knew it, and obviously so did Count Tuesday. Another blow fell, and the man left him there, shaking in agony. Grant growled and *forced* his body to still. The Count could have put him out of his misery at any point, but decided to toy with him instead.

Grant needed to figure out why he was able to take such a pounding, so he glanced to the side and quantified the changes to himself.

Name: Grant Monday
Rank: Wielder
Class: Foundation Cultivator
Cultivation Achievement Level: 8 -> 9
Cultivation Stage: Late Spring
Inherent Abilities: Swirling Seasons Cultivation
Health: 162/184
Mana: 6/6

Characteristics
Physical: 89 (Cultivation Stage Maximized. Gains will be retroactively applied when all stages are aligned.)
Mental: 23 (+1)
Armor Proficiency: 29 (+1)
Weapon Proficiency: 46 (+2)

His jaw was clenched too hard to say any words audibly,

which was a good thing. He would have gasped at the information aloud if he had been able to. *This* was the most shocking thing he had experienced today, including the lightning. The two hits had only taken twenty-two points of his total health. When he had first gained his Wielded Weapon, that would have been nearly half of his total. Now it was only a small fraction.

Apart from the blunt damage, the yellow lightning effect didn't leave any damage over time. Count Tuesday stepped closer. "Have you had enough yet? I don't have time for your games. You have a little skill, I give you that, but you are no match for the might of House Tuesday."

"N… never." Grant sucked in a ragged breath and got up unsteadily. What other choice did he have? If he didn't get the opportunity to confront and defeat Lord January, then he would surely die. At least if he died now, no one else would see his humiliation. He wouldn't need to put his friends through the fear of watching him die in the fighting pit in front of all the Lords and Ladies.

Grant swayed and barely kept his footing. He ducked and dodged, but try as he might, he couldn't get a hit in against his opponent. It took everything he had just to stay out of the way of the spectrum-shifting shaft, and yet Count Friday yawned—actually *yawned*—in boredom. Grant was breathing heavily and wasn't getting anywhere. His stamina was dropping fast. As he dodged once more, the Count lunged forward and the club connected with the exposed flesh of Grant's ankle.

"Ahh!" The club must have been blue at the time of the hit, because a deadly cold quickly spread up his leg and began sapping his ability to move the limb.

"It's over. That's the most potent effect I can create." Count Tuesday stopped and took a step away. Although Grant hadn't taken any damage, the debuff stated that his body would be completely frozen within two minutes, and would remain so for a further one minute. Within seconds his foot was numb from the cold. He dragged his freezing body away from the oncoming wrath of Count Tuesday. With no other options, he swung February Twenty Nine at one of the huge piles of randomly stacked gear in the storeroom, hoping to create a distraction.

For a long heartbeat, it didn't seem as if it would move. Then the pile suddenly dropped and toppled onto the bulk of Count Tuesday… who was taken to the ground with a shout of alarm, and buried. The falling items started a chain reaction, and more and more of the poorly stacked goods and crates began falling, until almost nothing was left to fall.

"Is he… dead?" There was only silence. Grant knew that he should get up and attempt to run, but he stood transfixed by the sea of crates, and within thirty seconds, his body would be frozen into a rigid position for at least a few breaths.

The silence was broken by a deafening roar. Count Tuesday slammed his weapon upward and exploded out of the mass of crates, his multi-hued eyes glowing. Grant wasn't in the mood to fight any more, and he knew that he wasn't going to get another chance if he let this man break free.

Acting on instinct, relying on his many hours of focused training, the dull blade of February Twenty Nine shot forward and sank into the massive chest of Count Tuesday… who hadn't even bothered wearing armor when he faced off against the annoyance that was Grant Monday.

Count Tuesday looked in wonder at the length of steel poking out of his chest, then down at Grant, before his eyes closed… for the last time.

Grant's body froze, literally, as the debuff went into full effect. For an agonizing instant before the effects of the Wielded Weapon faded along with the death of its Wielder, he held onto February Twenty Nine as it remained where it had penetrated Count Tuesday's body. He wanted to look away, but he was physically unable to do so.

He had done this. For the first time, he had thought it over and made the conscious choice to take another person's life. He had killed the leader of the Peacekeepers of the entire District of January. Was his quest *worth* taking someone else's life to save his own? Maybe he could have found another way to confront Lord January?

After the endless instant, his body thawed, and a single tear rolled down his cheek. He forced himself to move; if he broke down now, he'd never get back up. Grant slapped away the offered ability of the Weapon without looking at it, too caught up in introspection. "If I follow this path, I'll have a mountain of corpses to climb. I could leave here now, find a town, and blend in with the locals. I'll get fat and have fun as a Monday, enjoying the remainder of my days. At least this way, no one else would get hurt. No one but… me."

"No. *No*!" He yanked his sword back and wiped it clean on the corpse before him. "If I give up now, everything I have done will be in vain. Count Tuesday's death? Meaningless. How could I go off and have fun, knowing that I killed him for a task I then abandoned?"

He burst out of a rear exit in the workhouse and into a quiet alleyway. The immediate danger was gone, but he wasn't out of the woods yet. Grant felt like he was trapped in a maze. Windowless walls soared up, shrouding the alleyway in darkness. "If only I had a set of stealth armor!"

Not ten minutes later, trumpets blared. Not in the familiar call for breakfast, lunch or dinner; no, this din was loud and persistent. He knew what it meant, even if those he passed didn't. "They've discovered Count Tuesday's body."

He picked up his pace, not sure where to go, but wanting to get as far away from the poorhouse as possible. Someone down an alley called out, "I think he went this way!"

Marching footsteps were muffled by the mossy cobbles, but somehow, the Peacekeepers were on his trail. Grant broke into a run, slipping immediately and almost losing his footing as he tried to take a shortcut. "*There*! I think I see him!"

Grant didn't risk looking back. He picked up his pace and came out in a bustling market; knocking over two shoppers. All three of them went sprawling to the ground. Angry fists and shouts ensued as he mumbled an apology before descending into the throng of bodies milling around.

"Hey. Watch it!" A servant carrying a basket wasn't amused when Grant bumped into him. A moment later, the servant went flying as a House Tuesday Peacekeeper barreled into him, spilling the contents of his basket across the cobbles. Orange vests approached from all sides. Grant stayed low, not having time to sift through his pack to find the scarf.

There, a door that was slightly ajar! Grant squeezed through the opening and found himself in a stable, surrounded by stable hands that were too engrossed with their tasks to pay him any mind. There was no obvious way out that he could see, apart from a wooden ladder to the upper level of the stables. He took the rungs of the ladder two at a time, and for a moment, could have been back home at the farm. Hay bales stacked neatly, fodder for the horses… he took a moment to catch his breath and sat heavily on one of the bales.

"Did you see him? I'll check in here." A noise came from below. Grant didn't even dare to breathe. Any noise would give away his position. "Not down here."

"Well, you better check up top, just to be sure! Can't let a murderer get away." Grant was frozen in indecision. He tried to squeeze between two bales. Sandwiched there, a piece of hay tickled his nostrils. He only had to remain hidden for a couple of minutes till they moved on to search another building—

"Achoo!"

Sword Saints.

"Up here! I think he's *here*!" Footsteps clomped up the ladder, which groaned from the unaccustomed weight. Grant darted out, his hiding place compromised. He made a dash for a window and leapt out headfirst, not knowing what was waiting on the other side.

He landed in a heap on the castle ramparts, shocked that someone had been allowed to build such a tall building right next to the defensive wall of the keep. It worked to his benefit, but… he took his mind off it. Not his problem. To his right lay the castle keep, buildings, and a whole lot of angry House Tuesday Vassals. They were ransacking shops and pushing peasants aside as they searched… for *him*. On his left, on the other side of the crenellated walls, lay a sheer drop.

Footsteps smacked off wooden boards as someone approached the window of the hay loft. He considered jumping amongst the mass of bodies below, but half of them were out for his blood. He'd have to put the House Tuesday hounds off his scent. A plan forming, Grant jumped up on the wall and lowered himself over the other side, dangling into the abyss, his fingers straining to hold his weight. Two voices he didn't recognize grew louder as they approached until they were right above him.

"I'm sure he was here…" The first voice was very confused.

"Well if he was, he would have jumped back down into the market. He wouldn't be daft enough to jump over the castle wall now, would he?" Person Number Two growled at the first.

"I suppose not?"

"C'mon." The second person stated in exasperation. "That's how Lord January deals with the criminals, you know?"

Person number one had clearly not been in this position for very long. "What do you mean?"

"He forces them to jump from a platform. Right over the wall they go, down to the bottom of that crevice. Listen here… quiet-like. This goes to *no one* else, but I know you're pretty new. Fact is, Lord January's got a sick sense of humor, left over from the war a thousand years ago. He promises the convicts that if they flap their arms hard enough, they'll fly."

"They *believe* him?" Person One sounded doubtful.

"He's *the* Lord January." Person Two— who Grant was really starting to dislike—chuckled, "You can sometimes see their little arms flappin' as they disappear."

Grant watched as a glob of spit flew over the wall and into the darkness below. When he was sure they were gone, he tried to pull himself back up. However, the trifecta of gravity, his size, and his fatigued fingers weren't having any of it. One by one, he felt his fingers give up. He scrambled fruitlessly, trying to grip on to something as his body slid down the steep wall. "This wasn't how I-!"

Then he, like the criminals before him, flew.

His flight was short lived, as his body connected painfully with a tree branch that creaked alarmingly. It had grown out of the wall, which had clearly not been cared for in a long time. He clung on for dear life and gulped as he stared into the depths. Vertigo overwhelmed him. "How long can I last like this? There's no way to climb back up. I can either stay here and die of starvation, or drop into the darkness. Who knows… maybe I'll learn to fly on the way down?"

"I just *had* to pick up the sword, didn't I?" He lay there, quivering appendages wrapped around the tree limb, feeling strangely at peace. Grant closed his eyes and loosened his grip. He was calm. All he could hear was the wind, distant cries and shouts from the castle, the trickle of water nearby, and the smell of the people of the city. That was not a happy smell.

"Wait… the trickle of water?" He hadn't noticed it before. He searched around and found a rusty iron grate near the tree branch. The smell came from the foul brown liquid oozing out of the sewer grate and into the darkness.

"A sewer!" He'd never been so happy to smell sewage as he was in that moment. Grant pulled himself along the branch and used February Twenty Nine to lever open the grate, which swung open with a screech. Rather than try to jump directly into the opening—impossible from this angle—he pulled himself onto the corroded metal grate directly. His hands dug into the rust-coated metal, and his legs flailed around until he managed to pull himself through and into the welcoming, if smelly, opening.

As he lay in the waste from peasant and Noble alike, his laughter echoed along the sewer pipe. Not wanting to stew in the stench for longer than he needed, he got up and took his first tentative steps into the darkness.

CHAPTER THIRTY-EIGHT

After stumbling blindly through the rancid tunnels, a soft light coming from ahead was almost blinding. Grant heard the sound of muffled chattering, so he slowly unsheathed February Twenty Nine. "I'm ready for whatever lies ahead. I can do *anything*."

He wasn't sure if he was reassuring himself, just trying to find the courage to keep moving, or if he truly felt ready to attack something, anything, and everything. The light grew brighter and the chattering louder. He paused; it didn't sound like a monster, but… people? "Why would there be people all the way down here?"

"*Momma*! A monster!" A small child scampered from behind a wooden crate and hid behind what Grant presumed was his mother. February Twenty Nine glowed with the reflected dim light in the area, making him realize he was brandishing his sword in front of a group of filthy beggars almost as thin as he was. Grant instantly lowered his weapon and waved his free hand.

"Please," pleaded the woman as she clutched her filthy child, "don't hurt us!"

"I'm so sorry," Grant fully sheathed his sword and waved his hands furiously, "I would *never-*"

**Thud*

Debuff added: Unconscious.

Grant came to an unknown amount of time later. He had a throbbing headache, and he just barely remembered something hitting him from behind. Someone must have snuck up behind and walloped him with an entire *tree* to get through his armor and knock him out in one go. He fumbled for his sword, but found his movements restricted.

"You won't be needing a weapon," a gruff voice informed him brusquely. "What are you doing down here? A bit of *hunting*?"

Grant spat to the side as he strained against his bonds. "Why would I want to come down to this cesspit to *hunt*?"

"Mind your manners! It may be a cesspit, but it's *our* cesspit." Grant struggled to sit up with his wrists bound. By how the restraints bent when he pushed, he *could* probably break the bonds and dispatch the group without breaking a sweat, but he needed more information. Sarge's recent courses had been forcing him to *think* his way out of situations, rather than just react. In fact, he had even managed to gain a mental cultivation characteristic point, if he had read his status correctly. "How did you find us down here? We guard the entrances from intruders… but no one ever comes here with good intentions."

"I came… over the wall." Grant admitted as he again started to strain against his bonds. They started to creak right away. Good.

"Eh? What do you mean, over the wall?" The man scratched his patchy beard.

In the dim light, Grant couldn't make out any of their names. "Come closer, so I can see you better? I jumped the wall to escape House Tuesday. Somehow, I managed to hit a branch as I fell, and well… here I am."

"We're not falling for your tricks. If we come closer, you'll be able to tell who we are! Can't trust a Monday!" The man spat at him. "Running from House Tuesday, *indeed*."

"Listen. I'm not a normal Monday. I'm… I…" Grant decided to share some information, since these people clearly distrusted the Nobility as much as he did. "I'm going to destroy Lord January and go to February. I just want to get out of here and earn my freedom. I'm warning you, if you refuse to let me go, it won't go well for you."

"Lord… January? You plan to *kill* him? The man is pure evil," whispered the woman. "He has thrown so many of us over the wall for nothing but entertainment."

"No one is coming for *us*, are they?" The man leaned in and held a rusty blade at Grant's throat.

"Marcus… *Leap*?" Grant's eyes widened in astonishment, after reading the nametag.

"No!" The woman cried, "He knows who we *are* now! He'll bring others… what will we do, Marcus?"

Suddenly, it all made sense. House Tuesday Peacekeepers had mentioned that Leaps were being thrown over the wall. Samuel, Freda, and Marcus Leap's name tags were displayed as they came into the light; their dirty faces devoid of hope. Freda looked at Marcus with hard eyes. "We should kill him, shouldn't we?"

"I… I can't do that." Marcus lowered his blade. "It would make us no better than them."

"I mean you no harm. I promise." Grant mustered as much sincerity as he could.

"How can we *possibly* believe that?" Marcus snarled, striking Grant across the face with the hilt of his rusty sword. Apparently, he was not above *hitting* him, just killing him. So far. Luckily, the hit did nothing but hurt the other man's hand. "Ow! What in the name of the tyrannical Regent are you made of?"

"You have *nothing* to fear from me." Grant figured that

honesty was the best policy. "Before I was called Grant Monday, I lived in New Dawn. My name was… Grant *Leap*."

"How stupid do you think we are? That's not possible. Once a Leap, always a Leap." Marcus no longer seemed angry; he was deflated, like the fight had gone out of him entirely.

"I understand. I was like you. I worked relentlessly for no benefit, until I came across this sword, February *Twenty Nine*." Grant stressed the sword's name as he nodded at it. Marcus glared at him, walked to the blade, and slowly unsheathed it. The name etched in the blade glinted in the torchlight.

"The fabled Leap sword!" Freda cried out, dropping to her knees and pulling her child to her. "*The* Leap! He is *the Leap*! He's finally come to save us, and all Leapkind!"

Notification: Now friendly with Leap faction (updated from Unfriendly)
Effect: 10% discount during trade with Leap Faction.

Grant wasn't sure if he should be happy that faction discounts existed, or angry that this was the first time he had ever *heard* of one. He had been around for *years*, and had never even seen a *hint* that there were blanket benefits like this. "Whoa… hold up right there. I'm no one's else's savior. I'm only trying to save *myself* and get stronger."

"Please, come with us." The woman ignored his comment. "Everyone will be excited to meet you!"

After untying Grant—Marcus glared at Grant when he saw how frayed the ropes were—the three adults and smallish child followed the path toward an unknown destination. The torch Marcus carried provided little illumination, casting long, ominous shadows. However, Grant paused as the words really sank in: he was almost frozen by what he had just heard. "Everyone…? How many of you are there?"

Marcus was the one to begrudgingly answer him. He was

clearly used to keeping this information to himself. "There are only twenty-three of us left… not including you."

"I didn't realize there were so many Leaps… anywhere," Grant admitted uneasily. Marcus was *much* older than him. How long had he suffered?

"There are probably more, hiding on the fringes of society. Outcast, unwanted, unloved." Freda's head dropped as she sighed.

"Calm yourself." Marcus tenderly put an arm around Freda. "Our life isn't perfect, but at least we found our way here… and each other."

Grant felt a little uncomfortable sharing the couple's tender moment. Luckily, he wasn't forced to do so for much longer.

"Here we are." Marcus opened an iron door that **screeched** as it yielded. All chatter in the open room ceased as they entered. Many troubled faces turned toward Grant. Eyes darted around as people contemplated running and trying to hide from the newcomer. Most sat around a table made from planks of wood balanced on old wooden crates. The cavernous space smelled musty from the damp, and of roasting meat. "Don't worry! He's a friend."

"Ain't no *Monday* a friend to Leaps!" one of the bolder residents spoke up as he reached for a weapon. "Why did you bring him here?"

"He's a Leap in disguise! This man…" Marcus clapped Grant on the shoulder, and Grant realized that he was strong enough that the impact didn't even budge him. This was the first time that Grant actually felt *strong.* "…has the fabled three hundred and sixty-*sixth* Wielded Weapon, February Twenty Nine. He has the *Leap Sword*!"

"He's the one from the prophecy, I *know* it!" Freda's zealous declaration created rippling murmurs of discontent from the group. Clearly, no one believed that this was the truth. She whispered, "Go *on*, Grant. Show them."

Several people yelped in surprise and shrunk back as Grant reached for his sword. The steel sangas he unsheathed his

Wielded Weapon. He held either end of the Wielded Weapon and slowly walked forward, careful not to further antagonize the already skittish group. There was a collective gasp as the weapon's name glinted in the light. "It's true. He's the *one*! He has the legendary weapon of our people!"

Another of the group responded, "Not so fast. He could have killed the real Leap and stolen it from the corpse!"

Several people joined in on this voice, demanding Grant be bound while their questions were answered. Women and children cried in alarm at the sudden turn of events and screamed for people to calm down; Grant was still carrying naked steel. Finally, Marcus could bear it no longer. "Wait! We'll take him to Auld Leap; *he* will be able to confirm if Grant is a Leap or not! If he's not, he'll have to take a leap out of the sewers, sharing the fate of so many Leaps that came before us."

Grant looked around at the fearful people and rolled his eyes. He raised his sword, slamming it back into its sheath. If it came down to it, he would cut his way out of here, but he would play along for now. "I agree to your terms. Show me the way."

The faces around him held an equal mixture of hope and fear. If this was a ruse, their life would soon be over, but maybe… just *maybe*… he was the one they were waiting for? One whisper rang out through the room as he vanished into the tunnel.

"Is he really… *the* Leap?"

CHAPTER THIRTY-NINE

They descended a seemingly endless set of stone steps. "We must be under the castle by now. This is where you keep your *elder*? Seems kinda... damp."

"A bit to go yet." Marcus led him through a crack in the wall. It was a tough squeeze; Grant had to take off his backpack and crouch down to get through the opening.

"Where are we going?" He felt nervous now. No one lived down here. Perhaps Marcus was just looking for a quiet spot to dump his body? The orderly layout of the brick-lined sewers had given way to roughly hewn stone walls, indicating that they were no longer in the sewer system.

"You have to wear this now." Marcus took out a black cloth and folded it in half.

"I'm not wearing that. You want me to get lost down there, never find my way out? Gonna hit me on the head again when I can't see you?" Grant's hands twitched toward his Wielded Weapon, and Sarge responded with a tsunami of bloodlust, practically *begging* him to show these fools how weak they were.

"It's just for our protection! Regent, lad, what have you been through to make you so angry?" Seeing that his words were having no effect, Marcus sighed and spoke in a softer tone. "There are secrets down here that few *Leaps* are even aware of. If you don't know it exists, you can't give away the information if you are captured."

Grant huffed but accepted the face covering. He could feel his heart thumping in his chest as he gave away the little control he had over the situation. "At least hold onto me. If I slip here, I'll break a leg or worse."

Marcus guided Grant down the rough steps. Even so, he almost slipped a few times on the slimy, uneven surface. He could hear water dripping from the walls, and tried to keep track of all the twists and turns as they veered off down different paths, but quickly got confused. His fate was now firmly in Marcus's hands. "Are we almost there?"

"We're here now." Marcus unexpectedly took the cloth off, and Grant squinted into the darkness as he tried to get his bearings. From what he could tell, he was in a… cave? The torch light reflected off a pool of water in the center, but that was the only noticeable landmark.

"You can wait outside. Thank you, Marcus," a strange voice called. Marcus nodded, bowed toward the water, and quietly left.

Grant carefully scanned the area. Even with his higher cultivation achievement level, he couldn't tell where the voice was coming from. It sounded ancient, and rumbled like the rocks. "Is the cave talking to me? Is it alive?"

"What are you waiting on, Grant? Join me in the pool." Grant squinted again, barely able to make out a round, egg-shaped lump at the edge of the pool.

"I won't bite… hard." The voice chuckled, making Grant remember Madame Mercredi's strange habits. Perhaps being weird was just something that old people were prone to doing? Grant stepped forward until he could make out that the egg was in fact an ancient bald head covered with wrinkled folds of skin. The ancient man was submerged past his neck in the steaming water.

"I'm fine right where I stand, many thanks." The young man sniffed the strong odor of eggs that emanated from the water, finding not a single spark of interest for joining in. "Don't want to get my armor wet; it takes ages to dry."

"Grant, I wasn't *asking*. Remove your armor and join me. Clothing isn't permitted in the Pool of Foresight. Also, you stink! I can smell you right through the sulphur." Once more, Grant sighed at the memory of Madame Mercredi.

"I had an unfortunate crawl in the sewer earlier." He had evidently become accustomed to the stench of sewage. "I'm not taking a bath with a naked old dude. I just came to have a chat with Auld Leap—I assume you—and then I'll be on my way."

"You can leave if you wish. If you want to talk with me, to be accepted by our people, then you will join me in the pool." Grant sighed at the declaration and decided to just go along with the crazy old man. Maybe the water would wash away at least the surface layer of his stench. He supposed egg stink was better than… whatever was caked onto him. The backpack, armor, and sword clattered to the ground, the sound echoing around the chamber. Naked and wildly uncomfortable, he trudged directly into the water. As his foot broke the surface, a soothing feeling crept over him. Ripples of blue and white light emanated from the water as it was disturbed.

"Ahh…" A sigh escaped his lips as he sank into the inviting water. Bubbles fizzed and popped against his bare skin, effervescing until he was totally submerged. He floated in the comforting darkness. He didn't ever want to leave the bliss of the pool. His aches and pains faded away, along with his worries. Eventually he broke the surface to take a deep breath.

"You never forget your first time!" Auld Leap chuckled in the darkness. Grant sat on the opposite side of the pool, head bobbing above the surface. For a moment, he had almost forgotten the old man, but he tensed up at the reminder that he was somewhere he didn't want to be.

With a pop, a bubble broke the surface of the water. Grant stared at the bubble in horror, wondering where it had originated. Rather than dissipate, it broke free from the surface and floated upward. He stared into the rising bubble and squinted; he was sure he could see… himself? Not as he was now, but as a carefree child running through the fields.

The bubble popped, and he turned to view another of the curiosities. This time, he gasped as he witnessed himself lying in a pool of congealed blood, huge lacerations covering the entirety of his body. Maybe he was okay…? Then a dragon with a sword sticking out of its head belched fire; flames washed over his prone form… leaving behind only a pile of ash.

A third bubble appeared; this time, Grant was spinning and battling some unknown person wearing massive gauntlets. He wore an impressive-looking robe and moved with more speed and precision than he thought possible. The bubble-Grant let out a silent roar and drove his sword into the eye of a shocked… young woman? What in the world? The bubble popped, leaving Grant with more questions than answers. He was shaken, and looked at the old man with fearful eyes. "What was *that*?"

"Possibilities. Paths in the forks of prophecy." Auld Leap sounded serious for the first time. "You are in what was once a wonder created by Regent December himself, the person lauded as the most powerful Spatial Magic user. The man who created the barriers that split the very world."

"Will I… will I die from the claw or breath of a dragon? I saw myself turned to ash!"

"Possibly. There are an infinite number of paths, Grant. The decisions people make determine the fate of the world. Most choices have little impact on the direction of prophecy, but added together, they create a lever that can shift every single event through all of time. Whether you eat a donut or an apple for breakfast makes little difference in the grand scheme of things, though it may make a difference to your waistline!" Auld Leap cackled to himself, then let his face shift into stoic stillness as he locked eyes with Grant. "Other decisions, like picking up

February Twenty Nine, are critical nodes, ones where many paths converge and fork from."

"You believe me then? That I'm a Leap?"

"You *are* a Leap. Of that—and much more—I am sure. If you *weren't* a Leap, you would have died the moment your toe touched the water."

"*What*?" Grant struggled to get to his feet, but the old man didn't bother to calm him before speaking further.

"Leaps are special and rare, Grant. We contain a thread of magic which links us with the world, both the past and the future. Long ago, in a time before even the Wielder Wars, Leaps *ruled* the world of man. We harnessed and bent the power of this dimension to our will, the only people that could access *every* aspect of cultivation magic. We were the Timeless class of cultivators, a part of the world that faded and returned only after four years of recovery. We distilled the very essence of time into weapons; weapons that could enhance our powers and prowess to ever-greater heights. Using these shards of time, our cultivation ability soared… allowing us to achieve what used to take centuries in mere decades."

"Weapons?" Grant looked curiously at his sword. "You mean to tell me that some ancient Leaps created the Wielded Weapons?"

"With power often comes corruption. The Leap familia came to an end after a terrible tyrant was overthrown, a ruler who had created a sword representing the lost day. A weapon that could suppress even the most powerful weapons already in existence, and steal their power." Throughout Auld's story, he never reacted to Grant's agitation. "Those coming after... well, they attempted to erase all knowledge of Leaps from the collective memory. All records, every trace of the true abilities of Leaps, were wiped out and replaced with abject hatred and distrust of anything to do with us."

"This is unbelievable." Grant paused and looked at the old man suspiciously. "Really unbelievable. How do *you* know so much?"

"Knowledge in the wrong hands can be very dangerous, Grant. Those with power do whatever they can to hold on to it. If they realized what a Leap actually *was*, they would actively hunt and eradicate every last one of us, rather than settling for making our lives miserable for mere sport." The old man sighed and settled back with a content expression.

"I have spent my long life in this pool. Its power sustains me and grants answers. A thousand years ago, I was an intrepid explorer, searching the hidden halls and ancient sites that predated the Lords of the Months. Once the barrier was erected, I was stranded here. Back then, there wasn't a castle on the mound of stone above. The castle and its keep were built on the ruins of an ancient site, where the Regent had been testing his powers upon this pool. Even now, it holds a thousand *thousand* threads of prophecy. I do what little I can to influence events, including gathering what few Leaps I can to a place where they are safe, for now."

Grant's eyes lit up with understanding. "Did you lead *me* here?"

"No, Grant. You are in complete control of your own destiny. The path you follow is beyond my power to control. I can only observe." The old man smiled softly. "After February Twenty Nine chose you, all of the prophecies related to you went dark. I'm now blind to what happens next, though apparently, *you* can still see glimpses of what awaits you. Prepare well."

"This is a lot to take in. I'm just an orphan Leap that worked on a farm-"

The mutterings of the young man were cut off as Auld Leap splashed him in the face with the miraculous treasure of water they were immersed in. The sheer disrespect for the historic magic shocked Grant as much as an old man splashing him did. "Will you *help* us, Grant?"

"I don't know… if I can?"

"For us, for the people you have known, and never knew," the old man intoned, refusing to look away from Grant, no matter how the young man squirmed under the heavy gaze, "will you take a Leap of Faith?

Quest Notification: Leap of Faith (Epic)

Information: Leaps are downtrodden and despised throughout January. Will you risk it all to help Leapkind? Please note: not accepting this quest will result in the status quo being maintained. Leaps will continue living life as they are,

Reward: Liberation of all Leapkind. Exalted status with Leaps. 20% discount on all Leap goods. Other rewards are possible based on completion method.

Failure: A deep disgust and hatred for every Leap inserted into the hearts of the citizens across the District of January via propaganda. You will likely be the sole Leap enjoying freedom.

Accept / Decline

"So, if I accept the quest and fail, every Leap will probably die. If I decline, they get to survive. This doesn't sound like a good deal to me? At least they'd get to *live*-"

"This isn't living, Grant. This is surviving. Hidden in the sewers, searching through garbage to find the scraps that are wasted by others? We were once a proud and powerful people. I know how you were treated. Before you picked up February Twenty Nine, I lived your memories. If you successfully complete this quest, life for all Leaps will improve."

"I… I don't know." If he failed, he'd be responsible for the genocide of an entire people, his people, even if indirectly responsible. Would Grant help the other Leaps, young and old, at least to have the option of chasing their dreams? Should he risk everything that they had, for some rewards for himself? Wasn't accepting this incredibly self-serving?

"Take your time, child. But if you take too long in your deliberations, you'll miss the tournament!" Auld Leap laughed, then scooped water onto his wrinkled visage to moisturize his skin.

Grant had no time to think through every possible outcome of this quest. He needed an answer, now. "I accept this quest that has no instructions or clear path forward. I hope you are doing right by these people that trust you. I understand the consequences of failure, and I *also* hope that you didn't just force me to sentence an entire class of people to their deaths."

"Lovely! Now, get out and take those stinking clothes with you! A thousand years, I waited for you in this puddle. Prophecy didn't tell me that you'd smell of feces!" The old man laughed as he sent splash after splash toward Grant to chase him away. Ignoring the strange man, Grant got up and found himself *stuffed* with energy, his body unbelievably reinvigorated. "Remember, lad, there are thousands of paths forward… but only *one* will result in a desirable outcome for *everyone*."

Grant almost fell back into the pool in shock. "You could have told me that *before* I accepted the quest! What do I need to do? How do I complete the quest?"

"Give you *answers*?" Auld Leap chuckled at the thought. "Where would be the fun in that? Good luck, Grant! You'll need it."

CHAPTER FORTY

"It has been confirmed by Auld Leap. Grant is our savior!" Marcus bellowed as they stepped into the large living area which the Leaps had claimed for themselves. The room burst into cheers, with whoops and cries of happiness.

"That's *not* what he said!" Grant snapped at him, but Marcus and the others were too busy celebrating to notice.

"This calls for a feast!" a lady from the crowd announced. She was met with cheers and clapping. Grant sat and watched as people fussed around, preparing the large table. He assumed they would bring out some old scraps and morsels. He was hungry, but he didn't think he was hungry enough to eat plague rat.

In between hugs, handshakes, and pats on the back, the bodies moved around in formation, apparently with prearranged roles. A short while later, steaming bowls of rich stew, roast joints of meat, numerous types of potatoes, and a mountain of desserts came out. The variety rivaled that of Sir Friday's epic banquets, and may have even eclipsed it. Grant didn't recognize half the dishes that were brought out on steaming platters.

"From the castle. We managed to sneak in and steal a couple of old chef's outfits from the laundry room." Freda, who had become something of a celebrity for 'finding' the 'savior', offered him an easy explanation. "Every few days, we use those to go load up, but it's always a dangerous task."

"How do the outfits help?" Grant wondered with a frown.

"One of the outfits has been modified with lots of hidden pockets. Chefs can be rather large, and so are their clothes! When we waddle out, heavily laden with food, no one bats an eyelid. We just look like another obese chef, after all." Freda chuckled darkly, letting a hint of mischief show. "No one ever trusts a skinny cook, so it works out well."

Hope sparked in Grant's eyes. "Can I borrow one, or buy it off you?"

Marcus jumped into the conversation. "We'd really love to give it to you, but they're the only way we can get food these days. Only one has been modified to store food. The other wouldn't fit you. If we lost the modified one, we might not eat for *days*."

Grant sighed as he realized that his status as 'savior' only went as far as their next meal. These people, no matter their surnames, were typical Januarians. "I understand. You'd all starve. I wouldn't want that, but I do *need* to get into the castle for the exhibition tournament tomorrow if I'm going to get a chance to defeat Lord January. I guess… I have a scarf I can wrap my head in? I'll get through that…?"

"I wouldn't do that, if I were you!" Marcus barged into the conversation again when he heard what Grant was planning. "Security at the tournament will be stringent. They don't just let anyone wander in, especially not while Lord January is in residence."

"I have a problem, then. If I can't get past the guards, then I won't be able to fight in the tournament or defeat Lord January." Grant locked eyes with them, or tried to, but they kept looking away. He said nothing else, simply letting them come to their own conclusions.

"Well... after the feast, you can come to the castle with Marcus and I. We'll have to restock the pantry, and if we're lucky, we'll be able to find an outfit in your size from the laundry room!" Freda offered excitedly.

"All you think about are those silly *clothes*, Freda!" Marcus groaned at her offer, getting a not-very-playful smack in return.

"My *silly* clothing ideas are the only thing keeping us *fed*!" she huffed at him, clearly continuing a sore-spot argument they had hashed out many times.

Marcus ignored her warning. "Aren't you worried we'll get caught, or they'll miss the loss of yet *another* outfit? Seems too risky to me."

"What other choice do we have? If we don't replenish our stores, we'll starve. There are so many chefs, they won't miss a *single* outfit. As for the Nobles? They'll be busy feasting and partying. No one pays any attention to the army of chefs and servants running around. We'll go *tonight*. Come with us, Grant. You'll have to be careful while we sneak in the servant's entrance, but maybe you can just hide behind us."

"Won't people see our faces; our names?" Grant waved above her head, where her name was clearly displayed.

"We've thought of that. We wear oversized chef's hats and wear face masks. Lord January hates the system that kept him from becoming the Calendar King, so it's mandatory that all chefs and servers wear masks. If he doesn't *have* to be reminded of the system, like with Nobles, he does his best to ignore it."

Grant watched the group of Leaps enjoy their feast. People laughed, ate, and drank, resulting in singing and much merriment. He listened to the conversations and almost had to leave out of sheer shame. One woman was thrilled about the prospect of owning her own home, above ground, where she would wake up and be able to see the sun every morning. That was one of the *least* hopeful of the conversations, but with every passing moment, he was reminded of the fact that all of these hopes were all pinned on *him*.

He had to save them all for any of their dreams to come

true. That thought killed his appetite, which was just fine by him, for two reasons. First, he didn't want to anger Sarge, and secondly… it just didn't feel right devouring the last of their food. There was plenty of healthy food to satisfy his hunger. Frankly, if they all ate like him, the sheer excess would last them a full week of three meals a day.

He knew better than to say something like that. He had learned his lesson with Skinny: a thousand years of effort had made society the way it was right now. These people accepted him for who he was, and he was one of them. Yet… even now, the only way they would allow themselves to be saved was if he didn't cause too much of a change in their daily lives.

"This entire society needs to be torn down and rebuilt from the ground up." Grant finally understood what Sarge had explained to him weeks ago. His words held no heat. No anger. Only the purest disappointment.

**Bwapp!*

The laziest of trumpet calls signaled the start of Second Supper, since no one would be outside to actually hear the traditional clarion call.

"That's our signal to move," Marcus motioned for Grant to start walking. The man himself was dressed as an obese chef with a puffy white hat that had been dropping and covering his eyes since they started their trip. As they got closer to their destination, he started to sweat, making the hat stick to his skin and finally stop slipping.

"Let's go." Freda led the way wearing a similar outfit, but without hidden compartments. She pushed on a stone slab above their heads, which wobbled but didn't move. "Grant, give me a hand here."

Grant squeezed in beside her at the end of the tunnel. With a shove, the stone moved fully, scraping on the ground overhead. The last vestiges of sunset illuminated the tunnel as they exited the sewer one by one. He found himself in an old graveyard. Broken tombstones dotted the ground, along with more elaborate tombs for the wealthy. "Roll it back over, Grant."

He obliged the weary lady. As he shoved the stone, he realized that it was a headstone, belonging to a Marjory Wednesday. He read the inscription as he pushed.

Marjory Wednesday. Born 4th August 944 AB. Died 4th August 974 AB.

Wife, mother, chocolate lover. Chocolate Cake was her love, needing to breathe was her final downfall.

<Hey, Grant. Notice anything about *every single* tombstone here?> That was the only clue Grant was going to get out of him until he put in some effort.

As his eyes passed over the graves, he noted that every single one of them mentioned something about the way the person had died. Nearly all of them were 'accidental', but not a single one was from old age. "The inscriptions are lies, aren't they?"

<Utter lies.> Sarge confirmed with a combination of anger at the truth and pride in Grant. <Likely Lord January doesn't allow people to know the truth of how their consumption lifestyle kills them off.>

"Move it, Grant," Marcus whispered sharply as Grant fell into thought. "No time for daydreaming."

The streets and narrow alleyways were deserted. Grant stayed close as they rapidly closed in on their target, eventually coming upon a wooden door. When they paused a moment too long for comfort, Grant quizzed them, "What are we waiting on?"

"Waiting for the door to open," Marcus muttered around light gasping.

"How long will that be? I could be *spotted*!" Grant hissed at the man.

"Shouldn't be too long." Freda tried to placate him.

Long minutes passed, and footsteps closed in on them from down the alleyway. Grant could tell by the marching of the boots that they were most likely House Tuesday Peacekeepers. "We need to leave-"

The door swung open, and out stumbled a drunk Noble wearing voluminous pants and ruffled shirt. He nodded, and stumbled onwards with blurry eyes, eventually dropping his pants and leaning against the wall across from them.

"Halt!" A Peacekeeper bellowed at the man. "Public urination is against the law! *Ugh*! Why is it *green*?"

Grant and the disguised Leaps took the opportunity to slip in the door before it clicked shut. As it did, Grant couldn't help but laugh as he watched the inebriated Noble wave his 'weapon' at the guards. "I thought you said only servants used this entrance?"

"Um… usually." Marcus clearly wasn't in a talkative mood. "That fellow must have somehow found his way down here."

Grant followed Freda and Marcus through the mostly vacant hallways. A few times, he had to hide behind their bulky chef's outfits as servants scurried past, heavily laden with either full or empty platters of food.

"Here we are. The laundry room. Let's go." Freda turned the handle… but the door wouldn't budge.

"Freda," Marcus pointed at a shiny lock, "those bolts are new!"

"Oh, no… sorry, Grant. It looks like they've stepped up security since we were last here. Maybe they *did* notice the missing uniforms, after all."

"I'm sure we can find another way in." Though Grant tried to sound confident, he was anything but. The familiar sound of marching footsteps echoed along the hallway, and he froze in place. He could make a run for it, but the noise would bring more guards. He could fight his way out… he gripped the hilt of February Twenty Nine tightly.

The sword was as ready as always… but all he could picture

was Count Tuesday's accusatory eyes staring at him as the life went out of them. If he had to spill more blood, he would, but… once their bodies were discovered, the castle would be completely locked down. With a killer in the castle, the exhibition tournament could be postponed or canceled.

He couldn't risk losing his chance against Lord January.

Freda placed a hand on his just as he gripped the hilt. She shook her head, warning him not to unsheathe his sword. "Marcus… give him your outfit."

Marcus was already on it. Grant frantically shook his head in protest, knowing that Marcus was sacrificing himself. He threw the outfit at Grant, who—with no other choice—quickly donned the outfit, finishing it off with the puffy white hat and face mask.

The footsteps thundered in his ears. House Tuesday Peacekeepers rounded the corner, startled by coming across the group. The guard nodded and made to continue his rounds. "Oh, sorry. Didn't see you there."

"*Wait*! What do we have here? An almost naked, filthy *Leap*!" The last words were shouted, since they were almost drowned out by the ringing of weapons being drawn.

"We found it wandering the corridors in search of food," Freda answered the accusation quietly. "We were on our way to find someone to take it off our hands."

"Would you believe it…? A Leap, *here*, in our very walls. You'll have some questions to answer before you make the leap! We'll take it from here, chef. Good work." One of the House Tuesday guards planted a fist in Marcus's gut, and he doubled over in pain. Grant went to pull on the sword behind his back, but stopped after catching Freda's piercing stare.

They watched helplessly as Marcus was dragged along the corridor.

"By Lord January's beneficent bounty!" One of the guards shouted. "Double rations for catching a Leap in a place we can legally get rid of him! This might even mean a spot at Lord January's table? What do you think?"

"Let's go." Grant took charge, since Freda looked like she was on the verge of a breakdown. He needed to find a key, get a spare uniform, then find a way to save Marcus.

They hurried along the halls as quickly as they could without causing a scene, but each carpeted hallway looked exactly like the last.

"Don't worry; I've been here many times before," Freda announced, steel coming into her voice as she noticed Grant slowing down in confusion. They approached the duo of men joking and laughing, and Grant peeked around the corner to see the two men sitting, playing cards and eating.

An iron ring hung from one of the men's belts, a ring heavy with keys.

Grant tapped Freda's shoulder. "I'll go whack them on the head, then take the key. We can tie them up, and they'll be fine. A headache tomorrow, but-"

"*No*, Grant." Freda's voice was hard but also resigned.

"You can't sneak up on them, Freda. Even if you did manage to get behind them unnoticed, you couldn't-"

"Be quiet and stay *here*." She gave him a look that locked him in place, then walked forward. Grant watched helplessly as she approached the guards.

"Hey, who goes there?" The guard continued to munch on his sandwich while observing the chef closing in on him.

"Random Chef Number Five, sir. I really need your help!" Freda's acting was so good that Grant assumed she might have a high-leveled skill in acting.

"Huh. We're kinda busy right now. Guarding prisoners behind the door and such." He pointed to the steel door. "What do you need, citizen?"

"Chef is going crazy. Another Random Chef spilled soup down the front of his uniform." Freda's voice wavered at the end, not needing to hide the fear she was actually feeling right now.

The guard grimaced. "I wouldn't want to upset Chef

Gordon. He'll give you a good tongue bashing before a real beating! I don't see how *we* can help…?"

Freda leaned forward on their table invitingly. "Well… I need a favor. I need access to the laundry to pick up a new outfit for him."

Even though she was being as enticing as possible, the guard was shaking his head as soon as he heard the word 'laundry'. "No one is allowed access, I'm afraid. Not after a couple of uniforms went missing."

"Billy, Joel," she looked at both the guards, "I can make sure you're both allocated one of the best seats for the exhibition tournament tomorrow. After Lord January, I'll make sure you'll get first dibs at all the juiciest cuts of meat!"

Both gulped, licking their lips, but Joel's eyes narrowed right after. "Tempting… but I don't know. For all we know, you could be trying to con us!"

"If you can't trust a chef," Freda breathed huskily, "who *can* you trust?"

Grant gripped February Twenty Nine tightly, ready to charge in if things suddenly went south. Joel started to stand, reaching for a cudgel. "Why don't you show us what's under that mask and hat?"

"It's okay, Joel." Billy raised his hand to stop the other guard. "I'm sure it's fine. Anyway, I want a *really* good seat tomorrow, don't you?"

"I disagree… but as senior guard, the decision rests with you." Joel scoffed as Billy turned his eyes back onto Freda.

"Yeah, whatever." Billy eyed Freda, currently disguised as Random Chef Number Five, and pulled out a key. "Take this. If you're not back here in twenty minutes, we'll come looking for you. If we need to come find you, I'll throw you in with a Leap!"

"I'll be back in *ten*." Freda shuddered, apparently the correct response, grabbed the key and waddled back along the corridor in the bulky disguise. Around the corner, she collapsed against the wall and mopped her forehead. "He's… he's trapped in *there*?"

"Are you okay?" Grant's concern was waved away as Freda remembered their goal.

"We don't have time to chat. This key," she held up the shiny brass key, "must be back on the ring in under twenty minutes."

The chefs hurried along the hallways as fast as their bulky outfits would allow. To any observers, they just looked like any other chefs, rushing to fulfill the whims of the Nobles. Freda shoved the key in the lock, but it wouldn't budge. "It's the *wrong key*? That son of *Winter*!"

"Pause. Give it to me." She dropped the key into Grant's hand, while her own were shaking with the stress of having her husband locked up. He pushed the key in the lock and *gently* turned it. The lock clicked as the internal bolts opened. Inside, row upon row of clean white linen was hung to dry. Massive tablecloths that would eventually grace the banquet tables, huge bins of soiled tablecloths, and finally: the desired uniforms, which sat to the side. "Should I grab one of these?"

"No. If a high level chef or kitchen manager sees you wearing a soiled outfit, they'll make you strip and change immediately. They're proud of their role within the castle, and they're incredibly fastidious. The preparation and delivery of food is a sacred art, and being caught wearing a soiled uniform is a serious offense."

They searched frantically until they found one that fit him. He struggled out of the modified outfit and donned the new one, though it was huge and hung limply around his too-thin-for-society body. Freda shook her head and reached out, "Let me help you stuff it with cloth and linen."

When they were done, Grant finally resembled a properly obese chef. "Let's go."

"Hat and mask!"

Grant snatched them on the way out, then hurried back along

the hallway. He was profusely sweating, overwhelmed by the vast quantity of material surrounding his body. The modified uniform was light as a feather in comparison. He didn't know how, but the Leaps had managed to create compartments that didn't collapse when empty, maintaining the illusion of an obese chef. They were panting heavily by the time they returned to the guards and handed over the key. Grant had forgotten to hide around the corner.

"One minute to spare; we were about to come after you!" Billy grinned at them over his now-more-substantial pile of poker chips. It seemed as though the cards had been on his side. "Who's this?"

"Random Chef Number Seven, sir!" Grant instantly and monotonously replied.

"What's that in your arms? That isn't *one* uniform!" He pointed at the uniform bulked up by all its hidden compartments.

Grant and Freda shared a look. There was no way to hide the modified uniform now. Freda didn't stop Grant as his hand went for his sword, but she did grab the outfit and present the bulky clothing. "This is a new innovation, straight out of the laundry engineers' workshop!"

"Laundry… engineers?" The guards scratched at their heads as they tried to determine if she was messing with them or not.

Freda nodded vigorously, and Grant's hand slowly relaxed off of the hilt of his sword. "Oh, yes. They work day and night on creating new, innovative outfits. This one, for example, has hidden compartments for storing meals!"

"What use is that?" Joel stood up to examine the outfit, his piggy eyes scanning the entire cloth monstrosity.

"It's *obvious*, isn't it?" Freda tittered as though the guards were being intentionally obtuse to flirt with her. "A chef can only carry two platters of food safely! With this outfit, they can carry up to *ten* full platters!"

"Wow!" Billy poked at the material, near slack-jawed over the beauty of this magnificent garment. "It makes the chefs more efficient? They can carry more food and need to make less trips? It's... *genius*!"

"Before we forget, here's the key." Freda plopped the key into Billy's open palm. "I'll prepare premier seats for you fine gentlemen by Lord January's table. I might even be able to swing seats next to the big man himself!"

"Did you hear that, Joel? *Premier* seats!" Billy laughed and slapped his partner on his beefy shoulder.

Joel glowered at his boss, though he couldn't stop a smile from creasing his chins. "Yeah, yeah. You got lucky this time, like you did with the cards."

Grant and Freda took the opportunity to sneak off as Joel dealt another hand. Grant started chuckling as he pulled a face at his partner in crime. "Laundry engineers' workshop?"

"There could be one. It sounds like something that should exist!" Freda's serious tone only made Grant laugh harder. When they were finally clear, he stopped and presented the outfit to Freda. "Take this back to the sewers. I don't want to run into anyone else and risk having to explain 'laundry engineers' as well as you did."

<Their mental cultivation is probably a single digit,> Sarge sadly added.

Freda looked at the outfit, then back at Grant with a tearful expression. "But... I want to help. We still need to get Marcus back!"

He pressed the bulky uniform into her arms. "Our people can't afford to lose this. I'll get Marcus back, don't worry."

"Please find my husband, and... be careful." Accepting the situation with as much grace as possible, Freda gave him a quick hug and waddled off without looking back. Grant was alone again, but he didn't feel quite so confident without Freda's calming presence and knowledge of the castle's layout.

To calm himself, he tore open the interior of the chef uniform, making sure that his sword was ready to be drawn in an instant. It was time to get in position.

CHAPTER FORTY-ONE

Grant fumbled along yet another hallway that looked almost exactly like all the rest. At least this one had a portrait of Lord January to use as a marker, and if his memory served, that meant he was near the cells. Straining his ears, he confirmed his position when Billy declared, "I win again! Another game, Joel? I haven't taken *next* month's pay off you yet!"

"Forget it. Let's just do our rounds." A reinforced chair scraped as the guards started to get up. Grant didn't want to be questioned again. Once was more than enough, but a second time wandering the same stretch of hall would look suspicious. Grant recalled the Leaps talking about hidden passages during dinner, and that servants used them to zip between wings or floors in the castle keep.

He lifted back the painting looking for a switch or lever, but there was nothing. As footsteps approached, he headed in the other direction. Looking back, he tripped on a fold in the carpet. Tumbling to the ground, he tried to get up. In the outfit stuffed with linen, he felt like a turtle stuck on its back. He grabbed at a torch and used it to pull himself to his feet.

It clicked.

"Winter's son, I broke it. Someone..."

A section of the wall slid open. He wordlessly darted inside and pushed the false wall closed. Standing in the darkness, he heard muffled voices pass by on the other side of the wall. All was quiet a moment later, and he almost slumped in relief. Grant started feeling his way along the walls in the darkness, more than once having to stifle a sneeze from the disturbed dust. It seemed this particular path was not used very often, or at all.

By the time he finally found signs of habitation, he had gone up three flights of stairs. This certainly wasn't the way to the jail, but at this point, there was no way to find his way back. The faint sound of muffled voices drew his attention, and he was extra-careful not to make a sound. If he could hear them, they could hear him.

At this point, Grant had to move sideways due to the bulk of the stuffed outfit—likely why this tunnel was unused. He considered taking it off, but if he got lost in here, he'd likely never find it again. Then he'd *really* have a problem getting into the exhibition tournament in the morning.

Grant pressed his eye against a narrow gap and spied a meaty fist bedecked in familiar jeweled rings. He lifted his gaze to find the familiar face of Randall and gasped.

Randall's eyes darted around. "What was that?"

"I didn't hear anything, my Lord. It was probably just a rat." The familiar voice made Grant feel sick, especially as the conversation continued.

"Thank you for this information; it is more important than you'll ever know." Randall took a drink from a crystal glass and smacked his lips. "Once I inform Lord January, you will be known as *Sir* Skinny!"

"It would be an *honor*, sir." Skinny smiled as he too took a gulp of fine wine. "I *knew* there was something wrong with that brat. When he joked about being a Leap? It's never done."

Grant was nauseous. Skinny was here, sharing information with *Randall*, of all people? Try as he might, he couldn't understand *how* either of these men had come to be here. The last time he had seen Randall was back at the estate near New Dawn, and he had vanished during the fight with Sir Thirty-First. He thought back; Randall had often vanished, sometimes for months at a time, and had more money than his estate should produce. What was his actual role in the District?

"I *hate* Leaps," Skinny continued with a snarl. "To think I trusted him, *helped* him, even! I don't do this for the title; it's the right and just thing to do. Any honest Januarian would do the same."

Grant's head spun from the repercussions of what he was listening to. Skinny had betrayed him, and Randall now knew he was here.

"Quite right," Randall murmured contentedly while sipping on his beverage.

"Those *sympathizers*," spat Skinny, "were helping him intentionally, despite *knowing* what he was!"

"Don't worry. They'll be dealt with tomorrow, along with the Leap that was caught this evening." Randall promised darkly, spitting flecks of red wine over his oversized bib. "What a feast it will be! Come, Skinny. Or should I call you *Sir* Skinny, now?"

Grant watched the laughing pair leave the room, his heart breaking at the thought of Skinny betraying not only him, but his friends. For what? A title and a seat at Lord January's table. More than that, it bothered Grant that *Randall* was somehow here at Castle January.

Not knowing what to do, he found a wide spot in the passageway and resigned himself to an uncomfortable sleep on the dusty floor. The fluffy uniform offered a decent bed, and soon, he sank into troubled dreams.

It felt like only a moment had passed when trumpeting wrenched him from the grasp of nightmares. The cacophony signaled that the exhibition tournament was about to begin, and the spectators needed to take their seats.

"I overslept! I'll never get near the front now." He squeezed along the dark passageway, savagely pushing on every panel until one finally clicked. He landed next to a passing chef, who glanced at him with a critical gaze.

"You better clean yourself up. If the Head Chef spots you looking like *that*," the chef sneered as he pointed to Grant's dust-coated uniform, "you'll be punished severely. Especially *today*, of all days! What were you thinking, using the back passages?"

"Couldn't get through the crowd," Grant lied easily, wondering when it had become so effortless. He cringed as he remembered trying to convince a group of Vassals that his blood-coated sword had been used to scoop jam. Luckily, the chef had already taken off, scurrying through the hallway. "Regent's sword, I'm going to miss the event!"

Token in hand and disguised, panic still threatened to overwhelm him. Grant forced himself to take a moment and calm down. He watched a stream of servants, chefs, and Nobility pass. They all appeared to be going in the same direction, so he went with the flow, following the crowd down a flight of stairs. Along with the bustling swarm, he soon spilled out of the main entrance to the keep. People patiently lined up, waving tickets and wearing their finest clothes.

He did his best to dust off the uniform and wipe away the cobwebs. Bypassing the queue, Grant followed the other chefs and waiters. As a chef, he was waved through. Vassals of House Tuesday were arguing with the guards. "Come on, let us in. We're House Tuesday! Can't you see that?"

"I'm sorry, sir. Without your Vassal Weapon, we'll have to manually verify that each of you are who you say you are."

"How long will that take?" the Vassal sulked but stood to the side. "We'll miss the exhibition tournament. More importantly, the feast!

"Rules are rules. If you are really House Tuesday Vassals, you should *know* that." The guard glared at them, turning suspicious as he finished speaking.

"After Count Tuesday was murdered, we lost access to our power," a second Vassal whined.

"That's a real shame, but I still can't let you in without being able to prove who you are. Any more of this, and you can spend the day cooling off in a cell!" The guard's bellow drew attention, helping Grant merge with the line of chefs. Soon, he could no longer make out what the Vassals were saying.

A shadow fell over Grant. "What are you standing there for? Get over to the kitchen and help with starters!"

Grant looked up and tried not to panic as he saw the name boldly appear over the man speaking to him. Head. Chef. Gordon. The terrifying man loomed over him. "Your uniform…! If I didn't need all hands on deck, I'd have you *flogged*!"

"Yes, chef! Sorry, chef!" Grant scampered off in the direction of the kitchen. He wanted to take a seat close to the arena, but that plan had just gone out the window. The kitchen was a hive of activity as various chefs barked out orders in between plating dishes, frying, boiling, stewing, and roasting. The noise and heat within the suit was making his head spin. Grant felt like he would pass out at any minute.

He had to get out of there.

"What are you standing around for?" a chef snapped through his mask. "Take these eggs and make equal quantities of scrambled, poached, and boiled eggs." Grant stared down at the basket of eggs. He didn't have time for this. "Are you deaf or just slow?"

"Sorry." Sweat dripped down his forehead and nipped at his eyes. "It's my first day."

"First day or not, get to work, or it will be your *last* day! Ovens are over there, and you can heat up the water. Or is that too much for a *chef* on their *first day*?" The chef mocked him mercilessly. Grant went in the general direction the chef pointed, knocking into people and covering his uniform in tomato sauce.

Arriving at the range, Grant dumped all of the eggs into a

pot of water that was already at a roiling boil. The chef that had mocked him rushed over with a banshee-esque screech. "What are you *doing*? You really *are* dense, aren't you! I said to make *different types* of eggs. This lot is ruined!"

"I… I… I have to go." Grant stormed past the chef, who stared at the young man incredulously.

"Hey, come back! You'll never be able to keep a job if you give up right away!" The chef's tone was completely different from even a moment before.

Grant stopped. He knew the chef was right. Plus, if he left without a valid reason to be away from the kitchen, he'd be forced back here. "Sorry… it's all a bit much for me. I was hired from Sir Thirty-First's estate after my lord was killed, and it's my first time cooking in such a grand kitchen."

"Oh… I heard about that." The chef sighed and rubbed his sweaty neck. "Lord January sure is kind, trying to ensure that his supporters don't go without. You must have been through a lot to get here in time for the feast, and if you are just not up to proper cooking right now, get over here and work as my sous chef."

"I need forty pounds of these julienned for various stews and platters." Grant watched intently as the chef expertly diced and cut vegetables to add to a dish, then stepped in and started masterfully chopping the vegetables twice as fast as the chef had just demonstrated. Unsurprisingly, he was an expert at using bladed weapons to create perfect cuts by now.

"Would you look at *that*! You have some skills after all." The chef laughed as he watched Grant fly through the task. "That should take you at least an hour; I'll have someone running them to me. Hopefully you will be ready for the day, once you get your head on straight!"

Grant got light-headed as he chopped. The fat suit was unbearable; combining that with the heat of the kitchens… he felt like he would collapse at any moment. He could only hope that he would last long enough to get close to his target.

CHAPTER FORTY-TWO

"La~a~adies and *gentlemen*! Welcome to the exhibition tournament, to honor the generous Lord January; he who provides for all! This event is sponsored in part by Big Betty's Bakery, the premier bakery in Mid January," the announcer called out to the excited crowd. Fists pumped the air and cheers erupted throughout the massed spectators. Grant stood gawping at the throngs of people that had gathered. In his mind, 'thousands' of people meant nothing, but looking at it was enough to make his palms sweaty.

"What are you waiting for? Put the appetizers on the belt and get some more. There is no time to dawdle!" Grant plonked the dishes down on the conveyor belt and watched as the dishes snaked their way toward fat, grasping fingers. The first fingers to snatch greedily at the starters were Lord January's, followed by his entourage and Grant's obese former friend, Skinny. Grant could see his smug grin from here as he eagerly stuffed his face with the delicious treats. The betrayal stabbed deep into his heart. Still…

Not as deep as he planned to stab his sword in return.

"Get a move on! You're holding everybody up." An irate

server stood behind Grant. "Why are you even out here? Chefs should be in the kitchen, cooking. The clue is in the *name*."

"Would the competitors in the semi-final of the exhibition tournament please come forward and present their token to the panel of judges."

"Winter's bite, *I* should be down there now." From where he was standing, there was no clear path to the fighting pit; not in the oversized outfit, at least.

"Get back in the kitchen!" a deep voice demanded. He recognized it as Chef Gordon. "Don't make me warn you again—what have you *done* to your uniform!"

Grant rushed back to the kitchen in the suffocating outfit. In the next moment, he was expected to squeeze in alongside the other chefs and get to work. Pots bubbled and pans sizzled. The smells of delicious aromas infused the air. Grant licked his lips behind the face mask. His stomach rumbled as a reminder that he hadn't eaten anything today. He looked around, and when no one was looking, popped a few morsels from one of the starters into his mouth.

A shudder of pleasure shook his body, taste buds reveling in the unique combination of ingredients. He purposefully chose a healthy dish, not wanting to upset Sarge, but it was still *delicious*. Grant shook his head while savoring the flavors; he'd come to think of the mental construct as a real person that had real feelings.

Someone bumped into him and whispered, "I wouldn't do that again if I were you. If you're caught, you'll be *severely* punished. Wait till after the tournament is over. Chef Gordon will allow us to feast on the leftovers."

All Grant could do was nod. The chef could have easily reported him for nibbling on the starter. Rather than preparing the next course, he picked up another starter and made a beeline for the conveyor belt. He placed the dish down. Looking up, many in the audience were grumbling, and Grant could see why. The peasants in particular had to wait until the lords and ladies closest to Lord January had their fill before the dishes snaked their way to the lower classes in society.

"What are you doing out here again, chef?" Chef Gordon boomed across at Grant. He glanced around and spotted the head chef, whose fists were trembling. His face was beet red, and Grant knew that he was in serious trouble for breaching the kitchen rules for a second time.

"We only have three competitors coming forward for the semi-final," the announcer called out to the crowd. Dishes were finally making their way to the worst seats, calming the peasants. They were too busy stuffing their faces to complain about the poor view. "If the final competitor doesn't come forward, then the remaining contestants will face each other, with the winner of two bouts being crowned the champion."

A meaty fist clamped down on his shoulder. "You're coming with me, boy. I will teach you how to show respect.

"Stop." Grant's feet barely touched the floor as the powerful Chef Gordon dragged him back toward the kitchens and away from the arena. The head chef wouldn't listen, and instead clamped down harder.

"As punishment… you'll wash all the dishes after the tournament, by yourself!"

"What? That'll take days!" He was surprised by the penalty, having expected to be beaten or imprisoned instead.

"*Seven* days, if you do it efficiently and only take short naps."

"Oh no! Look!" Grant didn't have seven days to wait. "Over there. A giant rat!"

"Where? Not in *my* kitchen!" The fist loosened its grip as Chef Gordon's eyes darted around, hunting for the creepy crawly vermin.

Grant wriggled free and made a run for it. "My mistake; must have been a meatball rolling to the floor!"

"Hey, come back here!" Chef Gordon grabbed for him, but he'd already darted away. "Chefs aren't allowed to compete!"

"I'm not a chef," he called back, showing a rude gesture to the fuming head chef. Grant barreled into a Noble lady, struggling to move in the cumbersome suit. The lady face planted into a bowl of soup. "I know it's delicious, but you should try using a spoon!"

Grant barreled through the seated crowd, met with shouts and a shower of food tossed in his direction. He didn't have time to worry about anyone's hurt feelings or soiled clothes. In a flash, he stood on a table, tipping over a dish and catapulting the contents over startled front row spectators. Grant vaulted the low railing and attempted to land gracefully on the sand of the fighting pit… but instead crashed, then rolled, before finally coming to a halt against the wall.

"What is the *meaning* of this?" the announcer bellowed. "Chefs are not permitted inside the fighting pit. Present yourself to your superior *immediately* for disciplinary action!"

Grant, lying on his back, rocked his body back and forth and finally gained enough momentum to stand upright in the almost spherical fat suit.

"I'm *not* a chef!" He ripped off his face mask and threw the hat to the ground. Gasps went up in waves as the spectators realized who they were looking at.

"It's Grant Friday! The murderer is here!" a House Tuesday Peacekeeper bellowed, struggling to stand as he waved a drumstick as though it were his personal weapon. The audience cheered, enjoying the entertainment that accompanied their meal. To them, it was all part of a well-orchestrated show.

Grant looked around at the startled faces and over at Lord January's table. By the massive monarch's side, draped in chains, sat Sir Friday Twenty-Ninth, who had a grin on his face at the surprising turn of events. Grant wished he could save the man that had helped him, but right now, there was nothing that he could do.

"I have a *token*!" He fished out the golden token and held it up high for all to see. This brought another wave of gasps from the onlookers. They had to fan themselves to stave off meat-sweats brought on from over excitement. "I earned my place here, and anyone who tries to stop me is breaking the law!"

CHAPTER FORTY-THREE

While Grant struggled out of the fat suit, the judges conducted a heated debate. "This is *most* unorthodox."

"He's a *murderer*!" shouted one of the other competitors, a House Tuesday Vassal. "You can't let him compete!"

The announcer sighed dramatically and pushed his plate to the side. "We must check the rule book for direction in these unusual circumstances."

"*That* massive thing?"

Grant eyed the other two competitors that waited in the sandy arena with him. "Where's the final person?"

Looking somewhat nervous to find themselves next to a known murderer, the nearest contestant stated, "Last year's champion is allowed to participate in the feast until the exhibition tournament begins."

"They want to eat before fighting?" Grant shook his head at the thought. Someone was going to get *very* sick during this battle.

Uncomfortable, and becoming more so as he talked to the strange man, the Vassal gave Grant a funny look. "Everyone knows that food gives energy, and the greater the amount of food consumed, the larger the advantage bestowed. The champion always has a *huge* advantage over the others."

The other fighter stepped close, only wanting to be in the same space as Grant so he could shout. "Count Tuesday was a great man! His reforms reduced crime throughout the entirety of January! To think he was killed by a skinny beggar like *you*!"

The Vassal's screech was cut off by the squealing of a cart. Competitors and the audience alike craned their necks to get a better view, and the spectators started to pound on the tables with drumstick-wielding fists. "We want food. We want food!"

"Please, my fine ladies and gentleman." The announcer stood and held his arms outstretched, waiting for the audience to calm down before continuing. "Due to these unusual events, we have to consult… the rulebook!"

Four guards struggled forward with the massive tome, almost dropping it just as they managed to position it on the judge's table.

"*Yeouch*!" a judge yelped. He had been too busy eating and couldn't help himself from sampling another starter—causing his hand to become sandwiched between the table and the book. "My hand…! My *food*!"

"Enough. Let the games commence." For the first time, Lord January himself spoke, his voice surprisingly mellow. "People came here to eat, and be entertained, in *that order*."

"My Lord," the announcer pleaded with the ruler of the district. "We must first consult the rulebook!"

Lord January grumbled, but waved his hand and returned his attention to eating.

Grant was disgusted as he regarded the grotesque man. Grease dripped down the Lord's ponderous body. He couldn't even tell where Lord January's face ended and his neck began. The only powerful muscle that Grant could see was that of his jaw, relentlessly pounding anything that entered it into submission. The Lord of January was clothed only in a simple white robe that was loosely tied in multiple places; clearly regular clothes were no longer an option for him.

Grant turned his gaze away as the cover of the rulebook opened and slammed down. The judges peered closely at the words. An ancient woman hobbled forward, bopping the judges on the head with her cane as she made her way to the book. "Move it! As the Keeper of Knowledge, it's *my* duty to consult the rulebook!"

The judges settled down while she leaned over the book with a magnifying glass, occasionally motioning to the guards to turn the page. "Ahh, here we are."

More than one judge was startled awake by her scratchy voice, having drifted off to sleep as she painstakingly searched for the information. "Rule two hundred and forty-three. Competitors are allowed to participate in the finals of any tournament, so long as they present their token before the first battle commences."

"At last!" The announcer yawned as he stood up. "The rulebook clearly states that the competitor, Grant Friday, can participate in the exhibition tournament. He presented a valid token before the commencement of the first semi-final bout. Please, ladies and gentlemen, enjoy the feast. Additional desserts will be brought out as gratitude for your patience."

The competitors lined up as the audience cheered. "The first competitor, ladies and gentlemen, is a Vassal of Count Tuesday. House Tuesday Peacekeepers are *highly* skilled in martial training, and I'm sure he will give us an exciting fight!"

The Vassal of Count Tuesday waved his billy club at the spectators. His yellow armor gleamed in the colors of House Tuesday as the announcer continued, "Following the unfortunate passing of Count Tuesday, his mission is to bring honor to House Tuesday. As a genealogical Tuesday himself, depending on his performance here, he may become a candidate for the Wielded Weapon himself! Next, we have a Vassal of Archduke Sunday, one of the most respected Nobles in all of January."

The Vassal of Archduke Sunday presented himself. He was outfitted in lightweight, shimmering armor, and brandished two slender metal rods. They didn't look like particularly effective weapons, but Grant knew that they were imbued with Archduke Sunday's power, whatever that might be.

"Next up, ladies and gentlemen, we have a wildcard entry this year! The mysterious chef who made a dramatic entrance, Grant Fri… wait, *Monday*?"

The crowd booed and flung scraps of food from their plates at Grant. This was more like what he was used to back in New Dawn. As they pelted him with eggs, tomatoes, and cake, Grant finally wriggled and squirmed his way out of the unbearable fat suit. He let out a sigh of relief, and the audience gasped as his slim form was revealed.

With a ring of steel, he unsheathed February Twenty Nine and swished the eager blade through the air.

There was a round of applause. Grant grinned and bowed, excited to be taking part in the exhibition tournament. The prize of defeating Lord January was tantalizingly close now. Looking up, he saw that the additional promised dessert was being dished out to the ravenous spectators, and he chuckled to himself. "Why would I have ever thought that they were clapping for me…?"

"Last but not least, champion pie eater and all-round giant of a man; raise your glasses, ladies and gentlemen, to the incumbent champion and Prime Vassal of our venerable Lord January… *Randall Monday*!"

Grant's heart sank as the crowd went wild.

Randall lapped up the attention. He leisurely strode toward the center of the arena, hands raised in premature victory. The huge broadsword he carried looked tiny in his hands, and familiar jeweled rings adorned his fat fingers. "I'm glad you could make it, *Leap*. I was worried you wouldn't show. I don't have any cider for you today, but hopefully, we'll get the chance to play together."

Grant gulped. He had lost the ability to answer. Instead, he raised February Twenty Nine in an attempt to show he wasn't scared.

"That should be *my* sword, you little thief! You found it on my property. *Everything*, including *you*, belongs to me!" Spittle flew, and the whites of Randall's eyes turned a shade of yellow as he struggled to contain his rage. "I *will* have it back."

"Over my dead body."

Randall let out a deep belly laugh. "Naturally, but I'll have some fun with you first."

"Thank you for your patience, ladies and gentlemen. We hope you are enjoying your desserts. Let the semi-finals of Lord January's exhibition tournament commence! First up, we have the Vassal of the late Count Tuesday, versus…" the announcer paused for dramatic effect, "*Randall*!"

Grant watched from the sidelines as Count Tuesday's Vassal strode forward, twirling his club. It didn't look like much, but Grant remembered Count Tuesday's color-shifting Wielded Weapon all too clearly. That weapon could freeze, burn, electrocute, or poison its victim. However… that was gone now, and the Vassal only had a regular weapon.

The Vassal was large, but he resembled a chubby child in front of the immense form of Randall. The pair circled each other slowly. Count Tuesday's Vassal had trouble getting close to his competitor. Randall was wielding a blade that Grant had never seen before. From guard to point, it was around four feet long and two hands thick. For such a cumbersome-looking weapon, the man who Grant realized he had never actually known wielded it *effortlessly*.

Randall spun, avoiding the billy club as it licked out at him. The Vassal stumbled forward. Randall could have easily skewered him, but chose to flick the point of the blade against the Vassal's armor. The bindings parted like butter, and the armor slipped down, tripping the Vassal as it dropped over his feet. Randall yawned dramatically and waited for the Vassal to get into position.

Grant couldn't help but feel sorry for the demeaned Vassal. The man's face was red, from both humiliation and rage. He spun the billy club and circled around Randall. Then he made a move, one that Randall didn't anticipate. The Vassal flung a handful of sand in Randall's face, temporarily blinding him. The Vassal seized the opportunity and went to end the fight. His billy club slammed into his blinded competitor's jaw, but it did nothing more than momentarily cause ripples in the fatty folds of flesh.

"W-what?" Stumbling back, the Vassal gaped at his weapon in confusion. "My power… it's gone?"

Randall cleared his eyes and stabbed the sword into the arena sand. Cracking his knuckles, he strode toward the cornered Vassal. The trembling man had nowhere to run, and his weapon was ineffective against the powerful physical cultivator.

In a blur, faster than Grant thought possible, Randall planted a right fist into the Vassal's gut. Bent over and gasping for air, the winded man's face was met by the other fist. A powerful uppercut launched the large Vassal into the air, over the arena wall, and onto the table of a group of startled spectators. The audience threw food and booed. Randall pumped his fists, then bowed.

"It was all a fix!"

"This thing is rigged!"

"He shouldn't have won so easily," another screeched. "I paid good money for this seat. I expect my money's worth!"

The crowd was highly agitated, throwing cups and plates, along with scraps of food into the arena.

"Ladies and gentlemen, please… calm yourselves." The announcer held up his hands. The judges then huddled together and conferred amongst themselves. "After careful deliberation, and consultation with the keeper of the Rulebook, the fight has been deemed genuine. Count Tuesday's Vassal had apparently lost access to his power, putting him at a disadvantage against the highly skilled Vassal of Lord January. Therefore, ladies and gentlemen, we have an official winner! Randall, Prime Vassal of Lord January, will be the first competitor going through to the finals!"

As he went to leave the arena, Randall flashed Grant a

wicked grin. Grant's heart skipped a beat. If he won his fight, he'd have to face his old caretaker in the final match.

<Stop being afraid. This will be good tempering for your will.> Sarge snapping at him made Grant realize that everything would be okay. The sword was only a jerk when things were going well.

"Now, the Vassal of Archduke Sunday will fight Grant Fri—*Monday*, for a place in the final alongside the incumbent champion… after this small break!"

CHAPTER FORTY-FOUR

The spectators clapped enthusiastically, the sugar rush from the dessert having kicked in. Grant took a moment to check his stats.

Name: Grant Monday
Rank: Wielder
Class: Foundation Cultivator
Cultivation Achievement Level: 9
Cultivation Stage: Late Spring
Inherent Abilities: Swirling Seasons Cultivation
Health: 184/184
Mana: 6/6

Characteristics
Physical: 89 (Cultivation Stage Maximized. Gains will be retroactively applied when all stages are aligned.)
Mental: 24
Armor Proficiency: 29
Weapon Proficiency: 47

"Sarge, we never *did* get a chance to discuss how I got characteristics." Grant was hoping for something to take his mind off his nerves as he waited out the intermission between bouts. "Oh… also, what's my total cultivation time?"

Cultivation Time: 313:55 Hours (Time to Next Level 646.45 Hours)

<Oh, *now* you want to learn? I suppose it's better late than never.> Sarge drove into a lecture without more preamble. <Have you noticed that you're changing quickly? Remember that I told you the Swirling Seasons cultivation manual was one of the slowest, but that it just wouldn't matter if you were walking the martial path?>

"I do… a long time ago?"

<Whenever you increase your Cultivation Achievement Level, *Quintessence*—the energy of the heavens and earth—is forcefully absorbed into your body for each of the four methods that you can cultivate. This is why *you* are locked within a stage; you are achieving cultivation on all four aspects, which technically makes you a 'Foundation Cultivator'. This is the slowest and most difficult version of cultivation, as you cannot increase your highest cultivation without your *lowest* form of cultivation being within three stages. However, that Quintessence is held in your body, and filters throughout your system after breaking through.> Sarge paused to allow Grant a moment to catch up.

<*If* you manage to get your lowest cultivation to Early Winter, you will be freed from all restrictions and gain all characteristics as you earn them. You will also be known as a 'Dao Cultivator' and be able to defeat nearly all enemies on your own, becoming a true powerhouse.>

"Why doesn't *everyone* do that, then?" Grant gave Sarge the exact response he was hoping for, and the sword jumped on it.

<How easy was it to find even a single cultivation *method*, Grant? How about a full manual? Remember *that*, back when you were just a farm boy? Now, consider all those methods, and find ones that *don't* conflict with each other as you grow in

power. Do that before you get into the Summer ranks of cultivation, because you can't start cultivating a new method after that point. *That*, Grant, is why not everyone does it. In almost all cases, cultivating one or just two methods will be faster and make you stronger. Not everyone has a social status that allows them to defeat or kill every person they come across.>

Grant pondered that concept, and was about to ask another question, but Sarge stopped him by continuing. <As for how many characteristic points you gain, Wielded Weapons go against heaven's will, so the amount you can get away with taking is… *nearly* random, but they are bounded by a maximum and a minimum. The first five levels, you may gain anywhere from one to four points in weapon and armor cultivation, one to two points in mental cultivation… and a full one to *ten* points in physical cultivation.>

<But, on your fifth level, the potential gain increases by that amount *again*. Let's say you were looking at dice, as an easy example. Weapon and armor cultivation would increase by one four-sided die, mental by a two-sided die, and physical by a ten-sided die. You get another one of these 'dice' added on at level fifteen, then level thirty-five. See a pattern? I won't keep you waiting; the requirement *doubles*. What does this mean for you? It means that as you gain a more powerful *self*, you will literally grow stronger, *faster*. Levels are *everything* to a Wielder or Vassal; cultivation helps fill the gaps.>

"My mental cultivation is a lot lower than my physical cultivation, so that's why my physical cultivation is maxed out right now?" Grant looked at the 'locked' notification again. "So… there's no point in working my body harder?"

<Of *course* there is!> Sarge's words, though forceful, ended as a sigh. <Look at you. You're still at twenty-eight percent body fat. Seven percent loss in a month is amazing, and at this rate you'll be a *looker* by the time March rolls around, but you're holding onto impurities that need to be expelled before you are able to move at peak condition. Your balance is thrown off, and

all fine motor control is harder. Just wait until you are fit, trim, *and* have high physical cultivation.>

"I'm below thirty percent; the true test to see if someone is a beggar…?" Grant glanced at the ruler of the District and winced. "What do you think Lord January is at?"

<Eighty-seven percent, if I'm not off my mark.> Sarge paused for a long moment. <If I am correct, I can only think of a single reason why he's still alive. The sheer amount of time he's been cultivating means that he will have gained certain skills that keep him->

"Who's ready for *round two*?" Grant''s head jerked up, and he calmly strode into the center of the arena. Most of the spectators were banging fists on the tables, their chanting changed from 'food, food' to, 'fight, fight'. After being short-changed by the last bout, they were eager for entertainment. By now, most of their stomachs were full, or at least temporarily satisfied.

Grant bowed lightly in greeting to the Vassal. His decorum was met only by a roll of the eyes. The Vassal sighed, "Let's get this over with. Fighting a peasant is *so* beneath me."

"Can't you read?" Grant pointed at the nametag over his own head.

"You may *appear* to be a Monday, but you have 'lowborn' written all over you." Grant decided to stop being so nice. He thrust February Twenty Nine forward, planning to quickly end the fight. The Vassal managed to parry the blade, and as Grant's sword connected with one of the metal rods… a flash of light blinded him. He stumbled back in surprise, and the Vassal launched his own assault.

Right, left, right, the rods thudded off the Early Spring Medium armor Grant was wearing. Each painful hit would almost certainly leave multicolored bruises.

Damage taken: 15 blunt damage. (27.25 mitigated over three hits!)

Current health: 169/184.

Arms flailing left and right, Grant worked to bide his time until his vision cleared. When it did, he was met with the

Vassal's smug grin. The Vassal spun and waved his rods to the cheering crowd. Rather than waste the opportunity, Grant darted forward and kicked the back of his opponent's left knee.

The Vassal slammed to the ground. Grant's sword darted forward and caught the edge of the shimmering robe, tearing a strip from the material. Rolling away like a wheel of cheese left on a hillside, the Vassal escaped a follow-up attack and got to his feet. His teeth were locked together, and his eyes focused on his enemy. "Do you have no *honor*? Attacking me while my back was turned?"

"Honor is irrelevant. I want to *live*."

"I will teach you some respect, lowborn scum!" The Vassal ran at Grant, arms windmilling. Grant spun and took two excruciating blows to his back.

Damage taken: 11 blunt damage. (18 mitigated over two hits!)

Current health: 158/184.

"Face me like a man! You are a man, *aren't* you? You look more like a sick child!" The Vassal taunted Grant, hoping that he could blind the lad again.

"Legally, I *am* a child in this District," Grant called back sharply. "Does it feel good to attack a child, you brute?"

Grant turned and reflexively brought up his blade to protect his head from a barrage of attacks from the rods. He squeezed his eyes closed. A good call, since even with his eyes shut, white light flashed through his eyelids and forced him to see spots. While the Vassal attempted to blind him using his light manipulation powers, Grant took his knee and jerked it up into his opponent's crotch.

The flashes stopped, and the Vassal dropped in agony while the spectators laughed at the latest development. Grant felt a bit guilty after landing the low blow, and made the mistake of apologizing rather than finishing things. "That was too much, sorry. If you'd stopped trying to blind me, I wouldn't have had to do that."

"You would turn me into a laughing stock? Ridiculed by

peasants and nobles alike?" The Vassal slammed his rod into Grant's knee, getting a yelp of pain out of the younger man.

Damage taken: 3 blunt damage. (9 mitigated!)

Current health: 155/184.

"You leave me no choice, Grant *Monday*!" As Grant stumbled back, the Vassal of Archduke Sunday got up unsteadily and pressed the tips of the metal rods together. They fused with a flash, and he predatorily stalked toward Grant. The Wielder backed up, unsure what was coming next. Every hair on his body stood to attention as the Vassal closed the distance, and a high-pitched whine built in intensity.

Glancing around, Grant could see the audience clapping their hands over their ears with knowing expressions. Rather than attack, as was apparently expected, he remained patient. His skin felt as if it crawled with the feet of a thousand insects. The whine burrowed into the depths of his brain. His mind screamed back, demanding the noise to *end*. Grant held his ears. Many in the audience had collapsed, howling in pain, and those who hadn't were scrambling over the tables in an attempt to get away from the source of the sound.

And then it abruptly… ended. The ends of the rods parted, then started closing in on each other again. On a hunch, Grant spun and curled in a ball rather than watching them reconnect. A shockwave rocked the arena, which was illuminated by an incandescent light. Even tucked in a ball and shielded behind an arm, the light left an imprint on his retinas.

When Grant turned, he observed the Vassal, who was looking at the audience. Judges, nobles, peasants, all but Lord January were fumbling around, blinded. "Oops… I didn't… um… mean to do that. Your vision will return momentarily!"

Grant considered leaping the wall and charging at Lord January, but there was a chance that Lord January's guards would be fine by the time he had climbed the short wall. It was too risky. Instead, he ran forward and barreled into the Vassal, who was staring numbly at the blinded audience. Many were whimpering, others vomiting due to the distress caused.

The impact knocked the metal rods out of the Vassal's hands and sent them flying. Grant grappled the man, and they wrestled on the ground. He didn't have long to implement his plan. He pummeled his fists repeatedly into the side of the Vassal's head, until his opponent's eyes began to glaze over. Rather than leave him there, Grant dragged the dazed Vassal to the edge of the arena and kicked him across, before going back to the center, where he grabbed February Twenty Nine and panted heavily.

"He is... out of bounds!" The screech came from the ancient keeper of the Rulebook.

"I can't see anything!" the announcer cried out, feeling his way around like a blind person. "The brat is out of bounds?"

"Well *I* can see," she snapped back furiously, "the brat is fine. He won."

"Oh, yes. Look!" One of the judges rubbed at his eyes and pointed at the Vassal just as he attempted to make his way back into the designated area.

"Vassal of Archduke Sunday," Lord January bellowed, causing everyone to stop in terror. "I hereby disqualify you for stepping out of bounds, and for disrupting my feast!"

"Grant Monday is the winner!" Rather than countermand Lord January, the panel of judges nodded enthusiastically at the announcer's call. "He will face Randall, Prime Vassal of Lord January, in the final match!"

"But... I didn't..." The Vassal's head hung low with tears streaming down his face. "I didn't mean to blind everyone... only this honorless *peasant*."

"Please leave the arena," the announcer called with tightly controlled fury, "before we *drag* you out."

Now wasn't the time to sit on the floor and cry. The Vassal of Archduke Sunday didn't have to be told twice to leave and hide his shame. "We'll have a short break, ladies and gentlemen. The dining hall will be sanitized, and fresh food delivered to your tables. Please take this time to freshen up and recover from all the excitement."

The spectators filtered out, leaving Grant standing victorious in the center of the arena. Most of the people attending the event were quickly replaced by an army of mop-and-bucket-wielding cleaners. They had their job cut out for them, and they dove into the work of cleaning up.

It was almost time for the final match.

CHAPTER FORTY-FIVE

While Grant waited for the final round to commence, he tore into a plate of food prepared for him by the chef who had taught him how to chop vegetables. The man had handed over the small platter with a wink and a whisper of, "We're all rooting for you in the kitchen!"

Grant nodded in thanks. He didn't have the heart to explain that he wasn't actually a chef, and had more experience picking vegetables than cooking them. In any case, having the kitchen staff on his side gave Grant a much-needed boost. He needed all the help he could get in the upcoming bout.

He rubbed at the tender spots where the rods had connected with his body. Pressing lightly on a rib, he flinched in pain. If it was broken, there was little he could do to fix it. Binding it after the fight and getting plenty of rest would be the best tonic; no one had wandered over and given him a healing poultice.

The spectators eventually filtered back to their seats with their moods lifted as they witnessed the mountain of food prepared in their honor. Extravagant cuisine was available for all: even the lowest of the peasants would dine like kings.

"Chef Gordon has pulled out all the stops!" Every eye turned as Lord January made the unusual step of standing to address the audience. For a man of his stature, rising must have required a great deal of effort. Grant was almost taken in, but he realized that this was yet another fraud. A series of straining pulleys and winches made it appear as if Lord January had gotten to his feet, when in fact, behind the scenes, various staff were hauling on ropes to uplift their Lord. "I hope you are all enjoying the finest culinary delights that District January has to offer, as my *personal* chef is preparing the banquet. Give a round of applause… for Head Chef Gordon!"

The spectators dutifully clapped, genuinely delighted by both the quality and quantity of the fare on offer. All eyes were on Lord January as he continued addressing the crowd, "There can't be a feast without some *entertainment*, can there?"

"No, your Grace!" A filthy peasant woman, missing more than a few teeth, called out from the back row. Lord January laughed, having not expected an answer to the statement, then motioned to the guards.

Grant sat on the sidelines, wondering what kind of entertainment was planned. He could use a little fun about now. He almost choked on his celery when he saw a familiar mop of red hair appear.

Red shuffled forward, followed by Fergus and Derek. All dragged heavy chains with each step they took. Their eyes darted around in panic. Grant made a motion to jump up but stalled when Fergus gave a small shake of his head. He settled back in his chair, anxious about what was going to happen.

"It has come to my attention," Lord January boomed, "that these three, along with Sir Friday, conspired to *rig* the tournament!"

"What evidence do you have, my Lord?" one of the judges called, clearly well-prepared in advance to ask the perfect question at the right time.

"Our newest noble in January, Sir Skinny, shared details of

their plot!" Lord January called imperiously, waving his hand to showcase the massive man that sat beside him.

"It's true," Skinny blurted out around mouthfuls of food. "Grant Friday competed and won, but he is… *in fact…*"

Grant winced and waited for the truth about his Leap heritage to be made public knowledge.

"Grant *Monday*!"

"They've known that since I walked into the arena!" Grant shouted in return, getting *booed* as soon as he started speaking.

"I call for Grant Monday to be disqualified!" Lord January spat out blobs of food. His many chins jiggled in rage. The panel of judges nodded, going along with their Lord's proclamation.

"No!" Grant shot to his feet, ignoring the negative attention, much to the apparent surprise of the people gathered. "I deserve to participate. I have a token, and I *earned* the right to be here! The tokens were given *in secret* to the winners. No one *ever* said that I needed to use my real name to participate. I *demand* that you consult the rulebook!"

The judges sighed.

"The Rulebook will decide!" The old crone hobbled forward gleefully. Twice in one day, she'd been given the limelight. She'd *take* it! The book was still open from the earlier challenge, so she painstakingly began flicking through the pages. "Ah-*ha*! Here it is: rule twenty-nine. 'The bearer of a valid token has the right to participate in a tournament, regardless of magic used to hide identity, such as an illusionary spell or potion.'"

"But… this is an outrage." Lord January's chins quivered as his first contingency plan began to fall into ruins.

"The Rulebook has spoken! The matter is settled," she cackled, completely unintimidated by the rage of the most powerful person in January. Grant felt a wave of relief wash over him, but it didn't last long.

"Take him to the arena." Lord January pointed to Sir Friday. Lord January couldn't stop Grant, but he still held the fate of the young man's friends in his meaty hands. Guards escorted Sir Friday to the arena, with lances nudging him along. Lord January looked directly at the four prisoners in the arena. "I am a generous man, and I understand that you were misled by this traitorous Noble. Kill Sir Friday, and you can all go free!"

All the prisoners, apart from Sir Friday, looked around in panic. Sir Friday had clearly expected this. "It's okay. I knew the risk. You shouldn't have to pay for my mistake. Just... make it quick."

"No. I can't hurt you!" Red stumbled backwards after the chains were removed. His shiny hand axes were shoved into his hands. "I couldn't hurt a *fly*, let alone you!"

The crowd laughed, not expecting the giant with red hair to be such a big softy. Fergus and Derek's chains were removed and weapons placed in their sweaty palms. Derek was given a blacksmith's hammer, and Fergus two wickedly-sharp knives.

Sir Friday Twenty-Ninth's chains were removed and he was given his Wielded Weapon, the truncheon imbued with numbing power.

"I refuse to fight Sir Friday," declared Derek, tossing his hammer to the ground, where it kicked up a wave of sand. "I had *nothing* to do with this."

Fergus nodded, dropping his knives and glancing wearily at the audience.

"To make things more interesting, and *entertaining*," Lord January's laugh shook his body, and continued to do so for long after he stopped laughing at the scene, "I'll raise the stakes! If the audience is suitably entertained, I will spare... the Leap! If not, he will be giving us a flying lesson!"

"Leap? What *Leap*?" mumbled Sir Friday in confusion. Red and Fergus glanced over at Grant, thinking that Lord January was referring to him. A heavy velvet curtain was drawn back at the edge of the arena, which turned out to be an open air window directly over the deep crevice that surrounded castle January on three sides. Standing in the opening, wind gusting around him, was Marcus.

There was a sudden commotion from the audience. "No, *Marcus*!"

"What is the meaning of this?" The announcer called to a chef scrambling toward the Leap positioned toward the edge of the platform. Gusts of air from the looming chasm whipped at Marcus's hair.

"Freda!" Grant looked on in horror, unable to stop the events from unfolding. The chef was grabbed by guards before she could reach Marcus Leap. Her hat and mask were ripped off, revealing a petrified Freda Leap. The audience gasped at the surprising twist.

"Freda, my love... *why*? You should have stayed hidden. Who's going to look after...?" He didn't finish the sentence, terrified that his son would be exposed with even that much.

"Well, ladies and gentleman," the announcer's voice carried across the arena, "it looks like we have *two* Leaps to entertain us this evening. Will they make the leap into the void together, or will the prisoners defeat Sir Friday?"

"Leap, leap, *leap*!" The chant was taken up by the spectators. Grant didn't know if they were showing support for the Leaps... or wanted them to make the leap. From the look of disgust on the spectators' faces, he suspected the latter. With no other choice, and the fate of the Leaps in their hands, Red, Derek, and Fergus raised their weapons and slowly approached Sir Friday.

Red stayed back, unwilling to draw Sir Friday's blood. Seeing his friend so distraught, Derek strode forward and slammed his retrieved hammer into Sir Friday's side. Sir Friday made no attempt to defend himself, only grunting in pain at the heavy blow.

Fergus, understanding that the crowd desired entertainment, twirled the knives and screamed as he moved forward, slicing the knives against Sir Friday's armor. The spectators clapped, until they realized that the knives had only slashed the leather armor. There was no blood. The audience *demanded* blood.

Sir Friday nodded at Fergus, letting him know that it was

okay: he was already a dead man walking. Red tentatively walked forward and swung his axes at Sir Friday. Seeing his distress, Sir Friday dodged the halfhearted blows and bopped the glowing truncheon down on Red's noggin. Red went down like a sack of potatoes, his head completely numbed by the blow.

Derek swung the hammer at Sir Friday's leg. There was a loud crack as the bone snapped from the impact. Derek dropped the hammer, turned around, and threw up. "I'm so sorry, Sir Friday!"

Pain was etched on both Derek and Sir Friday's faces, each for different reasons.

Fergus approached the collapsed form of Sir Friday, whose leg was now twisted unnaturally under him. He looked up at the Leaps, then down at Sir Friday. Fergus's blades were shaking.

"Do it," pleaded Sir Friday.

Fergus raised his shaking hands. The crowd bayed at the sight of blood, simultaneously cheering and shoveling food into their excited mouths. Fergus dropped the knives and held his head in his hands. "I'm sorry. I can't do it. This isn't *right*!"

Boos erupted from the audience as they were deprived of their entertainment. Missiles of food and tableware showered the prisoners.

"Enough! The audience has spoken!" Lord January paused to toss back a milkshake like a shot of liquor. "The Leaps will make the leap… together!

Grant had to make a difficult choice. The ancient Leap, deep within the tunnels, had said the fate of the Leaps rested in his hands. The wrong decision would lead to the eradication of all Leaps within January. As he stood up, he hoped he was doing the right thing. He took a leap of faith, the name of the quest.

"Take me in their place!" Grant shouted over the din. All eyes turned toward him. "I was *born* a Leap!"

Several Nobles choked on their food, and dozens of delicate ladies fainted from the revelation. Lord January sneered down upon Grant from amongst piles of decadent food. "So I was told, Grant. Did you think my *Prime Vassal*, Randall, wouldn't share such important information? I *accept*! To the edge with you; let's see if being barely more than a skeleton is the secret to learning to fly!"

Lord January's declaration was met by cheers. The audience clearly wanted to be entertained. Grant turned to see Randall enter the fighting pit. He was wearing the suit of Mid Spring armor, the prize meant for the victor of the exhibition tournament. His broadsword's edge glinted in the light.

"Wait a moment, my lord!" Apart from donning the armor, Randall had spent time polishing his weapon and preparing for the fight… while Grant nibbled on a pie and followed developments in the arena. Classic misdirection. "Lord January, I demand *satisfaction*! I beg that you allow me the chance to quickly defeat this spawn, so we can *all* enjoy both the entertainment and the feasting."

"Oh, Randall… I…" Lord January paused to build suspense. "Agreed! I can't say no to my favorite Vassal, now, can I? After you've had your fun, the Leaps will be a-leaping!"

CHAPTER FORTY-SIX

"It's about time I *educated* you about your proper place in society, brat. You seem to have some funny ideas in your head. You *stole* my sword." Randall effortlessly tossed his broadsword from one hand to the other. "You are and always will be, a *Leap*. Lowest of the low. Let's *cut* those ideas out, shall we?"

Grant pulled his sword free and took a calming breath. "February Twenty Nine is bound to me, and will remain so while I live. The Leap Sword is mine by right."

"That's fixed easily enough… the 'you living' part!" Randall flashed his trademark wicked grin. Ring-bedecked fingers clenched around the hilt of the sword. "The sword was discovered on my property; therefore, it belongs to *me*. That goes for everything else on the estate, including your worthless life. I *will* have it back."

Grant gripped the handle until his knuckles turned white in an effort to stop his arm from trembling. Even as his heart raced and his mind panicked, he didn't want to give Randall the satisfaction of knowing he was scared. "Come on, Grant… you can do this. Just remember your training."

<Consider it a test. Defeat your kraken, take down the Vivian, and slay your life-long tormentor.>

**Toot!*

The trumpets signaled that the final bout of the exhibition tournament would commence imminently.

"Take your seats, ladies and gentlemen," the announcer called out. "Fill your glasses and plates, and get ready for the finale of Lord January's exciting exhibition tournament! Competitors Randall Monday, Grant Monday, do you accept the rules set out in the rulebook? Breaches of said rules will lead to disqualification and forfeiture of the match, as will leaving the arena before a victor has been determined."

Both Grant and Randall nodded. The announcer looked between them once more and nodded in satisfaction. "Then let the bout begin!"

They started to circle each other, weapons at the ready. The crowd shouted '*Randall,*' over and over. Surprisingly, that wasn't all. Grant could even hear *his* name faintly. That helped him get his frazzled mind under control, and he bent his will to ensuring his success. His once-caretaker caught the hard gleam in his eye, and started to taunt him. "Do you like my armor, Grant? A *lovely* set of Late Spring Medium armor. Oh? Didn't you know that the reward had been upgraded, since there was so much drama around the fighting this year? Shame. You know, there just wasn't much point in waiting to put it on."

Grant ignored the words and tried to study his opponent. The more he watched, the calmer he became. Acknowledging his feelings allowed him to overcome them. "I'm only scared because he terrorized me my entire life. I killed *Count Tuesday*. At my Cultivation Achievement Level, I should *easily* crush a… he's just a Vassal. I've got this."

"Oh. Look at the *anger* in those eyes." Randall let out a dark chuckle and stepped back. "I have a surprise for you, boy. You're not the only one who can use identify-shifting potions."

The air around Randall shimmered as he dispelled an active effect. His name didn't change, but the small red health bar suddenly began to grow. It reached the far right of his nametag, then a darker red bar appeared over the first… then a purple one. Grant stared slack jawed at the red skull next to Randall's name tag.

"You didn't *actually* think the Prime Vassal to Lord January was just a level three cultivator, did you?" Randall's smile showed too many teeth, all weathered heavily from constant usage. "Now, little ward of the District, I want nothing more than to sit down and feast with my fellow Nobles. Yet, the lesson you need is long overdue, and I want *my sword* back."

Grant slowed his breathing and focused on his training. He had known that Randall was a physical cultivator. Almost *every* Januarian had that particular claim to fame. The fact of the matter was that the only advantage that Randall had was lots and *lots* of health. He was a strong man, but damage output was calculated by *weapon* cultivation. Sarge had taught him well, and Grant would prove that right *now.*

Randall's sword swept forward in an arc. Grant ignored his residual fear and ducked, narrowly avoiding the whistling blade. He didn't expect such a fast attack. Regent's frosty breath, was he a *body* cultivator? Physical *and* weapon cultivation? Rather than dodge backward, Grant took the opportunity to retaliate, slicing the edge of February Twenty Nine across his opponent's tough leather pants.

The sword hit hard but didn't break through the tough leather. Even so, a sliver of Randall's health bar vanished as Grant's weapon cultivation sent damage past Randall's armor cultivation.

System logic for the win.

Grant's elation held out all the way until a knee launched him into the air, and he landed on the other side of the fighting pit inches from the boundary line. The young Wielder stared at the chalk line. He just had to cross it for the bout to be over, and he wouldn't have to be humiliated by Randall.

In his mind, he saw little Samuel Leap waiting for parents that would never return, and he realized that he couldn't give up. Even if he died, he would make sure that the people entrusting him with all of their hopes and dreams would know that he did his very best.

He turned to face Randall, who yawned and lazily waved his sword. "So, ready to give up, Grant? I wanted satisfaction, but there's no fun in slapping around a weak little twig."

Grant stood and settled into a defensive posture. Randall pulled a powder from his belt and sprinkled it on his sword, then snarled and leaned forward. A blistering attack was unleashed moments later. The broadsword hammered on the raised February Twenty Nine, and a blinding flash of light dazzled both competitors for a moment. "Randall has access to a blinding light power? How can that be? It must be that powder… his sword didn't flash in his last match."

He intentionally staggered, leading Randall to assume that he was dizzy from the brutal attack. The broadsword swung down, ready to cleave his head in half. Grant used the moment when Randall had settled into a horse stance to leap forward, through his bulky tormentor's legs.

"What the…?" Randall swung around to find his pesky opponent, abruptly letting out a shrill cry and wobbling. Grant's sword had been driven deeply into Randall's ankle. There was another flash of light as February Twenty Nine struck bone. Sticky red blood pooled on the sand, which greedily soaked up the sanguine liquid. The crowd roared in delight at the sight of *any* blood. Between the pain and the cheering of the crowd for the *Leap*, Randall was no longer amused. A yellow shade spread across his pupils, and he snorted like an enraged bull.

Damage dealt: 5.1 piercing (8 mitigated).

Grant scrambled back through the sand, kicking up a cloud in his haste. He had no idea how he had managed to deal so much damage. That armor was strong enough to block anything… *armor cultivation*! Randall's armor cultivation must be nearly nonexistent, if so much damage had gone right through the armor. He bet that if he hadn't hit the armor directly the first time, he would have done a *ton* of damage last time as well.

"Sarge, a physical and armor cultivator is known as a body cultivator, right? What's a physical and weapon cultivator called?"

<A berserker cultivator. They deal high damage, have lots of health, and never tire. Be extra careful; I'm looking forward to having lots and lots of lessons with you in the future.>

"Oh, I know you understand what I can do to you if I activate the earth. Yes, as a Vassal of Lord January, I have access to an elemental spell. But don't worry, I won't waste the precious resources my spell requires on you. I am going to take my time and slice you into thin, bloody *ribbons*. I'll make sure the pain *lasts* before I finally end it for you." The yellow light faded as the fear on Grant's face assuaged Randall's ego.

"Why do you hate me so much? I've never bothered you. All I did was look after the farm and try to stay out of trouble." Grant spat onto the ground between them, moving into a balanced stance. Defending was required, but he needed to take this Vassal's health down to nothing as well.

"I don't hate you, Grant. I *despise* you. It *sickens* me to look at your scrawny Leap body." Randall's lips curled up at some distant memory, and he decided to share. "When your mother abandoned you on my doorstep, I was *forced* by the laws of January to take you in and look after you until your sixteenth birthday. You're a Leap, not even five Leap years old yet. I've had to watch over you for the last nineteen solar years, and I'm *legally* required to look after you for *decades* to come! Nobles treated me as if I had a disease by just being associated with you, and I wanted to put an end to your disease… but House Tuesday knew about you."

"They've watched me ever since you were dropped on my doorway, *waiting* for me to break the law so that they could try to humiliate my Lord! Do you know how many investigations I've had to go through? Every time one of your little bullies would pick on you a little too *much*, Vassals of House Tuesday or one of their representatives would show up at my *house*! That day you came home covered in an itching potion? When you killed

Sir Thirty-First? He was there to investigate *me*, and you killed him! The irony was oh so sweet. You know… I could have forgiven you for everything if you'd just given me my sword. But no, you had to take *that* away from me too!"

Grant was shaken by the revelations. He shook his head and tried to calm his opponent. "I promise you, you don't *want* this sword. It's cursed, Randall."

Randall stalked toward him, trying unsuccessfully to hide his limp. The bright purple section on his health bar slowly ticked downward as blood seeped from the wound. However, at this rate, Grant would have to dodge attacks until tomorrow before the bar was fully depleted.

Grant almost paid for his inattention with his life.

The broadsword slammed against February Twenty Nine, causing vibrations that radiated violently outward from the point of impact. Calming his mind, Grant focused only on his opponent's position and that of the blade. He put all other thoughts out of his mind. The cheering of the audience faded away.

As the sword swept toward him, he managed to negate the power of each attack. Most of the time, he ducked, sidestepped, or dodged backwards, preserving his stamina. He remembered Sarge's lessons. This time, he wasn't against training dummies, but that had never mattered before. Through it all, he could feel his energy reserves quickly slipping away, and it seemed that his opponent was still fresh.

Despite his focus, more attacks got through than he managed to land on his opponent.

Health: 62/184.

Less than a third of his hit points remained. At this rate, he was going to die. Grant expertly parried an overhead attack. Too easily. He wasn't expecting the hand that shot out and closed around his neck.

"Ack!" Grant struggled to breathe as his body was lifted off the ground. The meaty fist slowly crushed his windpipe as the broadsword was drawn back for a final blow.

"This has been fun, Grant. You are actually more skilled than I expected. The skill you've gained in under a month... that was a nice touch." Grant could smell Randall's sour breath as he spoke next to his face. "I don't know how you did that. If you weren't a Leap, you might've made a decent fighter one day."

Grant's sword arm slashed against the Mid Spring armor, dealing more damage in seconds than he had managed the entire fight, but Randall just ignored it. The purple health bar faded away, leaving a dark red one. Even so, he lacked the power or leverage to swing his weapon effectively. His other hand clawed fruitlessly at the fingers suffocating him.

"I… give... up."

CHAPTER FORTY-SEVEN

A status announcement appeared. Grant could barely make out the words as his vision blurred.

Quest Failed: King of the Castle (Rare)

Information: You gave up, forfeiting the match. Randall's grip proved too strong for your weedy neck. No one will remember the second place contender in the exhibition tournament.

Failure Condition: You will struggle to breathe for the following week as your windpipe heals from its injuries. Visit a medic or level up to heal your injuries.

"Sorry, Grant. I can't hear you. You want to keep fighting? That's fine by me! Trust me, this is the most humane way to deal with you." Randall almost sounded sorry as he aimed the point of the blade at Grant's chest.

"Lord January is under attack!" Randall stopped mid-stab, even as the point of his blade pierced Grant's leather torso armor, distracted by the commotion at the high table.

"Stop!" The voice sounded familiar. Grant managed to turn his head as Randall's grip loosened. There, at the high table, Skinny stood with a steak knife pressed firmly against Lord January's neck. Lord January jerked his head back, making a sickening crunch as it connected with Skinny's nose. Blood sprayed from Skinny's ruined nose, but he held on tight.

Then the guards arrived and pulled Skinny off Lord January. The ancient monarch took a napkin and wiped the blood off his neck, revealing that the puffy skin was perfectly smooth, without even a trace of a wound. He gestured at the confused Skinny. "Take him to the gymnasium!"

"Not the gymnasium!" Skinny screeched in abject horror. There was a moment of silence as the audience held their breath throughout the nail biting event. "Wh-what's a gymnasium?"

"It's the section of the dungeon where you will be *forced* to exercise and placed on a strict diet of small portions of healthy food! The worst form of torture available!" Lord January smiled as horror grew on Skinny's face. "When you are as thin as we can *possibly* make you, you'll be beheaded for your treasonous actions."

The excitement over, Randall pulled back his sword arm to finish what he had started. Grant flailed around as Randall's grip tightened, his vision narrowing as the blood supply was cut off. Randall seemed so far away now, at the end of a dark tunnel. He was powerless to stop the elite enemy, his former caretaker, from snuffing out his life.

"Stop!" Grant's eyes flickered open as Lord January gave the surprising command. "Put him down a moment, Randall."

Randall reluctantly obliged, even as he cursed under his breath. He let Grant collapse to the sand, and Lord January sighed as he set his food to the side for a long moment. "Grant, I am impressed by your skills. Killing you would be… a waste. You may have started off life as a Leap, but you have managed to better yourself. That matters to House Monday. If you swear to serve me, you may enter my service as a Vassal. You will train under apprenticeship to Randall himself, restoring honor to both of you, as you are moved to Castle January to be lavished with the *best* training resources available."

It took a moment for Grant to compose himself after being half-strangled to death. "If I do, will you spare my friends?"

"I will spare their lives… all but Skinny. His attempt on my life indicates a devious plot to get close enough to attempt to kill me. This lot," Lord January waved at Sir Friday and Grant's three friends, "were his accomplices. They shall be sent for rehabilitation, a cell in which they will have plenty of time to reflect upon their past choices."

"The others?" Grant gestured toward the Leap couple, who were holding hands.

"The law is clear. They trespassed upon Castle January and stole from me. For the benefit of the District and society, they must be put to the sword… or take a leap." Freda sobbed upon hearing the judgement. Marcus held her close as the wind swept around them. "Plus… we need to be *entertained*!"

Grant looked around the room. People were merrily stuffing their faces, even though his and his friends' lives were on the line. To them, this was mere showmanship. Everyone clapped and applauded Lord January's generosity as he leaned forward to shovel cake into his face.

"This… what they have… was the life I wanted. I was just too poor to afford it. I didn't understand what it was; that there were other, *better* options." He scowled at the greedy, grasping hands of the citizens of January. Now that the offer was on the table, he contemplated his desires and wanted to run as far away as he could. The prospect of training under the yoke of Randall? That was just the gravy on the offered cake. "After careful consideration, I'll have to decline your offer."

More than one person choked in surprise, the rich food becoming wedged deep within their throats as they inhaled sharply. Cries of panic went up from around the arena. Grant used the moment of surprise to sneak attack the distracted Vassal, cracking the butt of February Twenty Nine against

Randall's temple. People screamed and fell over benches and tables, the panic proving contagious. He wasted no time in sprinting toward Lord January, whose mouth hung open limply, unable to process the fact that Grant had turned down his generous offer.

No one *ever* said no to Lord January.

After vaulting over the wall, Grant leapt toward the grotesquely obese form of Lord January, his sword aimed at his enemy's head. Time slowed as spectators panicked, the churning mass of bodies attempting to flee the confines of the arena dining hall. Grant looked like an avenging angel in the reflection of Lord January's glassy eyes, as they stared blankly back at him.

He didn't *want* to kill Lord January. He'd spilled enough blood, but by holding him hostage, he could both force the release of his friends and defeat the Lord, allowing him to progress to February. February Twenty Nine streaked through the air, its quivering target looming larger by the second.

Grant felt a thrill of excitement wash over him… followed by agonizing pain. Every nerve screamed simultaneously as the world went black. His body convulsed in midair. Sheets of lightning sprang from Lord January's fingertips, cascading over Grant's floating form. Lord January was lifted up by the pulley system, and he bellowed at the audience. "Everyone, back to your seats, *now*!"

Lord January's tone demanded obedience. Panicking peasants and Nobles scrambled to obey. Grant landed face-first in a custard pie, showering all those in the vicinity with globs of creamy dessert.

"I was *wrong*." Lord January's cheerful smile had finally vanished, replaced by a snarling mass of rotten teeth. "You clearly *are* a Leap. You will be joining your brethren today. Take them to the leaping platform!"

Grant, still spasming from the elemental magic, couldn't stop the guards from dragging his limp body toward the platform. He was joined by Red, Fergus, Derek, and Sir Friday.

They wouldn't even look at him, each stuck in their own personal nightmare.

"Let's get this done *quickly*!" Lord January snapped. "The Leaps first, followed by the conspirators, and lastly, *Grant*. He can look upon the results of his folly!"

The Leap couple embraced before being unceremoniously shoved off the platform and into the chasm. Their screams were lost to the wind as their bodies disappeared from sight. Red struggled, finally having found the courage to defend himself. He whipped the chains around, keeping the guards at bay. It took three of them to finally pin him down, as well as a boot to the face to shut him up. Laughing, the guards rolled his limp body off the platform.

"Red…!" Grant's heart shattered as his friend was thrown into the abyss. If he had just accepted Lord January's offer, his friends would have lived. They'd be sent to a prison of some sort, but at least they would be *alive*!

"It's not your fault, Grant." Fergus smiled at Grant as he shuffled toward the edge. "We each make our own choices in life. We chose to be here. Skinny's plan was risky, but we wanted to give you a backup plan, in case you didn't manage to defeat the Vassal. It didn't quite work out as we'd hoped."

Guards raised their lances and approached Fergus, but he walked proudly toward the edge. "If you don't mind, lads, I'll do it myself. See you on the flip side, Grant!"

CHAPTER FORTY-EIGHT

With a lopsided grin and a wink from his non-bleeding eye, Fergus raised his arms and fell back into the void. He didn't scream, and his body quickly faded from view. Grant hyperventilated, unable to process what was happening. One by one, his friends and companions disappeared over the edge. Cheers and clapping filled his ears, the audience thoroughly enjoying the spectacle. Derek didn't go as easily. Even chained, the brawny steelworker managed to take a guard with him, both toppling into the chasm below.

Sir Friday looked at Grant with sorrowful eyes. "I'm sorry, Grant. I only wanted to bring honor to House Friday. I want-"

He wasn't able to finish his sentence. A laughing guard bopped him on the head with his own Wielded Weapon, then gave him a vicious shove. The spectators erupted in laughter as the proud Noble slipped from view, his body tumbling head over heels.

Try as he might, Grant couldn't remain composed before his looming death. Even so... he'd rather die than be apprenticed to Randall. On his knees, he raised his head to watch Randall and Lord January approach. Lord January's morbidly obese body was carried on a litter by six straining, muscular guards.

"It is clear, after today's spectacle," Lord January began, "that we have a bit of an infestation. Every inch of the castle and the lands around it will be scoured. We'll find any Leaps that are hiding, and they will share your fate."

"Let me take *that* off you." Randall pried February Twenty Nine from Grant's iron grip one finger at a time. "Once you've made the leap, and you're dead, I should be able to access the sword's power."

Randall flashed a wicked grin at Grant. There was a large welt forming at the side of Randall's head from where the weapon had struck. The man's meaty, ring-festooned fist caught Grant under the jaw, lifting him into the air and over the edge. "That's for earlier."

"Flap your wings and fly, little birdy!" Lord January bounced his arms up and down in mockery. Grant scrambled to grab something, anything, but he was too far from the edge of the platform. Gravity took hold and accelerated him downwards. Laughter and the persistent aroma of cooked meat quickly faded away, replaced by the howl of freezing wind clawing at his body.

He squeezed his eyes, and fell for long seconds… then the howling of the wind stopped abruptly, and Grant felt himself drifting in a strange bubble of light.

"It *isn't* over, young man." Auld Leap's soft voice soothed Grant, and tension in his body left him as he drifted closer and closer to the ground, which was lit with the strange blue light that had filled the Pool of Forethought. "You made the right choice. If this didn't happen now, you would have been tested another time, perhaps with no one to catch you as you fell."

"What… this was *supposed* to happen?" Grant looked around as bubbles started drifting past him, showing him killing Randall, Lord January, making them submit, showcasing the two choking… all things that didn't happen.

"No." The answer on the wind caught Grant off guard.

"My boy, free will is a powerful thing. Nothing is *supposed* to happen. There is only what did, what did not, and what could have been."

"Then... how do you know that I did the right thing?" Grant asked the open air. "I lost the Leap sword!"

"You refused to give in. You did everything you possibly could to succeed, and it wasn't enough. Grant... that's *okay*." The words made tears of frustration start to run down Grant's face. "Sometimes, it just isn't enough, no matter how much we want it to be. Sometimes, like now..."

A new bubble floated up in front of Grant, showing Randall furiously attempting to force February Twenty Nine to bind to him. The sword was flashing, shifting between real and insubstantial as Randall gave in to fury and tried to take an ingot hammer to it. Soon, the man tired and threw the sword against the wall, standing and pulling up his pants. Only then did Grant realize that the man had been doing all this while using the toilet. Randall walked out of the room in a huff, leaving the sword where it was.

"Sometimes, you prove your worth, and walk the steps... of prophecy!" the voice echoed, and Grant's view shifted. A blue bubble appeared in front of Grant's face, this time showing a stern, ancient face. White hair, mustache, and beard were long but well-kempt. Words came from the bubble, and for the first time, Grant understood why Leaps were truly hated in January.

"My name... is Regent December. I am doing everything I can to save the world, so that one day, it may be healed. The easy road of January, part one of the prophecy of Year of The Sword."

"A great mind rots away in a prison of flesh, deeper thought and true genius sealed behind unending desire." The words continued to flow, and Grant was so mesmerized that he didn't even realize that he was already standing on his own two feet, on solid ground. "Innovation and technological singularities are ignored in favor of leisure; increases to the mind, all but forgotten. The people die younger and younger, the truth hidden behind false claims of accidents. Even if the deception is found, none search for deeper meaning."

"For they have *lost* all deeper meaning."

"The ancient Lord sits upon a throne he has become, his once-great mind begging for death, even as his body forces him to live. Each moment that he survives, his flesh dies and is reborn, returned to peak health… and he is made to endure. However, in a seeming fit of anarchy, one day, a descendent bearing his name—but none of his blood—shall end his reign of luxury." Regent December seemed to lock eyes with Grant at that moment. "Wielding the timelessness and legacy of the Leap sorcerers, and wearing the name of his enemy, this person shall give the people a choice. Survive… or live."

The bubble popped into a shower of blue sparkles, and Auld Leap stepped forward to stand next to Grant. The man was skeletal, his skin wrinkled beyond belief. He lifted a shaking hand and set it on Grant's arm. "My boy, for this moment to occur, you needed to forge a deeper bond of selflessness with your Wielded Weapon."

"I don't understand what's happening," Grant admitted freely, seeing no point in hiding his confusion from the thinnest person he had ever seen. "That prophecy; what does it mean? Is there more to it?"

"Of course there's *more*. Six parts in total, to be precise. Those are for another time, m'boy." Auld Leap started guiding Grant toward a door cut into the wall of the deep chasm they stood in. As they stepped through, Grant was greeted with a familiar sight: the Pool of Foresight, as well as all of the people that had taken the leap with him. "You needed to learn, and prove, that you were willing to give up your established norm. That you would go against your base instincts and work to better yourself… even with all external influences pressuring you to give up, just so your life could be *easy*."

A gentle hand guided Grant forward as the old man continued to speak. "You've taught everyone here that *surviving* isn't enough. You found self-determination and improved yourself, when everyone around you was satisfied with mediocrity. All of us are proud of you, Grant."

Quest update: Leap of Faith. You have forged a deeper bond with yourself, and therefore the Weapon of Power that has been bonded to you. You have unlocked a new Weapon ability!

Weapon Inherent abilities:

1) Weapon Absorption: This sword has the ability to absorb another Wielded Weapon's power, taking its ability into itself. Restriction: Only one weapon per Monthly series.

2) Weapon/Armor Synergy: When the Wielder is equipped with armor, this sword increases in potency and gains power. Increase is capped at the Wielder's cultivation stage, or average armor stage, whichever is lower. February 29 is now considered an 'Early Spring Medium' sword. Current maximum damage is: 8 (5.5 from weapon cultivation, 2 from weapon stage, rounded up.) Damage type is 'piercing' or 'slashing', depending on how February 29 is used.

3) NEW! Time is Space: you now have access to any of the powers of February Twenty Nine, no matter where the Weapon is. You may also call your Weapon to you, so long as you touch upon a place in the world where it once was while bound to you. Cost: 25% of mana pool.

4) Locked

As soon as he processed what had just happened, Grant stepped past his friends and put his hand on the floor where he had deposited his sewage-coated clothing during his previous visit… along with February Twenty Nine. There was a strange distortion in the air, and he reached for it while activating his newest ability. "Time… is Space?"

Mana flashed from his outstretched fingertips. His open hand clasped against cold leather, and Grant pulled back, retrieving his Wielded Weapon out of thin air. A collective inhalation rose from the group as the weapon caught the light, and the golden runes on the flat of the blade seemed to burn with the sword's name. Grant gazed around at all of his friends, people that had expected to die in order to help him, and took a deep breath.

"Let's go feed that tyrant some cold steel."

CHAPTER FORTY-NINE

Grant had originally planned on making his way into the Leap living area and recruiting everyone that he could convince for an all-out assault against the Lord of the Month, who was going to be hunting them in the near future. However, after ascending through the tunnels and the sewers with Marcus leading the way, they found only an empty space.

"They took my *boy*?" Marcus roared into the empty room. "How *could* they-?"

Freda stopped him with a gentle pull on the arm. "Marcus. They took him and fled for their lives. Someone must have tipped them off that Lord January is on the hunt for all Leap-kind. They took Samuel, yes, but that would do nothing but slow them down. They are looking out for him, and we have to trust that they have his best interests in mind."

The small group lapsed into silence as the enormity of the task before them suddenly struck. They needed to return to the surface, defeat Lord January and any of his Vassals... and do it all before their friends and loved ones were put to the sword. Grant shook off the melancholy and took a decisive step toward the exit. "For right now, we have the advantage. They think we are dead. The plot against them, defeated. Their enemies… on the run. We need to use that, right now."

"We're with you, lad." Fergus slapped Grant on the shoulder, and they started moving once more. "After the exhibition, there were going to be games and a feast to honor the new champion on the parade grounds. Lord January is sure to be there, because Head Chef Gordon has been tasked with providing the food."

"So, we know when, we know where… all we need to do now is figure out *how* to get at him." Grant was really enjoying having people to bounce ideas off of. He hadn't even realized how terrible keeping everything to himself was, and how badly it had been impacting his mental state. Having friends was… it was *incredible.*

"I might have an idea." Freda stated with a gleam in her eye.

Marcus groaned, "If this involves *uniforms*, Freda, I just may have to make you sleep in another room for a few weeks."

"Oh? You think *you* can kick *me* out of the bed?" Freda testily replied, much to the group's amusement. "It's something that's been tickling the back of my mind ever since I had a conversation with Grant and some guards about 'laundry engineers'. To use this plan… we will need to throw away honor and dignity, and recognize that what we will be doing will give us nightmares. Likely for the rest of our lives."

As she outlined what they needed to do, the others looked at her with a mixture of admiration, disgust, and fear. None of them wanted this devious mind working against them, and all of them felt at least a little bad for Marcus.

All of them barring Skinny and Sir Friday turned away from their original goal of reaching the surface, instead walking through the sewage lines that ran through the entirety of January's End. As they got further away from Castle January, where the lines had been updated and cleaned well over the years, they started to find themselves in rapidly-shrinking spaces.

Derek was the first person that could go no further, his bulk getting trapped in the tight space and requiring the others to rescue him. Though he was disappointed with the situation, the relief on his face was clear for all to see. The big man turned around, and went in search of a shower and a feast.

The others went as far as they could, but Red and eventually Freda were also forced to backtrack and find a different way to reach the parade grounds above. Eventually, it was down to just Marcus and Grant, and they soon were working to fit through the last stretch. Marcus babbled lightly as the tension grew, "I'm glad I always made sure to give Freda the extra serving; you'd have gotten lost in here without me!"

They were peering down a tunnel, where a light was shining through an open manhole. A wide pipe was being lowered in just as they reached the brighter area, and the two of them approached it apprehensively. Marcus looked up into it just as the pipe was secured. There was no way past it, only through it. "My lady sure has some smarts in her. Grant, this is where we part ways. I can't get into that, but I know you can. Let me give you a boost… and may spring warm your heart and fill your belly."

Grant nodded and tried to swallow around the dry lump in his throat. Marcus dropped down, and Grant stepped on him in order to reach up and pull his way into the pipe. A small blessing was that this was clearly a new sewage pipe, a novel innovation that was being rolled out for usage for the first time. Grant slithered through the just-barely-wide-enough flexible pipe, hearing muffled voices and fanfare as he went.

"Is that *supposed* to move like that?" A conversation right above his head made him nearly shout or stop moving. Both would have given him away, so all he could do was continue pulling himself along and hope for the best.

"No idea. It's hooked up to a 'pump', which I'm told is supposed to move it, but I thought the small windmill needed to be attached first."

"It isn't *on* yet? They warned that-" The voices moved

away and out of earshot, and Grant let out a sigh of relief. He slid along hurriedly, making decent progress, and eventually found that the pipe curved up. At the junction, he could just *barely* fit by putting his sword through first, then contorting his body in uncomfortable ways. He found himself in a strange, bowl-shaped room made entirely of a thin metal. Light came from above, as did the sounds of hundreds of people.

An announcer was speaking, but Grant only caught the last part of his prepared speech. "-Porta potties are located under your bench. Remember, all you have to do is flip the switch to use the facilities! You won't miss any of the exciting developments-"

Anything else that might have been said was drowned out as dozens of banging noises sounded above his head. He looked up, only saved from even worse nightmares by the fact that no more light was available in the room. All the shafts of light had been entirely blocked off by the bodies completely covering any gap. Grant dove to the side as the freshest of sewage splattered into the huge bowl, swirling around before draining into the hole he had just climbed out of.

"Welp. Not gonna be able to get out through there." Grant did his best to breathe lightly; the room was *hot* and now filled with filth. Water started to pour into the area, washing away anything clinging to the metal. In spite of the circumstances, Grant had to shake his head in admiration of the feat of engineering that went into making such a thing possible.

He already knew where he was going. Before he had lost all light, he had caught sight of one opening that was larger and more set apart than any other. Only one person would be sitting in a space away from the rest, and Grant hurried to get in position.

Whatever was going on out there sounded exciting to the crowd, and it appeared that a special course of food was being delivered. Grant continued to wait as the bowl heated and stank, needing to know for sure that Lord January was in position. It was only when the tyrant *flipped the switch* that Grant knew for sure.

Aiming at where the man's heart should be, Grant slammed his sword through the thin metal of the bowl as hard as he could.

Critical hit!

CHAPTER FIFTY

Damage dealt: 19.45 Piercing. Major bleed debuff added: -50 health per second!

Grant pulled back his sword and cut his way out of the flimsy metal. A strange, pained warble emitted from the direction where he had attacked. Slashing an opening, he pulled himself up onto the platform with Lord January. Blood was pouring out of the huge man, but the wound was getting noticeably smaller even as Grant looked on.

Not wasting another moment, he drove his sword deep into the mountain of flesh sitting before him. Again, and again, deep wounds were torn open across the Lord of the Month's back.

Damage dealt: 19.65 Piercing. Major bleed debuff added: -30 health per second!

Every hit was a critical hit. On his final attack, Grant drove the sword far enough that it slammed into something solid on the other side and stuck. His hands slick with blood, February Twenty-Nine slipped from his grasp as he tried to pull it back.

"What do you want, brat?" Lord January had turned his

head so that he could see the young man stabbing him. "Is that it? Are you tired already?"

"H-how are you not dying?" Grant's words were a whisper, but they might as well have been a shout in the dead silence that had overtaken the parade grounds. "Fatal wounds are *fatal wounds*!"

"A follower of tautology, are you? A thousand years of physical cultivation, eighteen hours a day. You do the math." Lord January actually paused to let Grant do the calculations. It didn't take too long, a testament to his advancing mental cultivation. "Then add in my life-saving skills and Mastered Regeneration."

"S-six and a half million hours of cultivation? You have a *quarter million* points of health?" Grant couldn't think of anything more to say.

"Close enough that it literally doesn't matter." Lord January sighed and glanced at the sword that had gone through his chest and pinned his plate to the table. "With your ability versus my skills and health, you could carve out my heart and I'd just grow a new one before I died."

"Are you not even going to defend yourself?"

"That's what my apparently *useless* guards and Vassals are meant for." Lord January looked around at the people closing in and casually waved them off before continuing in a mellow tone. "Now, answer me. Why are you doing this?"

"I… I want to live," Grant admitted as he reached forward and grasped the handle of his blade again.

"Not always what it's cracked up to be." Lord January spat a mouthful of blood to the side.

"I have a quest to heal the world. I think… I'm pretty sure it would drop the barriers." Grant's words made Lord January blanch, and pure fear could be seen in his face, the first time in the exchange that his expression had shifted at all.

"I could be *free* again?" The whispered words were completely outside what Grant had been expecting to hear. "I'd never survive… not like this. But if you're here… that means the barriers are failing either way."

"What do you-?"

"Who do you think *designed* the framework for adapting a Leap Sorcerer spell into a workable format for that *Regent*? You don't think I'd know the weaknesses? The failure points?" Lord January snarled as his hands reached for food to calm his mind. He stopped as if he had been shocked. "No… my training needs to restart immediately. This… one way or another, I'm a dead man if I stay like this."

"How could *anyone* kill you?" Grant stared at the flowing blood that had staunched itself in the few moments they had been speaking.

The question reminded Lord January of their current predicament. He frowned down at the gaping wound and sighed. "Every four years, for a *thousand years*, someone has come after me with this stupid sword. Every time, they die before I ever see them, and this thing is tossed in the vault until the end of the year. It really is a cursed blade, you know. If you don't pass its 'tests', it will turn on you and kill you on its own."

The offhanded explanation shook Grant, but he knew that he had passed at least one test of the sword. "I *need* you to submit to me, Lord January. I'm going to do whatever it takes."

"Why?"

"My quest. I need to kill, or defeat, all the Lords and Ladies of the month before the end of the year. If killing you is out of the question…"

"Ah… the sword steals our fragment? That must be the case. How else would you move through the barrier?" Lord January mused as blood pooled on his table, following along the blade. "I don't know if you have what it takes… but I don't care too much. Have a proper fight with my Prime Vassal, and if you win, I'll concede to you and go into secluded training for the remainder of this year. Do you agree?"

"I don't have a choice." Grant yanked on his sword, pulling it free with an organic **slurp**. "I accept."

The young man scanned the parade grounds, brandished his sword, then hopped over the low wall and landed on the grass near a few guards that were still wondering if they should skewer him.

System Sanctioned Duel! You have accepted Lord January's offer of a duel against his champion! If you win, you will have defeated Lord January by his own terms. If you lose… no terms have been set! Any outside interference or attacks on the opposing party will be returned to the attacker, and result in an instant loss for the side of the interferer.

The System cannot be tricked.

A discharge of lightning blasted past Grant's ear as Lord January bellowed in fury. The massive man had *barely* been able to turn his sneak attack against the young man to the side. A guard that had come too close was hit by the lightning and instantly collapsed as a smoking husk. "What is this…? A *duel*? I wasn't being serious; I was getting his guard down!"

Grant looked at the dead man, then back to Lord January, terrified of the power the man had just wielded against him. The Lord waved at the guards, eyeing his food hungrily. "Someone get Randall over here right *now*. Someone else, get this food away from me. I said *someone else*!"

The strange orders were carried out as swiftly as possible, and not even an hour later, Randall came *running* onto the parade grounds. The man was gasping for air, and he was frantic to learn what was happening. "My… Lord… the sword is gone! What's… *you*!"

Randall had locked his eyes upon Grant, and he lifted a shaking finger to point it at the young man. "You stole the sword *again*?"

Grant carelessly stepped further onto the arena floor and started walking around. The people watched him moving around for seemingly no reason, while Randall stared at him as if he were seeing a ghost. Finally, he felt comfortable that he knew the terrain well enough. "I'm ready."

<You got this, Grant.> Sarge told him quietly. <You totally won't mess this up and die for it.>

"…Thanks, Sarge."

Randall looked up at the expectant stares. "Wait, I was brought here to fight him? I don't have my armor, or-"

"*Now* you're worried about someone having an advantage of armor during a duel?" Grant scathingly called at his opponent. He leveled his sword at Randall's heart. "That didn't seem to be a problem earlier."

Randall's eyes flashed yellow, and he sneered at Grant with his stained teeth. "My Lord, do I have your permission to go all out against this brat?"

"I don't even care if there is enough left over to *identify* him." Lord January motioned to his litter carriers. "Get me back to the castle, now!"

The audience had no idea how to process all of these events. Lord January was attacked, *didn't* destroy his attacker, and was leaving behind food and entertainment? A thousand years had passed since the last time an event of this magnitude had happened, and the sudden shift terrified most of them. Others got angry. One member of the crowd tossed an apple at Grant, but right before it hit him… the apple stopped in the air and whipped back at the man. The projectile impacted with such force that the offending hand was cleanly blown off.

No one else tried to showcase their displeasure by throwing things.

Grant had only taken his eyes off Randall for a moment but was startled into action by an inarticulate *scream* from Sarge. He dropped and rolled just as a broadsword sliced through the air where he had stood, impacting the ground hard enough to send a pillar of churned earth into the air.

Now in a defensive position, Grant watched in shock as Randall's body finished fully coating itself in a yellow light. Steam was rising off the man, and although he wasn't moving any faster, he was clearly *leagues* stronger than he had been just a moment ago. "Oh, you're alive."

The casualness to the words made Grant want to run screaming, but he held his ground and hoped he could manage to fend off whatever this was. Randall stood to his full height, slowly straightening his spine one vertebrae at a time. "No one likes using this spell, Grant. But. It. Feels. *Good.*"

The huge man bent and *stomped.* Pure strength sent the man rocketing at Grant in a straight line, while a cloud of dirt showered the audience with rubble. Seeing that Randall would have no way to turn, Grant jumped and rolled to the side. He underestimated what the big man was able to do. Randall slammed his sword straight down, stopping his momentum and *pulling* to once more hurtle through the air at his target.

Unable to dodge in his current position, Grant frantically blocked the sword coming at him. With a tremendous **clang** of steel, he went flying backward, and February Twenty Nine went sailing through the air.

Damage taken: 22 blunt/slashing! (9.25 mitigated.)

Current health: 88/184.

Grant looked at his shaking hands as blood poured down them. He probably should have waited until his health had returned to more than one hundred before joining combat. Where he had held his sword, his skin was torn and the flesh was deeply bruised. Looking up at Randall, he was startled at the changes in the man before him. The Vassal had *shrunk*, his total mass having decreased by at least a quarter since the start of the battle.

"Do you know *why* no one wants to use the elemental spell of Impure Earth?" Randall breezily queried as he crossed the distance and yanked Grant to his feet. "While it instantly triples our strength and defense, it wastes vast amounts of resources to make that happen. It'll take me a year or more to get back to where I was. Even so… even so, it was worth it to ensure that my Lord's concerns were laid to rest right away. We've had our fun."

"Time to die."

CHAPTER FIFTY-ONE

Randall dropped his own sword and grabbed Grant's neck. The yellow light faded from his body; he had already proven that he had more than enough power to choke the life out of the smaller man, and this time, there would be no edict to save Grant's life. As he squeezed Grant's airway with his left hand, he cocked back the right and let fly with a heavy haymaker. It landed directly on Grant's nose, breaking it easily.

Damage taken: 2 blunt! (9.25 mitigated.)

Current health: 86/184.

"Huh, that was supposed to cave in your sinuses." Randall squeezed harder and reached up to grab Grant's skullcap and tear it off.

That was when Grant struck.

With an outpouring of mana, he activated Time is Space and pulled his sword out of thin air. He had made sure during his walk around the area to swing his sword around and touch as much *space* as he could with it.

Both of Randall's arms were raised, he was unarmored, and he wasn't expecting Grant to be in a perfect position. With a simple thrust, Grant drove his Wielded Weapon into Randall's armpit, following the subclavian artery directly into the man's heart. The huge man froze as blood stopped flowing through him nearly instantly, and his purple health bar dropped away like a stone. The dark red health bar was similarly emptied, followed by the final, normal, red one.

The battle had been decided in an instant, thanks to intense training and the arrogance of his opponent.

Randall collapsed backward, his grip on Grant going limp. The young man nearly tore his trachea as he forced air into his lungs, coughing heartily as his vision returned to normal. He landed on Randall's motionless form, and once more found himself staring into the eyes of a man that he had killed.

Even more so than with Count Tuesday, this death weighed on him and made his guts churn with disgust. He took another deep breath, and let it out softly. Reaching forward, he pulled his once-caretaker's eyes closed. "For what it's worth, Randall... I am sorry. Thank you for the small kindness you showed me in my life. I wish... I wish it could have been different."

Grasping his sword, Grant levered himself to his feet and sought for Lord January as the man attempted to make his escape to the castle. The entire fight had lasted under thirty seconds, meaning there was no time for the litter-bearers to move him.

Duel concluded! Winner: Grant Monday!

Terms of the duel: Lord January unconditionally accepts defeat!

Do you, Grant Monday, wish to absorb the power of January 1: Sword Grandmastery? Accepting Sword Grandmastery will override any previous Wielded Weapon power absorbed in the current monthly series. If not overridden by another weapon of the same month, this ability will return to its current Wielded Weapon at the end of the year, unless the quest 'Heal The World' has been successfully completed.

. . .

Accept / Decline

"Sarge... am I going to lose you if I take this?" Grant quietly voiced his concerns.

<I will slap you *silly* if you do not accept that prompt right this instant.> Sarge bellowed into Grant's mind. <That can get you an entire *two tiers* above my current training program!>

Grant hit 'accept' with a yelp, and a nimbus of light surrounded both Grant and Lord January. Golden light signified his increase from defeating a Lord of the Month, and a deep, earthy brown—the exact color of the best farming soil—was drawn out of Lord January as a huge pillar of light, which shot into the sky and vanished.

In the next instant, the column of brown light blasted back down from the sky, flattening the ground and corpse around Grant as though a ten-thousand-ton rock had just fallen from the heavens. Power and a strange authority coursed into him... and his sword. The Wielded Weapon reverted to the form he had first seen it in, and the dragon on the hilt began swirling around and finally spit out its tail. The now-open mouth stretched wide, and the brown energy was sucked in. When the last of it had vanished, the sword returned to normal.

Grant blinked as a new notification appeared.

February 29 now has the ability Sword Grandmastery, replacing Sword Expertise. Further information can be found on the Status Sheet.

Sword Grandmastery is requesting to use the Januarian Fragment of Life to send a message to District January. Allow? Yes / No.

"Um. Yes?" The very second that Grant accepted, tens of thousands of brown threads shot out of his sword, arching into the heavens and back down... then driving into the head of every human in the entire District of January. Grant wasn't spared.

A new Lord has begun his rule in January! All Hail Lord January: Grant Monday!

A terrible injustice has been done to the populace, and the desire of the Wielded Weapon, January One, to rectify this issue has been granted.

First, the previous Lord January has been fully and officially rejected by his Wielded Weapon. A new position of Nobility has been opened! See House Monday to join the running, though the final choice will be made by the head of House January in this District: Lord January, Grant Monday.

Secondly, know what the previous Lord January has done, and the truth on many matters.

What followed was images and knowledge from a millenia past: Lord January turning his population into a weapon against Leaps out of fear, shifting them from hardworking innovators into a hedonistic society, and granting a vision of how they would look and feel if they hadn't been influenced.

Quest Update: Heal the World (Legendary)

Congratulations, Grant Leap, you have defeated the first Lord of the Month, Lord January. As the new Lord January:

1) You have inherited the power of January, the ability to travel anywhere you have been before—within a District you are a Lord of—by slicing your sword through the dimension and picturing the destination. Each use costs 1 per movement. Charge:1/100,000.

2) You have gained the ability to open the boundary separating January and February by utilizing the Januarian Fragment of Life. Each use costs 1 per person. Charge:1/100,000.

3) You have gained the ability to send a message to anyone within the District of January by utilizing the Januarian Fragment of Life. Each use costs .1 per message. Charge:1/100,000.

4) You also have the ability to switch your name from Grant Monday to Lord January at will.

Only the wind could be heard as the people of January processed the information that had been forced into their heads. Then a man shoved himself away from the table and stood up. He wobbled side-to-side. "Everything… hurts. Why didn't I ever realize that everything *hurt?*"

That question broke the silence, and a roar of fury rose throughout the entire District. The deposed Lord looked around uncaringly. There was nothing they could do to him, but he had been hoping he would be able to hide his involvement. He hadn't counted on his own Wielded Weapon betraying him. "You allowed it to use the Fragment? Fool… what a waste."

Then the furious crowd turned on him, and the massive man was covered in thrown food, then attacked by various groups of peasants and Nobles alike. Lightning started spraying through the crowd, and Grant ran. He needed to get as much distance from the arena as possible before the Noble Houses realized that there was a weak Wielder they could challenge for the position of Lord January.

He had planned to meet up with his friends in the sewers, but they found him before he approached the gates. Fergus pulled him into a hug, then shoved him away. "You need to run. Go; get strong. House Tuesday is on the warpath. House Monday is looking to get the top position of their House back, and dozens of assassins have assuredly been given your name."

"But I need to-" Grant's concerns were waved away as Sir Friday limped forward.

"Listen, lad, wonderful changes are coming to District January. Terrible changes, but perhaps wonderful nonetheless." The Noble, the only *noble* Noble that Grant had met, clapped him on the shoulder, handed over a sack of Time, and gently pushed him toward the shimmering barrier in the distance. "No one will ever forget what you've done for us, but that is the issue… no one will ever forget. There are those that are happy with their life, and you have just shown them what could have been. They will hate you until the end of days."

"You need to flee to District February, or you won't last the night."

EPILOGUE

Grant stepped through the glittering barrier and fell to his face in a pool of water. He flipped over and lay on his back for a long moment as dried blood slowly stained the water around him. With a blink, he read over his current status and let out a long sigh of contentment and exhaustion.

Name: Grant Monday
Rank: Lord of the Month (January)
Class: Foundation Cultivator
Cultivation Achievement Level: 11
Cultivation Stage: Late Spring
Inherent Abilities: Swirling Seasons Cultivation
Health: 184/184
Mana: 9/9

Characteristics
Physical: 89 (Cultivation Stage Maximized. Gains will be retroactively applied when all stages are aligned.)
Mental: 34
Armor Proficiency: 44

Weapon Proficiency: 66

There was so much to do. Grant heaved himself to his feet, and got to it.

A man that wouldn't look out of place at a bodybuilding competition sprinted into a training hall where a young woman with pink hair was pounding a solid stone training dummy into rubble. "My Lady, there was a disturbance at the barrier to January."

"*January*? The grain and sugar suppliers? Who cares?" She blew a long strand of her pixie-cut hair out of her eyes. "House Thursday has already been instructed not to allow our people to eat *either* of those, and they are to be shuttled to March as they arrive."

"That's just the issue, Lady February. *No* shipments are coming through." The man held out a report, the muscles of his arm rippling as he presented the document. "There has been only a single ripple in the barrier. One Januarian apparently came through late last evening, but no one saw an issue as he moved deeper into our District. Only a few days later, when the delays became higher than normal, did anyone question *why* everything had stopped."

"Get to the point, or get out. Unless *you* are going to spar with me to help make up the time lost from my weapon cultivation?" Lady February's suggestion caused the huge man to blanch.

"House Monday is demanding an investigation." The words were almost stammered out, and the young woman groaned and turned away. Her mind was moving to her next training session, but the next sentence made her perk up. "Bureaucrat Monday believes Lord January, the leader of House Monday in District January, was murdered by whatever man escaped into our territory."

"Murdered? But..." She pondered the information she had available. "That ancient glutton should be nearly *impossible* to take down with normal methods. Do you think the rumor has merit?"

"I do," the man started leadingly, but the manic grin on the Lady's face made him freeze in place like a mouse staring at a snake.

"That means the killer must be able to *fight*! Find them for me, and make sure they participate in the remapping of the aristocracy!" Lady February turned her attention to the stone dummies set throughout the area, a wide grin on her face. She shot off, and the sound of a dozen explosions resounded through the area as she finally came to a stop at the last one, her fist an inch from its rocky face.

"I need a good sparring partner. Everyone that's offered so far has been... disappointing."

ABOUT DAKOTA KROUT

Associated Press best-selling author, Dakota has been a top 5 bestseller on Amazon, a top 6 bestseller on Audible, and his first book, Dungeon Born, was chosen as one of Audible's top 5 fantasy picks in 2017.

He draws on his experience in the military to create vast terrains and intricate systems, and his history in programming and information technology helps him bring a logical aspect to both his writing and his company while giving him a unique perspective for future challenges.

"Publishing my stories has been an incredible blessing thus far, and I hope to keep you entertained for years to come!" -Dakota

Connect with Dakota:
MountaindalePress.com
Patreon.com/DakotaKrout
Facebook.com/TheDivineDungeon
Twitter.com/DakotaKrout
Discord.gg/mdp

ABOUT MOUNTAINDALE PRESS

Dakota and Danielle Krout, a husband and wife team, strive to create as well as publish excellent fantasy and science fiction novels. Self-publishing *The Divine Dungeon: Dungeon Born* in 2016 transformed their careers from Dakota's military and programming background and Danielle's Ph.D. in pharmacology to President and CEO, respectively, of a small press. Their goal is to share their success with other authors and provide captivating fiction to readers with the purpose of solidifying Mountaindale Press as the place 'Where Fantasy Transforms Reality.'

Connect with Mountaindale Press:
MountaindalePress.com
Facebook.com/MountaindalePress
Twitter.com/_Mountaindale
Instagram.com/MountaindalePress

MOUNTAINDALE PRESS TITLES

GameLit and LitRPG

The Completionist Chronicles,
The Divine Dungeon,
Full Murderhobo, and
Year of the Sword by Dakota Krout

Arcana Unlocked by Gregory Blackburn

A Touch of Power by Jay Boyce

Red Mage and
Farming Livia by Xander Boyce

Space Seasons by Dawn Chapman

Ether Collapse and
Ether Flows by Ryan DeBruyn

Bloodgames by Christian J. Gilliland

Threads of Fate by Michael Head

Lion's Lineage by Rohan Hublikar and Dakota Krout

Wolfman Warlock by James Hunter and Dakota Krout

Axe Druid,
Mephisto's Magic Online, and

High Table Hijinks by Christopher Johns

Skeleton in Space by Andries Louws

Chronicles of Ethan by John L. Monk

Pixel Dust and
Necrotic Apocalypse by David Petrie

Viceroy's Pride by Cale Plamann

Henchman by Carl Stubblefield

Artorian's Archives by Dennis Vanderkerken and Dakota Krout

Made in United States
Troutdale, OR
07/24/2024